Showdown at Sutter Creek

A California Ranger Novel

By
Gary Crawford

 For information contact: Shalako Press
P.O. Box 371, Oakdale, CA 95361-0371
http:www.shalakopress.com

ISBN: 978-0-9961748-0-0
Written by Gary Crawford
Illustrations and cover art:
Karen Borrelli

Printed in the United States of America

Gary Crawford is a retired educator and author of the popular Sam 'Mac' McCloud, private investigator novels. He has also written three westerns.

Other Novels by Gary Crawford

California Ranger: Missing in the Mother Lode
Trepidation Trail
The Sam 'Mac' McCloud Series:
Immaculate Deception
Double Tap
Heidi's House

Acknowledgments

I would like to thank my editor, Judy Mitchell, for her corrections and suggestions. Her feedback was invaluable.

Thank you to Major Mitchell for his hard work and professional approach.

Thanks to Karen Borrelli for my creative cover design.

I am thankful for Shalako Press, a relationship I treasure.

Most of all, a big thank you to my readers for their support and encouragement.

Dedication

For my grandchildren:
Colton, Cade, Cuyler, Caylee, Cole, Jack and Thomas

"Here is *your* country. Cherish these natural wonders. Do not let selfish men and greedy interests skin your country of its beauty, its riches, or its romance."

President Theodore Roosevelt

Chapter 1

All eyes turned to watch the lone rider enter the small town. Back rigid, yet relaxed in the saddle, he looked straight ahead observing everything without seeming to do so. Though thriving from the gold mines of the Mother Lode, Amador City was so small that most of the town could be observed in its entirety from horseback at the top of a small rise. Unlike frontier towns of the plains, Mother Lode towns undulated with the terrain in the foothills of the Sierra Nevada Mountains and most of the foundations and walkways were large slabs of granite, limestone or whatever the most plentiful stone of the area was. Regardless of its small physical size, the town was bustling with folks attending to their labors and people seeking their fortune.

The rider reined in his magnificent red sorrel and allowed two bonneted ladies to cross the dusty street, the younger woman giving the handsome rider a bright smile; he received a nod from the older woman. Captain Seth Gentry of the California Rangers tipped his hat.

"Excuse me ladies, could you direct me to the marshal's office?"

"It's a half block down on your right," the older woman said. "You can't miss it."

"Thank you ma'am."

"Such a polite young man," the older woman said.

"And handsome, too," the younger one said, still smiling and staring at the broad-shouldered ranger astride the magnificent horse.

The sorrel tossed his head as if to acknowledge the compliments. Gentry touched spurs to the horse's flanks and continued down the small main street. An old-timer sat out in front of the general store whittling on a large stick. A pile of shavings was in front of him, the wooden stick a smaller version of its original self.

A couple of hard cases leaned against the porch post of the Mooney Saloon. Seth ignored their looks of disgust and continued past them to the marshal's office. He heard one comment to the other.

"That's all we need is another damn lawman around here."

Seth smiled to himself. Though a young man and recently appointed to the California Rangers by the governor, he had experienced men like these in every town. The reason Governor Thaddeus Brown had resurrected the rangers was to assist the overwhelmed lawmen in the state, overrun by gold seekers of every ilk. Along with the gold seekers came a plethora of men with less than honorable intentions.

As he arrived at the marshal's office Seth's mind flashed to the image of Darla Brown, the beautiful brunette daughter of the governor. His first assignment had been to assist the lawmen in the northern Mother Lode and to find the governor's daughter's missing fiancé. He had eventually found the man's body and discovered himself hopelessly in love with his boss's daughter.

Seth dismounted and tied his horse to a hitching post. He looked around the teeming little town and walked to the door of the marshal's office; his boots and spurs creating a rhythmic clack and jingle on the slab of rock.

*****

Ned Hayes and Virgil Smith watched the ranger ride down the dusty main street.

"It looks like he's a one-man parade," Ned said, spitting a dark stream of tobacco into the street. He ignored the spittle on his graying, previously red beard. The dark stain gave him a more menacing and unkempt look.

"That brother of yorn better get here quick like," Virgil said.

Disgusted, Ned said, "He'll get here as soon as he can. It's not like he can control when he will get out."

"It seems the longer we wait the more the law shows up," Virgil added.

Ned stared at his partner, wondering how he had gotten himself hooked up with such a dismal man. Then he remembered that friends were hard to come by in San Quentin; Virgil was getting more and more on his nerves. He, too, couldn't wait until his brother showed. He and his brother Eli were like two peas in a pod. Though they fought incessantly, their brotherly bond was as strong as a mother and her newborn calf.

"Why was your brother locked up?" Virgil asked.

"I told you before; he robbed a stage and got his dumb ass caught."

They both watched the new lawman enter the marshal's office.

"Well, I hope he's better at robbing banks," Virgil said.

Ned fought the urge to slap Virgil and gazed down the main street. The stage was due and its arrival was a curious interruption to a mundane and often irritating day. "I wonder why they brought in another lawman," Ned thought aloud.

"I don't like it," Virgil said.

Hayes glared at his partner. "I never found much you did like."

Virgil, with a grey-toothed sneer said, "You know as well as I do that I like money, whiskey, and women."

Ned glared at the slope-shouldered man. He fought the urge to knock him into the street. It seemed that life continually dealt him bad hands. Virgil was an irritant, but he was the only friend he had other than his brother, Eli. He stared at the closed door of the marshal's office. It was just his dumb luck to have another lawman show up when he was planning to rob the bank.

"Umm. . .umm, I'd like some of that," Virgil said, staring down the slight hill. "You can have the old one and I'll take the young one." He watched the two women approaching.

"Don't be stupid, Virgil; we can't bring no attention to ourselves," Ned said with disgust. "There still might be some old handbills about and we could get throwed back into the pokey."

Virgil ignored Ned and tipped his battered hat to the approaching ladies. "Good day, ladies," he said.

The younger woman looked down at her feet and the older woman's nose reached for the sky.

Rebuffed, Virgil grimaced. He glared as they passed by. "I betcha I could teach that old one a few tricks," he said, loud enough for them to hear.

"Shut up, Virgil," Ned said.

And then they heard the thunderous arrival of the charging stagecoach.

Chapter 2

Marshal Mack Wheeler was sorting through his most recent batch of hand bills when the door opened, the bright light causing him to squint at the backlit figure in the doorway. As the light faded with the closing of the door, the first thing that got his attention was the circled star on the man's chest. With raised brow he looked up into the face of a square-jawed young man.

"Marshal?" Seth asked.

"Yes, Mack Wheeler; I heard tell a ranger was coming," he said.

Seth smiled. "The governor's idea," he said. "Captain Seth Gentry's the name."

Wheeler nodded toward the pot-bellied stove. "Coffee's on, cup's on the peg. I got a wire that you was coming."

Seth walked over and poured himself a cup of coffee. He noticed the marshal's cup on his desk and refilled it for him. "Governor Brown always tries to be politically correct and please most everyone."

"Thanks," Wheeler said, watching the steam arise from his coffee cup. "What brings you into this neck of the woods? Have a seat."

The wooden chair in front of the marshal's scarred desk creaked in protest as the large ranger settled on it. He took a drink of coffee. It was strong like he preferred it. "Good coffee," he said.

"It's been simmering since sunup."

Seth took another drink. The coffee and the warmth of the stove on his back relaxed him. "The governor decided to assist the lawmen in the Mother Lode. With all of the gold-seekers and what comes with them, he wanted to give a helping hand."

Marshal Wheeler nodded, opening his right desk drawer. "I never met the governor. I just got this telegram for you and it's asking for a complete report from you. How many men are assigned to you?"

Seth took the telegram and smiled. He wondered if the governor was getting pressure from his daughter to ask about him. It also could be that he was getting political pressure from the legislature. The ranger looked down at his coffee cup. He took another drink and set it on the marshal's desk. "None, I'm it."

"The governor thinks that one man can do the job? Hells bells, the lode is up to four mile wide and 120 mile long. It extends all the way to Mormon Bar down Mariposa way."

Seth smiled over his cup of coffee. "You know politicians, they want crime to go away but aren't willing to pay for fighting it. Might cut into their fat salaries. The governor wanted to do something and pretty much hired me on his own. If we have some success, and we already have, he hopes to persuade congress to budget more money for the cause."

"We don't get paid enough as it is," Wheeler said, shaking his head.

"The governor wants you to know that he is trying to help. Is there anything I can do for you, marshal?"

"This whole area is full of bad characters with bad intentions," the marshal said. "I used to have a deputy, but he got hisself shot. Sheriff Bill Cartwright over Jackson way and Marshal Sam Clements down at Sutter Creek do the best they can with limited resources. We try to help each other out but we're spread pretty thin. What I'm saying is that we can use all of the help we can get. We'd appreciate you sticking around for a while."

Seth nodded. His old wooden chair squeaked in relief as he alleviated its burden and walked over to the stove and put his tin coffee cup on it. "I'll stick around a while. Got any recommendations on where to stay?"

"The Amador Hotel is just down the street. It's as good a place as any and my daughter Elizabeth works there. Beth is a fine girl and you can tell her I sent you."

"Thanks, and thank you for the coffee," Seth said.

The board floor of the marshal's office began to vibrate with the thunderous arrival of the morning stage, accompanied by muffled screaming and yelling.

"The stage--- sounds like trouble," the marshal said.

Chapter 3

Marshal Wheeler quickly went to the gun rack and pulled down a double-barreled shotgun. Ranger Gentry followed him out the door. A suffocating heavy pall of dust greeted the two lawmen as they exited the office.

"We been robbed and Jack's been shot," the driver yelled down as he steadied the lathered horses.

A crowd materialized as the Wells Fargo Agent came out of the office, retrieving his pocket watch from his vest pocket and checking the time as if getting robbed was a poor excuse for being late. "Did they get the strongbox?" he asked.

Seth looked down at the agent, a small bespectacled man with an arrogant manor. His total disregard for his wounded employee disgusted him.

"Somebody fetch the Doc," Marshal Wheeler yelled as he handed the agent his greener and climbed the front wheel to check on the wounded man riding shotgun. The weight of the heavy shotgun pulled the agents arms down and he grunted. It took all of his strength to hold on The slumped-over guard had been shot through the right shoulder and had lost a considerable amount of blood. He groaned as the marshal moved him to look at the wound. "He's alive," he said.

The doctor came hurrying down the walk with leather satchel in hand. "Get that man down here so I can take a look at him," he said.

"Seth, give me a hand here," the marshal said.

The marshal and ranger wrestled the limp and moaning man down and laid him on the hard walk. The doctor quickly tore open the wounded man's shirt and examined the wound. "Luckily it went through and through," the doctor said as he opened his satchel. "He's lost a lot of blood, though. Get some men to carry him to my office."

*****

Ned and Virgil observed the arrival of the stage. Ned looked over at Virgil. "You can stop fretting; Eli will be here in a day or two."

"How can you know that?"

Looking back at the doctor working on the wounded stage guard Ned said, "I'd recognize Eli's work anywhere."

"Is Eli crazy? He'll have the law looking all over for him. It's bad enough the law'l be all riled up over a robbery, and to make it worse he tried to kill the guard."

Ned grimaced. There was some truth in what Virgil was complaining about. His anxiousness for seeing his long absent brother had clouded the reality of his brother's downright cruelty. Eli was meaner than a cornered wolverine and would just as soon spit on you as shake your hand. Without believing it he said, "They'll be over it in a few days and on to something else."

They watched a group of men carry off the wounded guard.

"Let's go get a drink," Ned said.

"Best idea you had all day," Virgil grumbled as he followed Ned into the saloon.

"You can only have one; funds is getting kinda short," Ned said.

"If'n that brother of yours was the robber of the stage he best get here right quick afore we die of thirst," Virgil said.

The garter-sleeved bartender watched the two men approach. The saloon had emptied out when the stage arrived and the lonely echo of boots on the wood floor indicated a not too profitable day. The look of these two vagabonds certainly did nothing to dissuade the feeling of slowness and unprofitability.

"Two whiskeys," Ned said gruffly.

The bartender stared at the two men with hands still on the scarred wooden bar top. Only after Ned pulled a coin out of his pocket did he make a move to pour the drinks.

"Things is kind of slow around here," Ned said looking around.

"The stage don't get robbed every day," the bartender said as he poured two shots.

Virgil and Ned downed the whiskey. "Give us another," Ned said, bringing a smile to Virgil's face.

The bartender eyed the two-bit piece on the bar and waited.

"Well?" Ned demanded.

"You're shy some money," the bartender said.

Ned reached into his pocket and confirmed it was empty. He had a powerful desire for another drink. He looked over at Virgil.

"I'm broke," Virgil confirmed.

Ned sighed and took two forty-five cartridges out of his gun belt and placed them on the bar next to the coin. "Them's twelve cents apiece, you can keep the change," he said.

The bartender nodded, picked up the coin and cartridges and poured two more drinks.

Only after Virgil downed his whiskey did he say, "A gun don't do no good with no ammo."

Ned glared at his partner. "Didn't hear you complain before downing that drink."

"Thought didn't occur to me until I drunk it," he lied.

"Maybe you could swamp out this here saloon or muck some stalls so that you can return the favor of buying me a couple of drinks," Ned growled as his hand dropped near his revolver.

Virgil wasn't the brightest candle on the mantel, but the threat did not go unnoticed. He put a hand to his lower back. "I got a bad back; too much horse ridin' in my day."

The bartender stared at the two arguing men as he wiped some glasses with a bar towel. "I could give you boys another drink if you would empty those two spittoons out back."

"There you go, Virgil," Ned said, his lip turning up into a not-so-friendly smile. His hand moved closer to his gun.

Virgil's stomach turned as he looked down at the tobacco-covered brass spittoons. He looked up at his sneering partner.

"Hurry up and do it, Virgil, I got a powerful thirst," Ned demanded.

The bartender sat the whiskey bottle on the bar.

Ned licked his lips.

Virgil bent down and attempted to not look at what he was about to pick up and almost put his hand in the first spittoon. He forced himself to look, gulped back some bile that arose in his throat and picked up both spittoons and walked quickly to the back of the saloon.

Ned watched him walk out and turned back to the bartender. "That boy's short on brains and ambition," he said. "Pour me that drink, barkeep."

Chapter 4

The Sutter Creek Saloon bartender disgustedly looked over to the Faro table at the crude, boisterous cowboys as they made lewd comments and attempted to paw a saloon girl as she served a round of drinks. Saturday nights were busy and profitable when the cowboys came in off the range to blow off some steam and spend their week's wages. This group was the worst of the bunch, led by the son of the owner of the massive Circle J cattle ranch near Volcano. Buck Henry and his bunch tended to cause trouble and damage and would rotate their presence from Volcano, Jackson, Amador City, and Sutter Creek. Buck fancied himself a ladies man but his crude and obnoxious demeanor limited his success and only a great deal of money could persuade the occasional working girl.

Wiping bar glasses with a white towel, the bartender watched as Buck Henry eyed the little blonde girl at the bar talking to a rough looking old miner as she sipped on a watered down drink that the miner had bought her. The saloon girl laughed loudly at something the miner said, which irritated Buck, since the blonde was not paying attention to him.

"Hey blondie, get your ass over here and have a drink," he bellowed.

The woman and the miner briefly looked at Henry and turned back to the bar to continue their conversation.

"Blondie, I'm talking to you," Buck hollered.

The two at the bar ignored him.

Furious, Henry jumped up, knocking over his chair, the noise garnering the attention of the patrons of the crowded saloon, quieting them down to an awkward silence. He weaved unsteadily and gathered himself to his full height, two inches over six feet. The big man glared around the room and watched two men scamper out the door. He hitched up his gun belt and walked toward the couple at the bar, making an effort not to stagger. His fellow cowboys looked at each other, one of them shaking his head.

Henry grabbed the blonde saloon girl by the wrist and spun her around.

"Hey," the miner said.

"Shut the hell up," Henry bellowed.

"Ow, you're hurting me," the blonde said.

"What's your name, sugar?" Henry asked though clenched teeth.

The blonde girl struggled against Henry's iron grip. "Lola," she said. "Stop hurting me."

"Lola, I am Buck Henry. Me and my father own most of the land around here and when I tell you something you had better listen."

Henry saw movement out of the corner of his eye and turned to see the old miner pull a bone-handled knife out of a scabbard attached to a well-worn leather belt. He let go of Lola's wrist and grabbed the miner's arm in a vice-like grip. The miner struggled to move the blade forward but the larger, younger man held it still and then began turning the wrist, pointing the knife back toward the miner. Try as he might, the old man wasn't strong enough to stop Henry. The miner's face turned bright red from the strain and then the air left him as Henry drove the blade home.

Lola watched the miner's eyes widen with surprise and then heard him groan before he collapsed to the floor. She looked at the ginning Buck Henry, and then screamed.

The bartender yelled for somebody to get the marshal.

"I'll get the doctor," another said.

Keeping a watchful eye on Buck Henry, a man at the bar bent down and checked for a pulse. "You best get the undertaker, this ol' boys had it."

"You seen it, he pulled that pig sticker on me," Henry said to the bartender.

"Yeah, I saw it," the bartender said with disgust. He looked at Lola rubbing her wrist. "Why don't you just stay up Volcano way and leave these folks alone?"

"I don't see you folks minding Circle J cowboys spending their money here," Henry spat.

Marshal Clements burst through the door carrying a double-barreled shotgun. "What happened here?" he demanded.

"That old coot pulled a knife on me and he got a taste of his own medicine," Henry said.

Clements looked at the bartender. "That what happened?"

"Yeah," bartender answered.

Marshal Clements stared at Henry. "So, out of the blue this man pulls a knife and tries to stab you with it?"

"That's what he done," Henry nodded.

The marshal looked at the blonde rubbing her wrist. "Is that what happened, missy?"

Indicating Buck Henry, Lola said, "Elmer didn't like it none when he grabbed me by the wrist."

"You hurt this young lady?" the marshal asked.

"Naw, I's just tryin' to get her attention, marshal. I didn't mean her no harm," he said.

The marshal glared at Henry. "Get your boys and leave town," he said. "And do the good citizens of Sutter Creek a favor and stay away."

"Now, marshal, that's not right. The boys need to blow off some steam after a hard week's work."

"You'll be spending the night in my fine accommodations if you don't do as I say."

Buck Henry gathered his boys and they made their way to the door. "This ain't right, marshal."

Marshal Clements had the shotgun pointed at Henry's midsection. He didn't say a word.

Henry looked at the business end of the shotgun. The opening of the two barrels looked as big as side-by-side canons. He turned and walked out the door. "There will be another day, boys," he said as he stumbled out the door.

The doctor rushed in and bent down to check the pulse of the old miner. He looked up at the marshal and shook his head.

Marshal Clements walked to the door and watched the cowboys of the Circle J ride out of town. "That Buck Henry is no good," he said to himself. "I don't know who's worse, him or his Pa."

Chapter 5

Prudence Miller tapped on the governor's office door and entered, holding a telegraph message in her hand.

Governor Thaddeus Brown looked up from his desk over his rimless reading spectacles and watched the woman march toward him. He sighed. "What is it, Prudie?"

"We received a telegram from Ranger Gentry," she said.

The governor took it from her and read the short passage. He shook his head. "That boy isn't much for words."

"Well, he is keeping in touch like you asked," Prudie said in Seth's defense.

"All it says here is that he's headed toward Amador City. What am I going to tell Darla?"

The governor's secretary smiled to herself. She knew that despite the governor being the leader of the State of California, the leaders of the Brown household were his wife, Althea, and his daughter, Darla. His daughter was always asking about Seth Gentry and the governor seldom had much information to pass on to her. Darla incessantly asked about the handsome ranger and was insisting on returning to the Mother Lode to see him. Governor Brown knew that the Mother Lode was fraught with danger and had managed, so far, to keep his daughter reined in. It was becoming more and more difficult, however, and lately his wife had been increasingly sympathetic toward their daughter, even suggesting that mother and daughter could travel together.

The governor removed his spectacles and rubbed his temples. "Prudie, send a telegram to the marshal in Amador City requesting a complete report from Ranger Gentry when he gets there. Don't let Darla know about this."

"Don't let me know about what?" Darla Brown asked from the open doorway.

The governor groaned at his daughter's sudden appearance.

Prudie scurried back to the outer office.

"Hi, honey," the governor said.

"Well?" Darla asked.

Governor Brown took a deep breath. "I received a telegram from Seth today."

"So?"

"It just says that he is on his way to Amador City," the governor said.

"And?"

"That's it. That's all," the governor murmured.

"And you weren't going to tell me, father?"

"It's not that, Darla; I wanted to have more information to tell you and was going to send a telegraph to Seth for a full report so that I would have more."

Darla crossed her arms and tapped her toe. "Mother and I have been talking."

What's new? The governor interlaced his fingers on top of his desk.

"We could take a stage up to Amador City and see Seth and be back in just a few days," she said.

The governor sighed. "We've discussed this many times, Darla, and it is just too dangerous."

"You could go with us, father," Darla said.

Governor Brown took a deep breath. "I would, sweetheart, but 2,000 Chinese have struck the Central Pacific Railroad and that heavy-handed Charles Crocker has threatened to starve them out. That's just one of the major issues I have to deal with."

Darla pouted.

Prudence tapped on the door and entered. "Mr. Fargo is here and he says he needs to see you right away."

Governor Brown winced at the news. William Fargo and Henry Wells had a previously contentious relationship with Charles Crocker before they agreed to a high priced delivery contract over the Sierra Nevada Mountains using the Central Pacific Railroad. The governor had helped broker the deal and it had been a long, difficult process. "You'll have to excuse me, Darla; we'll discuss this with your mother tonight."

"Okay, father, hurry home tonight," she said, turning to leave.

"Send Mr. Fargo in, Prudie," the governor said. Being the governor and also a husband and father weighed heavily on his shoulders.

With hat in hand, William Fargo stormed through the office door. "Miss Darla," he said with a nod as he hurried by her.

"Hello, Mr. Fargo," Darla acknowledged.

"Thaddeus," Fargo said to the governor with a familiarity the governor did not like. "We've got big problems and I need to know what you are doing about it!"

"Sit down, *Will,* and tell me about it," the governor said, irritated. He didn't like Fargo coming in without an appointment and making demands.

Fargo plopped down in the leather chair in front of the governor's desk, laying his hat in the chair next to him. "Henry just found out that one of our coaches was robbed on the way to Amador City and one of our men was shot."

The governor nodded. "I hadn't heard, but it's not the first time."

"No, and I'm damn tired of it. The hills are crawling with desperados. We do the best we can to protect our passengers and merchandise, but we need more law enforcers."

"I can't argue with that," the governor said. "The politicians want to allocate the money toward their district's pet projects rather than fund more money for safety. They make demands without allotting the money for it."

"I've already talked to Crocker and we are going to pay those fat-cat politicians a visit and put pressure on them. We pay a lot of taxes and aren't getting our money's worth."

"That certainly couldn't hurt," the governor said.

"In the meantime, what are *you,* going to do?" Fargo asked.

Governor Brown picked up the telegram from Ranger Gentry and handed it to Fargo. "I've already taken steps," he said. "That's from Captain Gentry of the California Rangers; he's already on his way to Amador City.

Flabbergasted that the governor had taken some action, Fargo stared at the short message. "I commend your efforts, but only one man?"

"Obviously I had to be creative to resurrect the Rangers and I'm hoping I can convince congress to expand the program that we so desperately need," the governor said.

"Wells, Crocker and I will do the best we can to help you out governor," Fargo said.

The governor stood and put out his hand. "All help is appreciated, William."

Prudence had been eavesdropping through the still open door and entered with a serious look on her face. "I'm ready for you to dictate that letter governor," she said. "Have a nice day Mr. Fargo," she added, encouraging him to take his leave.

"Thank you," he muttered, taking up his hat.

Prudence smiled back at the governor after she watched Fargo leave. "You smoothed his ruffled feathers," she said to the governor.

Governor Brown sighed. "For the moment," he said. His thoughts returned to his wife, Althea, and his daughter, Darla. The pressure at home would be much worse than he just received from William Fargo.

Chapter 6

Marshal Wheeler and Ranger Gentry followed the stagecoach driver and Wells Fargo Agent into their office. "Tell us what happened," the agent said.

"When we come around Horseshoe Bend they was a man standing in the middle of the road with his six-shooter out. I was thinking about running him down but he shot old Jack and I reined in."

"What did the man look like?" Marshal Wheeler asked.

"I can't rightly say," the driver said. "He had one of them flour sacks over his head with holes in it to see out of."

"How about height, weight, clothing, anything else that might identify the thief?" Ranger Gentry asked.

The driver rubbed his whiskered chin. "I thought at first it might be Black Bart, but he never shot nobody. I seen Bart once and this guy had the same build, slender. But, he wasn't dressed near as nice. He looked worse for wear."

Wheeler looked at Gentry. "Not much to go on."

"He didn't seem nervous or nothing," the driver said. "If I was to guess, I'd say he done this before."

Seth shook his head and looked over at the agent. "What did the guy get out of the strong box?"

"The payroll for the Keystone Mine; we ship the gold out and they return with some cash."

With raised brow, Seth asked, "How much?"

"We don't usually like to divulge those things," the agent said.

"I'm only going to ask you one more time, or I'm going to ask the marshal here to put you under arrest for obstruction of justice," Seth hissed.

The Wells Fargo Agent took in a deep breath. "One thousand silver dollars."

Seth thought for a moment. "That'd be over fifty pounds."

The agent nodded.

"I seen him drag off the strong box into the woods," the driver said. "He musta known what was in the strong box; he didn't bother with robbing the passengers."

The ranger looked at the agent. The agent's furrowed brow showed concern and he was trying to figure out how a thief would know about the payroll on the stage. "How would one learn of the payroll being shipped?" the ranger asked.

The agent thought for a moment. "It's not a secret; all the miners know when they are going to get paid. The bank knows when the money is expected. It's also possible it was a random robbery: the hills are crawling with unscrupulous men."

Ranger Gentry looked shocked at the lack of caution taken to protect the payroll. "It seems to me that your payroll protection is a might light."

"Well, we only had one other attempt and that guy chose to run instead of shoot," the agent said.

"Unless the robber had a mule with him I'm guessing that he would have to stash some of the loot," the marshal said. "We need to go out to Horseshoe Bend and have a look around. My eyes ain't what they used to be. How're you at reading sign, Seth?"

"My Pa and a half-breed friend of his taught me to read sign of critters and men," Seth said.

"What are you going to do about this?" Agent Turley demanded.

Marshal Wheeler looked down at the irritating agent. “I’m going to do my job, Turley. I would suggest you check on the well-being of your employee.”

“I’d suggest you get to it, marshal; the thief could be miles away by now,” the agent said as he walked toward the door.

Seth watched the marshal clench his fists. He understood the frustration the marshal had. Pompous bureaucratic types could be mighty demanding and irritating.

“Come on, Seth, let’s take a ride out to Horseshoe Bend; it’s not too far from here,” the marshal said.

Chapter 7

As dusk settled over Sacramento, the governor strolled slowly toward his residence, lost in thought on how he was going to deal with his wife and daughter. There was no way he could tolerate the two of them traipsing up to the Mother Lode without him or, at least, further protection. If he could, he would have a whole patrol go with them. It would be better if he could talk them into staying home.

He ascended the wood steps of the warmly lit Victorian home and paused on the porch to take in a deep breath. The welcome aroma of cooking food greeted him and dulled the trepidation he felt before entering. He wished for a drink before he had to deal with the two strong females that inhabited his residence. He removed his hat and opened the door with a big sigh.

Their butler, Chen, greeted him with a slight bow and took the governor's hat and placed it on a tree in the hallway. "Go to parlor, I bring you drink," Chen said.

"Thanks, Chen," the governor said, relieved that he wouldn't be dealing with his wife and daughter right away. He entered the parlor and was surprised to see a man sitting there with a drink in hand. "I see you are enjoying some of my fine California Brandy," he said with a smile.

"Yes, Althea is the consummate host and she has invited me to stay for dinner," State Senator Phineas Hatfield said.

The governor had known the senator for many years and, most often, their politics meshed. Though the senator was from southern California and the governor's roots were in the north, on occasion their political focus was different, if not contrary.

Chen handed the governor his drink. The governor looked at the senator with suspicion. “Is this pleasure or business?”

Chen took Hatfield’s glass and refilled it then handed it back to the senator.

Senator Hatfield set his glass on a doily on the small, scalloped walnut table next to his chair and cleared his throat. “Both. I’ll get the business part out of the way and then I will enjoy some more of your brandy,” he said with a smile. And then he became serious. “As you know, the legislature, for the most part, was unhappy with your executive decision to resurrect the California Rangers. They felt you overstepped your authority and should have gone through the appropriate legislative process.”

Irritated, the governor said, “I’d still be waiting for their decision.”

Senator Hatfield held up the palm of his hand to continue. “That may well be, but, as you know, I smoothed things over and the successful events in the Mother Lode have given several of my colleagues political capital.”

The governor smiled. Leave it to the politicians to take the credit.

Chen appeared with the decanter of brandy and refilled governor’s glass.

“Thank you, Chen,” the governor said.

Chen gave a small bow.

The senator took a drink and cleared his throat again before continuing. “Since your, uh, little experiment has been successful so far, some fellow senators and I were thinking that we should add personnel to your rangers.”

The governor took a sip of his brandy. And suddenly he realized what had precipitated this turn of events. He smirked. “You all got a visit from William Fargo.”

“Well, yes,” the senator said, blushing at the governor’s astuteness. “The robbery and shooting indicates that we need more law enforcement personnel in the Mother Lode."

The governor nodded, restraining himself from saying 'I told you so'.

The senator continued. "Because of budget constraints we would have to start slowly and build from there."

"How slowly are we talking about?" the governor asked.

The senator took a handkerchief out of his pocket and dabbed the moisture on his forehead. "I think we can successfully add one ranger now and possibly more later."

The governor smirked. "One ranger; we wouldn't want the legislature to overdo it."

"Baby steps, governor, baby steps. We add one now and perhaps a number of them later."

"Uh-huh, perhaps," the disgusted governor said.

Chen reentered the room. "Dinner served."

The governor relieved the senator of his empty brandy glass. "We'll continue this over a snifter of Cognac after dinner, senator."

Chapter 8

Mounted and headed north, Marshal Wheeler said, "Horseshoe Bend's only a couple of miles from here."

Gazing up to the distant snow-capped Sierra Nevada Mountains with a cotton-like canopy of puffy clouds, Seth said, "I'm always amazed so much evil can exist in such magnificent country."

"Yep, there seems to be no end to it."

Up-slope the smoke of a distant campfire drifted with a slight breeze. "Could be our thief," Seth said.

"Could be. Also could be miners, ranchers, or farmers."

Seth nodded. He understood the marshal's point. Lawmen were so scarce that they couldn't go on wild goose chases. They had to be judicious with their time. Since he was here, however, he just might check the camp out on his way back to town.

"The Bend's just ahead," the marshal said.

Gentry loosened his holstered gun and scanned the mesquite and oak-strewn knoll. Just below the distant horizon stood a deer, motionless and staring in their direction. "Doesn't look like the robber is still in the area," he said.

Marshal Wheeler, gun hand dangling near his holster, said, "Just around this corner."

Seth checked his sorrel's ears for any sign of danger and reined in by the marshal. The two lawmen dismounted and looked for sign. The two-track road was well used and beaten down with no clear indication of what had happened.

"I'll take this side and you take the other," the marshal said, indicating the up-slope.

Seth nodded. With a thoughtful gaze, he looked down the road and up the knoll. The robber obviously had chosen this area for the robbery since the stage would have had to slow down for the sharp curve in the road. The robber would have a better view and advantage from above. His eyes were drawn to an outcropping of large boulders and he made his way toward them, taking his time observing the ground before him. His father and a half-breed friend had taught him that patience was of utmost importance.

As Seth neared the boulders, Marshal Wheeler hollered, "There's drag marks over here from the strong box."

The ranger smiled. The thief didn't want to be dragging the heavy box uphill. Behind the largest boulder was evidence of where a man had lain in wait. Several cigarette butts had been crushed by the heel of a boot. There was a large circle of bent grass where the man had been pacing around.

And then he saw it.

*****

Seth knelt down and looked at a clear boot print. The heel was worn down and there was a distinct circle in the sole where it was wearing through. The ranger placed his boot next to the imprint. The imprint was about two sizes smaller. He looked around and then studied the imprint some more. He moved his boot away. There was a deeper imprint left in the sand where he had been standing.

The ranger made a larger circle around the boulders and found the path the robber took down to the road.

"Found the strongbox," Marshal Wheeler said from behind some scrub oak.

"I don't suppose it's full of silver dollars."

"You suppose right," the marshal said. "It's empty as a saloon with no whiskey."

Seth joined the marshal. The strongbox had been dragged downhill and the lock broken open. He circled the area and found where the robber had tied his horse. The thief didn't take the time to cover his tracks and the ranger followed them downhill. In the dirt and debris the horses' hooves made a deeper imprint from the added weight of the robber's plunder. The direction taken was toward Amador City.

Working his way back uphill, Seth found the marshal sitting on the strongbox drawing on a cigarette.

"My knees ain't what they used to be, so I decided to take a break and wait for your report," the marshal said with a grin.

The ranger smiled back at the amiable marshal and sat down on a deadfall close by. "The robber loaded up the contents of the strongbox on his horse and it looks like he's headed to your town."

Marshal Wheeler took a drag on his cigarette and exhaled. "That's convenient; maybe we can catch him there."

"From the description given and what I've observed, we need to be looking for a small man with a worn sole of his right boot. I don't think he can get too far with that heavy load and we'll have to look out for a stranger spending silver dollars," Seth said. "His boot size is smaller than mine."

The marshal nodded. "Any of those things ain't enough to hang a man."

"True, but all of them put together would be enough to encourage the man to confess," Seth said with a chuckle.

The marshal stood up with a groan. "Let's get back to town and form a welcoming committee in case the man shows. We can tell Agent Turley where he can pick up his strongbox."

Ranger Gentry mounted his sorrel and the marshal looked on with appreciation. "That's some fine horse flesh you got there, Seth."

Seth patted the big horse's neck. "Red here is the best horse I ever rode. The governor's going to play hell getting him back."

"I was you, I'd keep rangerin' just to keep that horse," the marshal said as he touched spurs to his mount.

Chapter 9

Darla and Althea Brown watched the pompous Senator Hatfield enter the dining room. The governor's daughter and wife were accustomed to entertaining politicians and people of influence, many of whom they found rather distasteful. Visitors were often present in an attempt to gain favor from the governor, or vice versa. They gave each other a questioning look, wondering what the purpose of the senator's visit was.

"So nice to see you again, senator," Mrs. Brown said. "How is Hannah? It's been so long since I've seen your lovely wife, we must get together someday soon."

Chen pulled out the chairs for the Brown women as the senator and governor took their seats at the table.

The governor smiled to himself. He knew that his best asset was his beautiful wife. She could make anyone feel comfortable and make them feel as if they were the center of the universe.

The senator smiled. "She's just fine, Althea; she's down Stockton way visiting her brother with Jimmie. Her brother hasn't been feeling well lately."

A look of concern crossed Althea's face. "Oh, I hope he gets better soon. How's little Jimmie doing?"

Chen brought in a sizzling platter of fried chicken.

The senator aggressively stabbed some chicken and put it on his plate. "Little Jimmie isn't so little anymore. He's seventeen and about to go out on his own." The senator looked into the sparkling brown eyes of Darla Brown as he sawed away at his chicken with a knife. "He'd be a fine catch for Miss Darla, here."

Darla smiled a bright, insincere smile. "He's a bit too young for me, senator."

"Well, you could ignore a few years," the senator mumbled with a mouthful of chicken. "This is absolutely delicious," he added.

"I'm glad you like it," Althea said. "There's plenty more."

The senator reached over and stabbed another piece of chicken. Althea smiled to herself. What the senator lacked in decorum was offset by his enthusiasm.

As the senator wiped the juices from his plate with a piece of bread, Chen brought out a large sliced watermelon for dessert. With juice dribbling down his chin, the senator said, "I love watermelon."

The governor smiled. "That's the future gold of California, senator---agriculture. With our sunshine and fertile soils we could be the breadbasket of America. John Bidwell has done great work up Chico way."

"Maybe so, maybe so," the senator said as he took a large slice of watermelon. "Everyone is focused on our abundance of gold now."

"True," Governor Brown said, "but it is our job to look to the future of this great state. I'm glad the legislature is considering adding to our ranger force."

"Does that mean Seth is going to get some help, Daddy?" Darla asked.

Thaddeus Brown smiled at his daughter. "Eventually, honey; the wheels of politics can roll mighty slowly."

Everyone stared at the senator. He paused as he was about to bite into his watermelon. He cleared his throat. "The governor and I will be discussing this very thing after dinner," he said.

The three members of the Brown family continued to watch the senator in silence. Feeling uncomfortable, the senator put his fork down, as he realized everyone else was done with their meal.

"Come on, Darla," Althea Brown said, rising and grabbing some plates, "Let's clear the table so the men can go about their business."

Chapter 10

Agent Turley was pacing back and forth in front of the marshal's office when he finally saw the two lawmen ride into town.

"Looks like we got a welcoming committee," the marshal said to Seth as they reined in.

"Well?" Turley asked.

The marshal ignored the little man. "Let's get some coffee, Seth."

Turley followed them into the marshal's office. "I need a report, marshal. Did you find my money?"

Marshal Wheeler turned with hands on hips. "Turley, you're like a pesky mosquito. You're always buzzing around, irritating me."

"I have a job to do, marshal. What did you find out?"

The marshal scowled at the fidgety agent. "Fill him in Seth; I'm going to make us some coffee."

"You can pick up your empty strongbox at Horseshoe Bend. We put it behind a big oak tree," Seth said.

The agent guffawed. "That's all you can tell me?" he said pacing again.

Seth looked over at the grinning marshal. "No."

"Well?" the exasperated agent asked.

Ranger Gentry looked down at Agent Turley's boots. "The lowlife that stole *your* money was about your size and appeared to have your demeanor."

The agent stopped pacing.

"You can't possibly think "

"He also had a hole in the bottom of his right boot." Seth heard the marshal chuckle.

"How dare you imply I had anything to do with the robbery," the agent hissed.

"Let me see that right foot," Seth said, grabbing the agent's leg like he was going to shoe a horse.

Agent Turley lost his balance and gripped the edge of the marshal's oak desk. His spectacles were askew and he was sputtering as Ranger Gentry looked at the bottom of his right boot. Seth could hear the marshal laughing as he fed wood to the stove.

"Looks like you are in the clear, Agent Turley," Seth said, letting his foot fall back to the floor.

"I never," Turley said as he stormed out of the office.

Seth looked at the grinning marshal. "Just eliminated him as a suspect," he said seriously.

Marshal Wheeler laughed. "That pompous little twit has been a burr in my saddle ever since he showed up. You just made my day."

"It takes all kinds," Seth said shaking his head. "I been thinking, marshal, the robber had to have hidden the majority of that silver nearby. Can you think of any likely places?"

The marshal set the coffee pot on the stove and thought for a moment. "That's rugged county, Seth; it could be hidden in hundreds of different places."

Gentry nodded.

"There are dozens of stories and legends of hidden, undiscovered gold in these hills," the marshal continued.

"I've heard a few of them, but, the fact is that we have a lot of silver missing from the stage.

*****

Ned Hayes and Virgil Smith watched the Wells Fargo Agent storm out of the marshal's office. "He didn't look none too happy," Virgil said.

"Nope," Ned said as he squinted up Main Street. Well, looky here."

Chapter 11

Virgil followed Ned's gaze up the street. A small swarthy man on a tired horse rode down the busy thoroughfare. The rider was slumped over and it appeared that he would fall out of the saddle at any moment. He looked up from under the brim of his floppy hat and his eyes met Virgil's and then moved to Ned. And then he raised his eyes to the sign above the saloon, flashing a gray-toothed smile.

The rider eased himself out of the saddle and walked his horse over to the saloon's hitching rail and said, "Ned, how's it hanging?"

"Eli, good to see you," Ned said as he looked for Eli's saddle bags. "Traveling kinda light."

"Just now," Eli Hayes said. "Going to buy me a drink? My throat's mighty parched."

Virgil watched the small man seem to struggle to walk up the board steps.

Ned chuckled. "I hear yer the one with all the money."

Eli's eyes widened and he glanced around. "What do you mean?"

"Virgil and I heard about your unauthorized withdrawal of silver from the Wells Fargo Stage," Ned said.

"Don't mean I did it," Eli said.

Ned nodded. "Except that you shot the guard. That's got your signature all over it. You never lacked for wanting to shoot somebody."

Eli fidgeted. "Buy me that damned drink." He walked into the crowded saloon.

Virgil and Ned joined Eli at the bar. The saloon was packed with patrons, and no one seemed to notice the three men enter.

"Don't forget, you're buying," Eli said to his brother.

"You got more money than I do," Ned said.

Virgil watched the interaction between the brothers. Why had Ned seemed so taken by his loser brother?

"Don't be stupid," Eli hissed. "I stashed the loot. I can't be flashing silver dollars right after a robbery."

Ned grinned. Eli had just admitted to robbing the stage.

Virgil stared at the two. Though older and bigger, Ned seemed to defer to his smaller, younger brother. "I only got a dollar," Ned said.

Eli glared at Ned. "Well, use it then."

"Whiskey," Virgil said to the bartender.

"Make it three," Ned added reaching into the bottom of his pocket.

The bartender poured three shots and waited for the money to appear on the bar. Ned put his single dollar on the bar.

"Here's to better days," Eli said, downing the whiskey in one gulp.

"They better come quick; Virgil and I are about tapped out," Ned said.

Eli ordered three more whiskeys.

Ned glared at his brother as he pulled two silver dollars from his pocket. "I thought you said you stashed the money."

Eli smiled. "Well, I did grab a few to get by."

The three men hunched over their drinks. "You coulda paid in the first place," Ned said.

Ignoring his brother, Eli looked to see if anyone was in a position to overhear their conversation. "When we going to do this bank job you told me about?"

Ned leaned closer to his brother. "We got us another lawman in town. A California Ranger, and he and the marshal been stirred up by that stagecoach robbery. We're going to need to lay low for a couple of days and we have to wait for the gold shipments from the mines. We'll need to get some of that money of yours to hold us over."

Virgil grinned. Ned was plenty smart trying to weasel his way into finding out where his brother stashed the money. He fixed an expectant stare on Eli and watched him down another drink.

"I didn't know I was going to have to bankroll this operation," Eli growled. "Give me another, barkeep. Set these two boys up also."

"Virgil and I been waitin' for you and it's took all of our money," Ned said.

Eli squinted one eye at his brother and looked over at Virgil. "I can't be leading people to that money. I got enough on me for a couple of days."

"That's good," Ned said trying not to sound disappointed. "We may need more than a couple of days, though."

Eli finished off his drink. "I gotta get some chow. Where can I get a good steak?"

Ned eyed his little brother. He looked like a rat that had been foraging in the garbage. Eating at one of Amador City's finer establishments was out of the question. "Lulu Lamont's serves up a good steak, among other things," he said.

The trio lumbered north, oblivious to the citizenry giving the men a wide berth. "Them's nice places," Eli said with a sweep of his arm, indicating the Imperial Hotel and Amador Hotel.

"Expensive, too," Virgil said.

"Keep on going Eli, we got to make your money last awhile," Ned said.

They arrived at a white two-story frame structure that was tidy and welcoming. Lace curtains adorned the windows, but there was no sign indicating that this was a business establishment.

"What is this, a boarding house?" Eli asked.

"Something like that," Ned said, opening the door.

Sitting on a stool inside the door was a large, burly man. Next to him on a walnut table was a good-sized club. Behind him was a hat tree with a couple of holstered guns hanging from it. "You boys need to check your guns," he said.

"I don't rightly like giving up my gun," Eli said, glaring at the man.

Virgil and Ned began to unbuckle their gun belts.

"No gun, no service," the big man said.

An attractive middle-aged woman came sweeping down the staircase, her frilly dress rustling like leaves in an autumn breeze. "Is there a problem, Joe?" she asked.

"Little man here doesn't want to give up his firearm, Miss Lamont."

Eli's jaw had dropped when he saw the beautiful woman come down the stairs.

With hands on hips, Lulu Lamont said, "For the safety and well-being of my employees I have a strict rule of no weapons."

Y-yes, ma'am, I didn't mean no harm," Eli said, unbuckling his gun belt without taking his eyes off of the lovely brunette woman.

"What'll it be, boys?" Lulu Lamont asked. "A drink, dinner, or companionship?"

"Three whiskeys and steak dinners," Eli said, wishing he had brought more of the loot.

"Lulu walked behind the large oak bar and poured three drinks. "How do you want your steaks?" she asked, observing the trio and sniffing the close air.

"Cooked," Eli answered as he pulled several silver dollars out of his pocket and laid them on the bar.

The madam eyed the money. "If you boys are going to, uh, participate in our entertainment after your meal you'll have to get yourselves a bath out back; ten cents for a shave and fifty cents for a bath."

Eli thought about the money in his pocket and looked over to Ned and an expectant Virgil. "Maybe another time," he said.

Disappointed, Virgil wanted to protest but he knew he was not in a position to do so.

"Your steaks will be up in about ten minutes," Lulu said, leaving for the back.

Raucous laughter preceded two men descending the staircase, escorted by two lovely women, garnering the attention of the three men.

Chapter 12

Eli's eyes were drawn to the beautiful women in frilly dresses, and then they locked onto the eyes of the taller man of the two. He recognized the driver of the stage he had robbed.

"Something about that guy looks familiar," the driver said to the man next to him when he saw Eli at the bar.

The man shook his head. "I ain't seen him before."

The driver continued to stare at the little man as he descended the stairs.

Eli ducked his head and turned his attention to his drink. Even though he'd had his face covered during the robbery, he didn't want to attract unnecessary attention. Virgil focused on the two women coming down the stairs with the two men. The blonde was a small girl with sparkly blue eyes and the brunette was taller and more top heavy.

"I could go for some of that," Virgil said.

Ned turned from the bar to look. "Forget it, Virgil; you don't have two coins to rub together."

"Mayhap that brother of yourn could treat u\s since he's got all that money."

"Shut up, Virgil!" Eli said in a harsh whisper.

Lulu Lamont entered the bar. "Your steaks are up in the dining room."

The three men followed her into the dining room. Eli ducked behind his larger older brother to avoid the driver and his friend who had approached the bar.

As the men took a seat, Lulu sniffed the air. “If you boys are going to participate in our entertainment you’ll have to take a bath out back.”

“Not this day; maybe another time,” Ned said.

“Well, if you come back be sure and get cleaned up first,” she demanded.

Virgil grunted and tore into his steak. “Good,” he mumbled, juices dripping down his whiskered chin.

“Everything here is good,” Lulu Lamont said as she left them to their food.

“That’s a fine looking woman,” Virgil muttered, wiping his mouth with a dirty sleeve.

Eli peeked over his shoulder toward the bar. He was relieved to see the driver and his companion had left. He took a deep breath and cut a small piece of steak. “One of those two men was the driver of the stagecoach,” he hissed.

Ned turned to look at the bar to see that the men were gone. Virgil was oblivious, shoveling food into his mouth. He looked at Virgil and said, “I swear, a pig has better manners.”

Virgil looked up at Ned, drool dripping from his mouth, gave a food-packed grin and dove back in.

“I’ve lost my appetite,” Eli said.

Virgil stabbed Eli’s steak with his fork and deposited it on his plate.

Irritated, Ned thought “*I got to be rid of this guy.*”

Lulu appeared in the doorway. “Can I get you boys some coffee?”

“Bring three,” Eli said.

She returned with the coffee and said, “That’ll be $4.50.”

“Kinda expensive, ain’t it?” Eli said.

With a beautiful, bright smile, Lulu said, “Quality costs.”

Eli pulled out five silver dollars and handed them to Lulu. “Keep the change,” he said.

Surprised, Lulu Lamont looked at the five silver dollars. “Mister, you’re welcome back anytime.”

Chapter 13

In the parlor, Senator Phineas Hatfield accepted a glass of Cognac from Chen. He took a drink and smacked his lips and then he looked over at Althea in the dining room. "I have to say, Thad, you do appreciate the finer things in life."

The senator's glance over at his wife did not go unnoticed by the governor. He would prefer it if the senator would leave, but the senator had indicated to him there was more business to be done. The California Legislature controlled the purse strings and it behooved him to hear what the senator had to say. The governor took a sip of his Cognac and said nothing. Normally he would offer a good cigar to his guest, but he didn't want the senator hanging around any longer than necessary. "You had other things to discuss, Phineas?"

The senator set his Cognac on the table, interlaced his fingers and leaned forward. He cleared his throat. "Since we've added to your rangers, I would like to suggest a good man for the job."

The governor took a drink, staring at the senator in silence.

The senator twiddled his thumbs nervously, waiting for the governor to respond. When the governor said nothing, he continued. "Jimmie's of age for a job and he's good with a gun."

There it was, the coup de gras. He was being given another man for the rangers, not of his choosing. The governor searched his memory of last seeing Jimmie when he was about twelve years old. He stared at Phineas Hatfield. "He's not a man. He's just a boy," the governor said.

Senator Hatfield fidgeted in his chair. "You haven't seen him lately, Thad, he's all grown up. He'll be eighteen soon."

Governor Brown shook his head. "Being a ranger is hard work and can be awful dangerous, Phineas."

"I know, but I can assure you that he is up to it."

The governor's chair groaned in relief as he eased it of its burden. He clasped his hands behind his back and paced the room. And then he stopped and looked down at the senator.

Senator Hatfield raised his eyes to the large, imposing governor.

"Senator Hatfield, I won't say no. I appreciate your efforts to add to the ranger company and I'm sure Captain Gentry would welcome the help. However, I will not send a young man into harm's way unless I feel he is qualified to handle it."

The governor turned and walked across the room in thought and then returned.

Senator Hatfield wrung his hands and waited.

"When Jimmie gets back from Stockton have him come to my office for an interview."

Phineas Hatfield jumped up and shook the governor's hand. "Thank you, Thad, I do appreciate the consideration."

"One other thing, senator."

"Anything, governor, you name it."

Governor Brown smiled. The senator was so eager he decided to add to his demands. "I'm formally requesting that you work on getting me more funding and more men for the ranger company." As long as he had some leverage over the senator he was going to take full advantage.

The senator's smiling face turned serious. "I will make every conceivable effort to do so, governor," he said.

"Good." The governor guided the senator toward the door. "I'm looking forward to seeing little Jimmie again. You have a good evening, Phineas."

"Thank you governor, I'll get Jimmie in as soon as possible. Thank Mrs. Brown for the fine meal."

The governor watched the senator descend the porch and shut the door with shaking head. He walked slowly back into the dining room.

Althea Brown looked up from her sewing. "Finally get rid of that old wind bag?"

Smiling the governor said, "Yes; he not only wanted to hook up Jimmie with Darla but he wants me to add Jimmie to the ranger force."

"He's just a boy," the governor's wife said.

"Soon to be eighteen, though," he said. Boys a lot younger than that died in the war."

"The world can be awfully cruel," Althea Brown said sadly. "I do worry about Seth, so. Darla wants to go up and see him so badly."

The governor's shoulders slumped and he put both hands in his trouser pockets. He turned and walked back into the parlor with a sudden desire for another drink.

Chapter 14

The noisy arrival of cowboys in the bunk house awoke Chet Wagner, foreman of the Circle J Ranch. As a lantern was lit, he sat up. “You boys are back a little early. Get run out of town?”

Len, one of the younger cowboys, was sitting on his bunk and pulling off his boots. “We can thank Buck for that.”

Wagner leaned back on an elbow. “No surprise there. Trouble is that boy’s middle name.”

“He didn’t have to kill that old guy, and over a saloon girl,” Len added.

“What happened?” Wagner asked.

“This blonde gal wasn’t paying no attention to him like he demanded and this old miner pulled a knife on Buck. Buck gutted him with the old guy’s own knife,” another cowboy added.

“Is he in the pokey?” Wagner asked.

“No, it was self-defense but it put an end to our evening. We couldn’t hardly argue with the marshal with a dead man lying on the floor,” Len said.

The foreman shook his head. “That boy is just no good. One of these days he’s going to meet his match.”

Len looked down at his stocking feet. “The sooner the better as far as I’m concerned. He’s as mean as a stepped-on rattler.”

Wagner stared at the young cowboy. “You better not let the old man hear you say that, or you’ll be out of a job.”

"Yeah, I know. Because they're blood he don't see how evil his boy is."

Chet looked around and whispered, "The old man ain't no angel neither."

"That's a fact," Len said, pulling the covers over him and lying down to face the wall.

"One of you boys douse that lantern," Wagner said, settling back in his bunk. As dark enveloped the bunk house he could already hear a chorus of snoring.

*****

John Henry was sitting comfortably in his large leather chair near the wood stove reading a book when he heard the front door of the ranch house open. He knew it was his son because the boy wasn't capable of doing anything quietly. Buck Henry stumbled into the parlor and stared at his father with bleary eyes. "Home early, aren't you boy?"

Buck Henry swayed from side to side. "That damn marshal run us out."

His father closed his book and set it on his lap. "Don't suppose he had call to do so."

"Not much, I was just making over some saloon fluff."

John Henry raised a brow. He knew his son and they always say that the acorn doesn't fall too far from the tree. As always, there was more to the story. "You best hit the sack; I want you to go to church with me in the morning."

Buck squinted at his father. He hated going to church with a bunch of sanctimonious hypocrites. "I want to sleep in tomorrow. I've been working hard," he argued, knowing it would be to no avail.

"We've been through this before. You know that I promised your dear departed mother that I would get you some bible learnin'."

Disgusted, Buck tromped up the stairs. The only redeeming thing about going to church was that there were always a couple of good looking women in attendance. As he stripped for bed he felt himself starting to stir when the vision of the preacher's daughter appeared in his head. Though young, she had blossomed like a beautiful flower in spring time. He smiled to himself as he lay down on the bed. Yes, that little girl needed to have herself a man.

Chapter 15

"Where you boys been staying?" Eli asked.

"We was at the boarding house for a while, but you took so long gettin' here we been camping outside of town," Ned said.

Eli stopped and stared at Virgil and Ned. "At least in jail I got two hots and a cot."

Irritated, Ned said, "You can go back to those accommodations if you have a hankering to."

"Well, I don't cotton to sleeping on the ground," Eli grumbled.

"You could go get some of that money you stole and put us into some lodging," Virgil said.

Eli sneered at Virgil. Despite Eli's small size, Virgil felt a shiver run down his spine. Eli's beady eyes were like a snake's. "Where'd you come across this dumb ass, Ned? He'd just as soon I got caught for the sake of his comfort."

Ned sighed. "Come on, I'll show you our camping spot."

Just south of town and near a small creek was a fire ring surrounded by empty tin cans. Despite his own unkempt appearance, Eli viewed the scene with disgust. "Leastways you boys could clean this up."

"Virgil, dig a hole and throw this stuff in it," Ned said.

"Why don't you do the diggin'?"

"You gotta do yer share around here. I can't be the one doing everything."

Grumbling, Virgil grabbed a camp shovel.

Eli shook his head, wondering what he had gotten himself into.

"Don't get too far away," Ned said. "Them Keystone Mine guards are mighty sensitive about their property. They're going to be even more unpleasant since ol' Eli here stole their payroll."

Eli sat on a deadfall and listened to Virgil digging and grumbling behind a mesquite bush. "What's your plan on hittin' the bank?"

Ned smirked. "I was thinking you would get here sooner and we could rob it after the payroll come in, but you beat us to it."

Virgil chuckled. He glared in the direction Virgil was digging. "That wouldn't have been much of a take split three ways."

"More than I got now," Ned said.

"I was jest tryin' to get a grubstake. I had no idea that there would be that much silver in the strong box," Eli said. "How does this payroll thing work?"

Ned thought for a moment. "The guards bring gold down and they ship it out and return with money for the payroll."

"What do they do with the gold when they bring it into town?" Eli asked.

Ned glared at Eli like he was an idiot. "Why, they put it in the bank."

Eli nodded thoughtfully. "What are they going to do about the missing payroll?"

Exasperated, Ned said, "Try to find it."

"What if they don't?"

Ned began pacing. "I guess they'll have to replace it."

"Uh-huh. What do they do with the payroll when it gets here?"

Frustrated, Ned stopped and scowled at his brother. "They put it in the bank until payday. The miners come in with vouchers and the bank pays them."

Eli rubbed his whiskered chin.

"I got that hole dug," Virgil said, interrupting Eli's thought process.

Irritated, Eli said, "An empty hole don't do no good. Put that garbage in it and cover it up."

"Since when is he giving orders?" Virgil whined to Ned.

"Just do it, Virgil, we're working on making you a rich man," Ned said.

Grumbling, Virgil spread his bedroll and started heaping the trash on it. The Hayes brothers watched in silence as Virgil joined all four corners and hauled the trash back to the hole.

"What are you thinking, Eli?" Ned asked.

"I was thinking that it would be a lot more profitable splitting our take two ways," he said.

Chapter 16

Marshal Mack Wheeler walked over to the gun rack in his office and took down a double-barreled shotgun. "Come on, Seth, let's take your horse down to the livery and you can accompany me on my rounds. We'll get you checked into the hotel and have some dinner."

"It has been some time since I had a good meal," Seth said rubbing his stomach. "I need to get Red some grain; we've been trailing some."

Seth unhitched his sorrel and led him down the street, walking beside the marshal. The air was clear and pleasant, the warm sun soothing, and the clop, clop of the horses' hooves was a welcome, relaxing cadence. Though seemingly relaxed, Seth noticed the marshal's eyes taking in everything. Lawmen didn't live to be old men without being alert to their surroundings.

"It sure is a nice little town you have here, Mack," Seth said.

"Most times, 'cept when folks are robbed and shot."

"Too much of that goes on nowadays."

"You don't need to worry about your horse; ol' Charlie at the livery likes horses more than people," the marshal said.

Seth chuckled. "Know a guy like that in Sacramento; can't blame them sometimes."

The two men entered the livery, taking a moment to adjust to the darkness of the barn. The strong, familiar odor of horses and hay filled their nostrils.

Seeing no one about, the marshal hollered, "Charlie, where are you, you old coot?"

"Hold your horses, marshal, I'm back here."

The two men walked deeper into the dark barn and found Charlie mucking out the end stall.

"I got some prime horseflesh for you to take care of," the marshal said. "This here is Captain Seth Gentry of the California Rangers.

Charlie reached out with a dirty, rough hand and shook Seth's. Seth had a broad smile on his face. Charlie could have been the twin brother of the liveryman in Sacramento. Short, bowlegged, and a scraggly grey beard; he was looking over Seth's shoulder at Red.

"That's a fine looking horse you got there, mister," Charlie said.

Seth laughed. Charlie even sounded like Buster. "Red's the property of the State of California; be sure and give me an invoice for his keep."

Charlie cackled. "Do that mean I can charge double?"

"If it's too much they'll take it out of my pay," Seth said, still smiling at the amiable little man.

"Well, we don't want that to happen; law's awful scarce in these hills," Charlie said. "No offense, marshal."

"None taken, Charlie. I couldn't agree with you more.

"Thieves is thick as flies in the barn," Charlie added.

"We plan on swatting a few," the marshal said.

"Don't you go worrying about your horse, ranger, I'll take good care of him," Charlie said, grabbing the reins.

"Give him some grain; he's earned it." Seth grabbed his saddle bags ,threw them over his shoulder and pulled his rifle out of the scabbard. "You don't have a brother named Buster, do you?"

Charlie rubbed his whiskered chin. "Not that I knowed of. Don't know much about family; I was raised in a whore house near Sacramento. My mother died some years later of disease."

Gentry looked at the curious little man and wondered if he and Buster were related. He would have to ask Buster about his past the next time he went to Sacramento.

"Let's get some grub Seth; I could eat a small steer," the marshal said.

Chapter 17

Governor Thaddeus Brown was reading an article at his desk about the impending completion of the Transcontinental Railroad and what it would mean to California's growth and commerce. California's population had already doubled since the discovery of gold in the Mother Lode and easier and quicker access would create a population boom never before seen by mankind. His feeling of dread was real and he knew that the government was ill prepared to handle it.

Prudence tapped on his office door and entered. "There's a James Hatfield here to see you, governor. He says he's the son of Senator Phineas Hatfield and that you are expecting him."

"Oh, yeah, Jimmie," the governor said. "Send the boy in, Prudie." He stood up from his leather chair to greet his visitor, stretching his limbs and walking around his substantial walnut desk.

The governor was a large man and he was stunned to see a young man taller than himself enter the room.

"Governor Brown, so nice to see you again," the young man said, extending a large hand to shake the governor's. The boys grip was firm.

"It has obviously been a while, Jimmie. You are all grown up."

"Yes sir," he said with a smile. "My parents still insist on calling me Jimmie, but in the real world I prefer James or Jim."

The governor chuckled. “I’ll try to remember that, but I might slip up once in a while.” He indicated for James Hatfield to take one of the leather chairs in front of his desk and he returned to his.

“My father tells me that Darla has grown into a beautiful woman,” Hatfield said as he placed his hat crown down on the chair next to him.

“She’s the apple of my eye, as they say,” the governor said. “Thankfully she took after her mother.”

“How is Mrs. Brown, sir?”

“Fine, just fine, my boy; thank you for asking.” As pleasantries were spoken the governor was appraising the young man. He was better built and more mature than he had expected. He had a strong jaw line and an erect, confident manner. He had bright, intelligent brown eyes and a politeness that indicated good breeding, despite who his father was.

“Your father tells me that you might want to join the Ranger Company,” the governor said.

“Yes, sir, the law has been of interest to me. My father wanted me to go to law school. I’m afraid I would find that a little boring and I can’t think of too many lawyers that I have met and liked. No offense, sir,” Hatfield said, looking down to his hands.

Governor Brown laughed. “None taken Jimmie, I, er, mean Jim. What makes you think you would want to be a ranger?”

“Well, sir, I can’t see myself sitting around in an office all closed up.” He looked around the governor’s finely appointed office. “Even one as nice as this one; I’ve always enjoyed being outdoors and moving around.”

Governor Brown leaned back in his leather chair. He was beginning to grow fond of this boy and James was saying things that he often thought about. Sometimes he envied Seth Gentry, moving about the country, meeting new people and not being stuck in one place. He thought back on how he had enjoyed his little foray with his wife and daughter up to Nevada City after Seth had discovered the murder of Darla's fiancé.

The governor interlaced his fingers on top of his desk. "Tell me why you think you are qualified to be a ranger, my boy."

James Hatfield squirmed in his chair. He wasn't the braggart type and felt uncomfortable talking about himself. "Well, sir, as I mentioned, I prefer to be outside. I've spent most of my boyhood fishing, camping, and hunting. I can handle a shotgun and have been known to knock down my share of ducks in the delta. I have hunted deer and elk with a rifle and am well practiced with a hand gun. I keep my guns clean and loaded and my knife sharp."

Governor Brown watched the young man carefully. Though uneasy, he exuded a confidence not unlike Seth Gentry.

Hatfield sat on the edge of his seat.

The governor rubbed his chin. "You ride a horse?" he asked.

"Yes, sir, since I could walk."

"As a ranger, in the line of duty it may be necessary to shoot a man. Shooting a man is a lot different than shooting a deer or a duck; they don't shoot back."

"Yes, sir, I know that. I don't reckon I would relish shooting a fellow human, but if he is a danger to me or others he will get what's coming to him."

The governor smiled. "Getting hired on as a ranger is serious business, Jim. It's hard and dangerous but can be rewarding. I like what you've had to say, but we must continue with the second stage of the interview process."

Hatfield nodded expectantly.

"Tell your mother and father that you are having dinner at the governor's house so that we can conclude the process this evening." The governor wanted his wife and daughter to see the young man and be part of the process. He stood and held out his hand.

"Yes, sir, I look forward to seeing your family again," Hatfield, said, shaking the governor's hand.

"Come by at dusk and have a glass of brandy with me," the governor said.

"Thank you, sir."

The governor watched the young man leave his office. He would be interested in Darla's and Althea's opinions of the boy this evening. And then his thoughts turned to Seth. "Prudie, have you heard anything from Captain Gentry?" he yelled.

"Not a word, sir," she responded.

The governor sat down at his desk and fidgeted with a pencil. He needed to hear from Gentry so that he could placate the Brown women.

"Prudie, send another telegram to Gentry in Amador City telling him to contact me right away."

Chapter 18

The warm glow of a large, brass chandelier greeted the ranger and marshal when they entered the lobby of the Amador City Hotel. Behind a small, dark wood counter stood a little man. He was impeccable in his dress with a high tight collar, small black tie, a neat pencil-thin moustache and slicked-back dark hair. He looked like a transplant from a big city hotel in the east.

Seth smiled. It seemed that liverymen and hotel clerks were produced out of like molds.

A look of disdain greeted them as the clerk surveyed the dusty ranger with the saddle bags over his shoulder and rifle in his hand. The hotel preferred to cater to successful men of higher class. The clerk's eyes then focused on the circled star on the ranger's chest and he seemed to relax a little. The trail-worn man was not a vagrant and he was accompanied by the town marshal.

"I need a room," Seth said, producing his letter of authority from the governor for the clerk.

The clerk put on some wire-rimmed spectacles and read the paper carefully, his lips moving with each word. With new respect, the clerk said, "Why, this letter practically gives you carte blanche."

"Yes, I guess it does. The governor seems to have faith in me," Seth said, picking up the quill pen and dipping it in the ink bottle.

The clerk watched Seth sign his name. "How long will you be staying, Mr. Gentry?"

"A few days, I reckon. I'll let you know."

"Yes, sir," the clerk said, retrieving a room key. "You have the second room on the right overlooking the street."

"Cecil, get us a table in the restaurant. Seth can drop off his stuff in his room and we'll be right down," Marshal Wheeler said.

"Will do, marshal," the clerk said. "There's a basin of water on the bureau if you care to wash up."

Seth smiled. "I could do with a little less trail dust."

"Your table will be ready when you come down," Cecil said.

The ranger and marshal ascended the stairs and entered a small but well-appointed room. The walls were decorated in bright, cheerful wallpaper. Seth placed his rifle in the corner and dropped his saddle bags on the bed. He pushed down on the soft mattress and chuckled. "A person could get mighty spoiled here," Seth said.

"Nothing too good for a proxy of the governor," Marshal Wheeler said with a grin. "You just might get so comfortable that you'll forget all about fighting crime."

Seth pressed down on the mattress again. "You have point there, marshal."

"Come on, Seth, wash up and we'll get a nice thick steak."

Seth looked into the foggy mirror. "You're right, marshal, I wouldn't want to scare the folks. I could use a shave and a haircut, too." He splashed water on his face and ran his wet fingers through his hair before toweling off.

"We've got a good barbershop in town and a bathhouse out back," the marshal said, opening the door.

Seth followed the marshal out and down the stairs.

The hotel restaurant was a popular place. One lone table was vacant at the back of the room. A pleasant middle-aged woman greeted them and escorted the two lawmen to the vacant table. Marshal Wheeler placed his shotgun in the corner and Seth smiled when the marshal took the seat with his back to the wall.

A pretty, young brunette with a big smile on her face brought them a menu and handed it to Seth. She looked into Seth's eyes as she gave him the menu and then she focused on his ranger star. "Who's your handsome friend, Daddy?"

"Bethy, this is Captain Seth Gentry of the California Rangers," Marshal Wheeler said.

"Pleased to meet you Miss Wheeler," Seth said.

Beth Wheeler extended her delicate hand and Seth accepted it. Her fingers were long and elegant and she held on to his hand longer than necessary. "Please call me Beth, Mr. Ranger."

"And you can call me Seth, Beth," he said with a chuckle, realizing their names rhymed.

"You're too young for him," the marshal grumbled.

"Am not," she said.

"Are too," her father said.

Beth pouted. "I just turned fifteen, and some of my friends are married already."

Seth smiled at the cute girl. Her pout accentuated her full lips. She looked like she could be Darla Brown's younger sister. "The man that captures your heart will be a lucky man indeed. You look much like the woman I've fallen in love with in Sacramento."

The marshal's daughter crossed her arms. Disappointed, she asked, "You're taken?"

"In a manner of speaking," Seth said. "I'm hopeful, anyway."

Beth smiled. "So there still might be a chance. I can wait, for a little while."

Seth laughed.

"Bring us two steaks and all the trimmings," the marshal said as he frowned at her.

"Yes, Daddy, coming right up."

Seth watched the young girl leave for the kitchen, her dark, shiny hair bouncing with youthful energy.

"That girl's going to be the death of me," Marshal Wheeler said. "I love her with all my heart, but I was never equipped to raise a little girl. Her mother died in childbirth," he said.

"I'm sorry to hear that, Mack," Seth said. "It appears to me that you've done a fine job."

"I hope so," he said. "She's a fine girl, but she is high spirited like a new born colt."

Seth smiled at the concerned father. Fleeting thoughts of Governor Brown and his daughter made him chuckle. "Mack, I think all fathers of girls have the same concerns."

"I'm afraid I don't find any comfort in that," he said as he watched his daughter skillfully carry out two large plates of food with sizzling steaks tantalizing the nostrils.

Beth Wheeler placed Seth's plate in front of him first. He thanked her and enjoyed the enchanting smile he received in return. "My pleasure, Mr. Ranger, er, Seth," she said with a little curtsy after placing her father's plate in front of him. "Let me know if you need anything else."

"Thanks honey," the marshal said.

The two lawmen ate in silence. Seth watched the marshal scan the room as he ate, a necessity of the profession. Being a lawman meant that you had to be vigilant at all times.

"That's a fine steak," Seth said, wiping his mouth with a cloth napkin.

"The best in town." The marshal smiled at his daughter, who was bringing a pot of coffee.

"We have some fresh, hot apple pie, Daddy," she said as she walked by with a coffee pot.

"I shouldn't," the marshal said rubbing his full belly.

"How about you, Seth?" she asked.

Seth sat back in his chair. "I am partial to hot apple pie."

With a perky bounce she said, "Coming right up!"

After sipping his hot coffee, Seth said, "You are a lucky man, Mack. If I have a daughter someday I would be proud to have her be just like Beth."

Beth returned with two plates of steaming apple pie.

"I hope your daughter minds better than this one," Mack grumbled as his mouth watered.

"I knew you couldn't resist, Daddy," she said, smiling brightly.

Seth was about to take the last bite of his apple pie when he heard gunshots.

Chapter 19

Eli Hayes tossed and turned in his bedroll. "I weren't made to sleep on no hard ground," he said. "Prison was first class accommodations compared to this."

"Quit yer complaining, Eli, if you hadn't taken so long gettin' here we wouldn't have to be sleeping on the ground," Ned said.

"It's not like I had a key to my cell," he whined.

"Maybe if you hadn't been holdin' up stages we would have got the bank robbed already," Virgil chimed in.

Eli glared at Virgil. "If it weren't for me we would have no money at all."

Ned sat up. "You boys get some shut-eye; we got things to do tomorrow."

Mumbling, Eli turned his back to the other two men. He stared into the dark night. Perhaps he should just collect the rest of his silver and be done with these two. How long would that money last? If they made a big score at the bank he could be set up for life, especially if he dumped the other two. He could hear his brother breathing heavily and Virgil's snoring was irritating him even more. His thoughts turned to the whores he had seen at Lulu Lamont's. Uncomfortable, he rolled over onto his back. He licked his tongue over dry lips and rubbed his crotch. He put his other hand in his pocket and felt the two silver dollars he had left. As quiet as possible, he stood up and strapped on his gun belt. He needed a drink.

Eli gravitated toward the raucous Mooney Saloon. The piano was banging out a tune he did not recognize and numerous voices were raised to be heard, occasionally pierced by the shrill laughter of saloon girls plying their trade. As Eli entered he took a cautious look around before walking toward the packed bar. Even with his small stature he had to squeeze in between two large men that had their backs to each other. When he bumped one of them, the man turned and glared down at him. He was the stagecoach driver that Eli had robbed.

"You be needin' to watch yourself little man," the driver said.

Eli's close-set dark eyes looked like those of a rattler about to strike. His hand moved closer to his holstered gun.

The sneer on the driver's face disappeared. There was something menacing about this little man. "I seen you at Lulu Lamont's," he said.

Eli ignored the man and demanded, "Give me a whiskey, barkeep," tossing a silver dollar on the scarred wood bar with his left hand.

The garter-sleeved bartender eyed the bright silver dollar , then reached under the bar for a bottle and poured a shot of the dark amber liquid.

"I was talkin' to you little man," the driver said.

Eli knocked back the shot of whiskey, keeping his gun hand near his leather holster and turned to the larger man. "Mind yer own bidness." He turned back to the bar "Give me another."

The stage driver grabbed Eli by the shoulder and turned the little man toward him. "Hey, I'm talkin' to …"

Eli Hayes grabbed iron and shot the driver in the chest. The concussive explosion deafened ears and the smoke and stench of gunpowder filled the air. High-pitched screams from the saloon girls added to the chaos. The pianist had stopped playing. Dead silence followed and the driver lay on the floor under a cloud of gray smoke. Hayes had quickly downed his second whiskey and retreated out the door before the bartender and patrons fully realized what had happened. Eli slowed to a brisk walk and kept to the dark shadows in an attempt to not draw the attention of anyone that may be out this time of night.

*****

One of the saloon girls yelled, "Someone get the Doc!"

A bearded miner at the bar knelt down and felt for a pulse. "Make that the undertaker; he's dead."

Marshal Mack Wheeler and Ranger Seth Gentry burst into the hazy room with guns at the ready. "What happened here?" the marshal asked, with his shotgun sweeping the room.

The miner stood up. "I think there was some words and a guy drew and shot him."

"Where is this guy?" the marshal asked, looking around at the patrons. It was obvious most of them didn't want to get involved and there was an abundance of shrugs and blank stares.

Marshal Wheeler looked over at the bartender. "He drank his whiskey and just walked out," the bartender said.

The marshal looked over at a fully occupied card table with a couple of saloon girls hanging about. "Seth, go over there and verify what happened and get a description of the shooter. I'll take the bar."

"Sure thing marshal," Seth said.

After questioning the patrons and getting mostly vague answers, the two lawmen had a general description of the shooter. "I may have seen that guy ride into town," the ranger said. "He met up with two others and they went into the saloon together."

Marshal Wheeler looked over at the bartender with raised brow. "I never served that guy before. He had the look of a weasel and I would have remembered. You can check with the daytime guy in the morning," he said.

Marshal Wheeler nodded and looked over at Ranger Gentry. "Let's scout around outside and try to find somebody that saw this yahoo leave."

The two lawmen exited the saloon and stood on the dark walk looking for any bystanders. Across the dusty street was a toothless old man sitting on a bench outside the general store taking a draw on a corn cob pipe.

"Let's see if ol' Tinker's peepers saw anything," the marshal said as he led Seth across the street. "Tinker used to be a handyman of sorts but has slowed down even more than usual," he chuckled.

Tinker removed the pipe from his mouth and gave the marshal a toothless grin. "If my hearing is not playing tricks, it sounded like there was trouble in the saloon," he said.

"You heard right, old-timer," the marshal said. "A man got shot and killed. Did you see anyone leave after you heard the shots?"

Tinker put the pipe in his mouth and took a thoughtful puff. "They's always comin' and goin's. If'n I had some money I wouldn't mind getting myself a taste," he said gazing up at the marshal with a questioning look and then looking at the saloon door.

Seth forced back a smile. He reached into his leather vest and pulled out a silver dollar and held it in front of the old man. "The State of California would be happy to buy you a drink if you can help us out."

Tinker removed his pipe and stared at the coin. He licked his lips and looked up at the ranger. He squinted as if to focus on the ranger's circled star and reached for the coin. Seth closed his fist and withdrew it. "Information first," Seth said.

The old man took another draw on his corn cob pipe. He looked disgusted when he realized it had gone cold. He licked his lips again. "I seen some men enter the saloon not long afore the shooting."

Seth nodded and opened up his hand. "How about after the shooting?"

Tinker thought for a moment and nodded. "I seen the little one leave shortly after, but he didn't seem in no hurry." He reached for the coin and Seth closed his fist yet again.

"Which way was he headed?" Seth asked. "Did he mount up or continue to walk?"

The old man looked to the south. "That-a-way; he walked until he was out of my sight."

Seth held out the coin in his open hand and the old man grabbed it before he closed his fist again. "Thanks, Tinker, we appreciate your help."

"Let's take a little walk and see if we can find anything else out," the marshal said.

Chapter 20

Chen answered the knock on the door. A young man stood on the porch with hat in hand. ‘I’m James Hatfield; the governor is expecting me,” he said.

The houseboy took the young man’s hat and said, “You come in.”

“Thank you.”

“Go to parlor, Mista Brown in there,” Chen pointed to a room to the left of the foyer.

Hatfield quickly glanced around the well-appointed home. He had been in many fine homes with his father and he had expected the governor’s house to be larger. He had heard his father talk about the grandiose mansions some of the politicians wanted to build but many of them felt that the money could be better spent elsewhere.

“Come in, my boy,” the governor said, rising out of his comfortable chair and closing the leather-covered book he had been reading. Next to the warm light of a lamp on a scalloped end table was the glowing amber of a glass of brandy. “Have a seat,” the governor said, pointing to a chair across from his.

“Thank you, sir,” the young man responded, waiting for the governor to sit back down before he did so. The warm room and the book-lined shelves next to the governor were comfortable and welcoming. The aroma of food being prepared in the kitchen tantalized his nostrils. His stomach growled and he hoped that the governor had not heard it.

“How about a glass of brandy?” the governor asked.

“I’m not much of a drinker, sir.”

The governor went to the sideboard and poured a small amount of brandy into a glass. He held it out to the young man. “Just a taste; one must develop a passion for the finer things in life,” he said with a smile. “California wine and brandy are the lasting riches. Gold will eventually peter out, but sunshine and grapes can go on forever.”

“Yes, sir,” James Hatfield said, accepting the glass and sniffing the strong fragrance. He took a small sip and forced himself not to grimace. He had tasted beer before but had never tried any stronger spirits. The burning sensation traveled to his stomach and then he felt the warmth spread from within. He welcomed the relaxing sensation and looked at the governor expectantly.

The governor sat back in his chair and took a sip of brandy. “I must say I was concerned when your father suggested that you become our second California Ranger.”

Hatfield said nothing.

“My concern was on several levels,” the governor said. “One, of course, is that you are the son of a member of the legislature and I wouldn’t want anything to happen to you. And I didn’t want to be accused of nepotism. I was also concerned about your youth and lack of experience and ability to do the job. I would want you to be of assistance to Captain Gentry and not a hindrance.”

Jim nodded and took a polite sip of his brandy. He was feeling some of the tension leave him and was starting to enjoy a more relaxed state.

The governor observed the young man. “What do you say about my concerns, my boy?”

Hatfield cleared his throat. “Well, sir, I don’t plan on getting hurt or getting myself killed. I know my father is a politician and I would hope that people don’t hold that against me. No offense, sir.”

The governor chuckled, “None taken.”

“And, though young, I can handle myself and I think that I could be of help to Captain Gentry. Two guys watching each other’s back are better than going it alone.”

The governor smiled. The young man was smart and he liked his response.

Althea Brown entered the parlor removing her apron. "This is little Jimmie Hatfield? My, my, you have grown up."

Hatfield leaped to his feet. "It's been a while, Mrs. Brown."

The governor said, "He's not Jimmie anymore, Althea, he's James or Jim. It's more befitting a grown up."

She laughed. "I'll try to remember that," she said as she took Hatfield by the arm and led him into the dining room. "Dinner's about ready and Darla will be down in a moment."

The governor chortled. "That's a moment in female time; we probably have time for another drink," he said, following the two into the dining room.

"Oh, Thad, stop it," his wife said. "You're going to give our guest the wrong impression of us Brown women."

Governor Brown noticed that the young man was astute enough not to comment. *Smart boy, he thought.*

The clamor of feminine feet could be heard coming down the stairs. Darla Brown swept into the room. James Hatfield's jaw dropped. She was gorgeous.

"This can't be little Jimmie?" Darla asked.

"Yes, honey, he's all grown up," her father said.

Darla quickly moved around the table and gave the starry-eyed young man a sisterly hug.

Hatfield blushed, and stammered, "Uh, hello Darla."

"It's Jim now, Darla. He wants to join the California Rangers and give Seth a helping hand," the governor said.

"Mother, told me," Darla said. "I couldn't imagine little Jimmie Hatfield could be much help to Seth, but now that I see him, maybe so. If anything happened to Seth I would just die."

Hatfield finally closed his mouth. Again in his life he wished he was a little bit older. Darla Brown was the most beautiful young woman he had ever seen. "I hope that

Governor Brown hires me," Hatfield said. "I would appreciate the honor of helping Captain Gentry."

Darla's bright smile disappeared. With a serious expression she looked over at her mother. "Mother, I'll help you and Chen in the kitchen."

Althea Brown nodded and followed her daughter into the kitchen. She could tell something was on her daughter's mind.

Hatfield's eyes followed the two women as they left. "You're a lucky man, governor."

Governor Brown smiled. "Yes, yes I am, my boy; but sometimes I wish I had a son. I am hopeful someday that Seth Gentry will be my son-in-law. He's one of the finest young men I have ever met."

Hatfield watched the governor look off into the distance. He hoped that he would have the opportunity to gain the governor's respect like Seth Gentry had.

Neither had any idea about the scheming going on in the kitchen.

Chapter 21

Marshal Wheeler and Ranger Gentry split up, each taking a side of the main street. It was late and there were few people out and those that were weren't exactly sober. Other than Tinker and the witnesses in Mooney's Saloon they gained no new information and found no sign of the killer. They met at the end of town and peered into the dark night.

"If the killer had a horse he could be long gone," the marshal said.

Seth looked up into the star-filled sky. "Not much moon and its awful dark. He may not be too far away. He might hole up somewhere close. If we get an early start we might just catch up to him if he continued this way."

The marshal nodded. "Sutter Creek is only a few miles that way; we can take a ride in the morning and if nothing else I'll introduce you to Marshal Sam Clements."

"Sounds like a plan," Seth said.

"We'd best get some shut-eye," the marshal said. "When you get back to the hotel please tell my daughter everything is okay. Without a mother she worries about me."

Seth entered the hotel and walked over to Cecil at the counter. He glanced at the dark restaurant. "Is Beth still about?"

"She's about done; she's helping clean up in the kitchen. She's a little young for you ranger."

Gentry glared at the little man, fighting back the urge to grab him by the collar and pull him over the counter. He clenched his teeth and said, “I have a message from her father.”

Unconvinced, Cecil said, “Yes, sir, you can go on back.”

“Have somebody knock on my door before dawn; the marshal and I have early business,” Seth said.

“Will do,” Cecil said.

Seth walked through the dark restaurant to the kitchen thinking that Cecil and Agent Turley were two peas in a pod. Despicable little men; he disliked thinking poorly of people but sometimes they earned it.

Beth Wheeler was wiping her hands on a towel when Seth entered the kitchen. Her face lit up. “You come back to escort me home, Seth?”

He grinned. “I can certainly do that, Miss Beth. Your father asked that I stop and tell you everything is alright and he went home for the night.”

With a little pout she said, “Oh, I was hoping you came to see me of your own accord. Daddy does worry about me so.”

Seth thought about what the marshal had said. Obviously they both worried about each other and loved each other very much. “If I escort you home your father won’t shoot me, will he?”

The young girl laughed. Her laugh was hearty and like the laughter of a small child it made a person feel good. “He just might but I’ll do my best to keep that from happening.”

Seth chuckled. “Well, as long as you protect me,” he said as they left arm in arm.

“So, tell me about my competition in Sacramento,” she said as they walked down a narrow, dusty street.

Seth stopped and looked into the sparkling eyes of the little brunette. “She’s much like you, only a little older. She’s beautiful, with large dark brown eyes and a bright smile. You could be her younger sister.”

Beth smiled. “You think I’m pretty?”

"Yes, I do."

"What's her name?" she asked.

"Darla---Darla Brown."

They began to walk.

"So, if things don't work out between you and Darla I might have a chance in a year or two?"

Seth wasn't sure how he should answer that. So he didn't.

"I have a friend that is sixteen years old and married to a man that is twenty three," she said hopefully.

"Well, I'm older than that and you aren't yet sixteen," he said.

Beth turned to start up a path toward a little cottage with a neat front porch. Light was emanating from the curtained front window. "Daddy always waits up for me. I'd invite you in but he is armed," she said with a grin. She stood on her tiptoes and kissed him on the cheek. "Good night."

"Good night," Seth said, embarrassed by the show of affection from the young girl.

"Thanks again for escorting me home," she said as she opened the door.

Seth watched her walk in and close the door as Marshal Wheeler asked his daughter who she was talking to.

Chapter 22

Back at camp, Eli crawled into his bedroll. Virgil and Ned were still snoring and hadn't missed him. Even though it was a chilly night, he felt sweat run down the side of his face. He wished he hadn't killed the stagecoach driver. He had killed people before and that did not bother him, but it was the complication of having the law looking for him while they were planning this heist that would set him up for life. His brother had expressed his desire to be rid of Virgil and split their take two ways instead of three. He would be much better off not splitting it at all. He fell asleep planning on what he would do after they got the money.

The next morning Ned was relieving himself behind a thick mesquite bush when he saw two men with stars on their chest ride by, and he heard bits of their conversation. Apparently there had been a murder in town and they were on the hunt for the killer. They were discussing what the killer looked like and that they were provisioned to be gone a couple of days. He finished his business and hurried over to his brother's bedroll. Eli was snoring loudly and Ned knelt down and shook him forcefully. His brother snorted and rolled on his back. Frustrated, Ned kicked him in the ribs.

Eli grunted and sat up. "What did you go and do that for," he complained.

"Did you go into town last night?" Ned asked.

"What of it?"

"I just seen two lawmen ride by talking about a shooting last night. They's looking for the killer and he seems to look just like you."

"I know I shouldn't have done it, but the stagecoach driver made me mad and I thought he was gettin' awful close to figuring out that I was the one that robbed the stage."

Ned began pacing.

Virgil sat up in his bedroll. "You brothers don't let a body sleep," he complained. "I was you, I'd get breakfast going."

Ned stopped and looked at Virgil. He fought off the urge to kick him too. "Make yerself useful, Virgil. Make a fire and some coffee; I got some thinking to do."

Grumbling, Virgil pulled on his boots and set about collecting firewood.

Ned looked over at his brother. He had lain back down and pulled his bedroll up to his shoulders. "By god, Eli, if you don't get your ass up right now I'm going to kick you again."

Eli sat up with a groan. His narrow eyes pierced right through his brother. He started to say something and thought better of it. He turned his boots upside down and then pulled them on. He strapped on his gun, glaring at his brother the whole time.

Ned watched Eli carefully. Even though he was his brother, he knew that Eli's temper got the best of him, just like last night. Killing to Eli was like swatting flies. He was beginning to think that Eli was more trouble than he was worth. *If he could just get his hands on the silver that his brother had stashed.*

Virgil had gotten the fire started and the coffee on. He rubbed his stomach. "I sure could go for some vittles."

Irritated, Ned began pacing again. Eli was sitting on a deadfall and watched. "What's got you all worked up?"

"It seems every time I turn around, you're getting in trouble. Now you've upped and shot somebody else and the law's looking for you."

Eli shrugged. "It'll blow over in a few days."

Ned stopped and stared at his brother. He shook his head and began pacing again. He needed to think and make a plan.

The pleasant aroma of boiling coffee filled the air.

Ned stopped and looked at Virgil. It seemed Virgil couldn't do anything on his own. Ned had to do the thinking for him. "Virgil, get the cups and there is a slab of bacon in my saddlebags yonder."

"How come I got to do everything around here," Virgil complained.

Virgil went to Ned's saddlebags. Ned glared as he fought off the urge to strangle him.

Eli scratched his crotch and sat on a deadfall to roll a smoke.

Even though Eli was his brother, in the short time he had been here he had irritated him something awful. Virgil's constant complaining wasn't helping either. If they didn't rob the bank soon he just might shoot them both. He had to figure out a way to get Eli to come up with the money he had robbed from Wells Fargo. That was it! He broke out in a big grin.

"What you grinnin' about?" Eli asked.

"I got a plan, Eli, I got a plan."

Chapter 23

Governor Brown's wife and daughter were, as usual, consummate hosts. Their beauty and charm always made dinner guests enjoy themselves and it was obvious that James Hatfield was taken by Darla. It didn't hurt that Chen and Althea were excellent cooks. Hatfield's eyes almost never left Darla, but she seemed oblivious to the attention. The governor often wondered about the women. Were they aware of the attention? Were they just used to it or just practiced in ignoring it? Would they notice if they didn't receive extra attention because of their good looks? Darla seemed exceptionally bubbly tonight. Was it because she was being noticed by the handsome young man?

The governor unconsciously shook his head.

"What's the matter, Thad?" Althea asked.

The governor looked over at his wife and dabbed his lips with a napkin and then smiled. He was always amazed how in tune she was with his thoughts.

"Nothing, dear, just thinking about young Jim here and his desire to become a ranger."

Darla set her fork down. "Daddy, I think it would be wonderful for Seth to have some help. From what I see Jimmie would be the man for the job."

Hatfield smiled. He didn't mind Darla calling him Jimmie. The familiarity was comforting.

"What do you think, Althea?" the governor asked.

Althea Brown gazed over at the young man. "Well, I wouldn't want anything to happen to *Jim*, but I wouldn't want anything to happen to Seth either. Two are better than one and they can watch out for each other."

Governor Brown nodded. "Okay, Mr. Hatfield, come by my office tomorrow and we'll go over the details of your employment."

"Thank you, sir, you won't be sorry," Hatfield said.

"Just don't get killed. Phineas would have my hide nailed to the wall of the legislature."

"I promise you I will do my best to stay alive, sir," he said, chuckling.

"Darla, let's help Chen with the pie and coffee," her mother said.

The women left for the kitchen and the governor leaned over to whisper to young Hatfield. "Those women can be mighty troublesome, especially when they go shopping, but I can't imagine my life without them. I'm close to losing Darla to another man and I've been feeling pangs of loneliness already."

"She's delightful, governor; I wish I was a little older right now," Hatfield said.

The governor smiled. "Don't be wishing the years away, my boy, they go by mighty fast."

Althea and Darla Brown watched Jim Hatfield take his leave with smiles on their faces.

"What do you ladies think of young Hatfield?" the governor asked.

"He's a delightful young man," Althea said. "It would be nice for Seth to get some help and they can look out for each other. I just hope nothing happens to either one of them."

The governor nodded. "Yes, he appears capable. I'm going to make him an offer of a probationary position pending Seth's approval."

Darla smiled at her father, the consummate politician. If James Hatfield did not work out it would be Seth making the decision, not her father, avoiding any blame from

Phineas Hatfield. However, if it worked out the governor could take all of the credit.

"How soon would Jimmie be joining Seth?" Althea asked her husband.

Governor Brown rubbed his chin. "If the boy can be provisioned in a day or so I would say right away. I want to make sure he gets a good horse and everything he needs to be successful."

"Good, Darla and I will get packed. We're going with him."

"You're what?"

Darla ran up the stairs to start getting ready and to avoid the fireworks.

"Yes, Darla and I want to see Seth and we've never been to that part of the Mother Lode," Althea said.

"No! It's just too dangerous," the governor said, shaking his head.

"Jimmie will be with us and Darla and I can take care of ourselves," the governor's wife said stubbornly.

"He's just a boy," the governor said.

"You thought he was good enough to join the rangers."

"Althea, that's rugged country up there and it's full of dangerous and evil characters."

"We can't go through life with our heads in the sand like some kind of Ostrich," she countered.

With slumped shoulders the governor poured himself a drink. He knocked the whiskey back in one big gulp. "If you were to leave Sacramento without me I would be worried sick the whole time," he said.

"Don't be silly Thad, we'll be gone just a week or so. We'll have James and when we get to Amador City we'll have Seth to watch over us. Besides, the way the young man looked at Darla, I don't think he will let anything happen to her."

The governor poured another drink. He stared into the bottom of the glass. He could argue with politicians successfully but never seemed to be able to win an argument with his wife. He took a drink. Worse yet, as his daughter got older they double-teamed him often. "I don't like it and I can't get away right now."

"We'll be fine," his wife said.

The governor sighed. "At least take the Barouche. I don't think you two need to be riding that far on horseback. Jim can drive you."

Althea walked over and gave her husband a hug. "Don't forget, I can shoot if need be."

"I know," he exhaled, "I just don't want you to be in a position to have to do so."

Darla clambered down the stairs. "I'm almost all packed mother."

The governor eyed his beaming daughter. She was smiling and she radiated excitement. He knew then that he could not refuse her seeing Seth Gentry. He would have to ensure that young James Hatfield would defend the lives of his wife and daughter with his own if necessary.

Chapter 24

"What's yer plan, Ned?" Eli asked.

Virgil stared at the two brothers with anticipation. He was tired of being the flunky. He was looking forward to getting rich and moving on.

"I just seen the two lawmen ride out of town looking for your ass," Ned said, glaring at his brother. "It's time you get to your money from the stage robbery and we hit the bank."

"But we ain't sure if the stage will bring the new payroll today or if the mine will make a delivery," Eli said.

"I think today will be the day," Ned said. "We won't have a better chance than now and we'll just have to take our chances. Them two lawmen seemed like they was going to be gone for a while."

Virgil grinned with a grey-tooth smile. "No matter what, we'll be better off than we are now."

Irritated, Ned scowled at Virgil. Virgil was like a burr under his saddle working its way in deeper and deeper.

"I don't know; maybe we should wait and be sure," Eli said.

Ned glared at his brother. "So you can do something else stupid and get the law all riled up again?"

Eli's hand moved closer to his holstered revolver. He resented his brother talking to him that way. If it wasn't for him they would have no money at all. His fingers twitched and he forced himself to hook his thumbs in his gun belt. He would wait until they hit the bank and then move on.

Ned had seen his brother's hand move toward his gun. His brother often got in trouble because of his short fuse. Though he was blood, he couldn't wait to be rid of him and Virgil as soon as he could get his hands on the money. He couldn't believe that he had been looking forward to seeing his brother. Eli's impatience would, hopefully, work in his favor.

Silence hung heavily in the air.

Virgil fidgeted and then he said, "I'll pack up and saddle the horses."

"You do that Virgil. We'll follow the stage into town when it comes by," Ned said, staring down his brother. "That is after Eli goes and gets his silver."

Eli's hands came off his gun belt and he opened and closed his gun hand. Ned moved his hand slowly toward his gun. Tension coursed through their veins.

Virgil set about saddling Eli's horse first so that he could leave to get his loot from the robbery. He didn't know what he would do if the brothers shot it out right here. There was no way he could rob the Amador City Bank by himself. Then Eli yelled at him.

"You got that horse saddled yet, Virgil?"

"Jest about done, Eli," he said, tightening the cinch.

"I got a fair piece to ride to get that money and I need to get back afore the stage comes through."

Ned sighed and his shoulders relaxed. With great effort the plan he had laid out was started.

Virgil brought Eli's horse to him.

Mounted, Eli said, "Now don't you boys go robbin' the bank without me."

Ned and Virgil watched Eli ride north of town.

"Maybe we should foller him," Virgil said.

"No, Eli's an edgy sort and if he got wind of us he might not get the money, or worse, he might start shooting. He'll be back, not wantin' to miss out on the money from the bank."

"That brother of yours is kinda scary," Virgil said. "And not the stablest guy I ever met."

Ned watched his brother disappear over the horizon. Virgil had hit the nail on the head. Eli wasn't too stable and he was scary because you never knew how he would react. Doubt creeped in and he wondered if they could pull off his plan successfully and without being killed.

Chapter 25

Marshal Wheeler and Ranger Gentry rode into Sutter Creek with no sign of the little man that had killed the driver of the Wells Fargo stage. "We'll stop in and see Marshal Clements and have a look around the town," Wheeler said.

"I wonder if the killer doubled back on us," Gentry said.

"It's possible; there's dozens of logging roads, mining trails, old Indian trails, critter trails, and so on. He could have headed back to Plymouth or up to Volcano."

Seth nodded as the marshal dismounted in front of Marshal Clements' office and tied his horse to the hitching rail. Seth did the same. As usual, the two lawmen got curious looks from passersby. Seth tipped his hat to two ladies and he received smiles in return.

Marshal Wheeler shook his head. "If you was to stay in one place for any length of time you'd be fighting off them females with a broomstick."

Seth smiled and said nothing as they entered the marshal's office.

Marshal Sam Clements looked up from his old worn oak desk and said, "Kind of strayed down the road a piece, Mack."

Wheeler shook his hand. "This here is Captain Seth Gentry."

Clements shook Gentry's hand and stared at the circled ranger star on his chest. "I heard the governor wanted to resurrect the rangers."

Seth chuckled. “I’m it.” He liked Sam Clements right off. He was a middle-aged man with a greying moustache. He was of average build and his eyes sparkled with mischievous intelligence.

“Well, we can take all the help we can get. There’s no shortage of law breakin’ in these parts,” Clements said, tilting his head toward the fully occupied jail cells.

Marshal Wheeler walked over to the cells and looked the prisoners over. All were rough looking and unkempt and some were obviously hungover. “You on the bunk; stand up, I want to take a look at you.”

A small man grumbled and did as he was told.

“How long’s this fella been here?” Wheeler asked.

“Slim’s been here a few days. He pulled a knife on a feller in the Mint Saloon.”

Wheeler nodded. “Can’t be our man, then; we’re looking for a smallish man that shot and killed the Wells Fargo stagecoach driver in Amador City yesterday.

Clements rubbed his whiskered chin. “Can’t say as I seen any strangers of that description.”

“Appreciate you keeping an eye out, Sam,” Wheeler said.

Sutter Creek’s town marshal nodded. “I was about to make my rounds. Why don’t you boys join me and we’ll stop at the café for some vittles.”

Marshal Wheeler looked over at Seth. “We didn’t have no breakfast,” he said.

Seth smiled at the two expectant lawmen. “I am hungry and would appreciate a tour of your fair city.”

“All right, then.” Marshal Clements slapped Marshal Wheeler on the back. “Having company on my rounds will be a treat. And having three lawmen circle the town will irritate some of the bad element no end,” he said with a smile.

Marshal Clements walked over to the gun rack and took down a double-barreled shotgun. He broke it open and checked to see that it was loaded.

"You got two other guns with you, Sam," Wheeler said.

Clements nodded. "I never go without this greener. It's saved my hide a time or two."

Wheeler and Gentry followed the town marshal out the door. He turned right and headed north, the trio's boots echoing down the hard walk. At the sight of the three lawmen together, some men of questionable character scampered away. Seth heard Marshal Clements chuckle to himself.

The town marshal looked over at the smiling ranger. "This town of yours brings back some fond memories of when I was in Nevada City," Seth said.

"I been there. Nice town," Clements said. "Too bad about Frank Burke, he was a good man."

"That's what I heard," Seth said. "The boys that killed him won't kill anybody else."

"That's good," Clements said.

A piano was pounding as they approached Brody's Saloon. A grey bearded old-timer was sitting on a rough-hewn bench outside the door puffing on a corn cob pipe. Marshal Clements stopped and spoke to him. "All things quiet, Rusty?" he asked.

Narrow sparkling eyes looked up at the marshal. He took the pipe out of his mouth and with a toothless grin said, "'cept for that pianie. I swear old Turk hits more sour notes every day."

Marshal Clements chuckled. "Rusty here is our unofficial town mayor. He keeps his eyes and ears open for trouble."

Rusty turned serious. "Can't do it when you lock me up for a couple of nips."

Clements looked down at the old man. "You know I do that for your own good."

The old-timer cackled. "It's nigh on to noon; I think you should pay up on my watchin' fee."

Marshal Clements reached into his pocket and took out a coin. He flipped it to Rusty and said, "Don't drink so much that you can't do your job. And I got no room for you to sleep it off."

"You can count on me, marshal," Rusty said with a twinkle in his eye.

The three lawmen continued on their rounds. "Seems like every town has an old-timer like that," Seth said smiling.

Wheeler chuckled. "Yes, Sam has Rusty and I have Tinker."

Chapter 26

"Prudie, have you heard from Seth Gentry?" the governor asked his secretary.

"Not yet, governor."

"Dang it, doesn't he know how important it is to keep in touch?"

"I'm sure he does; you know how difficult it is to receive and transmit messages up there in the wilderness," she said.

With his hands clasped behind his back the governor began pacing. He stopped and looked down at Prudence Miller behind her desk. "Do you think we should send another telegram to stress how important it is that he responds?"

Governor Brown's secretary interlocked her fingers on top of her desk and looked up at him. "I'm sure he will get back to you just as soon as he is able to." She knew how the Brown household worked and was quite sure that he was getting pressured from his wife and, especially, his daughter. Sure enough, the governor explained.

"Althea and Darla want to accompany James Hatfield up see Seth, and you know that I can't get away right now."

"I'm sure that they would be okay," Prudie said. "Besides, they would be accompanied by a ranger." In truth, she felt that the two women were foolish to be venturing into dangerous territory.

"He's just a kid," the governor said.

"He looks very capable to me, and if you didn't think so you wouldn't have hired him," she said in an effort to reassure the governor.

The governor turned to the sound of the outer office door opening.

"I hope I'm not interrupting," Hatfield said.

The governor stared at the boy for a moment. Was this young man truly capable of protecting his wife and daughter? "No, no my boy, please come into my office," he said.

"Miss Prudie," the polite young man acknowledged the seated secretary.

Prudence Miller smiled brightly at the handsome young man. "Nice to see you again, James."

With hat in hand, Jim Hatfield followed the governor into his office.

"Have a seat, my boy, we have much to discuss," the governor said, indicating the leather chair in front of his desk.

"Yes sir." Hatfield placed his hat on the chair next to him.

"After my discussions with you, and having consulted with higher-ups, I have decided to offer you a position in the California Rangers on a probationary basis."

With raised brow, Hatfield asked, "Higher ups, sir?"

The governor chuckled, "Mrs. Brown and Darla."

"Ah, yes sir." Hatfield smiled back at the amiable governor.

The governor's face turned serious. "The State of California will provide you with every tool necessary to be successful. You will be under the direction of Captain Gentry and, of course, the office of the governor."

"Yes, sir," Hatfield said, watching the governor clasp his hands together on top of his desk and lean forward. "I appreciate the opportunity, sir."

The governor studied the young man and then opened his right-hand desk drawer. "I have here your authorized commission placing you in the California Rangers on a 120-day probationary basis. At the end of that time you will be considered permanent unless Captain Gentry or I revoke it in writing on or before the 120 days are up."

"Yes, sir," Hatfield said.

"Included in this authorization is your ability to spend some of the state's money on a limited basis. You also can pick out a horse and tack at the livery. I suggest you go see Buster on Front Street after we conclude this meeting."

"Will do, sir," Hatfield said.

Governor Brown opened his left-hand drawer and pulled out an envelope. "In this envelope is your first month's pay in advance and fifty dollars in expense money. Be sure to keep an accounting of the money you spend so that we can replace it." The governor handed the envelope to the young man and opened his center drawer.

Without looking inside the envelope, Hatfield put it in his shirt pocket.

The governor pulled out a circled star and placed it on the letter of authorization. "If you accept these terms, raise your right hand."

Hatfield's right hand shot up.

"Repeat after me. I, James Hatfield, do solemnly swear to defend the laws and citizenry of the State of California from all enemies, and observe and obey the orders of the Governor of the State and officers appointed over me. I will be honest and truthful, so help me God."

After Hatfield repeated the oath, the governor smiled and shook the young ranger's hand. He then personally pinned the star on Hatfield's shirt.

"Thank you, sir, I promise you I will do my best."

"I'm sure you will, son," the governor said. "Now, for your first assignment," he said, heavily sitting back down in his leather chair.

Feeling the unfamiliar weight of the badge on his chest, the young ranger looked at the governor with wide-eyed expectancy.

Governor Brown moved to the edge of his chair, interlaced his fingers on top of his large walnut desk and looked deeply into the eyes of the young man.

Hatfield could tell that this was serious and he felt his heart rate speed up. He clenched both fists on his lap and waited in anticipation.

The governor cleared his throat. "Seth Gentry has captured my daughter's eye." He stopped, parsing for words. He cleared his throat again. "Uh, my wife and daughter are insisting on going up to the Mother Lode to visit him. They fail to realize the full danger of such a trip and refuse to acknowledge that Captain Gentry may be busy carrying out his duties."

Ranger Hatfield nodded, wondering where this was going. He had been around politicians most of his life and knew that they often beat around the proverbial bush.

The governor leapt up and started pacing with his hands behind his back. "Jimmy, the bottom line is that I don't want them to go and I can't get away right now."

"Yes, sir," Hatfield said.

"I'm sure you observed that the Brown women can be very stubborn and persuasive."

"Yes, sir," Hatfield repeated.

The governor stopped and looked at the young man. With a deep sigh he said, "Since you have come into our life once again and are now a California Ranger, they want you to escort them into the high country."

The young ranger didn't know what to say so he said nothing.

"Well, what do you think, Jim?"

Ranger Hatfield thought for a moment. "I work for you and this state, sir, and I will do as directed."

"I don't like it," the governor said.

"I understand, sir."

"I assume you have driven a buggy," the governor said.

"Yes, sir, many times," Hatfield said.

The governor sighed and sat down heavily. He rubbed his temples with his hands. Almost in a whisper, he said, "Those two women are the most precious and important people in my life. I don't know what I would do if something happened to them."

The gravity of what the governor was saying added weight to the circled star on the young man's chest. He watched the bowed head of the governor and the rubbing of his temples. "Sir, if you direct me to escort your family to the mountains, I promise you I will protect them with my life."

Governor Brown looked up into the serious face of the young ranger. The man had hit a soft place in his heart. Hatfield sounded like he cared as deeply about his wife and daughter as he did. "I believe you would, James. I am reluctant to burden you with this, not because of your ability, but because of the circumstances. There are too many evildoers in those gold-laden hills. You must be suspicious of people's intentions."

"Yes sir, because of my youth people often under estimate my abilities. I assure you I will get the ladies to Seth safely."

The governor took a deep breath. The young ranger sounded confident and it was somewhat comforting. "When you pick out your horse at the livery, let Buster know that you will also be taking the barouche."

"Yes, sir, I'll do that."

"Provision yourself at the general store and take into consideration that there will be three of you for a few days. Make sure you have all the ammunition and tools you need to protect my family," the governor said.

"I'll do that immediately, sir. We can leave at first light," Ranger Hatfield said.

"Yes, they are all packed and ready to go."

"How long will your wife and daughter be staying?"

"They told me a week. I hope it is no more than that."

Ranger Hatfield stood and looked down at the worried governor. “One question, sir; how are they returning to Sacramento?”

Chapter 27

Eli Hayes warily approached the area where he had hidden his silver contraband. He reined in at a small rise and looked at his back trail. It would be just like his brother and his stupid friend to trail him and attempt to get their hands on his money. He waited several minutes before he allowed his eyes to stray over to a large burned-out oak tree. He had dropped his saddle bags into the dark hollow and brushed away any evidence that he had been there.

Eli looked down the trail to see if anyone was approaching and then looked to his back trail again before approaching the tree. He dismounted and cautiously approached his hidden bounty. He reached down into the hole. He didn't feel the smooth leather of his saddle bags. Panic set in. Had somebody discovered his hideaway?

Hayes looked around the tree for evidence of someone having been there. He saw nothing. A bead of sweat appeared on his brow and his heart raced. He pulled a Lucifer out of his shirt pocket and scratched it across the trunk of the oak tree. He reached down into the dark hole and to his relief he saw the saddlebags at the bottom. The hole was much deeper than he imagined. He was studying how he could retrieve the bags when the fire nipped at his fingers and he fanned the flame out. He licked his sore fingers and thought about how he could get the heavy bags. Eli was too short to reach them but his slight stature meant that he could drop into the small dark hole.

Eli went to his horse and took the rope off the saddle, wrapped it around his waist and the other end around the saddle horn, took one more glance around and climbed up into the black hole. His short legs dangled in the air. He pointed his toes in an attempt to touch the bags or the bottom. He felt nothing. His fingers were hurting from the flame and the edge of the ragged bark he was holding on to. How far down was it to the bags?

Hayes took a deep breath and let go. He dropped a couple of feet and one foot landed on the saddlebags, twisting his ankle. He grunted as the pain worked its way up his leg. He looked up at the light at the top of the tree trunk and hoped his unfamiliar horse did not panic. Though in tight quarters, he managed to remove the rope from his waist. The horse he had stolen must have been a cow pony and held the rope taught. In order to not lose the tight rope, Eli strained to tie it to the saddle bags.

Having secured the bags of silver, Eli took a few moments to catch his breath and then painfully shinnied up the rope, pulled himself over the jagged edge and flopped to the ground on his back. Breathing heavily, he looked up at the rock-solid horse. *I stole me a good one,* he thought to himself, always willing to take the credit.

Eli struggled to get up and after a couple of attempts got mounted. His effort and small stature had taken its toll. He slowly backed the horse up, the rope straining against the heavy weight and rubbing on the jagged edge of the burned-out tree. It wouldn't do to have the rope break and have to dive back into that charcoal hole.

He stopped the horse's reverse progress when the heavy leather bags caught on the edge. Eli dismounted and strained to lift the bags out of the burned-out cavity. He collapsed against the base of the tree and leaned against the bags of silver. After catching his breath, he looked around to make sure no one had seen him retrieve the loot. With effort, he pulled himself up, untied the rope, and reeled it into a loop to put back on the saddle. He went back to the oak and bent his knees to place the saddlebags over his shoulder. He straightened up with a loud grunt and stumbled over to the horse. Breathing heavily, he took a few moments before exerting maximum effort to swing the bags behind the saddle.

"Whoa," Eli said to the horse as it sidestepped from the sudden added weight. He secured the bags and again struggled to pull himself into the saddle. He scanned the surrounding area and walked the heavily laden horse back toward Amador City.

There was no avoiding going through town to reach their campsite. The citizenry of Amador City stared at the soot-laden little man as he attempted to ride through town unnoticed. What was so different about him that made people stare like he was some kind of freak?

As Eli approached camp, it irritated him that Virgil and Ned were standing there looking down the road as he approached. He knew the two men would love to get their hands on his money.

"You have to crawl down a chimney to fetch the money?" Ned asked.

"What do you mean?"

"Yer all covered in soot like you rolled around in a fire pit."

Eli dismounted and led his horse over to a mesquite bush. He tied the reins and quickly removed his saddlebags.

"Ya need some help?" Virgil asked the struggling little man with an obvious limp.

"No."

"You best go down to the crick and wash up," Ned said eyeing the saddlebags.

"Virgil, I need coffee. I'll be right back," Eli said, shouldering the saddlebags.

Ned's shoulders slumped as he realized Eli was taking the silver with him.

Virgil was about to protest Eli giving him orders, but stopped when Ned shook his head and said, "Go ahead, Virgil."

Ned and Virgil glared at the little man as he staggered under the weight of the silver as he descended the steep grade to the creek.

"I'd sure like to get my hands on some of that money." Virgil wiped his sweaty hands on his pants.

"Just make the coffee, Virgil, we'll deal with that later," Ned said, watching Eli drop the saddlebags, look around and kneel down to the cold water.

Eli took a drink and then splashed the icy water on to his face. It was shocking and invigorating. He stood and removed his shirt and shook it out. He dropped his shirt on the saddlebags, glanced around and knelt back down to the creek. He bathed his body, paying particular attention to his black hands and face, and then slicked back his straggly hair. He shivered in the chilled air.

Ned, still watching his brother, mumbled, "That boy sure is scrawny."

"What's that?" Virgil asked as he set the coffee pot over the fire.

"Nothing," Ned said.

Feeling better, Eli shook out his shirt and put it on, bent his knees to lift the heavy saddlebags, and with great effort ascended the incline to camp.

The distant cacophonous arrival of the Wells Fargo Stage interrupted Ned's thoughts on how he could relieve his brother of the silver.

Chapter 28

It had seemed that he had just closed his eyes when he was violently shaken awake. Foggy and bleary-eyed, Buck Henry looked up at his father. His head hurt and his mouth tasted like he had eaten a large amount of cow pie.

"Get up, its Sunday go to meetin' day," his father bellowed.

Buck Henry groaned. "You go without me, Pa."

"We go through this every time, Buck; you know what I promised your dear Ma."

Buck pulled the pillow over his head.

John Henry grabbed the pillow and swatted his son with it. The sudden and unexpected blow made his headache feel ten times worse. Buck moaned as he rolled to the edge of the bed. As he sat up, the room seemed to swirl around him.

"The boys already saddled the horses. Get yourself cleaned up; you won't have time for no breakfast," his father said with disgust.

The thought of food made Buck's stomach turn. "Don't want none," he said.

Buck's father left the room, slamming the door behind him. The concussive shock seemed to echo in his skull, and he winced in pain. *He can be such a jerk,* he thought to himself. He staggered over to the water bowl on his dresser and splashed his face. He squinted at his image in the foggy mirror. What he saw didn't make him feel any better. He slicked back his hair and wet his shaving brush before dipping it into the soap mug. He stropped his straight razor and carefully went to work with a shaky hand. In an attempt to avoid thinking about how bad he felt his thoughts turned to the preacher's daughter.

Buck winced in pain as he cut his cheek with the razor and his thin blood ran down his cheek. He grabbed a towel and pressed it against his face. He needed to focus on his task at hand.

"Hurry up Buck, we've got to get going," his father yelled from downstairs.

"I'm almost ready, Pa," he yelled back, increasing the pounding in his head. He dabbed at the cut and finished shaving. He dressed in his Sunday best, took a quick look in the mirror and hustled downstairs. He didn't want any more grief from his father.

"Let's go," John Henry told his son.

Buck took the reins from a ranch hand, looked over at the corral and didn't like what he saw. Ranch hands were perched on the top rail with smirks on their faces. He had the urge to pull them all off the rail but a stern look from his father told him to mount up and ignore them.

The jarring horse ride to church didn't do Buck's disposition any good. He breathed deeply of the fresh air in an attempt to clear his head. As they neared the church his thoughts turned again to the preacher's daughter.

*****

Priscilla Peabody stood on the steps of the little white church next to her father, greeting the parishioners as they arrived for services. Endicott Peabody never enjoyed life more than on his Sundays with his daughter and his flock. In the past he would stand outside and say farewell to the church goers after his sermon, but when he realized that his beautiful daughter with her sweet disposition was so welcoming he decided to greet them as they arrived also. Endicott and Priscilla had lost their wife and mother to cholera some years ago, requiring the young girl to grow up quickly. She was a bright, delightful young lady.

Preacher Peabody looked down at his daughter and his heart was full. Priscilla's dynamic and cheerful personality seemed to brighten the grumpiest person's day. He had noticed in recent months, however, that she was garnering the attention of men, young and old. It seemed like she had developed womanly curves overnight and though he wished it weren't so, some of the male members of the church were not desirable suitors for his daughter. Peabody didn't like to think poorly of other men, but it seemed that some were inherently bad despite his continual attempts to instill goodness in everyone.

Endicott Peabody's smile waned at the arrival of John Henry and his son Buck---two of the very men he had just been thinking about. John owned the largest cattle ranch around and Preacher Peabody struggled to find any redeeming quality in the man. With guilt, the only one he could think of was the generosity he showed at the passing of the collection plate. He knew that Henry was keeping his promise to his departed wife and he admired him for that. Then there was his son Buck. Buck was uncouth and a bully. It was as if he was the devil himself.

The preacher watched the two men tie their horses at the hitching rail and walk toward the church. Since firearms weren't allowed in the house of God, it was the only time he ever saw the two men unarmed. Being unarmed didn't cut down on Buck Henry's swagger, and he stared at Priscilla and licked his lips. He looked like a vicious animal about to prance on his prey. The preacher noticed his daughter's eyes narrow, but to her credit she kept the smile on her face as the men approached.

"Miss Priscilla, you look lovely as usual," John Henry said, tipping his hat.

"Thank you, Mr. Henry," Priscilla said with a small curtsy.

John Henry shook the preacher's hand and Buck took Priscilla's hand in his and held it for what seemed like a long time. He looked longingly into her eyes and wet his lips again. Priscilla strained to not show the results of the shiver that ran down her spine. She averted her eyes and looked over his shoulder at three approaching men down the street.

Buck Henry turned to see what the young lady was looking at. The three men approaching were heavily armed and there were bright flashes of sunlight off of their badges. While not a fearful man, Buck Henry's heart skipped a beat at the sight of three lawmen coming down the street. Were they coming after him?

The sudden appearance of so many lawmen caused Buck to drop Priscilla's hand and follow his father into the church.

Endicott Peabody brightened at the arrival of the lawmen. Though not a fan of guns and violence, he found comfort in the presence of Marshal Clements when the Henrys were around.

"Preacher Peabody, this here is Marshal Wheeler from Amador City and this is Captain Gentry of the California Rangers," Clements said.

The two lawmen shook Peabody's hand.

"This is my daughter Priscilla," he said with pride.

"Pleased to meet you, ma'am," Seth said, tipping his hat. The preacher's daughter was a pretty little blonde with a splash of freckles on her face. Her golden hair shone brilliantly in the morning light.

Priscilla did a curtsy and smiled brightly.

"If you fellas are coming to church you'll have to do something with that hardware," the preacher said. "You know I don't allow weaponry in the House of God, Sam."

Sam Clements smiled. "I know that Endicott; we're making the rounds after breakfast. We might just stand in the doorway for a bit and listen to your words of wisdom."

The organ music emanating from the interior of the church stopped, indicating it was time for the preacher to deliver his sermon. As he guided his daughter toward the door, he turned and said, "As you know, Sam, once a month we have a church picnic after services. Today the women are prepared to put out quite a spread and it would be our pleasure to have you three join us."

Marshal Clements smiled. "I've never had better fried chicken than Maude Adams'."

"That's a fact," the preacher said as he and his daughter disappeared into the church.

The three lawmen ascended the church steps, looked inside the cool darkness, and watched the preacher guide his daughter to the front pew and take his place behind the pulpit. The churchgoers looked up expectantly. "It's a glorious day in God's house; let us pray. Heavenly Father, we thank you for this day in which we choose to follow your word and strive for a pure heart."

Preacher Peabody raised his bowed head and looked directly at Buck Henry. Henry was gazing at the preacher's daughter. Peabody continued without again bowing his head. "May we be devoid of avaricious ways. May our wants and desires be just and pure, Amen."

"Amen," the parishioners responded in unison.

The preacher looked over his congregation. "The sermon today encompasses some of the Ten Commandments. Thou shall not covet. . ."

Marshal Clements turned away. "Let's continue our rounds so we can get back to the picnic. There's no hurry, ol' Endicott can be awful long-winded."

The three lawmen walked down the small hill to the quiet town. While most of the townspeople were in church it was important to make sure that no evildoer would take advantage of people being absent from their homes and businesses.

"Did you boys notice the two large fellas that entered the church as we arrived? One older than the other," Marshal Clements said.

"Sure did," Ranger Gentry said as Marshal Wheeler nodded.

"That was John and Buck Henry, the owners of the Circle J, the largest spread around here. Bad things seemed to happen when those two are about. Buck killed a man in the saloon last night over a dancehall girl. Witnesses said that it was in self-defense."

"At least they go to church," Marshal Wheeler said with a small smile.

Sam stopped and looked at Mack. "Being in a barn don't make you a horse any more than being in a church makes you a Christian."

"I've known a few that think going to church cleanses them of their weekly sins," Wheeler said.

"That's a fact," Clements said. "That Buck Henry fancies himself a ladies man, but most won't have anything to do with him unless he pays a high price for their company. He has designs on the preacher's daughter."

"That's troublesome. She seems like a sweet little girl," Seth said. "I don't abide a man that would mistreat women."

"Women are scarce enough and most western folk treat them with deference. Buck Henry, however, lacks character and is a bully. It seemed the preacher's sermon was aimed at him," Clements said.

The three lawmen continued down the main street, checking locked doors and peering into the almost-empty saloons. When at the end of the dusty street they scanned the area and crossed to work their way back on the other side. The three men were silent, left to their own thoughts, accompanied by the echo of their leather boots on the solid walk.

As they arrived to the bottom of the hill, Clements pointed to covered picnic tables in the shade of two giant oak trees. "Church will be out soon and you'll see quite a banquet," he said. "It's usually the biggest social event of the month."

At that moment the preacher and his daughter appeared outside the church door, followed by the noisy exit of the parishioners. They were buzzing with excitement and the women busied themselves preparing the food.

Then they saw John and Buck Henry stop in front of the preacher and his daughter.

Seth didn't like the way Buck held Priscilla's hand. She seemed to be trying to pull away and Henry wouldn't let go.

Chapter 29

Governor Thaddeus Brown considered himself a smart and thoughtful man. When Ranger Hatfield had questioned how his wife and daughter would return from their trip to Amador City, he felt a fool. He had been so worried about them leaving he hadn't considered who would accompany them back. Since he had hired Phineas Hatfield's son, perhaps now was the time to put more pressure on the legislature to increase the rangers and appropriate more money for law and order. California was growing exponentially and now was the time to move forward.

Excitement was in the air as Chen piled the ladies' bags in the foyer as they waited for Ranger Hatfield's arrival. The black of night was greying as the sun was about to rise over the peak of the Sierra Nevada Mountains in the east. Governor Brown sat at the table with a cup of coffee, waiting for his wife and daughter to come down the stairs. Their excited arrival made him smile and made him fearful at the same time. As usual, the two women looked lovely, dressed much nicer than the governor would have liked.

"You two are dressed awful fancy for hitting the road," the governor grumbled.

"Oh, Thad, you worry too much," Althea said.

"She's right, Daddy, we can take care of ourselves," Darla added.

"He here," Chen said, opening the front door as the sound of horse and buggy filled the room.

Governor Brown walked over to his wife and put his big hands on her shoulders. He looked into her sparkling brown eyes and said, "You two be careful." And then he kissed her on the forehead.

The governor turned his attention to his daughter. "You keep those guns handy in case of trouble."

"Yes, Daddy," Darla said. "I have the .32 and mother has the Derringer."

Thaddeus Brown smiled at his pretty daughter. He had taught her to shoot at a young age and even though he wouldn't admit it out loud, Darla was a better shot than he was.

Ranger Hatfield helped Chen load the buggy. Tied behind the buggy was a spirited buckskin horse.

"It looks like Buster fixed you up with a fine mount," the governor said.

"Yes, sir, he's a dandy," James Hatfield said with a wide grin. "I rode him around the riverfront. He's a fine horse."

"You get provisioned to your satisfaction?"

"Yes, sir, and Buster said since I am driving the governor's wife and daughter, I should take this," Hatfield said, holding up a double-barreled shotgun.

The governor smiled. "That old coot always was partial to my wife and daughter; me, not so much."

Hatfield grinned back at the governor. "He said you would appreciate the added protection and that you were going to buy him a new shotgun to replace it."

Governor Brown shook his head. "That old geezer is awful sly; I don't know if I've ever been able to outsmart him." The governor studied the buckskin. "Buster sure knows his horseflesh. I've wired ahead and made reservations for rooms at the Inn in Sloughhouse. If you get an early start in the morning you should make Amador City by mid-afternoon tomorrow."

"Yes, sir," Hatfield said, helping the ladies into the buggy.

"You know what you have to do Ranger Hatfield."

"Yes, sir, get your wife and daughter to Amador City safely."

"I want you and Captain Gentry to return with them. I want you two to help get more funding and personnel for the rangers."

James Hatfield's eyes widened. Inexperienced and young, he wondered what he could do to help the governor. As he watched the governor and his family say their goodbyes he remembered that his father was a member of the legislature and had helped him get the ranger job. Also, there would be two rangers making sure his wife and daughter returned safely. Hatfield smiled to himself. The governor was a smart man.

*****

The women looked straight ahead with their hands folded in their laps as Hatfield snapped the reins and the buggy lurched forward, the sky having turned into an orange glow as the sun was about to peek over the mountains.

Hatfield glanced back at the women and saw the misty eyes of the governor's wife and the beautiful beaming face of his daughter. He felt the heavy weight of responsibility on his shoulders. He looked side to side as he drove and realized that it was as if they were a one-buggy parade.

The people that were on the streets of Sacramento preparing to begin their day's labor stopped and stared at the elegant vehicle driven by a young man with a circled star on his chest. Women pointed to the two ladies in the passenger seat.

This must be how royalty feels, Hatfield thought, not sure that he liked the feeling. He would prefer to be on his horse heading to the high country to help Ranger Gentry. As they left the city limits for Jackson Road the women started talking, and they never stopped.

Chapter 30

"Pack your gear," Ned said, eyeing Eli's silver-laden saddlebags. "We be needin' to get away quick like after we hit the bank."

Eli struggled with the heavy bags and Virgil rushed over to help. Reluctantly Eli allowed him to swing the bags up and he tied them down to the saddle. "Don't you boys get no ideas about my money," Eli said. "You jest concentrate on that there bank's money."

Ned stared down the street. "I wish we knew if the gold and payroll were waiting for us. We got to take our chances while the law is out of town. They could be back any time."

Incredulous, Eli stared at his brother and then over at Virgil. They were both dumber than rocks, he thought. Ned always came up with ideas without an adequate plan or sufficient knowledge of the situation and Virgil spent all his time wanting money, but relying on others to get it for him. Eli found that shooting first and asking questions later worked best. After they robbed the bank he would be shed of these two and be on his way.

Ned mounted up. "Let's go get our money." He watched his small brother struggle into the saddle. "It's a good thing you ain't very big with all that silver you're carrying."

Eli glared at his brother and took the thong off his revolver and loosened it in the holster.

"Don't you go shootin' crazy, Eli, I don't want no posse tryin' to track us down," Ned said.

"You think they're going to sit back and let you jest take their money?"

Ned watched Virgil loosen his revolver. Virgil was nervous as a cat being approached by a cur dog. "We go in with guns drawed, but no shootin' unless we have to."

Riding three across, the men rode slowly down the dusty street. Ahead and to the right was the Wells Fargo office and next door was the Bank of Amador City.

Tinker, from his usual chair, observed the three-horse parade move slowly down the main street. *There's trouble if I ever seen it,* he thought. He squinted his old eyes through his pipe smoke and attempted to focus on the smallest rider. "I seen that guy before," he mumbled to himself.

A bonneted woman crossed the street in front of the riders. She glanced at the trio, averted her eyes and scurried to the other side.

The three men dismounted, looked around, and tied their horses to the hitching rail. "Virgil, you stay with the horses and watch my saddlebags," Eli said.

Ned glowered at his brother. He didn't like his brother giving the orders but he saw the sense in what he said. They couldn't lose their horses and somebody had to watch Eli's saddlebags.

"You don't let nobody near them horses or saddlebags," Eli added. "If you do I'll hunt you down and slit your throat."

Relieved that he didn't have to go in the bank Virgil said, "Don't you worry none."

"That's comforting," Eli said, taking another look around. He and Ned stepped up to the walk and drew their pistols.

The two men entered the bank. "This is a hold-up," Ned yelled. "Put them hands in the air if you 'preciate living."

A small man held his hands in the air behind the bars and counter.

From the back of the room a heavy middle-aged man came running out. “What’s going on?”

Eli, startled by the sudden appearance of the man, shot him in the chest. The concussion of the explosion echoed through the bank, and the clerk behind the counter ducked involuntarily. Shocked, the banker, with blood appearing on his chest, stopped in mid-stride and then collapsed to the floor. Eli swung his gun back to the clerk and the clerk raised his arms higher. Heavy smoke and the smell of gunpowder permeated the air.

“Don’t shoot, I got a family,” the nervous clerk said.

Incredulous, Ned looked over at his brother, “What you go and do that for, Eli?” he asked.

Ignoring his brother, Eli said, “Put yer money in a bag and hand it over. Where’s the safe?”

The clerk grabbed a cloth bag and opened his drawer. As he stuffed the money in the bag he said, “The safe’s in the back, but it won’t do you any good. The President hadn’t opened it yet.”

“Get him to open it, then,” Eli ordered.

The clerk handed him the money bag. “Can’t,” he said with a nervous twitch, staring at the business end of Eli’s revolver.

“What do you mean, he can’t?” Ned hollered.

“This fella here shot him and he’s the only one here that has the combination,” the clerk said, staring down at the Bank President on the floor.

Ned hurried over, knelt down and rolled the man over. Blank eyes, empty of life stared at him. He stood up and walked back to the closed safe and tried the handle. It wouldn’t budge. From the back of the room he stormed up behind the clerk and said, “You are telling me that the only one with a combination is that man over there?”

“Yea. . .yes,” the jittery man said. “He doesn’t like to open it until it’s time for the stage or payroll shipments.”

Ned glared at Eli, went around the counter and swung the barrel of his pistol across the back of the clerk’s head.

The clerk collapsed and fell to the floor. Ned checked the man's cash drawer to make sure that the clerk had emptied it. Ned had hit the man out of frustration and he didn't want Eli killing another man. "Let's get out of here while we got a chance."

Eli walked over to the window. "Coast is clear."

Ned looked at his little brother. "What did you have to shoot that guy for? Now we can't get into the safe."

Eli ignored his irritating brother once again.

Ned holstered his gun. "Put that gun away and walk out casual like. We might get out of town before people find out about this."

Irritated at being told what to do by his brother, Eli holstered his gun.

"Hand me that sack, I'll put it under my vest," Ned said.

Eli hesitated and then handed it over. Ned tucked it in his vest under his arm and they attempted to act casual as they left the bank.

Wells Fargo Agent Turley came bursting out of the office door, followed by Tinker who had reported the shot.

Scared, Virgil pulled his gun and fired in their direction. Luckily for the old-timer and agent, Virgil was a poor shot with a six-shooter. The two men dropped to the walk and looked up to see the three horsemen gallop out of town in the direction of Sutter Creek.

"Maybe they'll ride right into the marshal and ranger," Turley said. "We'd better check the bank," he added helping the old-timer up.

Tinker followed the agent into the bank. Fear and gun smoke filled the air. They saw no one at first; then they spied the banker on the floor. Turley rushed over and checked on the banker. "Dead," he said.

Turley walked behind the counter and found the clerk on the floor. "Unconscious, big lump on his head," he said. "Tinker, go get the Doc and I'll buy you a drink when you come back."

Tinker nodded. "Buy me a couple of drinks and I'll fetch the undertaker, too."

"Okay," Turley said, "get going." He examined the cash drawer and found it empty. He looked over at the closed safe and walked to it, trying the handle; locked. He studied the situation. The clerk probably had not more than one or two hundred dollars in his cash drawer and the robbers had gotten nothing out of the safe. "Not much of a take to be hung by the neck," he mumbled to himself.

Agent Turley stepped outside to wait for Tinker and the doctor. He took his spectacles off and cleaned them with a handkerchief. With the marshal out of town he considered what should be done. He put his spectacles back on and looked over at where the robbers had tied their horses and he remembered how Captain Gentry had mentioned looking for sign.

Turley heard the clamor of boots on the walk and observed the doctor hurrying toward him, followed by Tinker and a couple of other locals. The agent sighed. The entirety of the small town would know about the bank robbery in a matter of minutes.

Turley realized what he must do.

Chapter 31

Buck Henry saw the three lawmen approaching and let go of Priscilla Peabody's hand. "Let's get something to eat, Pa," he said to his father, walking toward the shaded picnic tables.

Seth watched the two big men walk away. He tried to think the best of most people while retaining a lawman's curiosity. Being suspicious of everyone got in the way of a pleasant life, but being vigilant kept you alive. Marshal Clements had pointed the two men out earlier, but he liked to make his own judgments. After further observation he decided he didn't like the Henrys and concurred with Clements' assessment. While Buck Henry's actions were subtle, he could tell that Henry was the type of man that did not appreciate or respect women.

An attractive middle-aged woman approached the three lawmen. "Who's this handsome man?" she asked, smiling at Seth.

"Margaret, this here is Captain Seth Gentry of the California Rangers. You know Mack, of course," Clements said. "Seth, this is my wife, Margaret."

Gentry tipped his hat. "Pleased to meet you, ma'am."

Marshal Clements took his wife by the arm. "Let's get these boys some grub," he said.

Margaret Clements hooked her arm into Seth's and they moved toward a long picnic table teeming with food.

Seth inhaled deeply. "It certainly smells wonderful," he said.

"After lunch you must have a slice of my apple pie," Margaret said.

"Margaret bakes the best apple pie around," Wheeler said, licking his lips.

"Why, thank you, Mack. Sam, you did invite Seth and Mack to stay the night, didn't you?"

"Well, I hadn't gotten around to it. I'm not sure what their plans are," Clements said.

"That's very kind of you, Mrs. Clements, but I'm going to search around and look for bad men and get the lay of the country," Ranger Gentry said.

Disappointed, Margaret Clements looked over at Mack Wheeler with a questioning look.

Marshal Wheeler glanced over at Seth. "I'm not as young as Seth and I sure do cotton to your cooking," he said. "I kind of give up sleeping on the ground," he added.

Seth smiled. "You stay, Mack. I'll scout the countryside and join up with you tomorrow morning."

"You boys get to eating and I'll put some food together for Seth to take with him," Margaret said.

"That's not necessary, ma'am," Seth said.

With hands on hips she said, "What is necessary is decided by me, and you are taking some of this food with you, young man."

Gentry smiled. "Yes, ma'am, whatever you say."

Determined, Margaret Clements marched off.

Sam Clements shook his head. "I can't remember the last time I won an argument with that woman."

"I think you are a lucky man," Seth said with a smile.

"Come on boys, let's get something to eat," Marshal Wheeler said.

As the lawmen approached the cloth-covered table adorned with enough food to feed a small army they heard a high-pitched protest from a woman at the end.

"You leave me alone, Buck!" Priscilla Peabody shouted.

Seth saw Buck Henry tugging on Priscilla's arm in an attempt to pull her toward him.

"Give ol' Buck a little kiss."

Ranger Gentry walked briskly over to the struggling pair. "I don't abide the mistreatment of women. Let her go."

Still holding Priscilla's arm, Buck sneered, "This is none of your business, lawman."

"You're wrong, boy; it is my job to protect the citizenry of California."

Henry let go of Priscilla's arm and turned to face the ranger. Priscilla rubbed her arm to lessen the pain and get circulation back.

Reverend Endicott Peabody appeared and asked Priscilla, "Are you okay, honey?"

"I'll be alright, father," she responded.

Buck Henry and Ranger Gentry's eyes did not waiver from each other. Seth saw Henry's hand drop to where his gun would usually be holstered. His hand clenched involuntarily as he realized he was unarmed.

"Who you callin' boy?" Buck asked with clenched teeth. "You guys are all alike, hiding behind little tin stars, harassing unarmed folks."

Seth smiled. "I haven't known you but for a short while, but I recognize a bully when I see one. I think it's time you were taught your propers." He unbuckled his gun belt and handed it to Marshal Clements.

Buck Henry broke into a large grin. The big man had never been beaten in a fight.

"That boy has no sense of honor, Seth; he'll kill you if he gets the chance," Marshal Clements said.

Marshal Wheeler looked over at Buck's father. John Henry had been watching with an evil smirk on his face. Even though his son often made mistakes, Henry thought of him as a young stallion, spirited and not quite tamed. John Henry had used a heavy hand raising his son and as Buck grew and got older, the beatings had occurred less often; and the truth of the matter was, John had grown to feel that his son might retaliate someday and he wouldn't be able to stop him.

Endicott Peabody stepped in-between the two big men. "It's the Sabbath, boys, let there be no violence."

"Step aside, Peabody, I'm going to tear this ranger apart," Buck said with clenched fists. "He's got no right sticking his nose in my business."

The pastor glanced at the crowd. The disturbance had interrupted the picnic and curiosity overshadowed hunger. He looked at the determined faces of the two would-be combatants, and an idea came to mind. The good reverend recognized an opportunity when he saw one. When the idea of the church picnic had been proposed he realized that such an event would encourage more people to attend church and further line its coffers. In his best preaching voice he said, "Gentlemen, again I remind you that it is the Sabbath, and it is a day of worship and fellowship. I propose you put your anger aside this day and we enjoy the fruits of our labors."

"Your labors, Peabody? All you do is spew hot air," John Henry said. He wanted to see his son destroy the ranger.

"Look here, Mr. Henry, these people deserve a peaceful and enjoyable day. If these two gentlemen insist on fisticuffs I say we reconvene tomorrow morning and have an organized event---Marquess of Queensberry Rules. I'll ask Marshal Clements to referee."

There was a murmur from the crowd and Buck Henry broke into a grin. He had no idea what Marquess of Queensberry Rules were, but it didn't matter. He wouldn't have followed them anyway. "I'll be here," Buck said, wringing his hands.

John Henry saw an opportunity to make some money on the side and nodded his head.

"You name the time, Mr. Peabody and I'll be here," Seth said, not taking his eyes off of Buck Henry.

It was disconcerting to Buck that there was no fear emanating from the ranger. Men were usually intimidated by him. Though a little shorter and less barrel-chested, the ranger had broad shoulders and a narrow waist. The ranger's movements were fluid with little wasted effort. Even so, the ranger's confidence probably came from a lack of knowledge about his abilities and his aptitude for violence.

"Ladies and Gentlemen," Preacher Peabody raised his sermon voice. "I would like to announce that tomorrow morning at ten o'clock we will have a boxing match with Mr. Buck Henry and Ranger Seth Gentry, Marquess of Queensberry Rules. This will be a benefit for the church and admission will be twenty-five cents. The event will take place here in the flat area near the horseshoe pits."

Startled by the quick planning of the preacher, Seth said to Clements, "Your preacher certainly is an opportunist."

Sam Clements smiled. "He's definitely enterprising."

Ranger Gentry felt movement near his right arm. He looked down into the freckled face of Priscilla Peabody. "Oh, Seth, I am so sorry to get you into this. Buck will try to kill you."

"It's not your doing," Seth said. "It's time that boy got taught a lesson."

"I'm afraid for you," she said.

"Don't be," Gentry said.

"Come with me, I'll get you a plate," she said, tugging at the ranger's arm.

Seth glanced back at Buck Henry; he was seething, with both fists clenched, smiling like a hungry wolf about to attack its prey. He turned his attention to the little blonde and said, "It'd be my pleasure to join you, Miss Priscilla."

Buck made a step toward the ranger but was held back by his father. "You can take care of him tomorrow," he said. "Let's get some grub and then I'm going to place some bets."

"I can't wait to get my hands on that guy," Buck said, turning and following his father.

Chapter 32

Except for the constant chatter, the ride to Sloughhouse was uneventful. Ranger Hatfield assisted the ladies down from the buggy and unloaded their luggage. The Inn was modest, but neat and clean and had a small restaurant to the right of the lobby.

A young boy assisted Hatfield with the luggage. An older balding man with gartered sleeves turned the ledger for Althea Brown to sign in. "It's such a pleasure having you stay with us Mrs. Brown," he said. "We were so honored when we received the telegram reserving the two best rooms we have."

"Thank you, Mr. . . ."

"Jackson, Andrew Jackson," he said.

Althea Brown smiled as she dipped the quill pen.

"I know, my father loved American history."

"How's the food here, Mr. Jackson?"

"It's the best in town," he said with a chuckle, "though it is the only place in town."

The governor's wife handed the pen back to the amiable man.

"Thank you, ma'am," he said as he turned his attention to Darla Brown. "I must say your daughter favors you."

"I consider that a compliment," she said.

"Yes, ma'am, it surely is," Jackson said.

"Tommy, take the ladies' luggage upstairs," Jackson said to the young boy. He turned to the ranger. "You can put your horses up out back. There's feed and water and a small corral." He handed the room keys to the governor's wife and she passed one over to Ranger Hatfield.

"We're going to freshen up, James; come and get us in about an hour and we'll go to dinner," Althea said.

"Yes, ma'am," Hatfield said and he went out to tend to the horses. After unharnessing the horses from the buggy and unsaddling the buckskin, Hatfield forked some hay and found a bit of grain in a small shed. Young Tommy appeared and climbed up the corral rail.

"Where you all headed?" the young boy asked.

"Amador City," Hatfield responded. "I'm joining up with Captain Gentry."

"Them two women sure are pretty," the boy said, looking at an upstairs window of the inn. "How come you're taking them with you?"

Hatfield smiled at the curious young boy. It seemed that it wasn't too many years ago he was just like him. "Well, Tommy, the governor's daughter has set her eyes on Captain Gentry and her mother is accompanying her."

"Ah, I bet that's disappointing for you," he said with youthful perception.

Still smiling, Hatfield said, "Darla is a mighty fine looking woman alright."

Tommy's attention turned to the circled star on Hatfield's chest. "How do you become a ranger?"

"To be a ranger you have to have character; that means you have to have strength, honor, and integrity. Even before you achieve skills in the use of firearms you must be honest and live your life by the Golden Rule. Do unto others as you would have them do unto you."

"So, you need to be a good person."

"Yes, Tommy, you must solemnly swear to uphold the laws of California and protect its citizens. Hopefully we'll have a much larger ranger force in the future."

"Maybe I'll be one of them," Tommy said.

Hatfield tousled the young boy's hair. "I think you would be a good one."

The boy smiled at the ranger. "You think so?"

"Yes, I think so. Now I have to clean up before dinner." Hatfield reached into his shirt pocket and pulled out a silver dollar. He handed it to Tommy and said, "Rub down the horses."

Tommy's eyes were as big as the silver dollar. "A whole dollar! I'll take good care of them, ranger!"

Ranger Hatfield retired to his room to rid himself of as much trail dust as possible. The nerves of youth arose as he slicked back his wet hair and studied his image in a small mirror. The enormity of escorting and being responsible for two of the most important and beautiful women in the State of California was weighing on his shoulders. Being vigilant and concentrating on driving the buggy had kept him busy, but now he was about to escort the two older women to dinner and it had his stomach in his throat and his heart racing. He hitched his gun belt, took in a deep breath and took one last look in the mirror before leaving to knock on the Brown's door.

He should have known better.

Darla answered the door and peaked through a small opening.

James Hatfield blushed with embarrassment. He could see a bare shoulder above the garment she was holding in front of her.

"Oh, Jimmie, we aren't ready yet. Wait just a minute and you can come in," Darla said.

"I…I don't think I should," Hatfield stammered.

"Oh, nonsense, I'll be dressed in a minute," Darla said, closing the door.

Hatfield fidgeted and looked down over the rail at the several people entering the inn. Women looked up at him and turned and whispered to each other. It was obvious that word of the governor's wife and daughter's arrival had spread rapidly.

The door opened and Althea Brown said, "Come on in James, we are almost ready."

"I, uh, don't know if I should, ma'am."

"Oh, nonsense, you are like family."

With hat in hand and a red-as-a beet face, Ranger Hatfield entered the room. The young man wished he was anyplace but here. Behind a small screen he could see Darla and he heard the rustle of clothing as she continued to dress. He attempted to look away and he caught the young woman's image in the mirror. He quickly looked away, the image burned into his mind. Miserable, he pulled out a handkerchief and wiped his brow.

Althea Brown watched the young ranger with a small smile on her face. It was obvious that his experience with women was limited.

"I'm almost ready, mother," Darla hollered from behind the dressing screen. If the governor had been there he would have been able to inform young Hatfield that 'almost ready' was a misnomer in the Brown household and meant that you could usually have one or more drinks before departing.

James Hatfield stood on one leg and then the other fidgeting with his hat. Althea wanted to put the boy at ease and invited him to sit in the rocking chair in the far corner.

"Thank you, ma'am," Hatfield responded and scurried to the chair.

"You haven't been around women folks much, have you?" Althea said.

"No ma'am, just mostly my mother."

"Well, we don't bite and Darla and I will give you some pointers during our time together."

"Thank you, ma'am; that would be appreciated. I do hope to find the right girl someday."

Althea Brown smiled. "You're a fine young man, James; in due time the right one will come along."

"I hope so, ma'am."

Darla Brown stepped out from behind the screen and Hatfield's jaw dropped. "You are right pretty, Miss Brown," he said.

"Why, thank you, Jimmie, ah I mean Jim," she said doing a twirl. "Do you like my dress?"

Hatfield swallowed and said, "Yes, it's very nice."

Althea smiled at the blushing ranger and said, "Women like compliments, Jim: remember that."

"Yes, ma'am."

"Let's go eat, I am famished," the governor's wife said.

Jim leapt up and opened the door for the ladies.

"Thank you," Darla said with a slight curtsy.

The trio entered the dining room. All eyes watched them be seated at a candlelit table with a white tablecloth. After the two women were seated, Hatfield sat down across from them, placing his hat in the chair next to him.

"For being in the middle of nowhere, this is quite nice," Darla said, beaming.

Hatfield stared at the two women across from him. The candlelight danced in Darla Brown's lovely dark eyes and he thought how lucky Seth Gentry was to have such a woman. He turned his attention to Mrs. Brown and thought how lucky the governor was.

"I said this is quite nice," Darla repeated.

"Oh, yes it is," Hatfield responded. "Sorry, I was lost in thought about how lucky Governor Brown is to have you two in his life."

"Ah, that's very sweet of you to say," Althea said.

A portly woman approached and said, "It's so nice to have you here, Mrs. Brown; our special tonight is steak, and we also have lamb chops."

"Thank you, I'll have the lamb," Althea said.

"The same for me," Darla said.

"Steak, medium rare." Hatfield's stomach was growling.

Althea Brown smiled. "Just like a man; have to have your beef."

"Yes, ma'am."

The pleasant solitude was suddenly interrupted by the arrival of two drunken ruffians.

Chapter 33

"What did you have to go and shoot that banker for?" Ned asked Eli.

Eli Hayes shrugged his narrow shoulders. "A man comes at me, he's got to pay."

Dumbfounded, Virgil looked over at the little man as they rode south toward Sutter Creek. "He didn't have no gun."

Eli, with a blank stare, said, "You never know, Virgil, it's better to be safe than sorry."

"Your kind of caution is going to have a posse dogging us," Ned said disgustedly.

"Not only that, we didn't get no loot from the safe," Virgil said.

Ned, in the lead, reined in. The two riders following stopped. He glared at his brother. "You cost us a lot of money, Eli, and you are going to bring the law down on us. You shot the lookout on the stage and killed two men in Amador City. Our take from the bank looks small and I think the right thing for you to do is divvy up that silver you took from the stage.

Eli's gun hand was unseen by his brother but Virgil saw his hand move closer to his revolver. There was no doubt that Eli was a dangerous character.

Through clenched teeth Eli said, "That's my money Ned, and mine only."

Only the creak of leather was heard as Ned studied his brother. It had been a big mistake involving him in his scheme. He and Virgil should have taken the bank on their own. Without another word, he spurred his horse and moved down the trail.

The three robbers road in silence until they reached a small oak-studded knoll above Sutter Creek. "There'll be law here," Ned said, "so we'll head up Volcano way. Nobody will know of the bank robbery yet."

Eli said, "I sure could go for a drink."

Disgusted, Ned said, "Ever' time you get a drink it costs someone their life and brings us grief."

"I can't be pushed," Eli said between clenched teeth.

"Live by the gun, die by the gun," Ned said to his brother. "And if that don't happen you die by the rope."

Wide-eyed, Virgil stared at the two brothers, wondering if this was it.

Eli sneered. "You was with me. Your neck can stretch, too. I say shoot first and ask questions later. I'm going into town for that drink."

The loud click of a revolver hammer pulled back made Eli turn in the saddle slowly. Virgil was holding a gun pointed at his back.

"Your brother's right, Eli, we don't need no more trouble," Virgil said.

"Pulling a gun on me can be mighty dangerous to your health," Eli said. "I'm going to get a drink, Virgil, and you ain't about to stop me."

"The way I figure it, you haven't been no help to me and Ned, and I don't think the law would mind me plugging you right now," Virgil said.

Eli stared at the gun in Virgil's hand. Virgil wasn't too bright but it didn't take brains to pull a trigger. "I'm going to get that drink, Virgil."

"You drop them saddle bags on the ground afore you go," Virgil demanded.

"Now why would I do that?"

"We don't want no one to get their hands on that silver."

"You ain't going to try to steal *my* money, are you?" Eli asked.

Not wanting any more trouble than they already had, and not wanting the silver to leave his sight, Ned said, "He's got a point, Eli; you don't want someone to get a hold of the loot."

Eli glared at his brother. "Well, I need that drink. At least allow me a few dollars for that," he said, reaching into his saddlebags.

The muzzle of Virgil's gun dropped a few inches, glad that he was getting his way.

In a blur, Eli pulled a .32 caliber Smith and Wesson from his saddle bags and Virgil briefly saw a stab of flame before darkness enveloped him. The shot had taken him in the forehead.

Ned fought to control his horse from the sudden violence and he watched Virgil's body slowly fall to the ground. The top of Virgil's head had been blown off; he looked like he had been scalped by an Indian.

"Dang, I was aimin' for his heart; that .32 sure ain't very accurate." Ned glared at his brother. Even for him, the sudden violence was a shock. "You didn't have to do that," he said.

"Easiest way to increase our profit by a third," Eli said. "Besides, that guy was irritatin'."

Ned looked at his brother with revulsion. Despite the fact that Virgil had gotten on his nerves, the sudden violence of his brother's ways disturbed him. But, what his brother said was true; he had gotten rid of Virgil and it was now just the two of them. He dismounted, went through Virgil's pockets and stripped him of his guns. He then dragged him into the bushes and piled some leaves and brush on top of the body.

"I'm going to town," Eli said.

His brother stared at the saddlebags tied to the back of his saddle. After what he had just witnessed he had second thoughts about suggesting that he leave the silver with him.

He gathered up the reins of Virgil's horse and pointed to a flat grassy spot near the creek that flowed towards town. "Let's set up camp down there and I'll go into town with you," Ned said, taking up the reins of Virgil's horse.

Ashes enclosed by a circle of rocks were evidence of past campfires. There was green grass for the horses and a pleasant clear creek chuckled by. An ancient old oak tree provided shaded relief from the afternoon sun.

Staying mounted and leaning on the pommel, Eli watched his brother silently strip the saddle from Virgil's horse and hobble him in a patch of grass near the creek. Ned then went through Virgil's saddlebags to be sure that they weren't leaving behind anything of value for thieves and such. It became obvious that the only things Virgil owned of value were his horse, tack and his gun.

Ned shook his head. How can a man live his whole life and be worth practically nothing? He thought of his own situation and realized he wasn't any better off than Virgil was. He had tried mining for gold. He had little luck and found no pleasure in the cold water and hard work. He had been a cowboy for a short time and suffered from long days in the saddle, choking on dust riding drag, the pay being little for the effort involved. It was then he came to the conclusion that you could make more money using your head than your back. He had no real skills, however, and below average intelligence. Eventually he felt he had no choice but to turn to crime and relieve other people of the rewards of their labors.

Eli fidgeted in his saddle, the creaking of leather interrupting the pleasant sounds of the rustling grass in the wind and the gurgle of the creek.

Looking over to his little brother, Ned felt more agitation. The absence of Eli in prison had dulled the memory of his brother's irascibility. The odds of further trouble coming his way were compounded the longer he partnered with Eli. His gaze settled on Eli's saddlebags.

"We'd best hide them saddlebags of yours," Ned said. "You carrying them around would surely draw attention."

Eli spit tobacco on to the ground and sneered with grey teeth. "You sure been worried about *my* saddlebags."

"You know as well as I do that a man carrying his saddlebags around means there must be something of value in them," Ned said.

Ned's brother knew that he had a good point, and, after all, his brother would be with him in town. From atop his horse he looked around. In the dark shade of the massive oak tree was an outcropping of grey lava rocks. He dismounted and untied his saddlebags. He threw them over his shoulder and with effort, hiked up the hill to the rocks. He found a small indentation, withdrew a few coins and placed the bags of silver in the shallow hole and covered it with rocks. He studied his handiwork to make sure it looked natural and went back to his horse. "Let's get that drink," he said mounting up and reining toward town.

Eli's brother glanced over to the pile of rocks. "Looks safe enough," he said when he noticed Eli looking back at him. "Leastways anyone will know the campsite is took with Virgil's horse here."

'Uh-huh," Eli responded, spurring his horse into a trot. He knew he couldn't trust his brother any further than he could throw him. He had an uncomfortable feeling as he led the way with his trigger-happy brother behind him. He slowed down and let his brother come along side. He glanced over at Eli on his right. He realized he couldn't see his brother's gun hand, a very unsettling feeling when in close proximity. When he got a chance he would try to maneuver to the other side.

Dropping down a small rise, a beautiful, peaceful valley spread out before them, rich in green grass. Cattle grazed contentedly and in the distance was evidence of the outer edge of the small town of Volcano.

A spiritual feeling overcame Ned and he reined in. Eli stopped ahead and looked back impatiently at his brother.

"Maybe we should take up ranchin'," Ned said as he breathed deeply of the fresh air.

Eli shook his head and spurred his horse.

Ned reined his horse to the right.

Chapter 34

Ranger Seth Gentry left Sutter Creek at the south end and started his big red sorrel in a circle back to the north. Unlike the flatlands of the great valley, the surrounding area of Sutter Creek and Amador City was an irregular pattern of hills and valleys dotted with great historic oaks on a lush green canvas. Though pleasing, the undulating scenery did not allow the eye to see far unless the rider was on the highest peak and even then danger could be lurking in hidden valleys. Horse and rider moved slowly on the highest outskirts of the canyon and the ranger kept a close eye on the horse's ears for any sign of possible danger.

Topping out on one of the higher peaks, Seth caught a glimpse of the large framework of the Kennedy mine outside the town of Jackson. He wondered if the murderer and the stage robber might have continued into Jackson or on to Volcano.

Gentry guided his horse down to the clear cold water of Sutter Creek and let his horse drink while looking around the peaceful little valley. A meadowlark trilled its melodic song and all seemed well with the world. Seth knew that peace and solitude could be a fleeting thing and kept a watchful eye despite the pleasant surroundings. After John Marshall had discovered gold at Sutter's Mill, the rush for riches brought thousands of people to the Mother Lode. Many were good God-fearing people but, unfortunately, many were greedy and lacked morals and would do anything to get their hands on gold.

A few level spots along the creek showed evidence of past efforts to locate gold and of long abandoned campsites. Gold and the need for water had made the creek a popular place to set up camp in the past. Seth decided to follow the creek to the east, climbing gradually through the green grass and around the massive oak trees. While looking for sign, Seth's mind wandered back to his stint in Nevada City and then to the image of Darla Brown. It had been weeks since he had seen her and he longed for her touch and her company. These were dangerous times, however, and despite the need to see her he hoped she would stay in Sacramento until he could get away for a visit and report to the governor.

As he and the sorrel climbed higher he saw the horse's ears perk forward and he slowed the horse to a walk. And then he heard the rhythmic sound of a miner's pick on rock. The pounding stopped and then he heard the scrape of a miner's tin pan in the gravel.

The creek made a slight bend and Seth couldn't see who was working. He knew that it could be dangerous approaching a miner's claim and yelled, "Hello the camp, friendly coming in."

There was sudden silence. A few moments passed. "If friendly you be, come on in slow and careful like," said a voice with some years.

Seth walked the sorrel around the bend, with hands visible for the miner. The grey- bearded miner had taken up his rifle and it was pointed to the ground in an unthreatening manner. He squinted at the circled star on the ranger's chest and said, "Light a spell, I was jest fixin' to make some coffee and get a bite of grub. Don't get much law in these parts," he said with a cackle.

"Thank you." Seth dismounted and led the sorrel over to a lush, grassy spot.

"All I got is beans and bread, but I'm a pretty durn good cook if I say so myself."

Seth grinned at the grisly old-timer. "My name is Seth Gentry."

The miner wiped his hands on his shirt and held one out to shake Seth's hand. "The name's Zeke; don't get much company and when I do it ain't usually good."

The ranger smiled and shook the dirt-creased rough hand of the miner. "I'm hunting bad guys; you seen any lately?"

"No, thank goodness," Zeke said as he built up his fire and put coffee on.

Gentry sat on a deadfall and watched the miner busy with a pot of beans. "Getting any color?"

Zeke closed one eye against the rising smoke of the fire. "Enough to get by," he said, stirring the beans.

Seth inhaled. "Smells mighty good, Zeke," he said as his stomach growled loudly. He hadn't realized how hungry he was.

"I don't hear so good, but I heard that." Zeke chuckled. "I jest hope it wasn't in protest."

"Just the opposite," Seth said, realizing the old-timer hadn't once turned his back on him. Zeke was friendly but cautious, and it was obvious why he had lived to an old age.

"I've got some cold fried chicken in my saddlebags," Seth said, walking over to his horse. He watched the miner's rifle raise a bit as he kept an eye on him. When assured that Seth's intentions were good he set the rifle aside.

The old miner filled a tin cup with coffee and brought it over to Seth. He handed the cup to the ranger and squinted at the badge. "My eyesight ain't what it used to be; what's that say?"

Seth quickly took his hand off the cup and grabbed it by the handle. The burning sensation continued and he was amazed how impervious the rough-handed miner had been to the scalding hot cup. He blew on his hand and the miner chuckled.

"I like my coffee hot and strong," Zeke said.

Flexing his burnt hand, Seth said, "I'm a California Ranger, commissioned by the governor."

Zeke nodded. "We got a governor?"

Seth blew on his steaming coffee cup. "Yes, we do," he said with a smile. "Governor Thaddeus Brown."

"Never did cotton to politicians," Zeke said, dishing up a plate of beans. "Nor attorneys either. Come to think of it, the politicians I knowed of were attorneys."

Gentry chuckled and took a small sip of coffee. He liked strong coffee and you could float a horseshoe in Zeke's. "Good coffee," he said.

"I'm glad you like it," Zeke said. "Wait 'til you taste my beans. I got some cornbread but you got to eat it cold." He placed a chunk of bread on the plate and handed it to Seth.

Seth inhaled the steaming aroma. "Smells mighty good, Zeke," he said, his stomach growling once again. He placed some chicken on Zeke's plate.

Zeke hooted. "You best feed that stomach of yorn afore it disturbs the critters here about."

The two men ate in silence. The beans were as good as Zeke had claimed, reminding Seth of the aroma of beans being cooked on a stove by his grandmother many years ago.

"That's mighty fine fried chicken," Zeke said as he gummed a bite.

The ranger put the empty plate down and returned to his cup of coffee. A comfortable, satisfied feeling coming over him, a feeling he hadn't enjoyed for some time.

"There's more where that came from," the old miner said.

"Thanks, Zeke, I'm plumb full. That was very good. You may have caused a problem."

Zeke stared at the young ranger. "Problem?"

"I may have to hunt you up again when I get hungry."

The miner grinned a toothless smile. "You're welcome any time, Seth," he said.

Seth smiled to himself when he noticed the miner had turned his back on him to retrieve the coffee pot.

Seth accepted a refill. "Zeke, I'm hunting a smallish man that robbed the stage and killed a man in Amador City. Have you seen anyone that might match that description?"

Zeke rubbed a whiskered chin. "Can't say as I have, Seth."

"If you come across the like, be careful and get hold of me or Marshal Clements."

The old miner nodded.

"And you be sure to be careful," Seth added.

Zeke cackled. "I've lived this long being mighty watchful."

The ranger looked over the rim of his tin cup. "You did turn your back on me, maybe you're getting forgetful in your old age," he teased.

The old miner turned serious with piercing dark eyes. "I size people pretty quick like, but I'm never far from protection," he said pulling out a small derringer from his pants pocket.

Ranger Gentry smiled. "Those things can't hit the side of a barn."

"Don't you worry none son, this gun has done its job afore," the old miner said putting the derringer back into his pocket.

A lawman's natural curiosity wanted to ask more questions, but Seth thought better of it. He liked this old man and secrets of the past were his. "Tell me, Zeke, you ever heard of John and Buck Henry?"

Zeke looked up quickly from putting his little gun in his pocket. "Them two is bad---plain no good," he said.

"That's what I surmised," Seth said.

"Surmised?"

"That's what I thought."

Zeke nodded. "Them two tried to run me off a time or two, but I'm like a bad habit, not easy to be rid of."

Seth smiled.

"Why did you ask about them two?" Zeke asked.

"I had a run-in with Buck over his lack of manners and we're going to have a little boxing match tomorrow in Sutter Creek."

The old miner squinted at the ranger as if he was sizing him up for the first time. "I'll have to see that," Zeke said. "You're put together, but that Buck is a mean one and rules don't mean nothing to him. He'll try to gouge your eyes out."

"I figured as much," Seth said finishing his coffee.

"Where's this here fight to be?" Zeke asked.

"Over by the church in the morning; the good reverend has turned it into a fundraiser."

Zeke chortled, "That sounds like Peabody. He's always asking for money."

"I've hung around long enough. I've got to go looking for bad guys," Seth said.

"It was a right pleasurable visit. I'll see you tomorrow and you whup that Buck Henry good."

"Thanks for the beans and coffee."

The old miner watched the ranger gather his horse's reins and mount up. With a small wave the ranger rode off and Zeke stared after him. "I sure hope that boy don't get serious hurt tomorrow," he said to himself. "That Buck Henry is pure bad."

Chapter 35

The two unkempt wranglers stumbled boisterously into the dining room. The patrons stared at the two drunks with irritation. Andrew Jackson rushed in and made a futile attempt to escort them out. The larger of the two men swatted him away as if he were a mosquito.

"Come on boys, you're drunk and disturbing my customers," Jackson pleaded.

"Don't you worry none little man, we ain't going to cause no trouble; just bring us two of the biggest steaks you got," the large bearded man said. "Me and my brother here are powerful hungry," he added, looking around for an empty table. His eyes stopped at Darla and Althea Brown's table. He devoured their beauty and licked his lips. "Things is lookin' up little brother," he said, walking toward them. He seemed oblivious to Ranger Hatfield sitting across from the two women.

The big man's little brother trailed behind him. It was obvious that the smaller brother deferred to the bigger man.

"My, you two are the prettiest women I have seen in a coon's age," the larger brother said. "Since there ain't no place to set ourselves, my brother and I would surely like to join you."

Ranger Hatfield had watched the two ruffians with amusement. He had sized them up as a couple of obnoxious blowhards and nothing else. He had been bullied in school by boys like these and when he wound up taking them on, the obnoxiousness tended to go away, at least when he was present. As he became of age, though still in his teens, men such as these two took his youthful baby face as someone who was soft. Nothing could be further from the truth. Hatfield had big hands and was as strong as a railroad spike. Just above a whisper, he said, "You boys move along; the ladies don't wish to be disturbed."

The two brothers seemed to see Hatfield for the first time. The big one looked down at the ranger and said, "You butt out, boy or I'll throw you out."

Hatfield turned toward him and the candlelight gleamed off of his ranger shield.

"Looky here, Festus, we got a boy playing lawman."

Festus snickered. "He don't amount to much, Leroy."

"Since you boys are not welcome, I'm sure I can have Mr. Jackson package your steaks to go," Hatfield said.

Squinting, Leroy looked closer at Ranger Hatfield's circled star on his chest. "You headed to the big fight tomorrow with that other ranger and Buck Henry?"

With wide brown eyes Darla looked up at the big man. "What did you say?"

"They's a big fight in Sutter Creek tomorrow between a ranger and Buck Henry. The money's on Buck; he ain't never lost a fight and some of the losers didn't live to see another day. 'Fact I tangled with ol' Buck one time when we was youngin's; he's tougher than a keg of nails," Leroy said.

Nervously Darla said, "That doesn't sound like Seth; he wouldn't just fight like that."

"You don't know Buck Henry. It's either fight or be killed immediate," Leroy said.

Festus nodded in agreement.

"We been ridin' fence line and got word. Me and Festus are headed to Sutter Creek. We figger we can double our wages bettin' on ol' Buck."

Andrew Jackson appeared at the table holding a flour sack. "Here are your steaks, boys, on the house. Now please, no more disturbing my patrons."

Festus grabbed the sack. Leroy looked down at the little bald man then over to the two women. Range Hatfield stood up and Leroy was surprised to be gazing up at the young man, a good two inches taller than him. He quickly reconsidered his alternatives.

Leroy tipped his hat. "You have a fine evening ladies. Festus and I will take our leave and we'll look forward to seeing you tomorrow."

Althea Brown took a deep breath as she watched the two men leave. "I'm glad to see those two go," she said.

"Me, too," Darla said. "I can't believe that Seth was goaded into a fight with that Buck fellow."

"Those two boys were full of whiskey and bluster," Hatfield said. "You needn't have worried; I could have handled those two."

Althea Brown looked at James Hatfield, wonderment written all over her face. Was this youthful bravado or could this baby-faced young man actually do what he said?

The waitress and Andrew Jackson appeared at the table with sizzling plates. "Sorry for the delay. We needed to get rid of those two so that you could enjoy your meal," Jackson said.

"Thank you, Mr. Jackson," Althea said. "It smells delightful."

"If there is anything more we can do for you, please let us know."

Althea nodded and smiled as she watched Hatfield tear into his steak. Her smile turned into concern as she looked over at Darla, fidgeting with her food. "You need to eat, dear," she said.

"Mother, I just can't believe that Seth is going to fight some man like a barbarian."

With steak juice dripping down his chin, Hatfield said, "You don't know what the circumstances are, Miss Darla; perhaps he is just trying not to kill a man unnecessarily."

"Wipe your chin, Jimmie," Althea said.

"Yes, ma'am," Hatfield said with some embarrassment.

Darla said, "I hadn't thought of that, Jim. I should not pre-judge Seth's motives."

Althea looked over at her beautiful young daughter, recognizing that this was a teachable moment. "Darla, it is always best to learn the facts before coming to judgment."

"I guess you are right, mother," Darla said.

"Yes, ma'am," Hatfield mumbled, wiping his chin again. He looked longingly over at Darla's lamb chops. She couldn't have taken more than a couple of bites.

Darla set her fork down and watched James wipe up the last remaining juices of his plate with a piece of bread. "You can have the rest of my lamb chops," she said.

Hatfield smiled. "Are you sure?" he asked.

"Yes, I don't have much of an appetite. I just don't understand why men have to be so violent."

The young ranger reached over for Darla's plate. "Sometimes that's the only way to fix things," he said to her.

Althea looked at the distraught face of her daughter. "As you get older, dear, you will realize that there is no reasoning with evil. Human beings are imperfect and some are more so than others, sad to say."

"I guess so, mother, but I don't understand how men try to solve things in a manner that can get them hurt, or even killed."

Darla's mother reached over and touched her hand as Ranger Hatfield wolfed down the last of Darla's lamb. "Men are aggressive by nature, dear, and not all of them are reasonable. Seth is a good man and if he is to fight this Buck Henry fellow he must have a good reason."

"I just don't want Seth to get hurt, or worse," Darla whispered.

Hatfield stood up, his chair making a loud vibrating noise on the wood floor. He looked around at the now half-empty room. All eyes were on him and the two ladies at the table. He had been so engrossed in his meal that he had forgotten the governor's wife and daughter were major news. "I'll escort you ladies to your room; we'll need to get an early start tomorrow to get to Sutter Creek on time."

Darla sighed.

"Come on, dear, let's get some rest," Althea Brown said. "Tomorrow's a big day."

Chapter 36

Horse and rider slowly worked their way up the gradual incline following the boiling creek, bright sun rising from the high Sierras, shadowed by massive oak trees and the folds of the green lower hills. The big red sorrel easily followed a well-worn deer trail, allowing the erect-riding ranger to be alert to all things surrounding them.

When the vista opened up, Ranger Gentry could see the bright flashes of sun on quaking aspen trees with large snow-capped mountains in the distance. "This is mighty fine country, Red," the ranger said, patting the horse's muscular neck. The large sorrel tossed his head in agreement, the bit jiggling musically with the sounds of the rushing creek along with the pleasant song of a happy mockingbird.

Working their way higher, Range Gentry rounded a small bend, sighting circling shadows of vultures high in the bright blue sky. "Looks like we might have a dead critter yonder," he said to the horse. On lonely trails with only a horse for companionship Seth often found himself talking to his trusty steed. While very fond of his horse, Seth felt a stab of loneliness and his thoughts turned to the beautiful daughter of the governor. It still amazed him how quickly and deeply he had fallen in love with the vivacious brunette. He had met and appreciated beautiful women before, but this girl was different. At first, he had fought the intense feeling with all of his strength because he had been instructed to find her missing fiancé. To further confuse matters he had felt guilty when he found her fiancé had been murdered. The governor had told him that he didn't cotton to the man, but in deference to his daughter's feelings Seth was told to find out what happened to him. He had never met the man, at least alive, and felt a natural detachment that he felt wasn't fair to Darla's past feelings.

As Seth and Red closed in on the circling shadows the distinct odor of decaying flesh permeated the air. Red's ears perked forward and he whinnied in protest. Seth rubbed his big neck and said, "It's okay, boy; let's check it out." He heeled the big horse's flanks and urged him up a small incline then dismounted and ground-hitched his horse. He followed the stench, climbed over a small outcropping of lava rock and came upon a pile of disturbed leaves. A coyote or some other critter had been digging and feasting on something. Holding his breath, Seth brushed away some of the leaves and found that the remains were that of a man, a very dead man. Closer inspection did not reveal his identity and he was unarmed. That he was killed and robbed was a distinct possibility.

Seth walked away and took in some fresh air. He wondered if he would be able to find this man's identity. How many men had been killed or suffered accidental death in these mountains, their demise forever unknown by friends and family? His thoughts returned to the body of Darla's fiancé, thrown down a mine shaft with others like everyday garbage. The ranger shook his head. Life was cheap to some; evil people did not value it in others.

The ranger went back to his horse and led him to water and a patch of green grass. Then he went about carefully scouting the area in an attempt to find out what had happened here. It was obvious that there had been more than one horse in the area, possibly as many as three or four. The dead man had been with companions or was brought here already dead or to be killed. Drag marks indicated he had been taken or shot from his horse and hastily covered with leaves and debris.

Seth studied the imprints of the horseshoes for any distinct marks that could identify them.

And then he saw it.

Off to the side of the drag marks was the imprint of a boot, a smaller size than his with a rundown heel and a worn spot in the right sole. Could the dead man be the robber of the stagecoach? Gentry went back to the body and knelt down to look at the deceased's boots. He brushed away leaves and dirt. The dead man's boots were about the same size as the imprint, but they were even in worse shape and they didn't match the imprint he had just seen and had seen at the location of the stagecoach robbery. Gentry thought about the robbery. The thief had been quick to shoot the man riding shotgun. It was possible, even likely, that the robber was the killer of this man.

Why was this man murdered? What was the motivation? The ranger studied the dead man's face. He certainly didn't look like a man of means. Would he ever know who this man was? We all have a story--- the good and the bad, and he knew this one did too.

Seth circled in a widening arc and found nothing more of help. He walked over to his sorrel, took up the reins and looked back at the site of the dead man. He sighed and mounted up. "Let's see if we can find the little man with the holy boot, Red."

Gentry continued up the deer trail, climbing a small knoll and dropping down into a little ravine; the gurgling rushing creek off to his right was providing a pleasant reprieve from the scene of violence. Seth took in a series of deep breaths of fresh air in an attempt to erase the stench of the decaying body. The familiar scents of saddle leather, horse, and green grass made a gradual return and his horse seemed to become more spirited, happy to be leaving the smell of blood and death.

The sudden forward movement of the big horse's ears caused Ranger Gentry to rein in. He loosened his revolver in its holster and listened for any foreign sound. He sat very still, his hand near his gun, and scanned the tree and ravine shadows. A slight breeze whispered through the grass, the stream babbling pleasantly interrupted only by the occasional creak of saddle leather.

And then he heard a horse nicker and Red tossed his head, with a rattle of bridle and bit. Seth dismounted and shucked his gun, holding the reins in his left hand, and with caution he approached the direction he had heard the horse. Getting the scent of another horse, the unseen horse whinnied again. “I think we’re okay, Red,” Seth whispered. “A guy lying in wait would have quieted his horse.” Still, Seth approached with utmost caution. A fool drawn in could be a dead fool.

In a little valley there he was, unsaddled, with reins tied and all alone. With eyes and ears alert and a lookout for any sign of danger from his sorrel, Seth approached with care. There didn’t seem to be anyone around. It was strange to find a horse out here all alone.

As he drew near he spotted the saddle at the base of a large oak tree. Closer inspection revealed a dark spot of blood on the left side. “This must be the murdered man’s horse,” he said to himself and any horse that would listen.

Seth looked over at a circle of rocks with old grey ashes, evidence that this location had been used as a campsite before. Again, he looked over at the unsaddled horse, the grass shortened to a pale color. Why would they have left the horse here, alone? The only answer he could come up with was that the killers intended to come back. Where would they have gone? If they had gone back to Sutter Creek the chances were that he would have seen them. Or they could have looped back to Amador City or gone over to Jackson to the east.

Gentry gazed over to the south side of the creek. Zeke had told him of the old road that went up to Volcano. He had never been to Volcano but from what the miner had told him it possibly was the closest town from this spot. Before he studied on it further, Seth moved the lone horse to some tall grass, making sure the animal could access water from the creek. He moved Red to a similar spot nearby and began the slow process of reading sign.

The ranger studied the ground with the pleasant sound of rustling leaves in a slight breeze and the gurgle of the creek and the horses chomping away at the grass. As near as he could figure out, there were at least two other horses and he could find evidence of only one man dismounting---the same small-footed man that had possibly killed the man down the hill. Seth rubbed his chin. It was likely that the men had left to get some grub or drink, and planned to return to this campsite; the lone horse would tell any passersby the spot was taken. If he were to go looking for them he might just wind up chasing his own tail.

Walking up the hill, he was about to turn around for another perspective of the site when he saw it in the soft, shaded turf.

Chapter 37

Approaching Volcano, Ned and Eli dropped down into a large, peaceful bowl-shaped valley. The picturesque town was so serene that it felt spiritual, even to the two men who could care less about such things. Chaos was such a big part of the brother's lives that the serenity was threatening to them and they fidgeted in their saddles.

"Purdy little town," Ned said.

"It gives me the creeps," Eli responded.

Ned nodded his head. "Let's get that drink and get back to camp. I wouldn't want nothing to happen to that money."

Eli glared at his brother. *I bet you wouldn't,* he thought.

The brothers dismounted in front of the St. George Hotel. Ned brushed off some trail dust. Eli didn't bother.

A small clerk behind a tall counter watched the untidy men enter. It was bad enough that a bunch from the Circle J were here, now these two vagabonds. The hotel was the largest in town and preferred to cater to a higher-end clientele. He nodded toward the noise emanating from the saloon.

"Not too welcoming here," Eli said.

"Now don't you go killin' nobody," Ned said. "We're here for a peaceable drink and then we'll get back to camp afore dark."

Eli's piercing little black eyes looked like a timber rattler about to strike. With more control than usual he said nothing to his brother as he led the way to the packed bar. The noise abated as the patrons sized up the two newcomers.

"They don't amount to much," one of Buck Henry's men bellowed.

Eli's hand started toward his gun and Ned grabbed it by the wrist. "We got enough law looking for us; we don't need no more trouble," he hissed.

"I'd like to shut that blowhard's face," Eli said between gritted teeth.

The bartender had a bushy moustache and wore a bright white shirt with gartered sleeves. His eyes went to Eli's gun arm, still being held by his brother. "What'll it be gents?"

"Two whiskeys," Ned said.

The bartender nodded. "Coming right up. I advise you to stay clear of that bunch at the end of the bar. They're Circle J boys and big trouble. I'm hoping to get them out of here with as little damage as possible. Every time they show it takes a month to recover."

"We don't want no trouble," Ned said. "We just want them two whiskeys."

The bartender poured two shots to the brim. "That'll be one dollar."

"Kinda pricy ain't it," Eli said.

"Best whiskey in the county," the bartender replied.

"You can let go of my wrist now," Eli snapped. "I need it for whiskey drinking; I ain't going to shoot nobody."

As Ned released Eli's wrist the bartender scurried down to the end of the bar.

In two large gulps the brothers emptied their shot glasses. "Let's get one more," Ned said. He didn't mind spending his brother's money. He put up two fingers to signal the bartender.

"It'd be mighty expensive to drink in this establishment very long," Eli grumbled, reaching in his pants pocket for another silver dollar.

After seeing the money appear the bartender refilled their glasscs.

The brothers leaned on the bar, taking their time with their second drink.

"Leroy, you best slow down on that whiskey; we want to see the big fight tomorrow," Festus said at the end of the bar.

Throwing back the rest of his drink, Leroy said, "This is going to be easy money. I could whip the both of them with one arm behind my back."

"That ranger don't look like no pushover to me," another Circle J cowboy said.

"Them guys hide behind those tin stars," Leroy said, slurring his words.

Festus stared at his partner. The drink was making him tougher than he really was.

Cowboy Len, old for his young years, studied Leroy. He had never cared for the big man. He was just like Buck and his father. "What are the odds on the fight?"

Leroy squinted at the young cowboy over the rim of his glass. "The last I heard Buck's Pa was offering three to one odds. Chet Wagner's keeping the bets. My advice to you, youngin', is to put all you got on Buck."

Len smiled to himself. Then he got an idea. He had saved up some of his wages and he saw an opportunity. He had gotten a good look at the ranger, and if he bought a bottle for Buck tonight he could get him drunk before the big fight and place a wager against him.

Len raised his half-filled glass of whiskey in salute to himself in the big mirror behind the bar. He didn't like to waste his money on over-priced drinks and had been nursing this one for quite some time. Digging deep into his pocket he said, "Give me a bottle barkeep." As expensive as a whole bottle of whiskey was he was considering the purchase a small investment for a larger return. Len knew it was a gamble, but the odds seemed worth it. He knew most of the money would be placed on Buck and the odds would more than likely increase just before the fight.

Ned looked over to his brother. "I wonder where that fight is tomorrow; it might be entertainin'."

Eli nodded. "I'd like to see a ranger get his ass kicked."

The bartender appeared in front of them. "Want another, boys?"

Ned shook his head. "No, we got to get going. Where's that fight them boys been talking about?"

The bartender picked up a towel and dried his hands. "It's in the picnic area outside of Pastor Peabody's church in Sutter Creek. I hear he's turned it into quite an event as a fundraiser. It sounds like most of the county will be there, including me."

"The money's on a guy named Buck?" Ned asked.

"Yep; he's a jerk, but he's never lost a fight," the bartender said in a low voice. "Thankfully his father usually pays for any damage."

"Let's go, Eli," Ned said. "We want to get to that fight early to place a bet."

Eli started to leave and stopped. He glowered at his brother. "You ain't got nothing to bet with."

With an attempt at an amiable smile, Ned said, "Come on now, Eli, we got us an opportunity to have our investment grow. Remember, half that bank money is mine."

"Weren't much there," Eli reminded him.

"That's why we need to make it grow," Ned said.

"Well, we ain't bettin' any of my silver," Eli said.

We'll see about that, Ned thought.

Chapter 38

Before the greying of dawn, Ranger Hatfield and young Tommy were busy getting the horses and buggy ready for the trail by the light of a small lantern. James had the unpleasant duty of arousing the governor's wife and daughter by knocking on their door loudly. Mrs. Brown had responded that they were getting up and would be down for breakfast shortly. The ranger would soon learn that shortly in female time was different than his concept of a short period of time.

Hatfield was working on his third cup of coffee when the two women entered the room. The wait was worth it. They had to be the most beautiful women he had ever seen. Mrs. Brown's eyes sparkled with anticipation and the ranger jumped up to help her be seated.

"Thank you, Jim; you're such a gentleman," Althea Brown said.

"My pleasure, ma'am," Hatfield said as he turned to assist Darla. Darla had already seated herself and he noticed her pursed lips. "I hate to rush you, but Tommy and I will load your luggage and we need to hit the road."

Althea Brown smiled. "A biscuit and a cup of coffee will do. We can leave in a matter of minutes."

"What's the big rush?" Darla asked. "Just to watch two men brawl like ruffians?"

Darla's mother looked at the tense face of her daughter. "Men are a different sort of creature," she said. "We don't always know what brings them to violence."

"I think it's stupid," Darla said.

Ranger Hatfield entered the room. "The buggy's loaded; ready when you are."

Gazing out the window, Darla grumbled, "It's still night time."

Not wanting to add to her sour disposition, Hatfield said nothing.

With youthful impatience, Tommy said, "No, Miss Brown, the sun is about to peak over the mountains; it's lighter than you think sitting in here looking out."

Darla's disposition softened. Young Tommy was such a sweet boy. As she took one last sip of coffee she looked up at Jimmy Hatfield. He was a nice young man also. What drove men to violence? She thought of the massive number of people killed in the wars. What insanity to have brother fighting brother, father fighting son. Why must Seth Gentry fight another man? Had she misjudged his character? She rose from her chair and said, "Let's get this over with."

Hatfield looked at the beautiful, sullen face of the governor's daughter. He couldn't believe how someone who had so much could be so dour.

With a smile on her face, Althea Brown guided her daughter out the door. She looked over at Ranger Hatfield and said, "Over time young women tend to accept, if not understand, the doings of the male gender."

"Yes, ma'am," Hatfield said, not sure he understood. Women definitely were a puzzle. Tommy held the reins as he assisted the women up into the buggy. He took the reins from the young man and reached into his pocket for a silver dollar, passing it to the boy.

"Oh boy, Ranger, a whole dollar!"

Hatfield smiled. "You earned it Tommy. Remember what we talked about. I look forward to the day you join the California Rangers."

"Yes, sir," Tommy said with a grin. He stood and watched the buggy disappear into the distance, the dawning light leading them to Sutter Creek. Saying a prayer out loud he said, “Heavenly Father, please guide and keep those nice people safe.”

*****

Althea and Darla Brown rode in silence as Hatfield drove the team down the well-defined rode to the southeast. The morning was crisp and he breathed deeply of the fresh air tinted with the smell of deer brush and blue lupine, mingled with the spicy, soapy scent of tarweed.

The horses were trained to the trail, allowing Hatfield to keep a sharp eye and scan the horizon for trouble. The day brightened as the sun rose above the snowcapped peaks of the Sierra Nevada Mountains, the orange light turning bright white.

“What a gorgeous day,” Mrs. Brown said as she observed the morning spectacle.

“Yes, ma’am,” Hatfield said. “It doesn’t get much better than this part of the country,” he added. He glanced over to Darla, spine erect and hands clasped in her lap, wondering what it would take to bring her out of her morose mood.

The trio rode in silence, only interrupted by the clop-clop of horse hooves and the rattling of the long traces. The morning quickly warmed and dust rose from the trail. Darla Brown took a dainty handkerchief from her sleeve and wiped her brow.

“How much longer before we get to Sutter Creek?” Althea Brown asked.

Ranger Hatfield thought for a moment. It had been some time since he had been in this neck of the woods. “Well, ma’am, I would say we are about an hour from Amador City and Sutter Creek is just a few miles after that.”

Mrs. Brown nodded and looked over at the strained face of her daughter. Though concerned, she smiled to herself. Youth could be a wonderful thing but being young was burdened by the lack of life’s experiences. Darla had been living a privileged and somewhat sheltered life and didn't totally grasp the difficulties of the world, particularly when it came to men.

"I think we will be in Sutter Creek in plenty of time for the big fight," Ranger Hatfield added as he whipped the reins for the horses to pull up a slight rise.

Althea Brown watched her daughter wring the hanky in her hands. She looked at the Ranger. He, too, was young and somewhat oblivious to things around him. She sensed that the young man was excited about the impending fight between Ranger Gentry and Buck Henry and was unaware of the stress it imposed on her daughter. She knew that Darla was having some doubts about her feelings for Seth Gentry. "I don't think Seth is an unnecessarily violent man; I think he is fighting this man to avoid a killing," she said for Darla's benefit.

"Yeah, his own," Darla spat.

"No, I think Seth can take care of himself," Darla's mother said. "This fight is the least violent way to teach a bad man a lesson."

"Well, I think it's stupid," her daughter said.

Ranger Hatfield wisely remained silent.

"Would you rather Seth was involved in a gunfight where someone might get killed?" Althea asked her daughter.

Darla glared at her mother. "That would be stupider."

Althea Brown smiled. She had made her point. "Sometimes in life you have to make decisions based on the circumstances---perhaps even the lesser of two evils."

"Like choosing a man," Darla said.

Darla's mother laughed. "Quite often love does not necessarily follow logical lines."

"Men can be so dumb," Darla added.

Althea looked over at the silent ranger, keeping himself busy driving the buggy and looking about. "Yes, I suppose so, but we women aren't without imperfections."

"Women don't usually fight and shoot each other," Darla said.

The buggy turned to the right, dipping into a small ravine and then climbing a steep rise, a red dirt cloud following them.

Ranger Hatfield's eyes went from the wagon trail to the top of the rise. Sitting on horseback waiting for them were two men.

Chapter 39

Ranger Gentry looked down at the same small, worn boot print he had seen at the site of the stagecoach robbery. Was the robber a murderer, too? It appeared so. And where was the killer now? They had left the victim's horse here and good horseflesh was worth money, indicating that they would probably return to this site.

Seth looked up to the descending sun. It was about to disappear behind an oak-strewn hill to the west. Normally he would stay the night hoping that the men would return for the horse, but he had business to take care of in Sutter Creek in the morning. There was no guarantee the men would come back tonight and he could return tomorrow after he took care of Mr. Henry. He made sure the horse had plenty of grass and could access water then rode back down the creek.

As the ranger rode toward Sutter Creek from the southern end, he noticed a crude campsite just out of town. Whoever had been camping had vacated it and left it in poor shape. Most men that Gentry knew were better stewards of the land. It disgusted him that men could desecrate such beautiful country.

His original intent had been to spend the night camping out so that he wouldn't inconvenience Marshal Sam Clements and his family. As weariness set in he thought better of it and decided to get a room at the hotel.

As the grey dusk enveloped the town, Seth reined in at the hitching rail of the Hotel Sutter. Tired, he dismounted and wrapped the reins around the wooden rail. He retrieved his saddle bags and rifle. With some effort he mounted the steps and entered the hotel. A balding, middle-aged man looked over the top of his spectacles at him as he approached.

Having appraised the dusty man, the gentleman behind the counter said, “There is a less expensive hotel just down the street.”

“I’ll take a room here,” Seth said. He turned to make sure his ranger star could be seen and he pulled the governor’s letter of authority out of his pocket and shoved it under the bespectacled man’s nose. The counter man read it quickly.

“Yes sir, Captain. You can have the honeymoon suite at the end of the hall.”

“Just give me a regular room,” Seth grumbled. “Do you have someone who can take care of my horse?”

“Yes, sir,” the man said as he pulled a room key out of a row of cubby holes. “Room 10 is at the top of the stairs to the right. There is a wash basin and towel for your convenience. The privy is out back next to the barn and corral. Your horse will be there.”

Seth nodded, taking the key. “The big red horse at the rail is mine and I want him well taken care of. He could use a bait of oats if you got them.”

The counterman looked wounded. “Of course we have oats; we are the finest hotel in Sutter Creek. And, if you’re hungry we serve the best steak around in our restaurant.”

Gentry looked up the stairs. His boots felt like lead weights. “Get me a table; I’ll be back down in a few minutes.”

“Yes sir, Captain,” the balding man said as he scurried from behind the counter to get the table reserved and to get his horse taken care of.

Seth smiled. He was always fascinated at the reaction he got when he presented the governor’s letter. He adjusted the saddle bags on his shoulder and heavily mounted the stairs.

*****

Not far behind Ranger Gentry, Ned and Eli rode the trail from Volcano to Sutter Creek. "I'm telling you, Eli, betting on that big fellow is a sure thing. He ain't never lost a fight in his life."

"Nothing's a sure thing," Eli said.

"This is as close to it. Let's make some money; a smart business man grows his investments."

Disgusted, Eli reined in and glowered at his brother. "If'n' you think it's a sure thing bet that little withdrawal we took from the bank."

"Now, Eli, you knowed there ain't enough there to make us a whole lot richer. You got to pony up some of that there silver and we can be right comfortable for quite a spell."

"Ned, if we lost it we'd be right back where we started," Eli said. "I have a notion to take my silver and half the bank money and hit the trail."

Ned sighed. For a little guy, his brother had a big, thick skull. He tried another approach. "Eli, you got to be more enterprising, you can't always be shootin' people; someday it'll catch up with you and it don't do you no good being dead, or worse yet, being throwed back into the pen."

Eli seemed to relax a little in the saddle. His brother had a point. There was no way he was going back to jail and he certainly did not want to be dead.

"Come on, Eli, it's a sure thing."

An image of the women at Lulu Lamont's flashed through Eli's head. He licked his lips. It had been a long time since he had a woman and he sure could go for some more whiskey. If he lost all of his money he wouldn't be able to participate in any of these luxuries. On the other hand, if he added to it he could have himself quite a time. "I'll tell you what, Ned, I'll match the bank money and that's' it."

Ned guffawed, "That ain't hardly nothing."

"It's more than you got now," Eli said. "I'd be puttin' up all my bank money and *my* silver, too. That seems to be a good deal for you."

Ned stared down the hill. He couldn't believe how stupid his brother was being. If he could only get his hands on the silver he could be set for a long time. He was tired of arguing with his brother and was ready to be shed of him. He knew it wouldn't be easy. Eli was as deadly as a den of timber rattlers. He would bide his time and take advantage when the opportunity presented itself. "If that's the way you want it," he said. "Let's stop and pick up your silver."

As the two brothers crossed the shallow creek the campsite came into view and something was different. They both drew their holstered guns.

Chapter 40

John Henry hammered on his son's bedroom door. "Get up, Buck, we're going to make some money today and you need to get your breakfast."

Buck Henry groaned. His head was pounding like a blacksmith's hammer on an anvil. His father kept beating on his door. "I'm up," Buck croaked. The noise stopped but the throbbing in his head didn't. He rolled on his back and stared at the ceiling. It seemed to be moving in a circle. His mouth tasted like something had died in it. He closed his eyes, willing the sickness in his stomach to go away. It didn't help.

"Damn it, Buck, get up and get some breakfast," his father yelled.

With great effort, Buck Henry sat up. He fought back the urge to throw up. His head hurt worse sitting up. "I'm coming," he hollered as he staggered over to the wash basin in his room. He splashed water on his face and looked at the bleary-eyed image in the small mirror. "I need a drink," he said to himself. He looked over at his boots on the floor. He hadn't undressed the night before but he had no regard for his rumpled appearance. He staggered back to his bed and bent over to put on his boots. He almost blacked out and gulped back a small amount of acidy regurgitation that had found its way to his mouth.

Buck's father watched his son descend the stairs carefully, as if each step pained the big man. "You look like hell," his father said.

John Henry's son took a seat at the table and made no effort to respond. He rubbed his eyes and put his head in his hands. The cook brought out a large plate of steaming food and placed it under his nose. The sight and smell made him moan in protest.

"You've got to cut back on your drinking, boy," his father said.

Buck didn't respond.

"Eat up; you've got a big fight today."

"I'm not hungry," Buck grumbled.

"You best eat something; I don't want to take no chance on losing some money."

"I ain't lost yet," Buck growled.

John Henry shook his head at his pathetic looking son. He did remind him of when he was a young man full of piss and vinegar. He got up and went to the sideboard and poured two shots of whiskey. He downed one and brought the other to his son. "Here, take this for what ails you and then eat some food."

Buck took the shot from his father with a shaky hand and threw it back, enjoying the medicinal burn as it made its way to his queasy stomach. He did feel better, but the food still didn't look too appetizing. He looked up and saw his father staring at him. Buck picked up a fork and stabbed at some fried potatoes. He sighed and shoveled a small amount into his mouth. He chewed slowly fighting back the urge to spit it out. He sure could go for another drink, he thought.

As if reading his son's mind, John Henry said, "Eat some more and you can have one more drink before you get cleaned up."

Buck scooped some beans and stared at his fork. The promise of another drink gave him the incentive to force it into his mouth. He chewed and mumbled, "I don't see no sense in cleaning up before a fight."

His father picked up the drink glass and slowly walked back to the sideboard. "You need to get cleaned up if'n you want to impress that preacher's daughter.'

Buck licked his lips as he watched his father pour two more drinks. His father set them down on the sideboard and turned around.

"No drink until you eat some more," his father said.

Henry's son grumbled something unintelligible and he forked a runny egg, fighting back an urge to vomit. Even sober, he liked his eggs well done. He was certain the cook always served him runny eggs for spite. He forced it down and looked expectantly to his father.

"You've got to do better than that," John Henry said, not making a move to the whiskey.

Buck sighed and whisked some potato through the yellow yoke. He gulped another bite and looked longingly at the amber fluid in the glass.

John Henry picked up one glass and took a swallow. He smacked his lips, tantalizing his son. "A little more and you can have your drink," he said, treating his son as if he was still a little boy.

To make matters worse, the cook brought out a hot cup of coffee that turned Buck's stomach. "I don't want no coffee," he yelled at the cook. Ignoring the younger Henry, the cook left the steaming coffee in front of him, the strong odor wafting under his nose.

Disgusted, John Henry said, "Drink that coffee; you need to get yourself together before you fight that ranger."

Buck's stomach rumbled in protest. He stared at the glass of whiskey with bloodshot eyes and clenched his fists. He glanced at his father and said, "I don't know why you're all worked up; I'll take care of that ranger in a few minutes."

The senior Henry shook his head. How pathetic his son looked. Was this the day he would lose his first fight? There was always somebody out there that was better than you. "You best be careful, Buck, that ranger didn't seem to be scared of you one bit."

His son forced another bite of breakfast. With his mouth full, he mumbled, "I got forty pounds on that tin star; I'll put him out of our misery."

John Henry studied his son. Though like him in many ways, it was obvious Buck wasn't the brightest candle on the mantle. "Finish that coffee and you can have your whiskey. You need to get cleaned up and we've got to get going."

Buck forced the last of the coffee down with a grimace. His father handed him the glass of whiskey and with a still shaky hand he eagerly took it from him. With a moment's appreciation, he took a deep breath and downed it with one gulp. With closed eyes he enjoyed the comforting sting as it descended to his stomach.

The pleasurable moment was interrupted by his father's demand. "Now, get shaved and cleaned up and put on some clean clothes."

Buck knew that arguing with his father would do no good. Besides, despite feeling a little better, he still had a throbbing in his head from last night's activities. He was in a surly mood and was beginning to think about tearing that lawman from limb to limb. A small smile that appeared as a sneer showed as he rose to go back upstairs to his room.

John Henry watched his son slowly ascend the stairs. Maybe he shouldn't bet too heavily on his son this day. He would have to work on him and get him ready on the ride into town.

As the cook cleared the table, Henry walked over to the sideboard and poured himself another drink. Yes, he would have to make sure his son was in his meanest possible state before fighting the ranger.

Chapter 41

The sun silhouetted the two riders on the knoll blocking the trail. Ranger Hatfield knew that the chances of the two having good intentions were slim to none. His right hand dropped near his revolver, and he said, "Mrs. Brown and Miss Brown, be prepared to arm yourselves." He had a quick glimpse of the wide-eyed Darla Brown.

With no way around the two riders, Jim Hatfield reined in. "What can I do for you, friends," he said amiably.

"We ain't your friends, lawman," a surly looking man said, glaring at the star pinned on the young man's chest.

Ranger Hatfield smiled.

Leather squeaked as the two men squirmed in their saddles. The lack of fear from the young ranger was disturbing. "We was on our way to Sutter Creek when we saw y'all coming."

"We's meeting up with a couple of ol' boys we rid line with," the second rider said.

Keeping his hand near his revolver, Hatfield said, "A man can't have too many friends in this world; you boys should be more disposed to making new friends if it's Leroy and Festus you're talking about."

Confused, the second rider said, "What do disposed mean?"

"Shut up." His partner didn't want to try to explain a word he didn't understand himself.

"It means you two boys should make more friends and not be so grumpy all the time," Ranger Hatfield said, his smile getting bigger.

Darla Brown looked over at her mother. "What's Jimmie doing?" she whispered.

"Shhhh. . ."

"What we do need is that cargo you are carrying." He took his eyes off of the ranger for a moment and stared at the two women. "And we could use the cash you are carrying.

"I thought you two were going to the fight in Sutter Creek," the ranger said.

The two riders looked at each other. "We was, but we kept thinking about how unfair it was that you had two women and we don't have none," the first rider said.

"And you just being a youngin' and all, we jest figured to take them off yer hands," the second rider said, grinning a black-toothed smile.

Althea felt her daughter shiver next to her. Darla gripped the handle of the .32 the governor had given her for protection. She slowly pulled it out and put it on her lap. She was thankful for the many times the governor had taken her down to the Sacramento and American Rivers to practice. The governor had lamented that she was now a better shot than he was. That thought brought a small smile to her face, not unnoticed by the riders.

"What's so funny, missy?"

Althea answered for her daughter. "Well, Ranger Hatfield here is a very nice young man and he's been quite friendly. I know we need to get going and I was just wondering which one of you is the fastest draw. I think it is important that, to be fair, this young man should know what your names are and who to shoot first."

Both riders glared at the governor's wife, dumbfounded. "Why I is by far," the first rider said. And then he watched the woman raise a derringer and he heard the loud click of her pulling the hammer back. It was pointed at the first rider. “My name is Emmitt, ma’am and I’d appreciate you puttin’ that gun down.

“Ranger Hatfield, you take care of Mr. Emmitt if he draws that gun; I’ve got the other covered and I’m a very good shot,” Althea Brown said as she pointed the gun at the other rider.

Hatfield kept an eye on Emmitt as he peeked back at the governor’s wife holding her gun, steady as a rock. The second rider didn’t move a muscle. Emmitt’s gun hand inched closer to his holster. The ranger broke into a big grin. He eyed Emmitt and said, “I don’t cotton to violence and I’ve been right friendly to you two boys, but it appears we got the drop on you and you best go about your business. Mrs. Brown here tells me she’s quite the shot and to be fair to you boys, I’ve won several quick draw competitions.”

The fact of the matter was that the young ranger had been in only one quick draw competition at the state fair and came in second. The two men on horseback didn’t know the difference and it was true that young Hatfield had become quite a bit more proficient since that contest.

“Emmitt, that woman’s got that gun pointed at me and I don’t care how good a shot she is, I don’t think she would miss at this range. Now, don’t you go challengin’ that ranger.”

Disgusted, Emmitt glanced at the other rider. “That boy’s just a pup; you want me to back down?”

“Not back down, just save it for another day. Let’s get to that fight or we’ll miss it.”

Emmitt looked at the gun held steady in Althea Brown’s hand. He couldn’t see the smiling ranger’s gun and it was possible he was already holding it in his hand, giving him a distinct advantage. He eyed Darla Brown and licked his lips. Would he ever get a chance to be this close to someone so beautiful again? But he was an opportunist and not a large risk-taker and his partner had a point. Emmitt would never admit it, but he was more cowardly than brave and he covered it up by being a bully. “I’m going to let you off the hook, ranger boy, 'cause we got to get going. We'll meet again."

Ranger Jim Hatfield watched the two men rein their horses around and head down the trail. "I'll be looking forward to it," he mumbled. He looked back at the governor's wife. She still had the gun aimed at the back of her target as he disappeared over the near horizon. "Could you have shot that man, ma'am?"

"Without hesitation," Althea Brown said with conviction.

"Yes, ma'am, I think you would have," Hatfield said as he heard Darla take a deep breath of relief. For the first time he noticed that the governor's daughter had her gun in hand under a frilly hanky. The ranger was grinning. "Those boys certainly were outmanned," he said. "Or, should I say out-womaned?"

Althea Brown chuckled.

Darla Brown sighed.

Ranger Hatfield whipped the reins and the horses leaped forward, anxious to be moving on the trail. When they topped the knoll they could see the two distant specks of the riders. Jim was glad that the two men hadn't had a change of heart.

"I don't think we've seen the last of those two," the governor's wife said.

"No, ma'am," Jim Hatfield said, "Especially since we're headed to the same place."

"Yes, some stupid fight," Darla said.

Chapter 42

"Somebody's done moved Virgil's horse," Ned said to Eli as they rode into camp.

"Maybe some miner or rancher come by and seen it needed some feed," Eli said.

"Let's take a look around before we set up camp. There's been too many lawmen crawling around for my liking. In fact, I ain't seen so many lawmen until you came about."

Ferret-like, Eli's eyes bored a hole through his brother. He dismounted and looked around. Virgil's saddle was still under the oak tree. "Well, whoever was here was no thief. "

Still mounted, Ned said, "Don't forget that silver for the bet, and you best grab a couple extra for some whiskey."

Eli glared at his brother. It seemed he couldn't keep his mind off his silver. He trudged up the incline to the rock cluster and was relieved to see that his hiding place had not been disturbed. He glanced back over his shoulder to see his brother watching him intently. "Get a fire going, Ned; since we don't got no whiskey I could use some coffee."

Irritated at his brother giving orders, Ned dismounted and retrieved the Arbuckle's from his saddle bags, lamenting that he was the one with the coffee and his abrasive brother was the one with the silver. He gathered up some firewood and got a fire going, wondering what was taking his brother so long up the hill. The coffee pot was steaming before Eli finally returned. "What took you so damn long," he grumbled.

"I had to make sure my money didn't get stoled, and nature called," Eli said.

Ned knew that meant that Eli had moved his hiding spot. His brother's lack of trust further aggravated him. Eli hadn't been gone so long that the new hiding spot could be too far away, but if something were to happen to his brother it would make it that much more difficult to retrieve the silver. A darker mood descended on him as he heard the coffee begin to boil.

Eli watched his brother trudge over and get a rag and two tin cups. Other than making a fire and coffee, what did he need his brother for? Dividing profit reduced the return. When the time was right he would shed himself from what he perceived as an expensive anchor.

Ned tossed an empty cup to his brother, noticing him catch it with his left hand. He almost smiled; that's exactly what he would have done. You never needlessly occupy your gun hand. He grabbed the hot handle of the coffeepot with the rag and walked over to his brother. Eli held the cup out with his left hand and Ned poured. The urge to pour the scalding coffee on his brother came and went.

Eli watched his brother pick up the coffeepot with his left hand. They had been brought up on a hard trail and the difficulty of life made one cautious at all times. Just in case, his hand moved closer to his gun as he held out his cup. He and Ned had a brotherly connection, but their greed and need for survival was stronger.

The brothers, lost in their own thoughts, sat in silence and drank their coffee, occasionally looking at each other, wondering what the other was thinking.

Eli broke the silence. "We got any of that side of bacon left?"

The muscles in Ned's jaw pulsated and through clenched teeth he said, "Yeah, we got a little; we're going to have to resupply with our winnings."

"My stomach's thinking my throat's been cut; why don't you throw it on the fire?"

There Eli went again, giving orders. Ned's gun hand clenched into a fist and opened up. For once he felt sorry that Virgil wasn't around to do their bidding. When they were kids he and Eli used to draw against each other with unloaded guns to see which one of them was the fastest. It was always close and he wondered if he could take his brother now. He was bigger and a loaded gun was heavier. They could wind up killing each other and that wouldn't do either one of them any good. Ned took a deep breath and threw the bottom dregs in his cup into the fire. He retrieved the bacon, tossed it into a fry pan and put it on the fire.

"Give me some more of that coffee," Eli demanded.

Ned glared at his smug brother holding out his tin cup. He fought back the urge to knock it down. He took a deep breath and took up the pot. He ground his teeth as he poured into Eli's cup.

Never one to say thank you, Eli grunted.

"I hope you fetched enough of that silver to take care of bidness," Ned said.

"Don't you worry none," Eli said before taking a drink of coffee. "At least you make good, strong coffee."

Ned glared at his brother.

The aroma of cooking bacon filled the air.

Eli watched his brother stir the bacon and divide it into two plates. He wasn't surprised to see that Ned's plate was piled higher than his.

The brothers ate in silence, lost in their own thoughts, each wondering how they could be shed of one another. Ned didn't like the fact that Eli had most of the money and even if he parlayed some of it into winnings from the fight it wouldn't be all that much. He needed to find a way to get his hands on the rest of the silver.

Eli peeped over at his brother. Ned was more of a burden than an asset. What did he need him for? He would have his brother place the bet tomorrow morning so as not to draw any unnecessary attention to himself. Once they split their winnings and he recovered his seed money he would retrieve the silver and rid himself of the brotherly burden.

Ned noticed his brother's observation of him. What was he thinking? Eli was such a selfish little bastard. Even though the thought of killing his brother had crossed his mind a time or two, he really didn't want to kill his own brother. Things were gnawing at him and one of them was the idea that Eli probably wouldn't hesitate to kill him. Would it come down to kill or be killed? Any hesitation on his part could be lethal.

Eli wasn't a big eater. He stood and walked over to his brother and emptied the remains into Ned's tin plate. "Finish it off and then you can clean up." He set the dirty plate by his brother.

Ned's appetite overrode his irritation. For such a little guy, his brother could be an enormous pain. It seemed like he was giving more orders as time moved on. Money was power and his brother had most of the money. He sopped the bacon grease from his plate with a hard biscuit and plopped its entirety into his mouth. As he chewed the last of his meal he watched his brother lay out his bedroll. He looked up the rocky slope, wondering where the remaining silver was hidden. He observed Eli remove his gun belt and boots and crawl in; and then he saw him pull his gun out of its holster and place it near his right hand. If he were to go hunting that silver he would have to be mighty careful.

Chapter 43

Ranger Gentry awoke at dawn. He put his hands behind his head and thought about the day's work before him. It had been some time since he had fought a man and he was certain that he had not faced anyone as huge as Buck Henry. Sharpened powers of observation were essential to a lawman. Though he hadn't seen much of Buck Henry, he thought back on what he had observed. The man was large and a bully. His size and strength made him overly confident. Despite his bulk, the man had fluidity of movement indicating some athletic ability. He had been told that the man never lost a fight.

Seth smiled to himself. His father had often said that there was a first time for everything and that there was always somebody that could defeat you. So, what was it to be, Buck's first loss or his own defeat?

Gentry remembered the time when he was a kid his father took him to a boxing match. He recalled the excitement and rowdiness of the crowd as he stared at the formidable John L. Sullivan, 'The Boston Strongboy'. The man's strength, skill and toughness had impressed him and as the fight progressed his father had pointed out the boxing techniques that made the fighter so successful.

The next day, after the boxing match, Seth's father had practiced boxing with his young son. He chuckled when he thought of his father's half-breed friend laughing at the pugilistic rules and he proceeded to show Seth how an Indian would defeat his opponent. Of course the method was more wrestling than boxing and rules be damned. It was kill or be killed. Indians used the strength in their legs to defeat the opponent along with strangulation and attempts to blind the enemy.

Seth chuckled to himself. He was certain that Mr. Buck Henry had no intention of following the Marquess of Queensberry rules. Thankfully, not only had his father's friend taught him the ways of Indian fighting, he had taught him how to avoid and counter each potential lethal move. Since most Indians were not overly large people, he had also taught Seth how to use a bigger opponent's size to his advantage.

Gentry took a deep breath and rolled out of bed. He limbered up by stretching, twisting and reaching, continuing to breathe deeply. He peered into the mirror at his face bronzed by the sun. He rubbed his whiskered chin and lathered his shaving brush and chuckled to himself at the thought of looking his best for a fight that would no doubt be brutal. Seth was seldom fearful and he wasn't now, but there was an underlying anticipation and excitement as he stropped his razor and began to shave. Finished, he wiped the residual cream from his face and then stripped to his skivvies and gave himself a basin bath. He wondered if Buck Henry would be as considerate. He brushed his damp hair back with his hand, studied his image in the mirror and then retrieved his hat off of the bed post. Then he and looked at his holstered gun that was underneath his hat.

Normally it wasn't a good idea for a lawman to go unarmed, but today was different. Today it was his job to take care of Buck Henry and he would count on Mack Wheeler and Sam Clements to manage any other difficulties that may arise.

Seth bounded down the stairs and was met by Wheeler and Clements entering the hotel lobby. "You look more like you're going to Sunday meetin' than a fight," Clements said.

Ranger Gentry smiled.

"We thought we'd buy you breakfast before you get yourself all beat up," Wheeler said, grinning.

"I appreciate that," Seth said. A feeling of warmth came over him as he thought about what good friends these two men had become in a short period of time.

All eyes turned to the three lawmen as they entered the restaurant and they were greeted with a chorus of whispers. They took a table in the corner with Wheeler and Clements having their backs to the wall.

"I noticed you don't have your gun on," Marshal Wheeler said to Seth.

"Don't need it. I got you two boys to watch out for everything."

Clements smiled. "We can keep a rein on others but you have to be the one to take care of Buck Henry."

Seth nodded as a lady came over to take their order.

Wheeler ordered coffee, steaks, eggs and biscuits for all three of them. "I'm hoping that being church-sponsored and early in the day there won't be too many drunks nor much rowdiness."

"Being early don't slow some of them down," Clements said. "And then there is Buck's father; he don't need to be drunk to be rowdy."

Wheeler nodded.

Seth accepted his coffee and took a welcoming sip.

"You seem awful calm before facing a tough fight," Wheeler said to Seth. "Buck Henry will try to kill you if he can."

Seth took another drink of coffee and set the cup down. "I know that, Mack; I don't intend to get myself killed."

Marshal Wheeler stared at the young ranger. While the young man was put together with narrow hips and waist and broad shoulders he would be outweighed by 30 or 40 pounds and fighting a man meaner than a momma grizzly bear protecting her cubs. Buck Henry had never lost a fight and he had no regard for rules.

"If I was a betting man I would put my money on you, Seth," Sheriff Clements said, hoping he sounded believable.

Then Wheeler looked at Clements and wondered if he meant what he said or was just trying to bolster Seth's confidence.

Three big steaming plates of food were set before them. "Looks good," Seth said, smiling at the two concerned-looking lawmen. "Don't look so worried, I'll take care of Buck Henry; you two boys make sure that no one else interferes."

Wheeler and Clements began to slice their steaks, both wondering if Seth's confidence was misplaced. How could he possibly win? The ranger was a mild-mannered man outgunned by size and meanness.

As the three lawmen finished off their breakfast and welcomed fresh coffee, there was a sudden buzz of conversation from the patrons of the restaurant as they stared at the entrance. Seth regarded the look on the faces of Clements and Wheeler, jaws dropped and eyes as big as saucers.

With a slow turn Seth looked in the direction of everyone's attention and couldn't believe what he saw.

Chapter 44

Ranger Hatfield glanced back at the two Brown women as the buggy slowed at the top of a small rise. The two women, with backs straight and hands clasped in their laps, looked as if they were sitting in their parlor at home. Mrs. Brown looked at peace, but her daughter had pursed lips, still simmering over Seth Gentry's impending boxing match. James smiled to himself. He wanted to tell her that the stern expression would give her wrinkles, but wisdom prevailed.

Hatfield expertly touched the brake as they descended the small hill and the quaint little town of Amador City lay before them. Wood smoke drifted from tin chimneys, and a smoky pall covered the town; the pleasant stillness was interrupted by the echoing slam of a door and the ensuing bark of a dog. He glanced back at the two women again and it seemed that the site of civilization had relaxed Darla some.

"This is Amador City?" Mrs. Brown asked.

"Yes, ma'am," Hatfield answered. "I was here once with my father. We were in the area deer hunting."

"How could you shoot those beautiful animals?" Darla asked.

"Venison is good eating, ma'am," Hatfield said.

"I just hate violence and killing."

"Yes, ma'am, but people have to eat and protect themselves. Life is about necessity and choices," the young ranger said.

Althea smiled. Though Jimmie was young, he was smart beyond his years and she was more convinced than ever that he was a wonderful addition to the California Rangers. "James has a good point there, dear," she said, patting her daughter's hand that still held a frilly hanky tightly.

"I know, mother, but oftentimes it just doesn't seem necessary, like when men hunt for sport."

Young Hatfield nodded. "I don't disagree with that entirely," he said.

Darla sighed and seemed satisfied that she had made a good point.

Leaving Amador City the buggy climbed a small rise and then descended into a small valley. The air was crisp and clean and the rising sun brought warmth to the cool morning. Ranger Hatfield snapped the buggy whip above the horses and they climbed another hill. "Just a couple of miles to Sutter Creek," he said. "We'll have time to get some coffee and a snack."

Althea smiled. Young men seemed to have never-ending appetites.

"I'm not hungry, but some tea sounds good," Darla said as she looked ahead in anticipation.

Darla's mother patted her hand again. There was tenseness there and she knew that her daughter was becoming more anxious as they approached the town of Sutter Creek where Seth Gentry was. She knew that not only did absence sometimes make the heart grow fonder, but often there were seeds of doubt sewn because of a lack of contact and understanding. She squeezed her daughter's lovely hand in an attempt to assure her that things would be just fine.

Althea's daughter looked at her lovingly. "I hope this wasn't a mistake," she said doubtfully.

"Don't worry, honey, it will be just fine."

With skill, Jim Hatfield guided the buggy downhill into the quaint little town of Sutter Creek. People stopped and stared at the fancy rig driven by a young man with two beautiful women; such finery was not often seen. A bonneted woman pointed at them and spoke to her companion. Used to people staring, Darla and Althea Brown, posture erect, looked straight ahead as they took everything in.

Hatfield pulled the buggy over to a side street next to the Hotel Sutter. “My father and I ate here once and it was terrific,” he said. He helped the ladies down from the buggy and stayed alert to the surrounding area for any trouble. He chuckled to himself when he noticed that an audience had gathered, and he admired how graceful the women were as they exited the buggy. They had ridden several miles over some rough country and did not exhibit any discomfort. Obvious silence filled the air with only the whisper of rustling gowns and a slight murmur arising from the ogling crowd.

With straight backs and erect heads the ladies gathered their gowns and led the way to the hotel. Ranger Hatfield checked the horses and scampered after them, once again amazed at how the two women seemed oblivious to the onlookers, yet totally aware of their surroundings. An older gentleman watched them approach and moved quickly to open the door for them as if they were royalty.

“Why, thank you sir,” Althea Brown said, giving the man a bright smile.

The man tipped his hat. “My pleasure, ma’am.” He nodded at the young ranger following them, and his eyes paused as he noticed the circled star on the young man’s chest.

“Isn’t this lovely,” Althea said to her daughter as she stopped and looked around the lobby with its large chandelier overhead.

At the sound of the woman’s voice the bald clerk looked up and removed his reading glasses. *This is more like it,* the man thought as he observed the two classy ladies. “Would you like to register? I have our best suite available.”

Ranger Hatfield laughed. "I was so occupied with the thought of eating that I didn't think about staying here."

"Looks as good as any," Althea said.

"I dare say, madam, this is the best place in town," the clerk said.

"I'm sure it is," Althea said with a comforting smile. "We are going to get a bite. Please have someone retrieve our luggage out of the barouche and we will register when we are done."

The clerk seemed to relax. "Yes ma'am," he said with a smile. Nodding to the right he said, "The restaurant is right through there."

"Thank you, sir," Althea said. "Come on Darla, I've suddenly gained an appetite." She glanced back at Hatfield and winked.

The young ranger blushed at the governor's wife's familiarity and followed the two women to the restaurant. The more time he spent with Mrs. Brown the more he appreciated her wit, strength and intelligence. Again, he thought how lucky the governor was to have such a capable mate and partner. He was certain that Mrs. Brown had something to do with him getting the ranger job, also.

At the entrance to the restaurant the women stopped to let their eyes adjust to the dark interior and to look around the room. As a precaution, the ranger stepped ahead of them and gazed around as heads turned and silence enveloped the restaurant. All that could he heard was the clatter of forks and spoons being placed down. Even though he knew that the eyes were on the two women, Hatfield felt uncomfortable in the middle of all of the attention.

And then he saw a tall man stand up and walk toward them.

Chapter 45

Ranger Hatfield heard Darla gasp. The tall man was approaching with a smile and he quickened his steps as he got closer. The candlelight from a nearby table reflected off the badge on his chest. He brushed by the young ranger, grabbing Darla around the waist and lifting her off the floor in a twirling hug.

Seth set Darla down and gave her a kiss. Darla flushed with embarrassment. Seth was so happy to see the governor's daughter that he didn't notice a lack of warmth; he would later assume it was because of the display of public affection.

"It's so good to see you, Seth," Althea said.

Hatfield looked at the startled face of the governor's daughter and said, "Captain Gentry, I'm ranger Jim Hatfield."

Gentry still had his arms around Darla and stuck out a hand. "Welcome, Jim, we can use the help. Where did you pick up these two vagabonds?"

"Well, sir, the governor had something to do with it," Hatfield said.

"Seth, you need to let go of me," Darla whispered.

"Uh, I guess so," he said, turning to Mrs. Brown. "It's so good to see you, too, Mrs. Brown."

"Come on, Seth, call me Althea," she said, taking his arm.

"Let me introduce you to a couple of old codgers before you sit down," Seth said. He guided them over to the table where two lawmen sat with their mouths agape. "Okay you old coots, shut your mouths and let me introduce you to thc governor's wife, Althea Brown, and her daughter Darla and Jim Hatfield, our new ranger."

The two lawmen stood up.

"This old-timer is Marshal Mack Wheeler of Amador City and next to him is Marshal Sam Clements of Sutter Creek."

"Ma'am," they said in unison, ignoring the young man.

Althea Brown, having been involved in political life for many years, stuck her hand out to shake the two lawmen's hands, a gesture usually only men performed. Though clumsy, the two men shook her hand, looking like they were afraid they would hurt her. Althea smiled brightly. She always enjoyed this friendly discomfort experienced by men. *Wait until we get the vote!*

The two men fidgeted. "You can have our table, ma'am, the marshal and I are going down to the, uh, picnic area," Clements said.

"Thank you, marshal, that is most kind of you." Althea looked over at her daughter, who was glaring at Seth. She still had a stranglehold on her frilly hanky. Seth had a big smile on his face, unaware of how much trouble he was in.

Marshal Wheeler removed his pocket watch from his vest and said, "We'll see you in about an hour, Seth."

Ranger Hatfield turned to go. "I'll check on your luggage, Mrs. Brown, and be back directly."

Seth only had eyes for Darla as the marshals pulled out their chairs for the two women. After they were seated, Seth sat down opposite the Brown women.

When the lawmen left Althea said, "It's so good to see you, Seth."

The ranger looked over to the governor's wife. "It's good to see you, too, ma'am, but I must say it is a bit of a surprise." His eyes returned to Darla. Since she hadn't said much, Seth said, "It's good to see you, too, Miss Brown." He reached across the table to touch her clenched hand but she pulled it away.

"How can you fight that ruffian like some kind of animal?" Darla spewed.

"Oh, you heard about that," Seth said, somewhat confused by her manner.

"I don't understand why men have to be so violent," Darla said. "Somebody could get hurt, or even killed and for what?"

Seth reached across the table again and Darla let him cover her hand. Despite herself, she found his big hand comforting.

"Buck Henry is a bully and he *has* killed people," Seth said. "I'm not any crazier about violence than you are, Darla, but sometimes I have to do my job and I prefer not to have to kill people."

Darla sighed. "Yes, but do you have to fight him?"

Seth smiled. "Oftentimes a bully is a coward deep down and I have found that behavior modification works sometimes when they get a dose of their own medicine." Seth felt the tenseness in her hand relax a little.

Darla looked up at him with glistening brown eyes. "Worry and doubt overwhelmed me when I heard about this." She put her other hand on top of his. "I do know I love you, Seth, but now I feel fear for you."

"Don't worry about me." He chuckled. "It won't be any worse than you two women ganging up on the poor governor." Darla's nose went into the air. Seth was glad that Mrs. Brown was smiling.

"Daddy loves us and appreciates us, Seth Gentry," Darla huffed. "You should, also."

The big ranger looked over at the governor's wife and then back to Darla. "I do appreciate you, honey, and I think the governor is the second luckiest man in the world."

Her brow rose in confusion, yet a shiver ran down her spine because this handsome man had called her honey for the first time. "Second luckiest?"

He put his other hand on top of hers. “Of course, I am the luckiest man there is,” he said.

A tear raced down Darla’s cheek. “Oh, Seth, that is the sweetest thing.”

Ranger Hatfield hustled into the room and took the chair next to Seth. “I hope I’m not interrupting,” he said, “but I’m starving.”

“Jimmie, uh, Jim hasn’t missed a meal,” Althea Brown said with a grin.

Seth looked over at the young ranger and smiled. “I assume you can handle that hog leg strapped to you,” he said.

“Yes sir, captain.”

“After you eat I want you to accompany me to the, uh, church and watch my back. My pugilist has a father that is said to be even more unscrupulous than him. But more importantly, you are to protect these two women with your life if necessary.”

“Understood, sir,” Hatfield said.

Darla pulled her hand away. The women ordered tea and Ranger Hatfield ordered steak and eggs. Seth took some more coffee.

Seth continued, “After the morning’s events we’ll get better acquainted and I’ll fill you in on what has been going on up here.”

“Yes, sir,” Hatfield said, eagerly digging into his just-delivered breakfast.

“How is the governor, Mrs. Brown?” Seth asked.

“He’s just fine. He’s not too happy with us taking this little trip.”

“I can understand that,” Seth said, looking over to Darla as she raised her steaming cup of tea.

“I hope it wasn’t a mistake,” Darla said tersely.

Seth watched the stern young lady sip her tea. He wisely said nothing. He looked over at Ranger Hatfield, who was wiping some egg yolk with a biscuit.

Althea laughed. “Ah, to be young again.”

At least someone is in good humor, Seth thought.

Ranger Hatfield pushed a very clean plate away and took up his coffee. "One other thing, sir, we are to accompany Miss Darla and Mrs. Brown when they return to Sacramento."

"What? That would take both of us away from doing our job up here," Seth grumbled.

"Yes, sir, but that is the governor's orders."

"Now, Seth, crime can wait. Surely you won't mind being with Darla a little longer," Althea said.

Eyeing the governor's daughter, Seth said, "Well, there is that."

Darla huffed. "Don't sound so excited Mr. Gentry."

Seth chuckled. "If you only knew how much time I spend thinking of you."

Althea Brown smiled delightedly as she observed the two young lovers. She thought back on her younger days when the handsome Thaddeus Brown had spent all his spare time raining attention on her. He, like Seth, was dedicated to his career and political endeavors and she knew that it had taken a great effort to spend so much time with her.

Young Hatfield watched the dynamics of the two women and Captain Gentry with envy and trepidation. Darla Brown was a beautiful woman, but relationships were complicated and he knew that having the governor's ladies here at this time would not make the events of the day any easier.

"You've thought of me often?" Darla asked in a whisper.

Seth reached across the table and took her hand again. She had long fingers and soft, delicate skin. He looked up into her glistening brown eyes and pouty lips and felt his heart pounding in his chest. He rose out of his chair, leaned over the table and kissed her on the lips. Her lips were supple and moist and accepting.

Darla's eyes widened at the sudden display of public affection. Instead of pulling away she melted into the pleasure of the moment. Her heart raced and she gripped the big ranger's hand more firmly as if she didn't want to let him go. And she didn't. There was no way that she wanted this beautiful man to get hurt. She realized now, however, that the man was who he was and it was not her position to try and change him. She reflected on the conversations she had with her mother and how a woman needed to accept a man for who he was. If you were not satisfied and felt a need to change him then he wasn't the man for you.

Seth sat back down. Althea Brown grinned at the two flushed young people, recognizing true love when she saw it.

And then the heat of the moment was interrupted.

Chapter 46

Ned and Eli Hayes rode into Sutter Creek navigating the crowded streets. People were streaming toward the church on the hill in earnest, carrying picnic baskets and jugs and bottles.

"Don't think they've had such a big event in these parts," Ned said.

"I ain't seen this many people exceptin' behind bars," Eli said. "The *Q* is crowded with folks."

Ned stared at his little brother. "The way you been shootin' people you must be anxious to get back to your buddies."

"No, I ain't never going back. Except for maybe one pardner the rest in there would just as soon shank you as talk to you. They's more territory staked out in that place than in these United States."

"Then maybe you ought to start thinking about not shootin' people no more," Ned said.

Eli glared at his brother. "Nobody's going to tell me what to do, not even you, big brother."

Ned's spine stiffened. It was getting awful tiresome putting up with Eli. It was a mistake to have included him in his plans; old memories of disappointment and discontent were flooding back. His brother's absence while locked up in San Quentin Prison had softened those memories and he had even thought that his brother might be a changed man. If anything, Eli was worse than ever before. And his brother was the one with the most money. Ned's shoulders slumped in weary frustration. "We can put the horses over by that oak tree yonder," he said.

The brothers worked their way toward the ancient oak. Under the shade of the massive tree a big middle-aged man was attempting to coerce a small group of men to bet on the impending fight. "Come on you boys, three to one odds is awful good. Where are you going to find a deal like that?"

"John, you knowed your son ain't never been beat; three to one odds is like taking candy from a baby," an old miner said.

John Henry regarded the man as if he was scum. The old man went silent and seemed to wilt under the glare. Frustrated, Henry considered the remainder of the crowd. No one was reaching into their trousers to pull out any money. Buck Henry's reputation as an unbeatable bully was putting a crimp in his ability to make a profit. Henry sighed and saw his son talking to Penelope Peabody in the distance near the picnic tables, much to her discomfort. And then he saw two newcomers walking toward them. *Fresh meat.* Perhaps these two didn't know anything about his son.

Ned and Eli found it mighty silent when they approached the crowd after tying off their horses. Ned asked, "What's the deal here?"

Henry looked at the two men. They didn't seem too prosperous. "I'm giving two to one odds on the fight."

The brothers heard someone snicker in the crowd.

John Henry made a move toward his holstered gun and it became quiet again. "Since these tightwads are afraid to bet, I just increased the odds to an unheard of three to one that my son, Buck Henry, wins." He scowled at the group, knowing they dare not say a word.

"Robbery," an unidentified man whispered.

Ned looked around. No one was placing a bet. Apparently everyone was giving the Ranger almost no chance to win the fight. The crowd turned to watch two lawmen approaching.

"You causing trouble here, John?" Marshal Clements asked.

"No, marshal, just trying to do a little friendly wagering on the fight."

Sam Clements nodded. He scanned the gathering, his eyes lingering on the two strangers. Both looked down at their boots. "What are the odds, John?"

"A generous three to one."

"Not so sure Buck can beat the ranger?" Clements saw Marshal Wheeler smile.

"What are you talking about?" Henry sputtered.

"Everyone knows that Buck has never lost a fight," Clements said. "But, you don't seem very confident with measly odds like that."

"Three to one is great odds; no one has ever seen such great odds before," Henry said.

"Any takers?" Marshal Wheeler asked.

"Well, not much," Henry said.

"I ain't seen no one make a bet," the old miner said.

"Who said that?" Henry asked, turning to the crowd. He was met with silence.

Marshal Wheeler nodded and reached into his vest pocket for a half-eagle gold piece. "I'll make a bet on Ranger Gentry at ten to one."

John Henry's eyes narrowed. "Those are ridiculous odds; never been heard of."

"That's only fifty dollars if the ranger beats Buck. You afraid your boy is going to lose?" Wheeler egged the man on.

"Well, uh, I think Buck will win," Henry stammered. He looked into the expectant eyes of the growing throng of people. Sweat beaded on his brow as he thought about how his bets were almost always a sure thing. The odds didn't make much difference as long as Buck won and maybe this would get the money flowing. He did resent the marshal backing him into a corner, however, but the chances of Buck losing were slim to none. “All right, marshal, I’ll take your bet,” he said.

The crowd became restless and men were reaching into their pockets for silver dollars.

Circle J range rider, Len Smith, pulled two months wages out of his trousers. “Put that on Ranger Gentry,” he said to his boss.

John Henry glared at the cowboy. “You’re going against your boss?”

“Just a hunch,” Len said with a smirk.

“You might be finding yourself riding for another outfit,” Henry said.

“Could be,” Len said with a grin that irritated the boss man. It was about time he moved on anyway; he was fed up with the Henrys.

Ned murmured to Eli, “Ten to one odds, we need to make that bet.”

“Don’t mean nothing ifin’ that ranger loses,” Eli grumbled.

“We could make a killing, Eli,” Ned said.

“Or lose all my money.”

Frustrated, Ned clenched his fist. For a man who was willing to kill for money his brother didn’t have the guts to place a bet that could set them up for quite a while. “What if I was to tell you to hedge your bet,” he said.

With a blank expression Eli asked, “What do you mean?”

“Look, Eli, if we place a bet of one hundred dollars on the ranger and he wins we get one thousand dollars.”

“Yeah, but if he loses we lose one hundred dollars.”

Ned sighed. “Yes, but if we hedge the bet with a one hundred dollar bet on Buck we get the one hundred back if Henry wins.”

“But if the ranger wins we lose that one hundred dollars,” Eli said.

"Yes, but we would have won one thousand dollars." Ned couldn't believe that his little brother still looked confused and reluctant.

From the back of the crowd a woman's voice rang out. "I'll bet two hundred on the ranger," she said.

Silence enveloped the crowd and they turned toward the woman's voice.

Chapter 47

The scraping of the chair next to Seth Gentry turned his attention to Ranger Hatfield.

"Time to go, captain," Jim Hatfield said.

Anxiousness returned to the flushed face of Darla Brown. Her hand grasped and twisted her lacy hanky.

"Let's get a room, Darla, and join the boys later. Something tells me we'd best register, with all of these people in town." Althea gave Seth a slight wink and a smile.

Seth took Darla's hands. "I'm staying here too, and we can have dinner tonight."

Darla couldn't believe how calm and confident Seth seemed.

"Yes, we'll have a picnic for lunch, and dinner here tonight. I'll have the kitchen make us up a basket while we unpack," Althea said.

Darla looked into Seth's eyes and said, "I don't know how you tell someone to be careful when they are going into a fight, but, at least try to take care of yourself."

Seth smiled at the governor's daughter. "Buck Henry is a big bully and hasn't fought the likes of me. I have many skills that you don't know about and one of them is experience in the art of pugilistic combat."

"You call it an art?"

"Yes, though brutal, there is a certain beauty in boxing. It's much like ballet," Seth said.

"But you are hitting each other."

"Well, there is that," he said.

Darla sighed.

"Come on Darla, I've got the picnic ordered," Althea said, taking her daughter by the arm. As her mother guided her out of the restaurant Darla turned with an imploring look over her shoulder. Seth smiled and gave her a little wave.

"Captain, we're going to be late," Hatfield said.

"I don't think Buck will be going anywhere and a little anxiousness on his part could be beneficial," Seth responded as he watched the two ladies leave the room.

*****

Endicott Peabody was engrossed in collecting the twenty-five cents for the fight and his daughter, Priscilla, was working just as hard trying to keep a safe distance from Buck Henry. "You sure smell a fright; have you been drinking already?" Priscilla asked.

"Just a taste, a little hair of the dog that bit me last night is all."

"Shouldn't you be getting ready for your boxing match?" Priscilla asked in an attempt to rid herself of the obnoxious bully.

"What's to get ready for; I'll beat that ranger to a pulp in a matter of minutes.

The noise coming from the picnic area suddenly diminished and the women who were setting up tables stopped what they were doing. They were all staring down the small hill. Rangers Gentry and Hatfield were approaching and the women began to whisper amongst themselves. That was the man willing to take on Buck Henry.

James and Seth took in the festive look of the picnic area in the meadow below the church. Picnic tables were arranged so that there was a square open area in the center. The tables were covered with bright checkered cloth and the reverend was standing at a small opening collecting his donations. Priscilla Peabody was off to the side with a sour look on her face. Standing next to her was Buck Henry.

"Let me introduce you to the reverend's daughter," Seth said to Jim.

Priscilla's face brightened as she saw the two handsome rangers approach. Buck Henry scowled. "Hello Mr. Gentry," Priscilla said.

"Miss Priscilla, I would like you to meet Ranger James Hatfield of Sacramento way."

She put out her small hand and did a slight curtsy.

Hatfield took her hand and said, "Pleased to meet you, miss."

Buck Henry growled.

"And this is my opponent, Mr. Henry," Seth said with a smile.

"Please call me Priscilla, James," she said.

"And you can call me Jim."

"You two are interrupting here," Henry snarled.

"I thought it would be important to have Priscilla meet someone more her age," Seth said, still grinning.

"I'm going to tear your damned head off, ranger," Henry said, with spittle flying out of his mouth.

Seth sniffed the air. "Are you grumpy because you are hung over or is that your natural disposition?"

"Ladies and gentlemen, the boxing match will commence in ten minutes time. Please do not put any food or any other items on the tables until the match is over," Reverend Endicott Peabody announced. "If you have not paid your donation please do so now."

"Daddy always makes sure the church is taken care of first," Priscilla said as she looked down at her hand which was still being held by Ranger Hatfield.

"Oh, sorry," he said letting go of her hand.

Priscilla giggled. "That's alright, I liked it."

Hatfield blushed and watched Buck Henry storm off toward the crowd under a large oak tree. "I don't think he liked me very much."

Laughing, Priscilla said, "There isn't much Buck Henry or his father like."

"Well, he seems to like you an awful lot," Jim grumbled.

With large blue eyes that sparkled like deep pools in the morning sun, Priscilla said, "The feeling is not mutual and I try to avoid the man as much as I can, but I am a Christian and my father taught me to be kind to everyone."

"That is commendable," Seth said. "I guess I'd best go get ready for my little contest; stay here and wait for Mrs. Brown and her daughter."

"Yes, sir," Hatfield said as he turned back to the young, attractive daughter of the preacher.

"Who are Mrs. Brown and her daughter?"

"They are the wife and daughter of the governor," Hatfield said. "I accompanied them here from Sacramento."

"I did hear something about that," Priscilla said, crossing her arms over her breasts. "How old is this daughter of the governor's?"

Hatfield looked at the tight-lipped girl. He wanted to smile, but he dared not. Her freckles seemed to have deepened. Very endearing, he thought. Though relatively inexperienced when it came to women, he recognized possible feminine jealousy and competition. "Miss Darla is in her early twenties, I think, and she has her bonnet set for Seth."

Priscilla uncrossed her arms and took in a deep breath. Her facial expression relaxed and she licked her lips. "You'll have to introduce me to them."

"It will be my pleasure," Hatfield said. "May I escort you to the contest?"

The preacher's daughter took his arm. "Thank you, Jim, I would like that."

The young couple walked toward the growing horde of humanity encircling the makeshift arena. "I've never seen so many people," Priscilla said. "Too bad they all don't attend church."

Hatfield nodded. He was sure that the area had other churches that people could attend. Off to one side he spotted the two ruffians from the Sloughouse restaurant. Just beyond them he spied Emmitt and his partner from the trail. He reached down and loosened his revolver. He hoped there wouldn't be trouble but needed to be prepared just in case.

Priscilla's eyes widened as she noticed Jim Hatfield touch his gun with his right hand. Only then did she realize that the ranger had made sure that she was holding on to his left arm. Hatfield had taken on an expression of determination as he scanned the throng of excited onlookers. There was a sense of intense anticipation racing through the air. It seemed to be building to a feverish pitch and increased as the gamblers moved from the giant oak tree.

Hatfield gazed over at the approaching group and was surprised to see who was in the lead.

Chapter 48

Marching toward the makeshift arena was the governor's wife and daughter, Althea looking like a determined momma duck leading her ducklings. Huffing, big John Henry was attempting to catch up with Althea Brown. His obvious agitation brought a smile to Ranger Hatfield's face. Having spent a few days with the governor's wife and daughter had shown him how independent the women could be. Their strength, though present in many women, was more obvious than most and seem to be manifested uncommonly for the day. Often men thought that, like children, women were to be seen and not heard. Perhaps because the Brown women were around politicians much of the time they became more confident in their own way of thinking.

As they approached, Hatfield said, "I take it that man is Buck Henry's father; he seems awful determined to speak to you, Mrs. Brown."

Althea Brown didn't bother looking back over her shoulder. "I don't think he liked the idea of a woman placing a two-hundred-dollar bet with him at ten to one odds."

"You bet two hundred dollars?" Ranger Hatfield was incredulous.

"If Seth loses the fight father will be so upset," Darla said with a worried look.

The governor's wife's nose rose to the sky and she said, "And what if we go home with two thousand dollars more than we left with?"

"Two thousand dollars!" Hatfield shook his head in disbelief.

"Ma'am, I'd like a word with you," John Henry said, trying to catch his breath. "I don't want to take no money from a woman; people would think I was taking advantage."

Althea stared at the wheezing big man. "You are Mr. Henry, are you not?"

Henry flushed in anger. It seemed like this woman was talking to him like he was a nobody. "Of course I am; I'm the biggest and most important man in these parts," he sputtered.

Mrs. Brown stared at the man in silence as if she was trying to determine if what the man said was true.

After a time, she said, "Of course you are."

Uncomfortable, John Henry said, "I'd appreciate to return your two hundred dollars."

Darla and James became aware of the crowd growing around them, many watching with amused looks, some grinning at the unpopular John Henry's discomfort. Ranger Hatfield scanned the close group of people, noticing some characters that deserved watching. No matter how the fight turned out, there was going to be quite a large amount of money involved.

"You can't afford to lose two thousand dollars? If so, you shouldn't have been taking bets at those odds."

John Henry became hotter under the collar. "Of course I can, I just told you who I was. I just don't want to take no innocent woman's money."

"Are you afraid your boy's going to lose?" Althea asked.

"He ain't never been beat," he said.

"There's always a first time for everything, Mr. Henry."

"My boy is forty or fifty pounds heavier than that tin star."

Althea smiled. "Mr. Henry, you are, perhaps, a hundred and fifty pounds heavier than me, and I'm going to beat you out of two thousand dollars."

John Henry's jaw dropped. "Who are you, lady?"

Ranger Hatfield's eyes met Marshal Clements'. The marshal was grinning from ear to ear. "I been waitin' for someone to put that man in his place and by gawd it was a woman that did it," he said to Marshal Wheeler.

"That woman's got spunk," Marshal Wheeler responded.

"Ladies and gentlemen, the contest between Buck Henry and Ranger Hatfield will commence in five minutes time," Reverend Peabody announced. "Please clear the arena and take your positions."

Several men rushed over to John Henry to place last-minute bets, including Ned Hayes. Ned shoved his way through the crowd to get to the front. "I want to place a bet on that boy of yourn," he said.

"Welcome, friend," Henry said, knowing he needed to balance the betting. "Know that there is a ten percent fee on winnings."

"Why, that's robbery," Ned whined.

"You are in for easy money, my friend, my boy ain't never been beat," Henry said as he pulled out his tally book.

Ned handed over all of the bank money.

John Henry smiled. "You can buy me a drink with your winnings after the boy beats that ranger to a pulp."

Eli joined his brother with a sour look. "I don't feel good about this," he said. "That woman bet two hundred on the ranger; she must know something."

"Women don't know nothing about fighting," Ned said with disgust.

"Two hundred dollars is a lot of money," Eli said.

"We'll bet almost as much the other way. She's shootin' for the moon and we're betting on a sure thing."

Eli shook his head. "Nothing is a sure thing except for a bullet between the eyes."

"You need to have more positive thinking," Ned said.

"I ain't never had reason to," Eli said.

"Now you go place that bet on the ranger to hedge our bet," Ned said.

"Looks to me like we are going to lose either way," Eli grumbled.

"I explained all that to you, Eli, we ain't going to lose. You never seen such a sure thing in your life."

"I hate parting with hard-earned money," Eli grumbled.

"You *shot* a man for it."

"That's right, *I* shot the man and took the risk, not you."

Ned Hayes sighed and looked over to John Henry. "You best place that bet before the man stops taking them."

Reluctantly, Eli placed the bet on the ranger, much to John Henry's surprise. Except for the woman's bet and his ranch hand Len's bet, most of the money was on his son. Why would young Len bet against Buck? Did he know something about the ranger that they didn't? He didn't cotton to men that didn't ride for the brand. He reviewed his tally book and smiled. With his ten percent fee and winnings from the fight he would have a very profitable day. He looked up from his book and spied his son standing as close to Priscilla Peabody as he could get away with.

That boy needed to be concentrating on the job ahead of him.

Determined, he strode toward his son and heard Priscilla say, "Buck, you stink of whiskey; back off."

John Henry assumed that the whiskey smell was from the two shots he had for breakfast. The fact of the matter was that last night's whiskey was seeping out the big man's pores. "Come on, Buck, we need to take care of business," he said.

Buck, irritated at his father's interruption, acquiesced when he saw his father's stern face and his tally book in his hand. Other than power, nothing was more important to his father than money.

"When I take care of that ranger fix me up a plate of fixin's," Buck said to the preacher's daughter.

"I wouldn't count my chickens before they hatch if I were you, Buck Henry, and since when do I take orders from you."

Buck guffawed and followed his father toward the arena, removing his shirt as he went. He turned to the sound of excited onlookers to see his opponent approaching two beautiful women and taking the hands of the younger one. He stopped and stared. The young brunette was the most beautiful woman he had ever seen. He'd just have to kill this guy and have her for his own. Buck grinned, the spoils of war to be enjoyed. "Who's them two women, Pa?"

John Henry followed his son's gaze. "I don't rightly know," he said, "but the older one bet two hundred dollars on the ranger."

Buck Henry belly laughed and flexed his bulging muscles, aware of some unusual stiffness. This was going to be quite a day, he thought.

"I wish you would reconsider this fight," Darla said to Seth with pleading eyes. "And mother bet two hundred dollars on you."

"Well, I can't let your mother lose that kind of money in default," he said with a smile. He had the strongest urge to kiss her right then but didn't want to embarrass her in front of all these people who seemed to be giving the three of them all of their attention, with the exception of the young ranger and two marshals that were approaching.

"That Buck Henry may be a blow-hard, but he is put together," Marshal Clements said.

"Don't notice much fat on that boy," Marshal Wheeler said, amazed that Seth only had eyes for the governor's daughter and wasn't paying any attention to his nemesis.

Reverend Endicott Peabody and his daughter approached. "It's time to get the festivities started," he said.

Seth continued to gaze into Darla's eyes. It felt like his soul was touching hers.

"Ahem." The reverend cleared his throat. "Did you hear me Captain Gentry?"

"I heard you reverend," he said, not taking his eyes off Darla Brown.

Darla squeezed Seth's hands. "If you must do this, protect that handsome face, please."

"Okay," Seth said, bending down and kissing Darla on the forehead.

"One more thing," she said.

"Uh-huh."

"Beat the crap out of him," she said, clenching her little fists.

Seth laughed and headed to the arena.

Chapter 49

Buck Henry watched the ranger approach the arena absent the fear that showed in the eyes of his norma opponents. *The stupid lawman didn't know what he was i for.*

Seth didn't bother to look at his adversary a Reverend Peabody approached. "I have asked Sve Lindquist to referee the match; he did some boxing in his ol country of Sweden."

The ranger nodded and removed his shirt. A titte with feminine overtones arose at the sight of the shirtles lawman. Seth Gentry, though smaller than Buck Henry, wa chiseled as if he was made from granite. The lea muscularity shined in the bright morning sun, a sheen o sweat already appearing from the unseen warm-up, a ritua taught by his father and his father's friend to stretch an loosen his muscles for combat.

"He may not have Buck's size, but that boy is pu together," Marshal Clements said to Marshal Wheeler.

Wheeler nodded, "That he is, and Buck may b getting more than he bargained for."

Althea Brown glanced over to her daughter. Darla' hands were clenched and her face was as flushed as a rip tomato. "That's a fine looking man you've got there," sh teased.

"Oh, mother," Darla said, stomping her foot. "He' half naked for the whole world to see."

Darla's mother smiled. "What's the matter, don' want to share?"

Her daughter hissed, “I just don’t want him to get hurt; fighting is so stupid.”

“Boy, this is going to be something,” Hatfield said with excitement as he approached the two women, feeling a little guilty at paying more attention to the combatants than the two women he was supposed to be protecting, though he had also been observing the crowd along with the two marshals.

Frustrated, Darla said, “This is just barbaric.”

“I reserved seats at the picnic table over yonder for you ladies,” Hatfield said taking each one of them by the arm.

Althea looked in the direction James was taking them and saw no unoccupied seats.

They approached two old-timers and Ranger Hatfield said, “I’d like to introduce you to two friends of Captain Gentry’s---Zeke and Tinker. They’ve been saving your seats.”

“Oh, we couldn’t take these men’s seats,” Althea said.

“It’s been our pleasure, ma’am,” Zeke said. “Any friend of the Captain’s is a friend of ours.”

Tinker nodded and smiled, showing no teeth. “Not only is we proud to save your places, but we’re going to help young Hatfield here to keep an eye on you.”

Ranger Hatfield was grinning ear to ear. His fondness for the two old men was obvious. He attempted to help the two of them get up from the picnic table.

Both men shrugged off the young ranger. “We ain’t helpless, you know,” Zeke said.

“Just giving you two old-timers a hand,” Jim said.

“Well, we don’t need it,” Tinker said in disgust.

The Brown women had dazzling smiles on their faces. It was evident why Seth and James had a fondness for these two men. “I don’t feel right about taking your seats,” Althea said.

"They ain't our seats, ma'am, they's yours; we was just holdin' them for you," Zeke said. "We consider it an honor to help the governor's wife and Seth's intended."

"Intended?" Darla questioned.

"Why any fool within a barnyard's distance can tell you two is crazy in love with each other," Tinker said with a cackle. "And I'll tell you this; me and ol' Zeke here want to be invited to the weddin'."

Althea laughed. "If that happens you have my promise that you will be invited."

The two old-timers grinned at each other like two cats that ate the canary and then smiled at Darla.

Flushed with embarrassment, Darla couldn't believe her feelings for Seth were so obvious, especially to two old men that didn't have the eyesight of their youth. "Seth and I are just good friends," she said in a huff.

Zeke cackled. "Why a blind man can see you two is so tangled a band of renegade injuns couldn't tear you apart."

In an attempt to ignore the well-intentioned men, Darla looked to the arena. Her heart leapt to her throat when she saw the man called Sven heading to the center.

Sven Lindquist motioned the two combatants to join him. "You boys come here, by golly."

Buck Henry stared down the ranger as he joined the Swede. His evil glare always put fear in his opponents, but there was something different this time. Seth Gentry joined them with an eager confidence he had never experienced before. Buck curled his lip and snarled, "I'm going to break every bone in your body." Buck observed another unusual response.

Seth smiled. "Good luck with that, Buck; I would suggest that when I am done with you that you stop bullying people and start treating women folk properly."

Buck seethed.

"Now, now boys, you got to listen to my rules," Sven said. "You will follow the Marquess of Queensberry Rules. We will have three-minute rounds and one minute rest."

"Three minutes is all I need," Buck snarled.

"Yumpin' yiminy, Buck, listen to me," Sven said. "There will be no eye-gouging, kicking, choking or biting. In a clinch you are to separate when I tell you to."

Buck, further angered by the smile on Seth Gentry's face, growled, "Sure, Sven, whatever you say."

Seth had seen a hundred men like Buck. Most of them weren't as big, but many of them were just as mean and over-confident. Unbeknownst to Buck Henry, Seth had been observing him from afar. He had been taught to study his adversaries. He knew that Buck was right-handed, was surprisingly athletic for a big man and extremely confident; after all, he had never lost a fight. Buck was also a little slow. In a fight, quicker was always better. Seth had been trained to use a man's over-confidence and size against him. He also knew that good defense was the best offense. A man of Buck Henry's size would tire quickly and if he was illusive it would work against the bigger man and also frustrate him. It also pleased him to have smelled whiskey on the big man's breath.

"I'm going to wipe that smile off your face, lawman," Buck sneered.

"You pay attention, Buck Henry," Sven said. "Dat man wid hammer and bell will time and signal end of rounds. You may have helper in your corner by da stool. I will stop the fight if necessary, by golly."

"You ain't stopping no fight," Buck growled.

"You may regret that, Buck," Seth said, chuckling.

Buck Henry roared, and snot and spittle sprayed out of his red, puffy face.

The crowd grew silent. They had seen Buck's evilness before and they all feared for the ranger's life. What Henry didn't realize is that Seth had already begun the match, angering the bigger man to interfere with his judgment.

"You two boys go to da corner, the fight will start in one minute," Sven said. "When I call you togedder, I want you to shake hands and start at da bell."

Seth walked over to his stool. Marshal Wheeler stood there with a towel in his hand and a tin bucket of water and a ladle at his feet. "Remember, Seth, that man don't follow no rules. He will try to gouge out your eyes and kill you. You want to stay out of clinches; he has hurt many men with his bear hug."

Sitting on the stool, Seth looked back at the amiable marshal, giving advice on what he already knew. "I hear you, Mack." He looked across the arena. John Henry was in Buck's corner, no towel, and no bucket. *They were supremely confident that the fight wouldn't last very long.*

Chapter 50

Sven Lindquist signaled for the two fighters to join him in the middle of the twenty-five square-foot arena. The surrounding crowd was silent with tense anticipation. “You boys shake hands, by golly,” Sven said.

“Sure thing,” Buck said as he sucker-punched the ranger in the mouth and Seth went down. The bell hadn’t even started the fight yet.

Seth was sitting on the ground with the copper taste of blood in his mouth. Worse than a cut lip was his overwhelming sense of foolishness; he should have known better and from now on he would expect the unexpected.

“Dat’s against my rules,” Sven Lindquist said, “we will wait one minute before we start, by golly. If you do that again I will call the fight and declare Mr. Seth the winner.”

“You ain’t calling no fight,” Buck snarled. “I was you ranger I’d stay right where you are.”

“Cheating the only way you can win?” Seth asked as he stood up.

Buck clenched his fist. “I don’t need to cheat to whup you, ranger.”

Seth strode over to his stool and took the ladle of water from Marshal Wheeler. He rinsed his mouth and spit out water and blood and then took a small drink. He looked in the direction of Darla Brown and saw a horrified expression. He smiled at her with a big, pink-toothed smile and gave her a wave.

Darla turned to her mother. “He’s hurt already, and the fight hasn’t even started.”

"He'll be alright, dear," her mother said, patting Darla's tense hand, hoping she was right.

Althea felt her daughter start at the ringing of the bell.

"Don't play around with this guy," John Henry said as he pulled back the stool.

"I ain't playing, Pa," Buck said. He rushed to the center of the arena and was surprised to be met by the smiling ranger. No fear showed in his eyes. It almost seemed like the ranger was feeling humorous.

Buck attempted a big round-house right to the ranger's head. He had telegraphed the blow and Seth stepped inside the punch and jabbed with his left to the mouth, snapping Buck's head back. The big man's lips sliced against his teeth and blood streamed down his chin.

"I never seen so fast; his fist was a blur," Zeke said to Tinker.

"How's it feel?" Seth asked. "Maybe you should go back to your daddy and forget this whole thing."

Buck wiped his mouth with his forearm and roared, rushing toward the ranger.

Mission accomplished.

The ranger sidestepped Buck as if he was a matador.

Someone in the crowd yelled "Ole!" Loud guffaws came from the audience, further infuriating Buck Henry. His father glared into the crowd trying to identify the culprit.

Seth had learned his lesson. He did not take his eyes off of the big man.

Buck, irritated at the ranger's illusiveness, turned and circled, looking for an opening. Seth just stood there preserving energy and patiently waited for the attack. He often found that big, sometimes clumsy men were susceptible to counter punching.

The wary ranger had appraised Buck Henry and knew that he was mostly brawn and bravado with a bully mentality. He also knew he was a little slow of reaction and thought. Buck wasn't the brightest candle on the mantle.

Buck feigned another round-house right and when Gentry stepped inside he hit him with a straight left that shook the ranger down to his boots. Stunned, Seth backed off ,shaking his head. Perhaps he had underestimated the man's mental acuity. Buck was a veteran of many fights, after all. *Second lesson learned.*

Henry had an evil sneer on his face. He had just gained some confidence back and felt that he could out-muscle and outsmart the ranger. If he could just get his arms around the smaller man it would be all over. He moved in, watching the ranger's quick hands. He should have been watching the ranger's eyes. As he got closer, the ranger stepped toward him and hit him three times---solar plexus, right bicep, left bicep. Air left him and his arms seemed to knot up and his hands felt heavy.

"That boy knows how to fight," Clements said to Wheeler.

"Yeah, and he's awful fast. If Buck don't get him early he could be in big trouble."

Buck caught his breath and shook out his arms. He put his arms up to protect his face and made a move to pressure in. Seth sidestepped him once again and gave him a shot to the kidneys. "Ooof," Buck's air left him as both arms dropped and Seth hit him in the temple with a hard right.

Seth felt pain shoot up his arm. Hitting Buck Henry in the head was like punching an anvil. *Third lesson learned.*

The bell rang ending the first round and Sven stepped in between the two fighters. "To your corners, yentlemen," he said.

"That punch to my kidney was illegal," Buck whined to the referee.

Sven Lindquist shook his head in disbelief. Buck Henry of all people was complaining about illegalities.

John Henry's son sat heavily on his stool. Sweat and whiskey was pouring out of Buck and he was looking around for some water. "You ain't got no water?" he asked.

Buck's father looked at the boy, still bleeding from his mouth. "I didn't think you was going to fiddle-fart around."

"Get me some water in case I don't get him this round. That tin star is like bees buzzing around a hive."

"Well, stop being a hive and get him in a bear hug, but watch them fists," John Henry said. "You best stay away from them; he's faster than lightning."

"How am I to get him in a bear hug if I stay away from him?"

John Henry looked at his son as if he was dumb as a rock. "Just get a hold of that boy and squeeze the life out of him, now."

The bell rang for the next round.

Seth watched the man lumber toward him with more caution. He smiled. Buck's heavy chest was rising and falling in an effort to take in as much oxygen as possible. The ranger brought his hands up in a boxing pose angering Henry. Buck roared, snot running down his bloody nose and made a grab for Seth.

When Buck leaned in Seth let loose with a flurry of punches to Buck's damaged face. The big man rocked back on his heels and, to his surprise, the lawman backed away and assessed the damage. A cut appeared over Buck's right eye and swelling was becoming evident.

Zeke said to Tinker, "I ain't never seen so fast; Seth hit him four times before he knowed it."

"He still best be careful. That Henry can be like a buffalo stampede."

Gentry watched Buck wipe the blood out of his eyes with a forearm. Henry again feigned a round-house right and Seth stepped inside toward the massive fighter. Instead of swinging Buck stepped forward and wrapped his huge arms around the ranger and squeezed. Seth's arms were pinned to his side. The ranger wiggled like a snake in an attempt to loosen the grip around him but Buck's superior strength held.

"You're mine now," Buck sneered. As he crushed the lawman he could hear the air leaving him and heard the crack of a rib.

Seth couldn't breath and he could feel consciousness leaving him. He had to do something quick. He stomped down on Buck's instep with his boot, the big man grunted and his grip relaxed. The ranger sucked in a quick breath of air and then head-butted Henry in the face, flattening his nose, spraying blood. Buck let go.

Glistening with sweat and blood, the ranger backed away, drawing in as much air as possible, which was not an easy thing to do with the sharp pain he felt in his ribs. *Fourth lesson learned. Don't get trapped inside.*

Buck looked a sight. He was bleeding from above the eye, from his nose and out his mouth. Despite that, he knew that his grip had a crushing effect on his opponent.

To Buck's disbelief, leaning to one side, favoring his hurt ribs, Seth advanced toward him.

The bell rang to end the round and Sven stepped between the two men. Neither of them seemed to mind and both wearily walked to their corners.

John Henry handed his son a ladle of water and watched him drink it down. "Easy boy, you'll get waterlogged. You almost had him; finish him off in the next round."

Peering out of swollen eyes, for the first time Buck had some doubt. As his father worked on his cuts, he squinted over at Seth's corner and the ranger seemed relaxed and confident; Buck knew he had hurt him and he would either have to give him some good body shots or try to get his arms around him again. Buck tried to breathe through his broken nose without much success. He had to admit that the lawman knew how to fight and he would have to revert to some of his old tactics.

Seth was hurt and he knew it. The pain in his side was excruciating and he was making a valiant attempt not to show it. He also knew Buck was hurt and would be desperate to finish him in the next round. He glanced over to Darla and her mother. He saw tears running down Darla's cheeks. He had better finish this quick.

The bell rang and Sven signaled for the men to come out of their corners.

Marshal Wheeler toweled Seth off. "He's going to try to finish you off. He's tired and frustrated."

Seth nodded and moved in.

Chapter 51

Seth dragged himself off the stool, stood as straight as he could, and feigned total fatigue as he slowly walked toward the center of the arena, hands down by his sides.

Buck, also exhausted, not only tasted blood but smelled blood. He was physically tired and weary of putting up with Ranger Gentry. Deep down he had to give the man credit; no one had ever lasted this long fighting him. Determined, he cautiously walked closer to his opponent to see what would happen.

Nothing happened.

Gentry's hands were down and he looked all done in. Buck smiled with his swollen lips and said, "This is it lawman, if I didn't want to tear you apart I would say you should turn around and go sit down..."

Seth exploded with a barrage of lefts and rights. A roar went up from the crowd. Toe-to-toe they slugged each other with smashing blows. Buck Henry went down. Sven backed Seth off and began the count. Stunned, Buck sat there blinking his eyes to clear his vision.

"Come on, Buck, quit fooling around and get up," his father hollered. He watched his son struggle to get up, fall back down and then get up again.

Sven looked into the fighter's eyes. "I'm calling this fight," he said.

"Like hell you are," Buck said pushing the referee aside. He rushed the ranger, grabbing him from behind and lifting him off of the ground. Seth struggled. Being off the ground took away one of his defensive moves. Buck squeezed with all of his might, the pain from his rib injury causing Seth to cry out. The ranger snapped his head back, a crushing blow to Henry's face, causing him to loosen his grip. When Buck let go, Seth made sure both of his boots landed on top of Henry's, and off balance the ranger did a tuck and roll. Buck shook his head as if he could shake off the pain and squeezed his puffy eyes in an attempt to clear his vision. He saw the lawman struggling to get up and he staggered over. Seth saw the big man approach and rolled out of the way just in time to avoid a kick to the head.

Seth found the strength to scramble up. Sven was attempting to control Buck Henry. "You must follow the rules, by yiminy," he said.

"Shut up, I'm going to finish this now."

The bell rang ending the round. Buck ignored it and went after the ranger. The Swede made an attempt to stop him and was shoved out of the way. The crowd roared in protest. Buck staggered toward Seth with a roar, looking like an enraged gorilla. Ranger Gentry swung from his toes and landed a hard right to the jaw. Buck's eyes rolled up into his head and after a moment Buck went over backwards like a felled tree. The crowd became silent and they heard the big man hit the ground, a cloud of dust rising around the cataleptic man.

John Henry rushed out to his son and the people greeted him with a chorus of boos.

Sven started a ten count and Henry said, "You can't count him out, the round was over."

"He was the one that broke the rules, by golly," Sven said resuming the count.

Buck's father rushed over to the bucket of water and threw it into his son's face.

"What the…"Buck sputtered, "what happened?"

"You got your butt handed to you," his father answered, "now get up; you got another round to go."

Buck struggled to get up; on hands and knees he shook his head, spewing a spray of water. His father helped him to his feet and guided him to the stool. Buck sat down heavily. "I never saw it coming," he said. "I need water."

"You're wearing it dummy," his father said.

Through swollen eyes Buck glared at his father, wondering why he put up with him. John Henry gave all of the orders and made all of the money while Buck did most of the work. Buck did his fighting for him and for what?

Seth and the marshals watched the Henrys' corner with amusement. "Don't let him get to you," Mack Wheeler said. "Use your speed and finish him off."

The bell rang.

Buck was slow to get off of his stool and Seth stole a glance over to Althea and Darla Brown. Darla looked on in disbelief and Seth smiled when Althea gave him a wink signaling that this was it. Seth attempted a grin with cracked and swollen lips and met Sven in the middle of the arena. The late-arriving Buck Henry tried an intimidation snarl that sounded more like the mewing of a kitten. He was whistling through his broken nose and mumbled something through thick tongue and puffy lips.

"This will be the last round, by golly," Sven said, "it's time to eat."

For a change, Buck didn't protest. Changing tactics, he punched Seth in the face with a straight left that knocked him down.

"That's more like it, Buck," his father yelled. His son wasn't done yet.

Seth clambered up, shaking his head. *Fifth lesson learned, don't forget about the other hand.*

The combatants met in the center of the arena, toe-to-toe with an exchange of blows the likes of which no one had ever seen. How could two men take so much punishment? The crowd sounded its approval at the vicious exchange.

Open-jawed, Ranger Hatfield heard Althea say, "Seth's got him now."

Both fighters were taking a brutal pounding. "Buck's about to run out; his punches are slowing," Marshal Clements said to Wheeler.

Mack Wheeler nodded. "I just hope Seth has enough left to finish him off."

A hard right shook Seth to his boots and he took a step back to regain his wits. Exhausted, Buck was slow to close in, his chest rising and falling, gasping for air.

Seth decided this was to be it. He pretended to be hurt worse than he was. He appeared shaky and reluctant to continue, hands down. Buck grinned and went in for the kill.

As fast as a snake striking his prey, Seth struck Buck's face with a wicked straight jab with his left, snapping Henry's head back, followed by a hard right that put him down. The crowd roared its approval.

Seth stood over the huge man in victory, breathing heavily. Buck Henry was out cold. Sven Lindquist counted to ten in Swedish and then looked over at a disheartened John Henry. "That's it, by golly," Sven said.

"I've never seen anything so barbaric," Darla whispered to her mother.

"Yes, but I will have two thousand dollars to go toward your wedding," Althea teased.

Chapter 52

"What did I tell you, Eli; we just made some money," Ned said.

"We lost some, too, on that big guy."

Disgusted with his little brother, Ned went looking for John Henry. He found him scowling and counting out the beautiful woman's winnings. She watched the man's hands and money carefully. Althea Brown had known men that thought they could take advantage of women; after all, her husband dealt with politicians every day. Many men thought women were to be seen and not heard, belonged in the kitchen and birthing babies, and would be the demise of the country if they ever got the vote.

Ned watched the woman put her winnings in her bag. That was a lot of money for a woman to be carrying around, he thought. Perhaps there was an opportunity here. "Mr. Henry, I came for me and my brother's winnings."

Henry looked at Ned with disdain. "I'm out, you seen *that* woman takin' it all," he said.

Flushed with anger Ned said, "You ain't going back on our bet; I'll go to the law."

Big John Henry's fists clenched. He'd had enough of the law around here. "Simmer down, mister, you can ride out to the ranch and get your money there."

Eli walked up behind his brother, hand near his gun. "We got a problem, Ned?"

"This guy says he's out of money."

Henry saw the little man arrive. The man was diminutive compared to him and his son, but rattlesnakes weren't all that big and could be deadly. The little man had close-set eyes and a feral appearance.

"I could just shoot him, Ned, and find out if he's telling the truth," Eli said.

"You boys don't need to get riled; just come out to the Circle J tomorrow and get your money." Henry looked over at a couple of his hands tending to Buck. "I've had enough trouble for the day."

Having seen possible trouble across the way, Marshal Clements and Marshal Wheeler approached the trio. "Is there a problem here boys?" Marshal Clements asked.

"This man lost a bet and says he doesn't have any money," Ned Hayes said.

With raised brow, Clements looked at the brothers. "You two bet on the ranger?"

"We bet on both 'cuz the odds was good," Ned answered.

Wheeler smiled. The two men weren't as dumb as they looked.

"Is that right, John, you don't have the money?" Clements inquired.

"*That* woman over there took it all," he said, pointing out Mrs. Brown and her daughter.

"You mean the governor's wife took you?" Clements asked, laughing as the big rancher's face turned red.

"Governor's wife?"

Marshal Clements chuckled. "Her daughter's sweet on the ranger that beat your son to a pulp."

"What about our money, Marshal?" Ned asked.

John Henry took in a deep breath. "The marshal can vouch for me; can't you Marshal," he said between clenched teeth.

"This man's short on a lot of things; kindness, manners, and some say brains, but he is not short on money," the marshal said with a smile. Marshal Wheeler chuckled in the background.

Henry, flushed with anger, said, "You call that vouching?"

The marshal continued to smile.

"I told these two to come out to the ranch tomorrow and I would give them what they deserve," Henry said.

"I don't think I should have to do that marshal," Ned said; "why can't he just go to the bank?"

Clements raised a questioning brow.

Disgusted, Henry said, "Any money I have in the bank is tied up and, besides, my safe at the ranch is bigger than the one in the bank."

Clements chuckled. "Everything about John Henry is big; big ranch, big son, big mouth."

"That's uncalled-for marshal," Henry protested. He glanced over at his beaten son sitting on the stool with a cowhand flapping a towel to give him some air. John Henry shook his head. He looked over at the opposite side of the arena and saw the ranger talking to the governor's wife and daughter.

Marshal Clements turned his attention to Ned and Eli. "It looks like you boys will have to get your winnings at the Circle J tomorrow."

"I don't think that's right; what if he don't pay?" Ned asked.

"I would say that would be fraud and I could lock him up," Clements said, locking eyes with John Henry.

Henry got the message and stormed over to his son, who was slouched on the stool.

Priscilla Peabody scurried over to the marshals. Ranger Hatfield was following closely behind. "Food is ready," she said with youthful excitement.

"What you got following you, girl?" Mack Wheeler asked.

Priscilla flushed. "Ranger Hatfield said that Ranger Gentry is with the governor's wife and daughter and he was free to be of assistance."

"Uh-huh," Wheeler said as he watched the young ranger catch up with the preacher's daughter, gasping for air.

"I dare say, Miss Priscilla, you are awful hard to keep up with," Hatfield said.

"I beat all of the girls in school and most of the boys in foot races," she said, proudly raising her nose higher. "Come on, let's go eat," she said, taking the young ranger by the hand.

Before following the young couple, Wheeler said, "Buck's not going to like that much."

Clements nodded. He turned toward Buck Henry; he was glaring through almost closed eyes at the young couple walking away. "We'll have to tell that boy to watch himself."

Darla Brown was fussing over Seth when the marshals approached.

"Darla, I'll be okay," Seth said.

"Your face looks like ground up meat," she said as she dabbed at swollen bruises and bleeding cuts.

"You should see the other guy," Seth said with a chuckle and winced at her ministrations, bringing back memories of his mother's firm wiping of dirt off of his face as a child.

"This cut over your eye should be sewed up," she said as she cleaned it, much to Seth's discomfort.

Seth hadn't noticed Darla's mother had left until he saw her returning with a wet rag and a clean towel. She started sponging Seth's back and then his chest. "Raise your arms," she ordered with motherly firmness.

"Yes, ma'am," Seth said. These Brown women, besides being beautiful and smart, certainly could take control, he thought. He grimaced when she went over his hurt ribs.

Althea Brown toweled Seth off, seeming to take some hide with her. He looked to her right in an attempt to take it like a man and saw the two old-timers grinning at him. “What are you two old coots doing?” Seth asked with obvious affection. Zeke was holding his shirt.

“We was watching over yer women-folk.” Zeke said.

“That young ranger put us in charge,” Tinker said with a toothless lisp.

“They did a good job, Captain,” Ranger Hatfield said, arriving hand-in-hand with the preacher’s daughter.

Althea and Darla smiled brightly at the young ranger and his new-found friend.

“That was some fight, Mr. Gentry; I never seen the like,” Priscilla said. “My daddy is pleased to have raised some money for the church.

Althea dropped the towel on the stool and picked up her bag. Zeke handed Seth his shirt and Darla helped him into it.

Darla’s mother reached into her bag and pulled out some money. “Here, Priscilla, give this to your father for the church.”

Priscilla Peabody’s jaw dropped. “There’s over a hundred dollars here!”

Althea laughed when she heard Seth groan as he slipped into his shirt. “I may need the rest for doctor’s bills.”

“I’ll be alright,” Seth grumbled. He glanced across the arena to see two men and John Henry arguing and the two marshals intervening. “I wonder what that’s all about.”

“John Henry said that Mrs. Brown took all of his money and he couldn’t pay those two men that bet on Ranger Gentry,” Priscilla said.

The governor’s wife laughed at the big man’s discomfort. “I thought he was a well-established important man around here.”

“He was saying that they have to ride out to his ranch tomorrow for their winnings,” Priscilla added.

Buck Henry was still slumped on his stool in defeat. He squinted at his father and mumbled, “I need a drink.”

John Henry looked down at his son, attempting to control his temper. You're in no shape to hang around; let's get you to the ranch and you can clean up and have a drink there.

Buck turned his attention to Priscilla Peabody and the young ranger holding hands. He clenched his sore fists and swore under his breath. He didn't like what he saw and vowed to himself to do something about it.

Chapter 53

"Do you think you can eat?" Althea Brown asked Seth.

"Yes, ma'am, and I sure could go for a beer; thanks for asking." Seth could feel Darla tense up. "Miss Darla, could I accompany you and your mother?" he asked, holding out both arms with obvious discomfort.

"You make me furious sometimes," Darla said as she took his arm.

"Who, me?" Seth asked with the utmost innocence.

"Yes, you; you are so darn sweet and stupid," she said.

With a painful smile, Seth asked, "Stupid?"

"Yes, stupid to get in some barbaric struggle and get all beat up."

"You did see the other guy?"

"He's even stupider," Darla said, dropping her hand from his arm and stalking off ahead.

Seth heard Tinker cackle. He glared at the old-timer.

"They's no figuring women folk," Tinker said. "No offense Mrs. Brown."

Althea Brown smiled at the old man. "None taken, Tinker; women can be mighty complicated and men even more so."

"Yes, ma'am, I guess that is so," Tinker said.

"Especially when both are in love and don't quite understand it."

Tinker hooted and Zeke grinned from ear to ear. "I'm right partial to those young folks," Zeke said.

"Me, too," Tinker added. "don't forget us for the weddin'."

"We won't. We've grown fond of you, too."

As they approached the buffet table they found Darla piling food on two plates with vigor and she shoved one at Seth.

"Thank you, dear," he said.

"Don't you dear me, I'm still angry with you," she said.

Seth wisely kept quiet and took the offered plate of food.

Darla set her plate on the table and with hands on hips said, "You are the handsomest man I ever met, Seth Gentry, and you go and get your face all beat up." A tear ran down her cheek.

Seth melted and reached out for her. Without shame he hugged her in public, one hand still holding his plate behind her. Darla wilted into his arms. "I love you Darla Brown," he said.

Darla laid her head against Seth's chest and sniffed. "I love you, too," she said, "with all my heart."

When applause broke out they looked up. They had been so focused on each other they hadn't noticed people had stopped dishing food and a crowd had gathered.

Darla flushed with embarrassment. "We're making ourselves a public spectacle," she said with another sniff.

Seth wiped a tear from her cheek with his thumb. The two old-timers were watching with big grins. "Let's eat; Tinker and Zeke look like they are starving to death."

"Take my plate, mother, I'll dish up another."

"No, dear, you and Seth find a place and I'll get my own and join you. Come on boys, you can be my dates."

Like two old peacocks the old-timers puffed up and joined the governor's wife. Althea handed each of them a plate.

"You first, ma'am," Zeke said.

"Why thank you, Zeke, you are such a gentleman," she said, the flattery turning Zeke's face beet red.

"I learned him his proper's," Tinker said.

"Did not."

"Did too."

"Now, now, boys, I'm just pleased to have such nice gentlemen as my dates," she said. "Finish filling your plates and come join me.

Bonneted women whispered to each other and men stared at the attractive wife of the Governor of California.

"I ain't never felt so important," Tinker said to Zeke.

"They's not looking at us," Zeke said.

"They are too, they's jealous," Tinker said, chest out.

Althea could hear the discourse behind her and she had a beaming smile on her face. She looked around at all of the people having a good time and thought about how wonderful and profitable this trip had been. Her euphoria increased as she approached two joined picnic tables. Sitting close together were her daughter and Seth. Darla appeared more relaxed and happy. Across from Marshals Wheeler and Clements sat Priscilla Peabody and Ranger Hatfield.

Seth looked up at the approaching trio. "It's a good thing we have you two to look after Mrs. Brown; it seems Ranger Hatfield has been preoccupied."

"We are always glad to help, Seth," Zeke said.

"My dates have been most helpful," Althea said, as she settled herself across from Seth and Darla.

The two old-timers scrambled to sit on either side of Althea; Seth laughed and Darla giggled. "You've still got it, mother, I only have one date," Darla teased. "Maybe we can take your dates back to Sacramento with us."

Althea laughed. "It would make Thad jealous and I would just love it," she said patting Zeke and Tinker on the arms with each hand.

"Ah shucks, Mrs. Brown, we wouldn't want to cause no trouble," Zeke said, "besides I'm not much for city life."

"Don't be so formal, Zeke, you can call me Althea and that goes for you too, Tinker."

"Yes, ma'am," they said in unison.

"How long are you able to stay in our fair city?" Marshal Clements asked the governor's wife.

Althea noticed Darla nuzzling Seth. "Thad wanted us back within a week, but I might be able to stretch it out for a few days."

"That's wonderful; we are glad to have you."

Chapter 54

"I don't like it. I don't like it at all," Eli said to his brother.

Irritated, Ned asked, "What don't you like, Eli?"

"That guy not paying us our winnings."

Ned was silent for a moment and then said, "It might be a good thing."

"How is not getting our money a good thing?" Eli asked.

Ned rubbed his whiskers thoughtfully.

"Well?"

"First of all, we've got to ride out to the Circle J ranch tomorrow and collect our money."

"Don't seem right and I don't see that as a good thing."

"Think about it, Eli, it's an opportunity."

Eli shook his head. "Don't see it as nothing but a long ride to get our money we shoulda gotten today."

"John Henry has a big ranch and is a wealthy man. "We can case the ranch out and maybe add to our winnings."

"I don't know, you heard him say he has a safe bigger than the bank safe," Eli said.

"Safes open, and he has to open it to get our money." Ned looked at his brother like he didn't have a brain in his pointy head.

Eli gave a slight nod.

"That's not all," Ned added. "Who received that rancher's money?" He waited for his brother's answer.

"That woman," Eli responded.

"That's right, that woman don't need all that money; she's the governor's wife."

Eli's narrow eyes widened. "Them two women sure are purty. They's always surrounded by lawmen, though."

Ned sighed. "We don't rob them during the day, dummy; they've got to have a hotel room."

"Who's the dummy? You don't got no money and I do," Eli said, his fist opening and closing near his holstered gun.

Exasperated, Ned said, "you've got to use your brain instead of a gun all of the time."

Eli sneered. "You talk too much; a gun is more convincing and a lot quicker."

"You can't go around killing people all of the time, especially women, and more especially if it is the governor's wife and daughter. We'd have the whole state of California after us if them women got harmed."

Incredulous, Eli said, "I ain't going to shoot no woman."

"I should hope not; we can relieve those women of their money without hurting them."

Eli lit up with a grey smile. "We could put some scare into them; maybe even spend a little fun time with them."

"Don't be stupid, Eli. Focus on the money."

"I ain't had me a woman in a long time."

"Well, let's get us some money and we can go back to Lulu Lamont's."

Eli grinned. "Now you're talkin'."

"Let's get some of this free grub and get back to camp. We've got to ride to the Circle J tomorrow."

Marshal Clements watched the two brothers approach the food. He had been watching them for some time and the two of them looked like they were up to no good. He expressed his concerns to Marshal Wheeler. Wheeler watched the two pile food on their plates. "One brother is a little guy; you think he could be our stage robber?"

"Possible," Clements said. He looked over at Seth and Darla. "I'll mention it to Seth when we get a chance."

Wheeler chuckled. "I don't think Seth is thinking about the law right now."

"Can't say as I blame him," Clements said. "That girl and her mama are mighty pretty."

"And smart, too," Wheeler said. "Not too many people take John Henry's money."

Clements laughed. "And not too many men have beaten Buck Henry."

"Uh-huh," Marshal Wheeler said, "and that young ranger's going the way of the captain; he's enamored by that little daughter of the preacher's."

"Spring is in the air," Clements added.

Mack Wheeler thought of his daughter, Beth, back home. For many years it was just the two of them and someday a young man was going to come along and take her away from him. He sighed loudly.

"What's the matter, Mack?" Sam Clements asked.

"All this love in the air just got me thinking," he said.

Clements was momentarily silent then said, "Yeah, the birds are singing and the bees pollinating. Ah, to be young again."

Wheeler's wistful look seemed to deepen. "I was just thinking how hard it would be to lose my daughter, and feeling guilty about being so selfish. She's been my whole life and I love her so much."

"Ah, that's it," Clements said. "Don't be so hard on yourself; fathers and daughters are special. Don't think of losing her, but of eventually gaining a son-in-law and grandchildren."

"Grandchildren! Beth's much too young and so am I!"

Clements chuckled. "Time flies, Mack. Look at the Peabody girl over there; she's younger than your daughter."

Wheeler saw Jim and Priscilla holding hands and smiling at each other. They were a cute couple, he thought.

Near them were the other two lovebirds, Seth and Darla. Darla was softly rubbing the damaged ranger's face. His eyes met the sparkling brown eyes of the governor's wife. With a smile, she nodded in understanding. He gave her a slight nod.

Althea recognized the concerned sadness on the marshal's face. She knew that he was a widower and had a beautiful young daughter. "Life is quite a journey, Mr. Wheeler, enjoy the ride," she said.

"Yes, ma'am; sometimes it can be a hard, lonely ride."

The governor's wife smiled knowingly. "When it is difficult, it makes us appreciate our blessings that much more."

Mack contemplated her words. "The governor is a lucky man."

"Why, thank you, Mack, I think your daughter is lucky to have you as a father."

Mack Wheeler seemed to relax. "Thank you, ma'am, I'm very lucky to have her as a daughter."

Chapter 55

Ned Hayes kicked his brother in the ribs. "Get up, Eli, we're burning daylight. We got to go get our money."

"Do that again and you'll find yourself shot," he grumbled.

"Come on, coffee is on and I just slapped on a side of bacon."

Eli shook out his boots and pulled them on. "I still don't like the idea of us having to chase after our money."

"I don't either, but at least we got money coming," Ned said. "Like I said before, let's look at it as an opportunity."

"Yeah, to ride a lot of miles," Eli murmured.

"Saddle the horses and I'll get breakfast together," Ned said.

"I wish you would quit giving me orders, Ned."

Ned's jaw muscles worked. He was growing weary of his brother's negativity. His demeanor seemed to darken the brightest day. His slow-moving brother was doing as he asked with the reluctance of a Missouri mule. "Hurry it up, Eli, we got to get going."

Eli's shoulders sagged and his gun hand itched. If Ned wasn't his brother . . .

Eli took off up the hill. "Call of nature," Eli said over his shoulder.

Ned was certain his brother was retrieving the rest of his silver. When Eli came down the hill he regarded him with suspicion and handed a plate and cup to his brother as he approached the campfire. Eli perched on a large granite rock while Ned sat on a long log and they both ate in silence. They heard a horse coming up the draw.

"Hello the camp, coming in," a man yelled.

Eli set his cup down and loosened his revolver from his holster as he watched a big sorrel horse and its rider work their way toward them. The morning sun glimmered off the badge on the rider's chest. "It's that ranger that was in the fight," he said.

"Let me do the talking. We don't need no trouble," Ned said. "Good morning ranger, light a spell, coffee is on; that was some fight yesterday."

Ranger Gentry scrutinized the campsite, noticed the third horse and dismounted. "Thank you kindly," he said. "You boys camp hear before?"

Ned thought a moment, wondering why the ranger would ask that question. "No, first time; we're going up to the Circle J to collect our winnings. We bet on you to win."

Seth chuckled, wincing from his sore ribs. "You boys were some of the few that did."

"That woman sure cleaned up," Ned said.

Gentry pulled a tin cup out of his saddlebags and walked over to the fire, making sure his back was not exposed to the two men. He poured some coffee that resembled Mississippi mud and smiled at the strong smell. It looked like it could float a horseshoe. "I do like strong coffee," he said.

"What brings you out this way?" Eli asked, as Ned scowled at him.

The ranger took his time, blew on his coffee and sipped a taste with his left hand, leaving the other one free. "That horse over there yours?"

Ned looked over at Virgil's horse eating a patch of grass by the creek. "Never seen him before last night," he said, "I was wondering who would go off and leave a nice horse like that, and the saddle was under that tree yonder."

Seth nodded and looked over the rim of his coffee cup at the two men. “I saw you two arguing with John Henry yesterday.”

“He gave all his money to that woman and didn’t pay off his bet,” Eli whined.

The ranger noticed the dirty look from the little man’s brother. “I saw that horse here the other day and was checking to see if the owner had come to get him.”

“I ain’t seen nobody,” Ned said. “We did look in them saddlebags and they’s just a few garments in there, nothing of real value.”

Gentry knew that to be true, as he had checked them before. If there had been anything of value he was sure that it had been removed by the person or persons that did the horse’s owner harm. He took another drink and then threw the dregs on the ground.

“Eli, pack up, we got to get going,” Ned said.

“I swear, Ned, you keep ordering me around and I’ll put a bullet between your eyes,” Eli said.

Ned flushed with anger. He glanced over to the quizzical ranger. “We’s brothers and argue some.” He began helping Eli pack. The sooner they left the better.

“I’ll take that horse back to town and put him up in the livery; if you come across the owner you can tell him where it is,” the ranger said.

“Sure thing, ranger,” Ned said as the two brothers mounted and headed up the hill toward the bright rising sun.

“Soon as we get our money I need to go back to Lulu Lamont’s,” Eli said.

“Shh. . .” Ned said, “That ranger might hear you.

After putting his cup back in his saddlebags, Seth got the saddle from under the oak tree and saddled the missing rider’s horse.

“I was hoping we could sell Virgil’s horse,” Eli said to his brother.

Ned glanced over his shoulder down the hill and saw the ranger saddling it. "Better to lose out on that horse than hang from the gallows," he said.

"It jest seems that if you didn't have bad luck you would have no luck at all, big brother," Eli said.

Like hooking up with you, little brother.

Seth glimpsed the riders disappear over the hill. The two had not been good stewards of this campsite and he set about digging a hole and cleaning it up. His stiff muscles loosened as he worked and, though sore, he started feeling better. His thoughts turned to Darla and the goodnight kiss he had received. She was disappointed when he told her he was going to leave before breakfast and wouldn't see her until noon or after. He had given Ranger Hatfield orders to stay with the women. The marshals had their business to take care of and too many people were aware that Althea Brown had taken a lot of money off of John Henry.

He chuckled to himself when he thought of old Tinker and Zeke. He had given them a silver dollar each and told them to watch out for the women and the wet-behind-the-ears ranger. He had also asked the marshals to keep an eye out as much as possible.

Captain Gentry picked up the stray horse's reins and led him toward Red. The big sorrel nickered a greeting and then Seth saw it.

Chapter 56

The ranch hands at the Circle J ranch were pouring out of the bunk house; the clanging triangle had called them to breakfast. The talk of the morning was of the fight the day before. Some of them had to work and weren't able to witness Buck Henry's humiliating defeat and the enthusiastic descriptions of the fight by those who saw it gave pleasure to those who couldn't attend. The men appreciated having a job, but no love was lost on their two bosses; they were bullies who showed no compassion for their employees.

Cookie was as excited to hear the story as anyone and had outdone himself with the morning cuisine, adding steak and beans to the eggs and bacon. No one knew Cookie's real name but he was appreciated for his skill around a stove or campfire despite his neglectful personal hygiene. His ability to create a great meal off of a chuck wagon was renowned and contributed to the Henry's ability to retain good ranch hands despite their demanding demeanor.

On occasion, like around branding time, John Henry would throw a party and the surrounding ranchers and the people of Volcano would be invited. Though not well liked by most people, the locals were not averse to sharing the big rancher's food and drink. During such events Cookie would team up with the house cook, Elma Anderson, to put out a spread that was legendary in Amador County. The culinary spread included Cookie's ranch fare, Elma's Swedish dishes and pastries, Chang Lee's Chinese delights and Maria Rios' spicy Mexican fare.

The ranch hands would have liked to linger over food, coffee, and conversation but all were aware that the loss of the fight by Buck and the loss of money by his father would leave them with untenable dispositions. It would be better to ride fence than to put up with their irascible moods.

The festive atmosphere did not extend to the ranch house. Elma went about her business baking Swedish pastries as quietly as she could. The longer she could avoid dealing with the Henry men the better her morning would be. Elma had also implored her sometime helpers, butler Chang Lee and maid Maria Rios, to go about their business as soundlessly as possible. Not only were the surly men in foul temperament when they got home yesterday, they both drank a lot of whiskey and got into a horrendous argument. Eventually they both passed out and serenity again descended upon the domain.

Elma pulled a tray of butter kaka out of the oven with a towel in hand and put it on the counter.

"Some ting smell good," Chang Lee said, sniffing the air as he entered the kitchen.

"Shhh," Elma said, "you'll wake the men."

"What you cook?" Chang asked in a whisper.

"Butter kaka," Elma answered.

"Sound nasty," Chang giggled.

"Dis is cinnamon buns cake with almond and vanilla custard, by golly," Elma said.

"Muy Bueno," Maria said as she came through the door.

"Shhh," Elma and Chang hissed in unison.

"Que es?" Maria asked.

"Butter kaka," Chang said, "don't you know nutting?"

The trio heard movement upstairs. Their eyes widened with unwanted anticipation. "Maria, you help get breakfast," Elma said. "Chang, make sure there is nothing dim boys can complain." Chang and Maria got busy. Though the three of them spoke different languages and a little

English, they fully understood each other and the problems the morning might bring. After a night of drink and contention the Henry men were often abusive to those around them. The goal for the morning was to minimize the opportunity for complaint.

"Maria, get the sausage and eggs going and I will do pancakes," Elma said, scurrying about the kitchen. The strong smell of coffee permeated the room as the two women got busy.

John Henry's head pounded like a bass drum. Dressed, he went down the hall and hammered on Buck's door. "Get up Buck, you've got work to do today," he yelled. He heard nothing so he kept pounding, exacerbating his headache and disposition. "Darn it Buck, get your butt out of bed, you're burning daylight. I can smell breakfast cooking."

No answer.

Buck's father tried the door. It was unlocked so he entered the room and saw his rumpled son passed out on the bed fully clothed. John Henry walked over and shook Buck, causing him to moan and roll over on his side. His son smelled as bad as he looked. "Get up, Buck, breakfast is ready; clean up and get downstairs."

"I'm not hungry," Buck moaned.

"You best get some grub; you're working the line today," his father said.

"We got people to do that," Buck complained.

"You cost me a lot of money, so you're going to earn it back. Stay up at the line shack; I don't want to see your face for a couple of days." He stayed and watched his son struggle to get off of the bed. Buck sat on the edge of the bed holding his head. "Hurry up," his father said again and left, making sure he slammed the door, regretting it when the shock reverberated in his own head.

"Where's breakfast?" John Henry bellowed. "I can't find that Chinaman to polish my boots," he complained, entering the kitchen.

Facing the stove, Elma smiled. Chang had wisely made himself scarce. "Breakfast be ready in a minute, by golly," she said.

"Dish up the boy's too; if he's late to breakfast he can just eat it cold."

"Yes, sir," Elma said. She smiled as she dished up Buck's plate first and set it aside. "Sit down, Mr. Henry; I bring it right out, you betcha."

John Henry regarded the young Swedish woman. She had been indentured when she came to this country and he had bought her out from a friend back east. Spying the pastries on the counter he considered his purchase one of his smartest business moves.

Henry sat at the dining room table and Maria poured him a cup of fresh coffee. "Gracias," he said.

"De nada," Maria said with a small curtsy. "Bring Buck's plate out, Maria."

"Si, señor."

John Henry was wiping up egg yolk with a biscuit when Buck stumbled into the dining room. "Eat, it's getting cold."

"I'm not hungry; I could use a drink," Buck said.

"You know there's nothing but beans up at the line shack; you best get your fill now. I'll give you a drink after you eat," his father said. His son had been drinking too much and it had probably contributed to his defeat to the ranger.

Buck forced a bite of food, gulping it down and suppressed the urge to regurgitate. Maria poured him a cup of hot coffee. "I don't want no coffee," he growled. Maria scurried off, ignoring him.

A sharp knock came at the kitchen door and Elma opened it. It was the foreman of the Circle J, Chet Wagner. "Ja?" Elma asked.

Chet smiled at the Swedish girl. He loved her foreign language but usually had no idea what she was saying. "Tell Buck we are ready to head out. His horse is saddled and ready to go; we'll be waiting out back."

Elma nodded and regarded the door to the dining room. With a deep sigh, she entered and passed on the information to John and Buck Henry. Buck's father watched him play with his food then stood and followed Elma into the kitchen. He poked his head out the door and beckoned to the foreman. "Buck's going to be a while; come in for a cup of coffee."

Wagner faced the two cowboys holding the horses and rolled his eyes. He handed the reins to his horse to one of them and reluctantly entered the house. It was bad enough to be stuck with Buck for a few days, but now he had to hang out with both of them. Ranch hands weren't allowed in the house and as foreman he had only been in there a couple of times. He sat across from Buck and accepted a steaming cup of coffee from Maria, feeling uncomfortable at what he considered a fancy room and table.

"Maria, get that bottle of whiskey from the sideboard and pour a shot in Buck's coffee," John Henry said.

"That's more like it," Buck grumbled.

Chet took a deep breathe, sipped at his coffee and said, "Len was wondering about his winnings from the, uh, contest yesterday." The annoyance leveled at him at that moment from the two men made him want to crawl into a hole. He was met with a long silence. He raised his coffee cup and avoided making eye contact with his bosses.

Buck downed his spiked coffee. John cleared his throat and said, "Tell him I'll add it to his month's wages. Now you two get out of here and get to work."

The relieved foreman rose quickly, grabbed his hat and hurried toward the kitchen. Slower, Buck rose, walked by the sideboard, picked up the bottle of whiskey and put it under his vest. His father was about to protest, then thought better of it and let him go. It would be nice to have some peace and quiet around the house for a few days. "Stay out of trouble, Buck," he said.

Buck grunted and left through the kitchen. His father sighed, wearily stood and retreated to his office off of the parlor. He sat behind his large oak desk and through the window watched his son and ranch hands gallop up the hill toward the eastern fence line. He opened the ledger on his desk and stared at the numbers without really seeing them, lost in thought about the previous day's events and the amount of money he had lost. In all of these years he had never lost money like that and he didn't like it; *and to be outdone by a woman of all things.*

The unexpected arrival of horses, followed by hammering on the door and the muffled sound of men talking, brought him out of his reverie.

Chapter 57

Following the creek up a long draw, the Hayes brothers were relieved to be leaving camp and the ranger captain. “I didn’t like the way that ranger was lookin’ at us,” Eli said.

“Eli, you don’t like the way anybody looks at you; more often than not you wind up shootin’ them.”

“I didn’t like that he took Virgil’s horse neither,” Eli added.

Ned shook his head at Eli’s continued negativity. “Not much we could do about that, unless you wanted to confess to killin’ Virgil.”

“It just ain’t right.”

“Maybe not, but that’s just the way it is,” Ned said.

“After we get our winnings I’m thinking of ridin’ out,” Eli said.

Only the clop-clop-clop of the horse’s hoofs and the occasional squeak of saddle leather interrupted the silence of Ned’s contemplation. Being rid of his brother was mighty appealing, but his brother would have the majority of the money.

“When we get our money from that Henry fella, be sure to reimburse me my seed money,” Eli added.

Ned glared at his brother. “What are you talkin’ about? I put up my share of the bank money.”

“We couldn’t have won that bet without *my* money,” Eli said.

What a selfish little twit, Ned thought. “Where would you be ridin’ to?”

"Thought I might head south toward Mariposa. I heard they's pulling some gold out of there."

The brothers rode in silencc. Ned didn't mind the idea of being rid of his brother, but he needed to raise some money first. His thoughts turned to the governor's wife and the two thousand dollars she had won from John Henry. Perhaps it would be better if he stole that money himself. He wouldn't have to split it with his brother and Eli was awful quick on the trigger. If any harm came to the governor's wife or daughter they wouldn't be able to show their faces anywhere in the state.

The riders topped out on a small rise, reined in, and looked down at the Circle J ranch. The large ranch house was surrounded by numerous outbuildings, a corral full of horses, and cattle grazing in the distant pasture.

"Some folks got all the luck," Eli said.

Ned leaned forward on his saddle horn. "Maybe they worked mighty hard for what they got."

"Or maybe they jest was borned into it," Eli said. "We work hard and not much comes of it."

Disgusted, Ned glared at his brother. "Don't take much work to pull a trigger."

Eli ignored his brother and continued to stare at the ranch house. "It do look mighty peaceful down there. Let's go get our money."

The brothers galloped into the ranch yard trailing a cloud of dust. No ranch hands were about and Ned said, "I hope Henry is home. I'd hate to think we come all this way for nothing."

"And you said that I'm the negative one," Eli said, dismounting in front of the porch and climbed the steps to the front door. Ned followed and arrived as Eli pounded on the front door.

"What the . . .," John Henry said. He saw Chang move toward the entry through his office door.

Chang opened the door and saw two swarthy men standing on the porch. "Foreman not here, come back for job," he said starting to close the door.

Eli shoved the door open, knocking Chang back, arms circling to regain his balance. "We're not here for no job," he snarled. "We want our money."

Frightened, Chang said, "I get boss, you stay."

"Be quick about it," Ned said, watching the little china man scurry through the parlor.

Chang almost ran into John Henry as he walked through the office door to see what the ruckus was about. The little man was visibly shaken. "What's all of the fuss about, Chang?"

"Two men here want money," Chang said.

Henry walked back to his desk and took a small pistol out of the drawer and stuck it in his pants, hidden by his vest. "You take the women out back in case there is trouble."

Chang gave a quick bow of understanding and dashed out to the kitchen to find Elma and Maria. He told the two women of the possible threat and Elma peeked around the corner.

John Henry approached the foyer and saw the two men that he had lost the bet to. "You boys cut a wide path," he said.

"We been waitin' some time and rode a far piece for our money," Ned said.

Henry nodded. The little man's hand was closer to his gun than he would have liked. He didn't want any trouble and thought he had better diffuse the situation. "I'm sorry about that; as you know that woman took all I had on me."

"We come for ours," Eli said through clenched teeth.

Henry reached inside his vest for his tally book. Eli gripped the butt of his pistol. "Easy, fella, just getting my book," Henry said.

"Make sure that's all yer reaching for," Eli sneered as Henry slowly pulled out his notebook.

The brothers watched the big man open the book and trace a finger down the page. “Here it is; you boys wait right here and I’ll go get your money,” Henry said.

Ned and Eli watched the man turn and go through the parlor into his office. “Let’s go,” Eli whispered. The parlor had a nice rug that helped muffle their steps as they lightly walked toward the man’s office. Eli peeked in and saw the big man knelt down working the combination of a large safe. He held up his hand, signaling Ned to wait.

Eli drew his gun and Ned grabbed his brother’s arm. “No shooting,” he hissed. He watched Eli grab the gun by the barrel and when he heard the sound of the lever on the safe click and the door start to squeak open, Eli tiptoed in and brought the gun down with a vicious blow to the back of Henry’s head, knocking him unconscious.

“You didn’t have to hit him so hard,” Ned complained.

Disgusted, Eli snarled at his brother, “What did you want me to do, tap him lightly.”

“You might have killed him,” Ned said.

“I think he’s still breathing; help me move him out of the way,” Eli said.

The brothers each grabbed an arm and pulled Henry out of the way. Ned opened the safe door and started going through its contents. There were numerous legal papers and he tossed them aside. He found a small derringer and stuffed it into his pocket, unseen by his brother. He opened a large cash box and let out a whistle.

“What ya got, Ned,” Eli said, trying to look over his brother’s shoulder.

“Hang on a second, Eli,” Ned said, trying to block his brother’s view. He stuffed some bank notes into his shirt and took out two leather pouches of coin. He opened one of them up and found it full of gold. He closed the drawstring and opened the second pouch to find that it contained silver. He showed the silver to Eli. “Two pouches of silver; a good payday," he said, tossing the silver pouch to his little brother. "Let's get out of here."

The brothers mounted up and headed west. "That was easy," Eli said.

"I sure hope you didn't kill that man; if you did our lives won't be worth a plug nickel," Ned said. He liked the feel of the heavy pouch.

Chapter 58

Ranger Gentry squatted down in the soft sand next to the bubbling creek and saw the imprint of a small boot with a worn spot in the sole, identical to the print he had seen at the stagecoach robbery site. The men he had just talked with were the culprits and he considered what to do. He looked over at the abandoned horse he had intended to take to the livery in Sutter Creek and thought about the two men riding up to the Circle J ranch near Volcano and then he recalled the attention Althea Brown had gotten after winning a large amount of money from John Henry. Ranger Hatfield and the Marshals were in Sutter Creek, but Marshal Wheeler had talked about returning to Amador City and young Hatfield was being distracted by Priscilla Peabody. Seth felt a need to protect the governor's wife and daughter. He also had a strong affinity to good horseflesh and disliked the idea of leaving the neglected horse again. If he pursued the two brothers all the way to Volcano it would be possible to miss them coming or going. In an attempt to reach a decision, he thought about what the two outlaws might do. They might hang around Volcano for a while or go into Jackson and it was just as likely that they might return to this camp or go into Sutter Creek. He had overheard the little brother say something about a Lulu's; he'd have to ask Marshal Clements what or where that was.

Seth stiffly mounted Red, took the reins of the other horse and in a quick gallop traveled downhill toward Sutter Creek, feeling a pang of guilt for not going after the outlaws, but his remorse was overridden by the need to protect Althea and Darla.

As Gentry rode into the quaint little town, the citizenry noticed the riderless horse, wondering what had become of the rider. Seth left both horses at the livery and walked down the hill to the Hotel Sutter. Marshal Clements, working his teeth with a toothpick, walked out and greeted him.

"The ladies are inside," he said. "Mack left for Amador City."

Seth nodded. "Those two boys that won some money from Henry are the outlaws we been looking for. I didn't discover it until they had already left for the Circle J."

"I knew them boys were no good," Clements said. "Go get some vittles; I'll keep an eye out."

"Thanks," the ranger said, "I'm starved."

"Oh, and captain, that ranger boy is in a corner with Miss Priscilla, like two mourning doves in a tree."

"I'm hoping he's watching over the governor's wife and daughter," Seth said.

Clements laughed. "I think he only has eyes for the preacher's daughter, but I been helping out; I only came out because someone said that you had rode in with an empty horse."

"Thanks, Sam. I'll be along directly."

Seth entered the dark restaurant and paused to let his eyes adjust to the low light. Sure enough, over in the corner was Jim Hatfield all cozied up with Priscilla Peabody. He shook his head at the giggles emanating from the back of the room and scanned the restaurant for Althea and Darla Brown. When he spotted them he was pleased to receive two welcoming smiles.

As he walked over Althea said, "We've been waiting for you, Seth. We're having a spot of tea."

An involuntary groan emitted from the ranger as he took a seat next to Darla. Her face turned serious as she regarded his injured face. “Just a little sore from riding this morning,” he said.

“Sure, and that fight didn’t have anything to do with it I suppose,” Darla said.

Wisely, Seth said nothing.

“We’re going shopping this morning,” Althea said, to try to find something for Thad. He didn’t want us to take this trip but eventually acquiesced.”

Seth ordered coffee and breakfast. “A lot of people know about that large sum of money you won, Mrs. Brown; I hope you aren’t packing it around.”

“Well, I’m certainly not going to let it lay around for some thief to steal,” she said.

Gentry winced, his discomfort exacerbated by his swollen face. “You are an attractive woman, Mrs. Brown, and the governor’s wife, but neither of those things would preclude evil men from knocking you over the head and taking your money.”

“I can take care of myself,” Althea said.

“Your daughter could get hurt, also,” Seth added.

The governor’s wife went silent. She wouldn’t want Darla to get hurt.

“After breakfast I’ll escort you two to the bank and then you can go about your shopping,” Seth said as a sizzling plate of steak and eggs was placed before him.

“He’s right, mother, and we will make it obvious what we are doing so that the vagabonds know you aren’t carrying much money,” Darla said.

Althea nodded and took a dainty sip of tea.

Seth chewed on a slice of tender steak and eyed the corner of the room. He swallowed and said, “I don’t think young Mr. Hatfield has your best interests in mind; I’m going to have a talk with that boy.”

“Let him be, Seth, he’s young and in love,” Althea said.

The ranger cut a slice of beef and chewed. He gazed into the deep brown eyes of Darla Brown. Darla put her hand on top of his. “Mother’s right, Seth, let them be. I know how they feel.”

Gentry’s heart skipped a beat. He gulped and said, “I don’t want anything to happen to you two.”

Althea smiled. “Nothing is going to happen. Remember, we will have two rangers escorting us back to Sacramento.”

Seth put his other hand on top of Darla’s. “I’ve got some business to take care of first; I hope you ladies can occupy yourselves for a few days.”

“Don’t you worry about us; we love to shop and enjoy new environs. We are also unofficial ambassadors of the governor and the state and when we tell Thad we got him some more votes it’ll make his day,” Althea said, smiling brightly.

“The governor’s a lucky man,” Seth said, holding on to Darla’s hand. He looked at her long elegant fingers and delighted in the softness of her skin.

“I’ve been told that a lot lately,” Althea said.

Chapter 59

The ranch hands glared at the big man sleeping in the shade of a large fir tree as they mended fence. "That guy is as worthless as teats on a bull," said the hand who was stringing wire.

"That's a fact," Chet Wagner said. "Leave him be; he ain't causing us no trouble."

"There is that," Len said, "and he did make me some extra money by losing that fight."

"Careful, he might just kill you if he hears you bragging on that," Wagner said.

Two riders silhouetted the skyline as they topped a knoll riding down the fence line.

"Somebody coming; should we roust Buck?" a ranch hand asked.

Wagner considered the lump of humanity snoring under the tree. "Naw, that'd be like disturbing a grizzly from its winter hibernation." The two riders were drawing near and Wagner loosened his gun in his holster. As they neared he called out friendly like, "You boys huntin' work?"

Ned Hayes regarded the workers. "No, we was in Volcano and decided to venture a new way to Jackson. I hear they's a good game of cards at the National Hotel. We's heading downhill and was looking for a way around this here fence."

Wagner decided Hayes was friendly enough, and kept his eye on the smaller rider, his hand not straying far from his gun. "We done fixed all the fence to this point. Yer best bet is to follow that creek down yonder; it has a crossing and flows right into Jackson."

"Much obliged," Ned said and spurred his horse toward the creek.

As the two men galloped down the slope, Len said, "I seen them two boys in Sutter Creek at the fight between Buck and the ranger. I think they placed a bet with John Henry."

Wagner nodded. "My guess is those two is no good, especially the little feller; he looks meaner than a cornered possum. Come on, this fence ain't going to repair itself."

*****

Ned led his brother toward the creek, thinking about the fate of John Henry. Henry was a big man in these parts and if he was seriously injured, or worse, if he died, they would be hunted like a pack of dogs going after a 'coon. "You shouldn't have hit that guy so hard."

Eli's narrow eyes pierced his brother. "What's done is done; your best paydays are when I'm around big brother and I think you were right about that woman's winnings; we need to get our hands on it."

They rode in silence, only interrupted by the clip-clop of hooves and the squeak of saddle leather.

"We've got to figure a way to get that money so that no harm comes to those women," Ned said.

"So what if it does? No sweat offin' our back."

"We'd wind up dead for sure," Ned said.

"We all get dead sooner or later," Eli said.

"Well, I'd just as soon as it was later than sooner," Ned said, spurring his horse up a small hill.

"How come you told them boys we was going to Jackson?" Eli asked.

Ned shook his head. "Eli, if they come looking for us for what you done at the Circle J you don't want to let them know exactly where we can be found."

"What I done! You was there too big brother."

"I'm not the one that conked Henry on the head; might even be dead," Ned said.

"Since yer giving me all the credit maybe you should give me all the money."

Ned knew his little brother and it was necessary to listen to what he said. There was the obvious statement and the underlying reasons he said what he said. Eli was thinking along the same lines he was; to be rid of the other and have all the money. The irritation he felt being around his brother seemed to get worse every day.

The brothers rode in silence, lost in their own thoughts. The trail along the creek dropped down an incline and the town of Jackson lay before them. They crossed the creek on a small bridge and rode into town. The majestic National Hotel rose above them on the corner. "Let's get a drink," Ned said.

"Fancy place," Eli said.

"We'll have a drink, be seen and then get down the trail," Ned said. "Just don't cause no trouble."

"What you want to be seen for?" Eli asked.

Ned sighed, dismounted and tied his horse to the hitching rail. "We told them boys we was going to Jackson and if they come looking for us they'll think we are still here."

The brothers slapped some trail dust off and climbed the steps to the bar. When their eyes adjusted to the dim light they found the bar empty and a bartender polishing some glasses.

"Howdy, gents," the bartender said amiably, "what can I get you?"

Eli looked around the room. "Business is a little slow."

The bartender smiled. "It's a little early in the day; you can't find a place to sit down later on."

"We'll have a couple beers," Ned said.

"Good choice. Our beer is the coldest around; we got a basement and you probably saw that cold creek running out back." He set a frothy mug in front of each. "Staying in town?"

Ned smiled and took a long drink and then wiped the foam from his mouth with his sleeve. He knew that saloons were information centers, a lot quicker than a newspaper and many times more informative. "My brother and I are heading down Mariposa way; we heard they're pulling a lot of gold out of those hills."

"I've heard that," the bartender said, resuming his glass polishing. "They are still pulling quite a bit of gold out of the Kennedy Mine and the Pioneer Mine right here in Jackson."

Ned nodded and emptied his mug of beer. He saw that his brother still had half of his beer left. "Give us a shot of whiskey for the trail," he said.

"Another wise decision," the bartender said. "We have the best whiskey in the county."

Eli glared at the bartender. "I'm not partial to braggarts."

"Don't get your drawers in a knot, cowboy," the bartender said.

Ned scowled at his little brother, downed his whiskey and said, "Let's get out of here." He didn't want his brother causing any trouble, or worse, shooting someone else. As they rode out down the main street they passed a tree with a hangman's noose draped over a tall branch and he asked, "Why do you have to cause trouble?"

"That guy thought he was better than us jest because he pours drinks in a fancy hotel."

Ned deliberated on that. Did it really matter? And, there was his brother being negative, as usual. Eli was always darkening his mood. As soon as they got that woman's money he would split from his brother. Maybe he would go to San Francisco and have a good time. He glanced back at his trailing brother, his beady eyes seeming to pierce his back. A chill ran down his spine. He didn't like his brother behind him.

Chapter 60

Seth opened the door to the Sutter Creek Bank for Althea Brown and her daughter. It was not a secret that the governor's wife and daughter were in town, and when the bank manager saw them enter he eagerly approached the swinging gate and invited the trio to his opulent desk.

"It is an honor to have you visit us," Tobias Chandler said.

This guy should be a salesman, Seth thought. Chandler was a rotund man in a large grey suit and silk vest with a gold watch chain strung from pocket to pocket. He exhibited a large, disingenuous smile and the ranger wondered how people trusted him with their money. Seth pulled out a heavy leather chair for Althea and then another one for Darla before taking his own seat. "Apparently you are aware of Miss and Mrs. Brown's visit, and I am Captain Seth Gentry of the California Rangers."

"I certainly know who you are, Captain, and, yes, it has been the talk of the town that the governor's wife and daughter were here; and needless to say the spectacle at the church has been the major topic of conversation," the bank manager said. "How may I be of service?"

Althea Brown smiled sweetly at the pompous manager. "If I open an account, would your little bank be able to transfer the money to Sacramento on my behalf."

Seth looked down, hiding the smile on his face. Althea Brown had just put the man in his place. He took a peek at Darla and found her composed, with a rigid posture and hands clasped in her lap. The Brown women were experienced at handling self-important men.

The smile had disappeared from the manager's face. "I assure you, Mrs. Brown, we are one of the most profitable banks in the county."

"Of course you are," Althea said, "now answer my question."

The banker sputtered, "Though we are quite successful, we are an independent bank and when you return to Sacramento I can provide you with a bank note for the amount of money you deposit, less a small fee, of course," he added quietly.

Althea stared at the bank manager in silence.

Chandler squirmed in his chair uncomfortably. He cleared his throat and intertwined his hands on top of his large desk.

"I suppose that will have to do," Althea said, finally. "I have almost two thousand dollars here to deposit."

"My, that's quite a large sum," Chandler said. "I heard that the governor's wife had won quite a bit of money from Mr. Henry."

"You know John Henry?" Seth asked.

"As you may know, Mr. Henry is one of the wealthiest men in the county and we do have a business relationship with him, as do most of the banks in our surrounding area. He is on our board of directors as well as on other boards."

Ranger Gentry recalled that Marshal Clements had said that Henry told him his money was tied up in the bank and his safe at home was larger than the bank's. "Are you sure that Mrs. Brown's money will be safe? I was told that Mr. Henry keeps his money in a much larger safe at the ranch."

Tobias Chandler fidgeted and cleared his throat again. "I'm not at liberty to discuss the private manners of other customers, but I can assure you that Mrs. Brown couldn't place her money in a more secure situation."

Seth noticed the raised corners of Mrs. Brown's mouth. She had enjoyed Seth's jabbing of the manager.

Chandler signaled for a teller to come to his desk and told him to open an account in Mrs. Brown's name.

Althea removed the money from her bag. "Please put my daughter's name on the account also in case something were to happen to me."

Darla appeared startled; she had never considered something happening to her mother. "Oh, mother, don't say things like that."

The governor's wife patted her daughter's hands in her lap. "Honey, there is a business side of life you must always consider. If something happens to me or your father we want to make sure that you are taken care of."

"I just hate to think of things like that," Darla whispered.

"You already do, you just don't realize it," her mother said. "Think about the concern you had when Seth was going to have that fight. Remember your concern for your fiancé when he went missing in Nevada City?"

Darla looked down at her hands.

"Life is full of peril, sweetheart, and I am so glad that you have met Seth and you will have someone to meet life head-on with, when your father and I are gone," her mother added.

"Oh, mother!"

The three of them watched the manager return from the teller window. "Here's your receipt Mrs. Brown, with your daughter's name on the account as you requested."

Althea considered the receipt and stood to leave. The manager reached out and shook Seth Gentry's hand and Althea wondered if, someday, women would be treated equally. She recalled her many conversations with her husband and other politicians on how absurd it was that women could not vote just because of their gender.

After the women stood, Seth pulled back their chairs to give them room.

"Have a good day," Tobias Chandler said.

"Thank you," Althea said, letting Seth guide them out of the bank.

Seth sighed. "I feel better knowing that you aren't caring that large amount of money around anymore."

"A lot of people know I won that amount of money," Althea said, "but, not very many know that I put it in the bank."

She was right of course. Ranger Gentry knew that they were still in danger. Hatfield would have to keep an eye on the governor's wife and daughter. As much as he would enjoy being around Darla more, he needed to go after the outlaws.

The Brown women stopped at a shop window and started to go in. "You two be careful," Seth said, "I have to go talk to Ranger Hatfield."

"Don't worry, Seth, we'll be fine," Althea said.

Darla squeezed Seth's hand. "*You* be careful."

Seth laughed, "Giving orders already."

"Get used to it buster!"

Chapter 61

Dusk descended on the small line shack on the Circle J Ranch. It had been a long day riding and repairing fence, a never ending job on a large cattle ranch. Work didn't end at the fence line. Wood had to be cut and stacked, fire started, and water hauled. The cowboys didn't mind, as it was nearing the end of their workday and they could relax, and perhaps participate in a game of cards for a couple hours before hitting the sack.

The ranch hands went about their duties, having done this many times before, with one exception; Buck Henry sat idly at the table with his head in his hands feeling the pain of a hangover and of the physical beating by the hands of Captain Gentry. Chet Wagner often reminded the men that they were better off not having their bosses' son complaining and getting in the way. Buck Henry saw himself as privileged and he was a bully. His lack of participation in the work was the least of their worries; if he went on a rampage people could be hurt or even killed.

It was known that Len Campbell had bet against Buck and had won money from Buck's father and Len knew to avoid Buck as much as possible. He was fortunate to be known as the best cook and was busy getting a good fire going and assembling the makings for dinner.

"When's dinner ready, Campbell," Buck hollered.

"Won't be long, Buck," Len answered, not looking at him.

"I suppose its coffee and beans," Buck complained.

"I got some biscuits," Len said. "Elma gave me some afore we left."

"Great, cold biscuits," Buck snarled.

"This ain't the Sutter Creek Inn or the National Hotel," Len said.

Buck slammed his fist down on the table. "I didn't come here to eat no slop."

"Nor do any work, either," Len said.

Henry stood up, knocking his chair over. He started for Len with clenched fists. "By gawd, Campbell, I ain't going to take no lip from the likes of you."

The foreman stepped between the two. "Calm down, Buck, we got a long day tomorrow and these boys need to eat."

"No one can talk to me like that and get away with it," Buck growled.

Chet said to Len, "Get the grub ready. The boys are mighty hungry." He picked up Buck's chair and indicated for him to sit down.

"Hang on a second," Buck said, glaring at Campbell, and then went out the door. He had just remembered the bottle of whiskey he had in his saddlebags. When he came back in with the bottle, the most unpopular man in the shack just became friends with most everyone, except for the foreman and Len Campbell.

"Buck, put that bottle away," Chet Wagner said. "It ain't Saturday night."

"You can't tell me what to do, Wagner; who owns this ranch?"

"You're daddy does, Buck, and I'm running it," Wagner said.

Henry pulled the cork out with his teeth and guzzled some whiskey.

Wagner scanned the room. A couple of cowboys were licking their lips. He despised having Buck Henry here with his crew; wherever the man went he caused trouble and dissension. This whiskey bottle could be big trouble; the flip side was that if Buck got drunk he wouldn't be able to go out with the hands tomorrow. "Cork it and wait until after we eat. I don't want the boys having whiskey on an empty stomach."

In defiance, Buck took another drink. "Who says I'm sharing?" The loud click of the hammer on a revolver being pulled back silenced the room. Buck slowly turned at the ominous sound. "Ain't you supposed to be rustling grub?"

"Buck, you're like a burr under a saddle, irritating folks from all directions," Len Campbell said. "The only thing botherin' me about plugging you is that I would be out of a job; now I advise you to follow Chet's instructions."

Henry eyed the revolver in the cowboy's hand. The dark circular opening of the barrel seemed the size of a silver dollar. Buck corked the bottle and put it on the shelf behind him. "Now put that gun down; it might go off accidental like."

Campbell eased the hammer down and holstered his weapon. He turned to stir the pot of beans on the stove and Buck started to rise out of his chair.

"Stay where you are, Buck," the foreman said, "it's about time to eat."

Buck settled back down and glared at the back of Len Campbell. "It seems to me that *everybody* should be riding for the brand."

Campbell ignored the pointed comment.

The oldest cowboy, Joe Harbke, said, "Seems to me the only one that didn't do no riding today was you, Buck," his words whistling through missing teeth.

"Shut up and mind your own business, old man," Buck responded.

"You should treat your elders with more respect," Wagner said.

Harbke cackled and set tin plates on the table. "Buck would have to be awful lucky to live as long as I have."

Campbell grabbed a towel to put over the bean pot handle and took up a big wooden spoon and began dishing beans on to the tin plates, the cowboys joining Buck at the table. Everyone pretended not to notice that Buck got his beans last and they were runnier than the rest, splashing off the side of his plate. The ranch hands watched Buck with anticipation. The ranch owner's son was clenching his fist and snorting like an angry bull. Campbell scurried back to the stove without apology and took up the plate of biscuits. He deftly avoided getting near Henry and placed the biscuits at the far end of the table.

All the hands dove into their plate of beans only interrupted by the passing of the plate of biscuits. It arrived last to Buck Henry with one lone biscuit. Buck glared at the one biscuit and said, "You boys should have let more biscuits pass by so that I could soak up some of this slop. I'll be as generous with my whiskey."

"Here, you can have mine," Len Campbell said, tossing his biscuit into Buck's plate, splashing bean juice on the front of his shirt.

Furious, Buck said, "I'm going to kill you for that."

The following silence lay heavy in the small shack and was only broken by the intermittent sound of boiling coffee on the stove.

Chet reached over for Buck's coffee mug and put it next to his. "There ain't going to be no killing, Buck; bring us some coffee, Len."

Chapter 62

Captain Gentry rode Red up the Sierra Foothills toward the town of Volcano and the Circle J Ranch. He had asked Marshal Clements to keep an eye on the governor's wife and daughter and had asked the experienced marshal to give guidance to his young ranger. Jim Hatfield was a likeable young man, but as was the case for many a young man, his head had been turned by the attractive Priscilla Peabody. He needed the young ranger to be vigilant in his protection of Althea and Darla Brown.

Seth chuckled out loud and Red tossed his head as they worked their way up the crystal waters of Sutter Creek. He realized that he, too, had to often refocus when his head filled with pleasant thoughts of the governor's daughter. He had never met a woman like he---stubborn, intelligent and beautiful. He had been with a few women in the past and none of them held his interest like Darla Brown. Her sharp mind and spirit drew him in like a bee to pollen. Darla was strong and delicate and willful and sweet; an intricate intertwining of contradiction that he found fascinating.

Gentry and Red topped a tall hill and gazed down to a peaceful green valley with scattered cattle grazing. In the distance he saw puffy white clouds blanketing snowcapped peaks of the mighty Sierra Mountains. Seth sucked in a lungful of fresh air, enjoying the sweet scent of pine and California Chaparral. He leaned forward to pat the well-muscled sorrel. "This is God's country, Red," he said. As if in agreement, his horse nickered and tossed his head.

"According to Marshal Clements the Circle J is just a few miles yonder."

Ranger Gentry approached the large ranch house at an easy gallop. He saw no one about and just a few horses in the corral. He tied Red at the hitching rail in front of the large wooden porch. Seth scanned the yard and then went up the steps to the front door, his boots interrupting the acute silence. He knocked on the door and waited. No one answered. He knocked again and received the same results. Ranch houses often had more people enter and exit from back doors and Seth considered walking around to the back, but then he tried the door knob; the house was unlocked. The door hinges squeaked in protest as he pushed the door open. "Anyone home?" Seth hollered. He opened the door further and was greeted by a double-barreled shotgun pointed at his mid-section. His hands went up in the air. "Whoa, I'm friendly," he said.

"Que es, señor?" Maria asked.

"Mi, amigo," Seth said, "Ranger Seth Gentry."

"Who is it, Maria?" Elma entered the room wiping her hands with a towel.

"I'm Ranger Captain Seth Gentry, ma'am. I knocked on the door and no one answered."

Elma studied the ranger's battered face and considered the circled star on his chest. Satisfied she said, "Put the gun down, Maria. Did you come about the beating?"

"No, ma'am, this isn't about the fight I had with Buck. I'm trailing a couple outlaws and was wondering if anyone had seen them about."

"I wasn't talking about Buck. Two men beat and robbed Mr. Henry," Elma said. "Chang Lee went to fetch the doctor."

"I didn't know about that, ma'am. Could you describe the men to me?"

"I yust got a glimpse; two men, one smaller than the udder. They didn't look like nice men, by golly," Elma said.

"Sounds like the boys I'm looking for; how is Mr. Henry?"

"Muy malo," Maria said.

"Not goot; Chang, Maria and me put him on sofa in office." Elma added, "Come see."

Seth followed the two women into John Henry's office. He lay there unconscious with a cloth bandage around his head, his breathing shallow. Gentry surveyed the room and noticed the safe door was open. "Do either of you know what was taken from the safe?"

Elma and Maria both shook their heads.

"How long ago did this happen?" Seth asked.

"Two or three hours," Elma answered.

Gentry walked over to the safe and checked its contents. He didn't find much of value, mostly legal papers. A desk drawer was open and a small derringer lay on the floor. "Looks like those two took more than they had coming," he said.

They heard the arrival of horse and buggy through the open door. Seth walked quickly to the door and saw the buggy of the doctor and a Chinese man on horseback. The two women had followed him and Elma said, "That's Chang Lee bringing the doctor from Volcano."

The doctor grabbed his black leather medical bag and climbed down from the buggy. He was startled to see the big ranger standing at the top of the steps. "Name's Doctor Leonard; where's my patient?"

"In his office, doctor. I'm Captain Gentry of the California Rangers. I'm hunting the men that did this."

The doctor nodded then squeezed past the ranger and went directly to the office, having been to the house several times before. Seth and the two women followed behind. The doctor removed the bandage and examined John Henry. A moan emitted from the big man as the doctor felt around the wound. He then opened each eyelid and assessed his condition. He shook his head. "Mr. Henry's in a bad way;

there is a chance he won't make it. He has a severe skull fracture and may never come out of his comatose condition."

Elma had her hand to her mouth.

"What can they do, doctor?" Seth asked.

"Not a lot; they can take care of his needs, give him a spoonful of water once in a while. If he's still with us in a few days, give him a spoonful of soup on occasion."

The women nodded in understanding.

"Where's Buck?" the doctor asked.

"Mr. Henry was angry with him for losing the fight, drinking too much and losing his money; he sent him with the boys fixing fence," Elma said.

"Do you think Buck knew what was in the safe?" Seth asked.

The ranger nodded and thought about his next move. His first priority was to apprehend the two outlaws before they got too far away and disposed of their loot. "If Mr. Henry's condition changes, please notify me through Marshal Clements in Sutter Creek."

The doctor nodded. "I'll find someone to notify Buck," he said.

"Livery man say riders go south," Chang said.

"Thank you, Chang, I hope to catch up with them before they do any more damage," Seth said.

"Maybe go Jackson," Chang added.

"Very possible," Seth said, "and it's on the way to Sutter Creek."

Chang gave a quick nod and a slight bow. The ranger took his leave, deep in thought. *What would he do if he were the outlaws?*

Chapter 63

Len Campbell poured coffee at the table, keeping a wary eye out for Buck Henry.

"I don't want no coffee," Buck snarled. He rose abruptly and retrieved his bottle of whiskey.

"Go easy on that Buck, we have a long day tomorrow," the foreman said.

Buck glared at Chet Wagner. "I've told you before, Wagner, don't you be telling me what to do."

"It's for your own good."

"Right, and the health of others," he said, taking a drink from the bottle, wincing at the burning whiskey on cut lips. After another pull he let the bottle be passed around. "One drink for y'all, and none for Campbell; the rest is mine."

"That'd be the day I share a drink with you, Buck," Len said, causing Henry to ball up his ham-sized fists. The rest of the ranch hands seemed to shrink within, many of them wondering if Len was brave or just stupid.

Len Campbell wasn't stupid. He was enjoying needling the big bully and thought that Buck was the stupid one. Buck apparently didn't remember Len encouraging him to drink the night before the big fight. Buck might not be the brightest candle on the mantel, but he was very dangerous and he could never let his guard down around him.

The whiskey bottle made its way back to Henry and he took it to his bunk.

"If he finishes off that bottle he won't be worth nothing tomorrow," Joe Harbke said shaking his head.

"Let him be," Chet whispered, "he's more trouble than he's worth; I'm going to roll a smoke and then we best turn in."

Len and Joe cleaned off the table, both keeping an eye on Buck working on his bottle. Len had to smile every time Buck grimaced from the pain he felt from the beating he had taken.

Chet lighted his smoke, the flare of the Lucifer temporarily lighting the surrounding area. The distant lonely cry of a coyote and the musical song of crickets was not an unpleasant interruption to the peacefulness. He gazed up into the night sky at the prolific dusting of stars, the universe reminding man that he is only a small part of God's tapestry. Despite the hardship of life, it was nights like these that gave pause, and strength to continue on. Chet sighed and moaned from the stiffness of the day's labor that had set in, and rose from his seat.

The foreman entered the shack to a single burning candle providing just enough flickering light to find his bunk. The loud snoring of weary men greeted him. He peered over at Buck and found him sprawled on his back snoring the loudest of all, with the empty whiskey bottle lying on the floor. He usually enjoyed his work at the Circle J because of his authority and independence and camaraderie of the other hands, but when it was necessary to be around the Henrys it was unpleasant and burdensome. Until now he hadn't had to spend an extensive amount of time with Buck. As he removed his boots he hoped this was an anomaly that wouldn't be repeated. He lay back in his bunk and placed his hands behind his head. Despite the weariness of the day, sleep did not come easy. Being the foreman had its burdens and he thought of the miles of fence they had to check and repair the next day. The complexity of different personalities on his crew and his responsibilities weighed heavily on his shoulders. Then there was Buck Henry, the bosses' son who wouldn't recognize his authority, did very little work and stirred up trouble.

It seemed that he had just closed his eyes when the foreman was awakened by the rattling of pans and the welcoming smell of boiling coffee. He rolled out of his bunk with a stiff groan, turned over his boots and put them on. He looked out the window and saw the horizon greying before the dawn. Except for Joe and Len, everyone else was still sleeping in their bunks; Buck Henry sprawled on his back as he had seen him the night before.

Len smiled at Chet. "Sorry if we made too much noise."

"No problem," Chet said, "but I sure could use some of that coffee. Be careful you don't wake up sleeping beauty over there."

Joe looked over at the beaten and bloated Buck Henry with a cast iron fry pan in his hand. "I thought about putting this to use afore I put bacon in it," he cackled.

The aroma of frying bacon and hot coffee got the cowboys stirring. Being late to the table meant you would be starting the workday on an empty stomach. Not one of them complained about the re-heated beans. They often glanced over at the snoring Buck Henry, all hoping that he would not wake up any time soon. As each man finished he left to saddle his horse.

"What about him?" Len asked the foreman as he finished cleaning up. Both of them stared at the bully for a moment.

"Leave him lay," Chet said, "and no one pick up that bottle in case his father shows."

Riding fence was often hard work and the elements could be unforgiving, but this day was glorious. It was fair with a slight breeze and the spring flowers were in full bloom, the meadows carpeted with gold and yellow and purple flowers amongst the waving lush green grass. The creeks were running full and all seemed right with the world.

"I sure hope that blowhard don't show up," Joe Harbke said.

"If he did he wouldn't do no work," Len said. "All he does is cause trouble. I never enjoyed nothing more than that ranger takin' it to him."

Joe hooted. "Weren't that something."

"You boys quit your gabbin' and fix this fence," Chet said, attempting to hide his smile. He looked back over his shoulder in the direction of the line shack. He couldn't help but be relieved at not seeing Buck Henry approaching.

As the men packed up at the end of the day, Joe said to Chet, "Good, productive day."

Chet Wagner smiled at the old-timer. "Sure was, Joe." They all knew the unspoken relief that Buck hadn't shown.

Though tired and hungry, the hands rode back to the line shack with apprehension. None of them wanted to see Buck. As they approached the corral they were pleased to see that Buck's horse was gone.

"Looks like he mighta took out," Joe said.

"Let's hope so," Len said.

"You boys take care of my horse; I'm going to check inside," Chet said. "I'll get the fire going." Chet's shoulders relaxed when he verified that Buck had gone. "I wonder what kind of mischief that boy's off to," he said to himself.

Chapter 64

Ranger Gentry rode into the teeming town of Jackson. It was his first time in the Amador County Seat and there seemed to be an energy and prosperity that was missing in some of the Mother Lode towns he had been in, though every one of them had personality and he took the liberty of visualizing himself and Darla Brown settling in each one of them. Darla had expressed her fondness of Nevada City and had told him she 'adored' Sutter Creek. He smiled as he hitched his horse in front of the sign that announced the sheriff's office. The fact of the matter was that it didn't matter which town he was in as long as he was with her.

Seth entered the sheriff's office. Behind an old oak desk was a burly man with long grey sideburns and a sheriff's star on his vest. The man studied the circled star on the ranger's chest. "Sheriff Cartwright, I'm Captain Seth Gentry of the California Rangers," he said.

"Take a seat, Captain," the sheriff said. "Coffee's on; I'll get you a cup."

"Thank you, you can call me Seth."

The sheriff stood; he was at least six-foot-two-inches tall and had a barrel chest. "And you can call me Bill," he said with an amiable chuckle. "Your reputation supersedes you. Your fight with Buck Henry is the talk of the county."

Seth accepted a steaming mug. "News travels fast around here."

Cartwright sat back behind his desk. "John and Buck Henry, despite their wealth, are two of the most hated people in the county. Buck, in particular, is mean as a rabid bear.

He's trouble with a capital T. The news of someone whipping Buck was bigger than the news of a gold strike."

Gentry rubbed his sore jaw. "I assure you that it wasn't easy."

Cartwright studied the ranger's damaged face and nodded. "What brings you here?"

"I'm hunting a couple of outlaws. They're brothers that robbed the Amador City Bank, and robbed and beat John Henry," Seth said.

"I'd heard about the robbery, but not of John Henry; when did that happen?"

"Recently. I just came from the Circle J. The doc says that Henry may not make it. I was wondering if you are aware of two strange riders coming through your town."

"Not that I know of," Cartwright said, looking at a pendulum clock. "I'll gladly accompany you to ask around. The best place to start is the National Hotel and I'll buy you a cold beer."

Seth smiled and licked his lips. "I am a little parched."

"Let's go then," the sheriff said, sweeping his hat off of a hall tree.

The two lawmen received curious looks as they made their way to the impressive hotel at the end of the street. "Nice town you have here," Seth said.

"I was born and raised in this county," the sheriff said. "The towns have all grown considerably because of the rich gold strikes. As you can imagine, difficulties have increased with the growth; but it's a wonderful place to live and raise a family."

The duo ascended the tall steps to the hotel saloon. There was one lone miner at the bar and the bartender appeared happy to see them enter. "Cold beer, sheriff?"

"Make it two." This is Captain Gentry of the rangers and he would like to ask you a few questions."

"No problem," the bartender said as he poured two draft beers. "Coldest beer in town, ranger," he added.

Seth took a foamy sip. “Can’t argue there; tell me, have you seen two strangers ride through here recently?”

The bartender nodded. “One guy bigger than the other, trail worn?”

“Not very pleasant personalities,” Seth said.

“I wasn’t overrun by business, but I couldn’t wait for them to leave. The smaller one seemed to have a king-sized chip on his shoulder,” the bartender said. “There’s one other thing; for some reason I got the impression that they came in to be seen. They said they were heading down Mariposa way to do some mining.”

Seth thought about that. Mining was hard work and the Hayes brothers liked getting their money the easy way, by taking what was somebody else’s. It was apparent that announcing where they were going was a way to throw off anyone in pursuit. Where would they go from here? “How long ago did they leave?”

The bartender paused his wiping of glasses. “I’d say a couple of hours ago.”

A couple of hours would give the brothers time to be in Sutter Creek already, or even Amador City. Seth set his half-empty beer mug down. “I’ve got to go, sheriff; we can palaver another time.”

“Come on back anytime, Seth,” Cartwright said.

“Thanks for the beer.” Seth hurried out the door.

The old miner stared at the half-empty mug and the bartender casually slid it over to him. Having seen the look of determination on the ranger’s face, the bartender said, “I wouldn’t want that guy after me.”

Sheriff Cartwright watched the ranger ride out of town on his magnificent sorrel horse. “You got that right; pour me another beer.”

“Say, I saw that guy’s face; is he the ranger that whipped Buck Henry?”

Cartwright accepted a fresh mug and nodded. “The one and the same; he just informed me that those two boys you served beat up and robbed John Henry.”

"You don't say," the bartender said, resuming his cleaning of glasses. The two men watched the miner scurry out the door.

"That news will be all over town," the sheriff added.

"More like all over the county," the bartender said, "that old-timer will milk that news for as much beer and whiskey as he can. Things have been quiet of late."

Sheriff Cartwright nodded, and took a drink. He sighed and said, "Seems like when there is quiet it is followed by a storm."

Silence followed, the two men lost in their own thoughts. Both men enjoying the quiet camaraderie; the peacefulness was calming and relaxing.

The peace was interrupted by the sudden, impolite shoving of the door as someone bulled their way in. The sheriff looked at the reflection in the mirror and couldn't believe what he saw.

Chapter 65

"I got a hankerin' to ride over to Lulu Lamont's, Eli said as they rode into Sutter Creek. "I'd even be willing to take a bath for some of that trim."

Ned glared at his little brother. "Now ain't the time to be foolin' around, Eli."

"Come on, Ned, we got a little money and we should have a little fun."

"That's just it, we have a little money; we need to add to it and that politician's wife has a bunch she don't need."

Eli reined in. "Looky there, if it ain't that woman and her daughter." The brothers watched the Brown women exit one shop and enter another. "We could just go take her money right now."

Ned leaned on his saddle horn in thought. "There you go again, little brother, jumpin' in with no thought. You know that people don't cotton to women being mistreated; we have to be smart about this. We have to make a plan."

"We'll be having the law on our tail and we can't be foolin' around," Eli said. "I say we just go in there and get our money and hightail it out of town."

Ned watched Ranger Hatfield escort Priscilla Peabody into the same store. "Look at that, Eli, if we had done what you said that ranger would have walked right in on us."

"So, what, he's just a kid."

"There might have been gunplay and someone could have got killed," Ned said.

"Well, there would be one less lawman," Eli said.

Ned sighed. "Or one less brother," he said. Both brothers went silent in thought.

"You're so smart big brother, what are we going to do?"

"There's a saloon over there; let's get a drink and we can cogitate."

"That's my kind of planning," Eli said, leading his horse to the hitching rail.

The brothers ordered a beer with a whiskey back and sat at an empty table in the corner. There were only a few patrons this early in the day and the customers didn't pay any mind to the two vagabonds. "Don't see no dancin' girls," Eli lamented.

"Too early; drink while I think on it."

Eli drank and fidgeted.

"Sit still," Ned said, "you're interruptin' my thinking."

"That ain't my nature," Eli whined.

Several minutes passed and Eli went to the bar for two more drinks. He complained to the bartender, "We was at that table and no one come over for a drink order."

"It's early cowboy, stick around and we'll have someone by and by," the bartender said as he handed the drinks to the little man.

Eli returned to the table muttering, setting Ned's drink in front of him. "Well, what you got figgered, genius?"

Ned surveyed the room making sure that no one was in ear shot. "Them two women have a hotel room and no one is around them at night. We bust in tonight and politely ask them for their money and no harm will come to them.

Eli sneered. "Maybe we could have a little fun at the same time."

"Don't be stupid, Eli, every law dog in California would be on our tail; save it for Lulu's."

"Nothin' at Lulu's is as nice as them two women. They's beautiful and got class," Eli said wistfully.

"It just ain't worth it," Ned added. "I don't want no harm to come to those two. When we get that money you can have all them women at Lulu's and probably Lulu herself."

"All of them, including Lulu, don't together amount to that governor's wife and daughter."

Ned pushed his hat back and glared at his little brother. When his brother got his mind set there was no bending it. He was now convinced, more than ever, that when the two of them relieved those women of their money he would rid himself of his burdensome brother. The chances of him doing serious time in jail, or even getting hung, were a lot greater the longer the two of them stayed together.

Frustrated, Eli went to the bar for two more drinks. His brother didn't have the guts to get the most out of life. Things weren't going to be handed to you; life is not that easy. You had to take what you wanted. Most of the money the two of them had was due to his philosophy, taking from the stagecoach, the bank, and that rancher. Sure, he had to hurt or kill people to do it, but if he wasn't willing to do it they would have no money at all. What good was it to have a partner to split *his* money in half? Ned was blood and he didn't want to kill him, but once they got those two thousand dollars he was going to take his leave, perhaps to San Francisco. He put the two drinks on the table. Ned was lost in thought. It riled him that his oldest brother thought he was the smartest and the leader. He was the one of action and Ned often seemed to have paralysis by analysis. His brother, the mighty thinker, was slow as molasses. "What did you come up with, Ned?"

Ned scrutinized the room. Just above a whisper he said, "The way I figger it is that them women will be asleep about an hour after they go up to their room. Women are strange creatures, primping and fussin'. From what I've seen, morning or night you got to give'm lots of time."

Eli nodded and took a drink. "Seems like the long way around," he said.

"Yeah, but it's the best way; we don't want no alarm raised. We surprise them, get the money and get out."

"You make it sound easy," Eli said. "Things is never that easy."

"This could be the way I got it planned. There are two of us and two of them; we each grab one and make sure they don't make no noise and we demand the money if they don't want to get hurt. We gag and tie them up and take the money and run."

"I still say we should have a little fun first," Eli said.

"Think about it, Eli, ifin' we get caught with our pants down they'll hang us from the nearest tree. You saw that tree in Jackson with a rope hanging from it."

"Well, this ain't Jackson," Eli said.

"Close enough; let's find them women and find which room they are in."

Ned stood and Eli polished off his drink. "I'm ready for some grub," Ned said. "Maybe we'll find them at the hotel."

Chapter 66

Sheriff Cartwright turned to see Buck Henry standing inside the door. With the beating from the fight and with a severe hangover, Cartwright had never seen the rancher's son look worse.

"Uh-oh," the bartender said, "here comes trouble."

Cartwright chuckled. "His reputation do precede him."

"Sheriff, I ain't here for trouble, just needin' a drink," Buck growled.

"I'm glad to hear that, Buck. I wasn't in a mood to do any arrestin'."

"Whiskey, barkeep," Buck demanded. Without a word the bartender poured a shot, not wanting to engage in any conversation.

Buck tossed the shot in one gulp and demanded another.

"What are you doing in Jackson this time of day?" The sheriff asked.

Bleary eyed, Buck said, "None of your business."

With a stern look the sheriff said, "I'm the law in this county, Buck Henry. If I ask you a question you had best answer it."

"Give me another, barkeep," Buck said. "Relax, sheriff, I told you I wasn't here for no trouble. I'm just on my way to Sutter Creek and needed a drink."

The sheriff regarded the flushed and battered face of Buck Henry, deciding this boy was on a fast downhill slide. "How's your father doing?"

With the third drink in hand, Buck took a sip. "Ornery as ever."

"I meant health-wise; I heard he was beaten and robbed."

Buck started. "Don't know nothin' about that, I been riding fence. What happened?"

"A couple of fellas whacked him over the head and robbed whatever your father had in the safe."

Buck downed his whiskey and ordered another. "I'll be dogged; the old guy got some of his own treatment."

Sheriff Cartwright regarded John Henry's son with disgust. There was a total lack of sentiment from the young man, though he shouldn't be surprised. "I hear he's bad off and may not make it."

Henry accepted his fourth whiskey. "You don't say."

Cartwright thought about Sutter Creek and Marshal Clements; if Buck continued on in his condition there was bound to be trouble. "Maybe it would be best if you head back to the ranch and check on your father; Ranger Gentry was up that way and was curious what might have been taken from you father's safe."

Buck lifted his glass and squinted at the sheriff. After another drink he said, "Finally feeling better," running his words together as a result of the alcohol.

"What about it Buck?"

"Whata about what?"

"You going to check on your father, and what is missing from the safe?" the sheriff asked.

"How would I know; that old codger never let me see what he had."

The sheriff studied the slouching man. He never liked Buck Henry, or his father for that matter, but he even liked Buck less now, if that was possible. "Well, you going back to the ranch?"

Buck leaned on the bar on his elbows and seemed to be swaying slightly. Thoughts of his father were being replaced by the vision of Priscilla Peabody. There was something about that girl that stirred him something awful. The fresh freckle-faced beauty was so sweet, so innocent and unbelievably pure; he just had to have her. He clenched the fist that wasn't holding the glass. The idea of that young ranger beating him to her was tearing at his craw. It was time to ride to Sutter Creek.

Sheriff Cartwright watched Buck stagger out the door without a word. He hadn't even bothered to pay for his drinks. "He didn't pay," he said to the bartender.

"Didn't want no trouble. Besides, his father has a tab here."

"You'd best hope John Henry lives to pay that tab," the sheriff said, watching Buck ride out in the opposite direction of the Circle J. "That boy's up to no good."

The bartender nodded. "I'd be a rich man if I had all the money that boy has cost our drinking establishments in this county."

Cartwright walked back to his office, tipping his hat to some ladies on a shopping mission. The day was still young and the town of Jackson was quiet, and thankfully Buck Henry had left town. He locked his office door and walked to the livery.

Chapter 67

Arm in arm, Priscilla Peabody and James Hatfield strolled happily down the main street of Sutter Creek. Althea Brown and her daughter were enjoying a noon meal at the hotel and Mrs. Brown had encouraged Hatfield and the young preacher's daughter to enjoy the town. The governor's wife had insisted they would be safe in the hotel and that she and her daughter were going to their room after their meal.

"Looks like Jimmie has caught the love bug," Darla said to her mother.

Althea smiled at her daughter. "She's not the only one."

"Mother, please!"

"It is not like it is a disease," her mother said, "but it is a wonderful affliction. There is nothing like being in love."

Darla played with her food.

"Seth is an awful handsome man. I wouldn't toy with his emotions too long."

"I am not toying with his emotions, mother."

"What I mean, dear daughter, is don't be too hard on Seth about his chosen profession and being a *man.*"

"Men are dumb sometimes," Darla moaned.

"Sweetheart, you need to look at it a little differently. Men are *different* than women; and be glad that the genders are different."

"I know, mother, but it drives me crazy sometimes."

Althea laughed. "Don't you think women drive men crazy sometimes?"

"I guess, but women don't fight and shoot each other."

"It has been known to happen. I saw a girl fight in school one time that was downright vicious," Althea said.

It suddenly grew quiet in the hotel restaurant and all eyes were toward the door. Standing there in all their glory were Ned and Eli Hayes. There were three empty tables available and the waitress guided the unkempt pair to the farthest, darkest corner near the kitchen. The restaurant catered to a higher class of people and it was rare to see men of this low character enter the establishment.

"I don't like the way them people are staring at us," Eli grumbled to his brother as they took their seats.

"Don't worry what other people think, Eli; we are here for some grub and to keep an eye on those women over there."

Eli turned to look over his shoulder.

"Don't be so obvious," Ned hissed.

"Jest lookin'," Eli snapped.

The waitress took their order and the food was delivered quickly. The restaurant workers had been through this before and knew that the sooner unwanted guests were served the sooner they would leave.

Ned kept an eye on the two Brown women and soon realized that even though they were in the restaurant before them, they were having a leisurely meal. Much to Ned's consternation Eli kept looking back over his shoulder at the two women. "Eli, stop that, they will get suspicious."

"Them two women are lucky to be so good lookin'; I hate people who think they are better than me," Eli said.

"What little I seen of them two, I don't get to thinkin' that they feel that way," Ned said.

"I'd sure like to show them what a real man is like," Eli said.

Ned sighed; he was growing weary of his brother's narrow-minded ways. "When they leave we'll see if they go to their room so we know which one is theirs."

Suddenly there was the sound of gunshots. Darla's eyes widened. Her mother touched her hand as some people left to see what had happened. "It's safest to stay right here," Althea said.

A man stuck his head in the door and yelled, "The ranger's been shot!"

Chapter 68

Darla Brown screamed, “Oh, mother, someone’s shot Seth!” She stood up, frantic, and started to run out of the restaurant.

Althea grabbed her daughter by the arm. “The shooter may still be out there.”

“I don’t care, mother, I have to tend to Seth.”

“Pay the bill little brother, we’re gonna have to follow them women,” Ned said.

Mumbling, Eli reached into his pocket. “I’m always the one that pays.”

Darla ran outside and watched a small man with a leather satchel hurrying across the street to a crowd of people. “Oh, mother, he’s over there,” she said, picking up her dress to rush across the street. She unceremoniously pushed her way through the throng of onlookers.

Lying on the ground and bleeding from the shoulder was Jim Hatfield. The ladies’ fear for Seth was immediately replaced by concern for Jim.

The doctor tore open Hatfield’s shirt to look at the profusely bleeding wound.

The gathering parted for the arrival of Marshal Clements. “How is he Doc; what happened here?”

The young ranger moaned as the doctor turned Hatfield to see if the wound had exited out the back. The doctor looked up at the marshal. “I’ve got to take the bullet out; get some men to carry him to my office.”

“What happened, Jim?” the marshal asked again.

“Got shot,” he muttered.

"I can see that; did you see who did it?"

"Not sure. Is Priscilla okay?"

Darla and Althea scanned the crowd. "Don't see her," Althea said.

"Is Jimmie going to be alright, doctor?" Darla asked.

"As soon as I get the bullet out, but he'll take some time to mend," the doctor said.

"I seen the whole thing, marshal," Tinker said from the back of the gathering.

"That Buck Henry rode in to town drunk and meaner than a griz just out of hibernation. He just up and shot that youngin' and took Priscilla away."

"He kidnapped Priscilla?"

"Yes, sir, seen it with my own two eyes," Tinker said.

The marshal picked two young men to carry Hatfield to the doctor's office.

"Which way did he go?" the marshal asked.

"That way," Tinker said pointing north.

"I'm not the only one that shoots people," Eli said to his brother.

"Well, I'm glad it's not you that done it for a change."

Eli stepped back into the shadows and pointed down the street. "Looky there."

Riding into town was Ranger Gentry. He reined in when he saw the governor's wife and daughter. "What's the commotion about?"

"Oh, Seth, Jimmie's been shot," Darla said, her voice aquiver.

"I seen it, captain," Tinker said, "it was Buck Henry and he took Miss Priscilla."

"Took her?"

"Yes, suh, grabbed her right up and rode off that away."

Seth turned his attention to Darla; she was shaking like a leaf. "How's James doing?"

"Oh, Seth, at first I thought it was you when they said the ranger had been shot; now I'm so worried about Jimmie."

Gentry was learning that women often wouldn't answer a question directly. "What's his condition?"

"He was shot in the shoulder and the doctor is trying to get the bullet out," Darla said.

Marshal Clements walked toward them carrying a double-barreled shotgun. "I'm glad you're here, Seth. I'm going after Buck and would appreciate you watching the town."

"I'll go with you," Gentry said.

"No, I'd feel better if you stayed here, with the governor's wife being here and all."

"Have it your way, but I'm here if you need me. I'm going to escort the ladies and check on Jim."

The trio arrived at the doctor's office in the front of his home. The doctor's wife told them he was attempting to get the bullet out now and should be done shortly. She was delighted to have the governor's wife and daughter in her home and set about brewing some tea.

As they sat anxiously in the parlor waiting for the doctor, Darla said, "I hope Jimmie will be alright. Seth, it worries me so, this ranger business you two are in."

Gentry smiled and took her hand. "It could be worse. I could go into politics."

Althea laughed and Seth's comment brought a small smile to Darla's face. "He's got a point there, dear," Althea said. "Politics can be very brutal and stressful."

"Yes, but politicians usually don't get shot," Darla said.

"Tell Mr. Lincoln that," Seth said and immediately regretted it. Adding to Darla's worry wasn't the smartest thing to do.

The doctor entered the parlor wiping his hands on a towel. "I got the bullet out and the young man has lost some blood but I think he should be as good as new in a couple of weeks. He's resting peacefully and you can see him later when he comes around."

"Thanks, doctor," Seth said. He squeezed Darla's hand. "See there's nothing to worry about." He watched the doctor go over to the sideboard and pour a drink.

"Join me, Mr. Gentry?"

"Don't mind if I do, doc; I'm not too partial to tea, and please call me Seth."

The doctor nodded and poured another drink, handing it to the ranger as his wife entered with a tray of tea and some cookies. "Mrs. and Miss Brown, I am so pleased to have you as guests in my home. I just wish it was under more pleasant circumstances."

"Please call me Althea, and my daughter is Darla."

"And please call me Ruth and my husband is Bert," the doctor's wife said.

"This is Captain Seth Gentry of the California Rangers," Althea said.

"Yes, the captain has made quite a reputation around here in a very short period of time," Ruth said with a smile.

"Here's to better days." The doctor saluted with his glass of whiskey.

The ladies raised their teacups in response, wondering how much the doctor self-medicated.

Behind some bushes and in the dark shadow of a large elm tree the Hayes brothers observed the doctor's office. "I don't like waitin' around," Eli said.

"Have some patience little brother," Ned said.

"I don't like that ranger hangin' around neither," Eli added.

"Yeah, I wish he had gone with the marshal, but the women will be alone tonight."

Then the brothers saw Preacher Peabody rushing down the street and they stepped deeper into the shadows.

Chapter 69

Marshal Sam Clements worked his way up a small green valley following the heavy tracks of what he perceived to be a horse carrying a lot of weight. He estimated he was only a couple of hours behind Buck Henry. He had ridden up this valley before and he was thinking about what was ahead. There were a couple of old abandoned miner's shacks up this way and Buck would probably know about them. If he were to lose the tracks he would check on those shacks first.

The marshal watched his horse's ears for any sign of trouble as they topped a small rise to see the first shack near the crest of the next hill. Cautiously he reined in his horse and watched and listened. Except for the melodic trill of birds all was quiet. Despite the peacefulness the marshal did not approach the small cabin directly, swinging his horse off to the right near the tree line. This way he could observe the shack and check to see if anyone was hidden amongst the trees. Pine needles on the ground seemed to be undisturbed and the shack seemed to be unoccupied. He approached the right side of the structure, stopped and listened.

Silence. "Hello the house," he yelled, his voice echoing down the hill. "Marshal Sam Clements here, anyone home?"

The marshal was greeted with more silence, the birds no longer singing. He loosened the revolver in his holster and dismounted, keeping his horse between him and the building. Clements worked his way to the edge of a porch that had seen better days, knowing that once he stepped on it total quiet would be impossible. He removed the revolver from his holster and went up the steps on his toes. He halted when he heard scurrying inside. He held his breath and listened. He heard more rustling. There was a slight breeze and there was no glass in the front window. Perhaps it was just debris.

Clements eased toward the window, removed his hat and peeked in. The interior was dark and from what he could tell it appeared empty. He tiptoed to the door, turned the handle and then shoved it open, assuring that no one was hiding by the door. He stepped to the side to be safe. "Anyone home?" he called.

He was met by silence. He closed his eyes to adjust to the dim light and stepped in. Some rats scurried off, and Clements was greeted by quiet emptiness. He holstered his revolver and walked over to an open cabinet. There was no evidence that the place had been inhabited recently. The marshal sighed, scanned the room and turned to leave. Then he saw it.

On an exposed nail near the door was a piece of cloth. It appeared to be gingham as if from a women's dress. He removed it from the nail and looked at it closely, trying to recall if he had seen what Priscilla was wearing that day. Had Buck stopped here, and seeing the poor condition of the shack, moved on?

The marshal put the cloth in his vest pocket and continued on. He lost the tracks of Buck's horse in the rocky terrain and decided to set his horse in a gallop to the next shack that he estimated was six miles away.

Marshal Clements felt anxious. Hunting a man was always troublesome, but the added element of a young woman in danger made him more uneasy than usual. He came upon a small pond and let his horse drink, scanning the empty horizon. The shadows were lengthening, adding to the trepidation he felt.

After a lengthy ride the marshal saw the second shack in the distance. As he rode nearer he felt disappointment at not seeing any activity. There was no horse about but he still approached with caution. This shack seemed to be in better condition than the first and was a more likely spot for Buck to hole up. Clements swung wide in an attempt to avoid detection, riding up a small knoll to get an overall view. Behind the cabin was an empty corral. If Buck had been here it appeared that he had moved on.

Clements tied his horse to a manzanita bush and approached the structure on foot, moving with the utmost caution. He loosened his revolver in his holster and eased himself on to the rickety porch. He was met with absolute quiet. "Anyone here?" Clements announced his presence.

Silence.

With gun drawn, the marshal peered into the dark interior. Seeing no movement, he closed his eyes briefly and stepped inside. What he saw made him swallow back the bile that arose from his stomach.

Chapter 70

"What's happened to my daughter?" Endicott Peabody yelled. "Why are you not looking for her, ranger? They say Buck took her!"

"Take it easy, Mr. Peabody; Marshal Clements has gone after her. With the governor's wife and daughter in town and with a couple of killers on the loose he asked that I stay here."

"That Buck Henry is such an awful man; I heard he shot that young ranger," the reverend said.

"That's true; thankfully, it looks like Hatfield will make it."

"Those Henrys are just no good; they are disciples of the devil," the reverend said.

"John Henry won't be a problem for a long time, if ever."

"Why do you say that, captain?"

"He was beaten and robbed on his ranch and he may not make it."

"I'll pray for his recovery and the good Lord's forgiveness for what I just said. Please let me know if you hear anything about my daughter" The reverend shuffled off, slump-shouldered.

"I so feel for that man," Darla said squeezing Seth's arm.

"I can't imagine what he is going through," Althea said, "I would just die if something happened to you, Darla."

"It disturbs me how cruel the world can be," Darla lamented.

Seth stood. "Let's get supper so you two can turn in safely for the night. I've got to make the rounds, with the marshal out of town."

*****

Marshal Clements stepped out onto the porch and sucked in some fresh air. What he had just seen turned his stomach and he had to decide how to deal with it. Inside the shack he had stared into the empty blue eyes of Priscilla Peabody. Her dress was torn down to her waist and it appeared she had been choked to death. The marshal had never witnessed such a violent act against a woman and it shook him to his core. Women were scarce in the west and the code of the west said that a man was never to harm a woman. Even saloon girls and soiled doves were treated with respect by the most crude of men. Alas, there were always the few exceptions like Buck Henry.

As much as Clements wanted to pursue Buck Henry, he couldn't leave Priscilla; he would take her home and go after Henry later. He wrapped the young woman in his slicker and put her over his horse. "I wish I could do this in a more dignified manner, Miss Priscilla, but I don't have much of a choice," the marshal said, choking up. He mounted up, holding on to his precious cargo, and slowly made his way down the hill.

*****

Ned and Eli Hayes waited in the deep shadows outside the hotel. They could see the two women and the ranger through the window of the restaurant. "As soon as they're done, you stay here, Eli, and I'll sneak over and see what room them women go to. You keep an eye on that ranger."

The meal had been a solemn one. The shooting of James Hatfield and the kidnapping of Priscilla Peabody had caused a pall of concern and fear over the small town of Sutter Creek.

Darla put her fork down and gazed into Seth's eyes. "I'm afraid. I'm afraid for Jimmy and afraid for you."

"There's nothing wrong with that, Darla. Sometimes I think fear is a good thing. I have a lot of fear---fear of letting your father down, fear of dishonoring my parents, fear of not doing a proper job, fear of disappointing you, and most of all, fear of losing you."

"Phew, big tough Captain Gentry afraid!" Darla spat.

"Yes, and fear keeps me sharp and on my toes, just as your fear should keep you aware." Seth watched Althea nod. "I am sure your mother has her own fears."

"He's right, honey, fear is a part of life and as Seth so eloquently put it fear can be quite useful if kept in perspective."

Zeke poked his head into the restaurant. "Ranger, the marshal's riding down the street and he's got something slung over his horse!"

Seth grabbed his hat and hurried out the door. Marshal Clements was riding slowly toward him, with a grave expression. "What have you got?" Seth asked.

The marshal wearily dismounted. "Give me a hand, Seth, I'm plumb done in; it's Miss Priscilla."

"Ah, no…!" Seth lifted the body down from the horse. *She was so tiny and so young.* He carried her into the hotel and laid her down. The weary marshal followed, hat in hand.

"I found her in a shack up yonder, choked to death," he said just above a whisper. "Buck was long gone; looked like she put up a fight."

Althea and Darla Brown stood aghast in the shadows of the restaurant. "Poor Pricilla," Althea said, "and like you, she's the reverend's only daughter."

Darla took her mother's hand, tears streaking down her face. "Poor Jimmie. He's not only shot but will have a broken heart."

*****

Ned Hayes snuck up on the porch and peeked in the window. He had overheard that the small body wrapped in the slicker was Pricilla Peabody. There was a funereal atmosphere, and people were standing around crying. His eyes settled on the two Brown women. He stepped back into the shadows and waited. He felt certain that the women would retire to their room shortly. He leaned around the edge of the window and saw the marshal and ranger talking to each other in a quiet manner, unable to tell what they were saying. He saw the ranger turn to the women and say something. Mrs. Brown nodded and took her daughter by the arm and went upstairs.

Eli watched his brother turn and walk back toward him. “Well?” he asked.

“I seen the room they’s in, so now we wait until they turn in,” Ned said.

The brothers watched the marshal and ranger come out of the hotel and walk down the dark street. They overheard Marshal Clements say, “I sure hate to have to break the news to Endicott.”

Seth rubbed his eyes. “Hard part of the job; I hate having to tell Jim Hatfield about this when he’s able.”

“I don’t know which one is worse,” Clements said.

The lawmen walked in silence, lost in their own thoughts.

“I’ll stop at the undertaker’s and then head over to the reverend’s,” Clements said.

“Ranger Hatfield won’t be up to the bad news just yet, so I guess I’ll tag along.”

Marshal Clements stopped and nodded to the young ranger. “Appreciate it,” he said.

Chapter 71

The Hayes brothers watched the undertaker arrive and put the body of Pricilla Peabody in a black hearse.

"Such a waste," Eli said. "She was mighty fine."

Disgusted, Ned glared at his brother. "She was just a kid."

"A growed up kid," Eli said.

"Get your mind on the job at hand; we need to relieve the governor's wife of the burden of all that money she won."

"They must be asleep by now," Eli said, looking into the dimly lit hotel.

"We don't want to make no commotion. We got to be quiet as mice and get away without no one seeing us."

"I still think we should enjoy our spoils," Eli said, rubbing himself.

Flushed with anger, Ned said, "You keep that gun holstered and your pecker in your pants, you hear?"

"I sure get tired of you ordering me around."

"We don't need no more trouble; we get the money and get out of town. Go quiet to the window and see if the clerk is there and if he is, make sure he's asleep; if so, wave me in and we'll grab a key off the board to room 6 and sneak upstairs."

Eli glared at his brother; *there he goes again.*

After a moment, Ned watched his brother quietly approach the hotel window and look in. The clerk was sound asleep at the desk. He waved his brother up on the porch.

"You go get the key, and ifin' he awakes conk him on the head," Ned said. "Try not to kill him if you have to hit him."

The Hayes brothers tiptoed into the lobby; As Eli retrieved the key to room 6 off the board the clerk snorted, causing Eli to draw his gun, but the man remained asleep. Before mounting the stairs Ned whispered, "Stay to the sides so the stairs don't squeak."

"If you weren't so big they wouldn't be squeaking," Eli snarled.

They eased across the hallway and Ned placed his ear to the door of room 6 and took the key from his brother. He carefully inserted the key and when he turned it, the click sounded as if it were a gunshot in the still of the night. He paused and listened. He didn't hear anyone stirring so he slowly turned the knob. Holding his breath, he eased the door open, the hinges creaking. He peeked around the door and saw the governor's wife and daughter sleeping peacefully. Ned signaled for his brother to follow him into the room. As they crept into the room Ned put his hand to his mouth and pointed to Darla Brown. Eli nodded and Ned went around the bed to the governor's wife. When they were in position Ned whispered, "Now," and they grabbed the two women with their hands over their mouths to stifle any screams.

With wide, frightened eyes both women struggled. With his other hand, Ned pulled his gun and pointed it at Darla's head. "Listen very carefully Mrs. Brown; if you cooperated no one will get hurt. If you do not cooperate I will put a bullet in your daughter's pretty little head. Do you understand?"

Althea Brown attempted a nod despite Ned's tight grip over her mouth. She looked at her frightened daughter, who fixated on the business end of a large revolver.

"Now, Mrs. Brown, I am going to take my hand off of your mouth and you will quietly answer me; do you understand?"

The governor's wife attempted another nod. Ned eased his hand off, keeping his gun pointed at Darla's head. "Now, tell me where that money is that you won and your daughter won't get hurt."

"It's not here," Althea said.

"What do you mean it's not here?" Eli demanded.

Althea looked at the little man as if he was dumb as a post. Eli despised being looked down upon by those that thought they were better than him. He drew back his empty hand to slap the governor's wife. Ned grabbed his brother's hand.

"I don't take no sass from an uppity woman," Eli said.

"Where's the money, Mrs. Brown?" Ned sneered, pulling back the hammer of his revolver with a loud click.

"We put it in the bank," Althea said. "The ranger felt it would be safer there."

Eli glared at his brother. "Another fine plan, Ned; now what?"

Ned thought for a moment, and spotted some clothes hanging over a dressing screen. "She may not be telling the truth; we'll search the room. Mrs. Brown, be careful and go get them clothes and bring them here. No shenanigans or you'll never see your daughter alive again."

The governor's wife brought a petticoat over to Ned and laid it on the bed.

"Now tear off some strips of cloth."

Althea did as she was told.

"Tie your daughter's hands behind her back, nice and tight," Ned ordered.

Mrs. Brown hesitated for a moment and then did as she was told. The fright showing on her daughter's face made the bile rise from her stomach. She swallowed hard and tied Darla's hands as loosely as she could without being obvious.

"Eli, gag the young lady and tie Mrs. Brown's hands behind her back."

Even though she attempted to swell up, Althea cried out when thc little Hayes brother snugged her wrists so tight it was painful.

"One more time, Mrs. Brown---are you sure the money ain't here?" Ned asked.

"Like I told you, the money is in the bank."

"Gag her, Eli, then will take a look see."

The Hayes brothers tore the room apart. They emptied all the trunks and drawers, taking the drawers out and checking the backs and bottoms.

"Don't look like it's here," Eli said. "Maybe she told the truth; now what are we going to do, genius?" He wondered if his brother ever made a plan that worked out.

Ned hooked his thumbs in his gun belt and considered his options. If they robbed the bank there was no guarantee they would get the money and they could be discovered, or even killed. If harm came to the two women it might even be worse for them. He had the additional complication of his brother either harming the women or killing someone, especially if they robbed the bank.

"Well, smart guy, what are we going to do?" Eli said, caressing the cheek of Darla Brown. "Mayhap we just enjoy ourselves for a little while."

"I told you, Eli, no unnecessary harm is to come to those women. I got a plan; we'll just wait for morning when the bank opens."

Chapter 72

Dawn was brightening as Marshal Clements and Ranger Gentry entered the Sutter Creek Café. The mixed aroma of strong coffee and cooking food welcomed them as Clements took a chair against the wall at a table in the back.

Hattie Reutter, the owner, brought them coffee. “The usual, marshal?”

“Yes, Hattie, make it two,” Clements said.

“Coming right up,” Hattie said.

“Nice lady,” Seth said.

“One of the best, and she’s a great cook.”

“What’s the plan, today?” Seth asked.

The marshal took a drink of his coffee. “I’m going to ride up to the Circle J and see if I can locate Buck and check on his father’s condition.”

Seth nodded. “Maybe I should go with you.”

Hattie placed a steaming plate of steak and eggs in front of each of them.

The marshal started cutting into his steak. “I think it would be best if you would stay here,” he said. “I’d like the company and the help, but with your young ranger down and the governor’s wife and daughter here I would feel better if you stayed in town. You never know, those bank robbers might show and maybe even Buck would come to town. Buck might just figure we would be out looking for him.”

“You’ve got a point, Sam; I think I was just avoiding having to tell Jim Hatfield about Priscilla.”

Marshal Clements nodded. “Last night was the worst. When I told Endicott about his daughter, I thought he was going to die right there of grief. I sent someone for the doctor and stayed with him until he showed. The doc gave him something to knock him out. I can't imagine what he'll be like today."

"Another reason to leave town," Seth said.

"And another reason I want you to stay."

"Thanks, marshal."

"Think nothing of it."

The two lawmen lingered over coffee, lost in their own thoughts.

Finally, the marshal said, "I'd best hit the trail."

Seth took up his hat and rose from the table. "And I'd better get over to the Doc's and check on Hatfield."

"Maybe you should take the governor's wife and daughter with you; it might help."

"I wish I could; I'll let them sleep in. It's my duty to tell him," Seth said.

The two men stepped outside and both took in the fresh mountain air. "You've got a nice town here marshal."

"Except for the bad things," Clements said with a sigh. "I'll be back this afternoon; I appreciate you keeping the bad things corralled.

"Don't worry, you take care, Sam," Seth said as the two men split up.

The doctor's wife greeted Seth as he entered the office.

"How's the patient doing," Seth asked.

"Chomping at the bit. Says he wants out of here, but we're going to keep him another day. Come on back; maybe you could cheer him up."

Seth took a deep breath. "It won't be today."

The doctor's wife stopped and considered Seth's serious face. "Doesn't sound good," she said.

"It's not; is he able to handle some bad news?"

"Physically he is," she said, escorting the ranger to the back room.

"Hey, captain, you come to get me out of this place?" Ranger Hatfield said with eagerness.

Gentry shook his head. "No, they're keeping you another day."

"Aw, I'm fine." The young ranger sat up with a groan.

Seth observed James Hatfield. He was shirtless and had a large bandage wrapped around his chest and shoulder. The color in his face had returned and he was looking more like his normal self.

"Have you seen Pricilla?" Hatfield asked. "I haven't seen her since I was shot, though I was kind of out of it for a while." He considered the captain. Gentry seemed to be struggling for what to say. "Is something wrong, captain?"

Seth inhaled deeply. "There is no easy way to tell you this, Jim, but Pricilla is dead. Marshal Clements found her in a shack and it looked like she had been strangled. I'm so sorry."

Shock overtook the young ranger. "Dead…Pricilla is *dead*?"

"I'm afraid so," Seth said.

'Was it Buck, the one who shot me?"

"It appears so; the marshal went back after him, uh, after he brought Pricilla back home."

Ranger Hatfield struggled to get up, tears streaking down his face. "I've got to see her; I've got to help the marshal." But he moaned, clearly in significant pain.

Captain Gentry put a gentle hand on the young ranger's chest and guided him back, staying away from his bandaged wound. "You are not going anywhere this day; doctor's orders. I'll come by tomorrow and we'll figure out what we can do."

Ranger Hatfield was breathing heavily and wiping tears from his face. "Some tough guy, aren't I?"

Sympathy for the young man overwhelmed Seth and his eyes began to water. "Having feelings does not indicate a lack of toughness," he said. "In fact, empathy makes you a better man and a better lawman. If we didn't care about others we would be no better than the bad guys."

Jim Hatfield sniffed. "I can't believe she's gone," he said softly. "She was so sweet and vivacious and so young."

Gentry nodded. "I guess God was in need of another angel."

"He got a good one," Hatfield whispered.

Silence overtook the room. Seth put his hat back on and took hold of the door knob. "I've got to make my rounds for the marshal, but I'll be back tomorrow," he said, leaving Jim to his own thoughts.

Chapter 73

"What we going to do, Ned?" Eli asked.

"We can't have no shoot-out at the bank; they's just too many lawmen around these parts. We hunker down here and wait for morning and then I'll take Mrs. Fancy Lady to the bank for a withdrawal. You stay here with the young lady until I return with the money."

Eli glared at his brother in silence. What would keep Ned from taking the money and running? His brother thought of himself as the brains of the outfit, but every plan he came up with never seemed to work out. Ned was too soft and too unwilling to use force when necessary. It would be best if he went to the bank for the money. Then he had an idea to outsmart his brother. "Sounds like a good plan, Ned; I like the idea of being alone with the girl," he said stroking her arm as she attempted to shy away.

Althea Brown's eyes widened and she struggled against her restraints. She would rather die than have something happen to her precious daughter. She wiggled and moaned.

Ned observed Mrs. Brown's reaction to Eli fondling her daughter. When the bank opened he needed her to appear as normal as possible when they withdrew the money. Leaving Eli alone with Darla Brown would cause Mrs. Brown to be stressed and unpredictable. Perhaps it would be best if Eli accompanied the governor's wife to the bank. But, then again, Eli couldn't be counted on to be predictable himself. "I told you before, Eli, no harm should come to these women as long as they do what we say."

Eli Hayes licked his lips. “I ain’t going to jest sit around here; I’m going to have some fun,” he said with a smirk.

Althea was shaking her head, eyes wide with fright. Ned had an urge to punch his brother. Eli had no common sense. He was driven by the impulse for immediate gratification, which was one of the reasons he had a hair trigger.

“Yep, I think I’m going to have me some fun,” Eli added as he began to remove his gun belt.

Ned reconsidered his situation. There was no way that he could leave his little brother alone with one of the women. On the other hand, if he allowed Eli to take Mrs. Brown to the bank there was no guarantee that violence would not break out. He watched as his brother hung his gun belt over the bedpost. He sighed and pulled his gun from its holster, the whisper of leather and the loud click of the hammer being pulled back giving pause to Eli’s movement.

“Ned, what are you doing pulling a gun on me?”

“For the last time, Eli, no harm is to come to these women. Our lives wouldn’t be worth two cents if something were to happen to them. Now I want you to settle down and get some rest and you’ll be taking Mrs. Brown to the bank in a few hours.”

Eli’s gun hand twitched and he looked over at his gun. Maybe it was time to be rid of his big brother. He was tired of taking orders that never seemed to pan out. He clenched both fists, cognizant of the fact that his brother had the drop on him. His eyes took in the frightened women on the bed. What a waste it was to just leave them be. Then he regarded the cocked revolver pointed at his midsection. Circumstance dictated that now was not the time to go against his brother’s wishes. “I thought you said you was going to the bank,” he said.

“Changed my mind. I will watch over the young lady, but you better not be trigger happy; we need to get the money and quietly get out of town. Just leave your gun where it is and get some shut-eye."

Eli unclenched his fists and took in a deep breath. If he was the one to go to the bank he could just take the governor's wife and the money and leave town while his brother babysat the governor's daughter. "Don't get your drawers in a knot, Ned. I'll get the money from the bank," he said, taking a seat in a velvet chair and putting his feet up on the bed.

It disgusted Althea Brown to see the brother's dirty and worn boots on the bed next to her, but the situation seemed to diffuse and she relaxed a little as Ned holstered his gun. She regarded her daughter and gave her a wink for assurance that things would ultimately be okay.

Ned was exhausted. It seemed like every minute with his brother was fraught with tension. He wanted to tell his brother to get his boots off of the bed, but noticed he had tipped his hat down over his face and had begun to snore softly. The bound women seemed to relax some and lay down next to each other. He strolled over to the opposite corner from his brother and sat in a fancy chair that was short on comfort. He attempted to fight off sleep but the drowsiness overtook him and he nodded off.

The brilliant morning sun streaming in through the dusky window shown on Ned's face and his eyes snapped open. The morning had arrived without incident and he took in a deep breath. It seemed as if he was stiff all over and he stood to stretch out the kinks. The women were sound asleep and Eli began to stir at the sound of his brother rising out of his chair.

"Dang, didn't figure I was so tired," Eli said, setting his boots on the floor. "How soon you reckon the bank opens."

Ned checked his pocket watch. "About half an hour, I suspect. Get Mrs. Brown untied; we need her to appear as normal as possible."

Eli's nose flared and he bit his tongue. *There he goes giving orders again.*

It did not go unnoticed to Ned that his brother belted on his gun before undertaking the task of untying Mrs. Brown and awakening her. He also noticed that Eli was none too gentle in his handling of the woman.

Althea Brown rubbed her wrists in an attempt to increase the circulation. She looked sadly over at her daughter as she began to stir.

"Afore we take your gag off, Mrs. Brown, you are to remain quiet and do as I say or harm will come to your daughter; do you understand?" Ned said.

The governor's wife nodded.

"Take her gag off, Eli."

Eli glared at his brother, and then did what was asked. With a dry, hoarse voice Althea asked if she could have a drink of water as she attempted to lick parched lips.

"We don't have no drinking water; you'll just have to wait," Ned said. "Eli, get her something to drink when you go downstairs. Remember, Mrs. Brown, no shenanigans or you'll never see your daughter again. Now stand up and get your legs underneath you."

Althea did as she was told; her stomach was in her throat as she looked down at her wide-eyed daughter. "Don't worry about me," she rasped, "my daughter is more important to me than money."

Ned checked his pocket watch. "It's time, Eli; go get our money."

Chapter 74

Marshal Clements rode directly to the Circle J Ranch. He was certain that Buck Henry would have returned to the ranch and if he had already been there and gone he might discover what he was up to.

With caution, he approached the ranch house, taking in all of the surroundings. All seemed quiet as he gazed around one more time before dismounting. With the utmost caution, the marshal mounted the wooden steps and stopped to gaze back around. All was quiet. He loosened his revolver and knocked on the door.

After a moment the door opened slowly. "Ah, marshal, we been expecting you," Chang Lee said.

"Hello, Chang; why were you expecting me?"

"Mista Henry hurt and robbed."

"Yes, I heard about that. How is he doing?"

"He still sleep. Come in marshal."

Marshal Clements entered the foyer and removed his hat.

"Who is it, Chang?" Elma asked, entering with towel in hand.

"Howdy, Miss Elma. Mr. Henry not doing so well?"

"Ya, he is still unconscious. Not good, by golly; you see."

Sam Clements followed Elma through the parlor into a downstairs room with a bed in it. John Henry, pale as a ghost, was lying comatose with hands crossed on his chest. The marshal had to look closely to see that Henry was breathing. “Looks like you’re taking good care of him, Elma.”

“We do our best,” she said. “You see his office.”

“Sure, Ranger Gentry told me about the robbery.”

The door of the safe was still open and the drawers of Henry’s desk were thrown around with their contents strewn about. “The robbers do this?” the marshal asked.

From the doorway Chang said, “No, Mista Buck come in all drunk and angry. He say sometimes Mista Henry keep money in desk.”

The marshal nodded. “Where is Buck?”

Elma shook her head. “He took some bottles of whiskey, got a fresh horse and rode out of here, yelling and screaming, by golly.”

Maria Rios walked into the room. “Senor Marshal, he no care about his father.”

“Not surprised,” Clements mumbled. “Did Buck say where he was riding to?”

Elma shook her head. “No,” she said, pointing west.

“Chang, if you see or hear from Buck send somebody for me. It’s important.”

The china man gave a bow and Marshal Clements put his hat on. “If you people need anything or if there is a change in John Henry’s condition, please let me know.” He walked out onto the porch, took a deep breath, and scanned the yard. “If I was Buck Henry, where would I go?” Clements asked himself. He strolled over to the corral and looked at a horse that was done in. “The bastard didn’t even wipe him down,” he grumbled. “Anyone that would treat good horseflesh like that don’t deserve to live.”

The marshal leaned on the corral fence and thought about what Buck Henry might do. Buck had a mean streak a mile wide and wagonload of vices. One of the things Buck coveted most he wound up killing. He drank a lot and fought a lot. He didn’t get along very well with his father, but his father was near death. Rationale and common sense were lacking in the boy.

Clements started for his horse and was surprised to see Elma walking toward him. He tipped his hat and waited for her to speak.

"I yust remember someting," she said. "Buck, he was ranting and raving and didn't make too much sense."

The marshal nodded.

"He yelled someting about killing the man who did this to him."

"Anything else, Elma?"

"No, that is all," she said.

"Thank you," Clements said, mounting his horse. "Again, let me know if there is any change in John's condition."

The marshal set his horse to a gallop toward the west. The shadows were longer and the sun shone in his eyes. He tipped his hat down and thought about what the Swedish girl had said. It was possible Buck was going after the men that robbed and hurt his father. Perhaps he was going back to finish off Jim Hatfield, blaming him for the death of Pricilla Peabody. But, he hadn't even asked who had robbed his father and he had already shot Ranger Hatfield. *Seth Gentry; he was going to try to kill the Captain.*

Chapter 75

Sadness seemed to permeate the small town as Seth made the rounds for Marshal Clements. His gut was in a knot from the raw emotion of breaking the news to Jim Hatfield about Pricilla's death. He was attempting to be vigilant but the fact of the matter was that he felt like he was just going through the motions. He checked locked doors and peered into dark alleys and thought how he would feel if something happened to Darla Brown. Anger began to well up and replace the sorrow. Anyone who would kill a woman, a youthful, vibrant beauty, should be hung by the neck and be sent for celestial judgment.

Gentry looked over at the hotel. The light was still on in the room that the Brown women occupied and he had the urge to go see them. He let the thought pass as he realized it was getting on in the evening. He gazed down the darkening street and saw a weary horse and rider entering town. He soon recognized Marshal Clements and he was alone.

"How are things?" Marshal Clements asked.

"Fairly quiet," Seth answered.

"You break the news to Ranger Hatfield?"

"Yup, took it hard."

"To be expected," the marshal murmured.

"No sign of Buck Henry?" Seth asked.

Fatigued, the marshal dismounted and said, "He was at the ranch, got a fresh horse and took off. Have you eaten, yet?"

"No, having to break the news to Jim kind of took away any urge to eat. I could probably have something now."

"Good." Clements dismounted and tied his horse to the hitching rail. "I'm starved, but let's have a drink first. "I've had enough of the Henrys for one day."

Even the saloon seemed subdued after learning of Pricilla Peabody's death. The preacher's daughter could be counted on for pleasantry and brightness on the darkest of days. Pricilla had treated all people the same and her bright smile lightened the gloomiest of moods. Both lawmen stood quietly at the bar working on a couple of frothy mugs of beer, staring at their own images in the mirror.

"I saw John Henry," Clements said. "He's in a bad way and I don't think his son gave a hoot."

Seth nodded. "Figured such," he said.

"I been thinkin', though most men fear Buck, I don't think his life is worth a plumb nickel. Elma told me he took some whiskey with him and he's going to be mean and intolerable. The killin' of a woman is about the worst thing a man could do."

Seth nodded, took a drink and wiped foam from his upper lip with his shirt sleeve.

Clements continued. "While his life has been full of conflict, with chaos and evil in his mind, it's worse since you rangers come to town. He has always coveted Pricilla and Ranger Hatfield wooed her away; and he had never lost a fight until you come along."

Seth nodded. "Do you think Buck is on the run?"

"I been cogitating on that," the marshal said. "Maybe temporary, but I think he is going to come after you. Like I said, things have gotten worse since you rangers showed and he's already shot Ranger Hatfield. I also think he will rationalize that Pricilla's death was Hatfield's fault."

"Possible," Seth said, taking another gulp of beer. "He may come right to us."

The marshal took a drink. “We could chase after the boy; he tends to leave a path of destruction.”

The lawmen quieted with their own thoughts.

“We could separately go after him and cover as much of the county as possible,” Seth said.

Marshal Clements shook his head. “I don’t have a deputy and can’t leave the town uncovered.”

“It will be awhile before Ranger Hatfield is healed up,” Seth added. “I could go it alone.”

“You could; the funeral is tomorrow and maybe Buck will show. Let’s give it a few days and we’ll go from there,” Clements said, setting his empty mug on the bar. “I feel like I could eat a whole steer; time to eat.”

The following morning the two lawmen met for breakfast early to plan the day. The funeral would be at the church and they expected most of the town to attend. Since the doctor was going to release Ranger Hatfield for the funeral they chose three vantage points to cover the area, with Hatfield closest to the funeral. “I think that is where he would want to be and it’s the safest because of his injury,” Clements said.

Seth nodded as the waitress refilled their coffee. As the dull gray of dawn flared into a bright morning he said, “It’s as if God shared the brightness of Pricilla’s smile on this day.”

Clements regarded the solemn ranger. “Buck will pay,” he said.

The clanking of dishes and the murmur of morning conversation came to an abrupt halt as someone walked into the room. Seth looked over his shoulder to see the reverend scurrying toward them.

“Marshal, ranger,” the reverend said, “on this glorious day as we celebrate Pricilla’s life and her journey home, we are going to have a gathering after the funeral and I want you two to be there. Mostly for fellowship, but I don’t want there to be any trouble.”

"Don't worry, reverend, we'll be there," the marshal said.

"Can I buy you a cup of coffee?" Seth asked.

"No, thank you ranger, I have a lot to attend to. Let's break bread together later," the reverend said as he turned and hurried out the door.

"Poor man," Gentry said. "He seems to be holding together."

"Endicott Peabody is a man of faith," the marshal said.

"I'm worried about young Hatfield," Seth said.

Marshal Clements nodded. "Let's go get him and we can make the rounds. You and Jim can take the east side and I'll take the west before we head to the church."

Chapter 76

The doctor's wife greeted the lawmen.

"How's he doing, ma'am?" Seth asked.

"He's healing physically, but he's been mighty quiet," she said. "He's all dressed and ready to go. He needs to keep that arm in a sling for a few weeks."

They found Jim Hatfield waiting impatiently in a chair. "About time you got here," he grumbled.

Seth gave him a slight smile. "Ranger rule number one is to try not to get yourself shot."

"It's not like I was trying too," Hatfield retorted.

"Come on, ranger, you've laid around long enough; we got to go on our rounds before the funeral," Marshal Clements said.

With a stiffness he could not conceal, Ranger Hatfield arose slowly. "I could use a little help putting on my gun," he said, indicating his holster hanging on the bed post.

Seth strapped on the young man's gun belt. "Don't be expectin' this all the time."

"You find Buck Henry?" Hatfield asked.

"Trailed him to the ranch, where he got a fresh horse and a bottle of whiskey and left," Marshal Clements said.

"Give me a couple of days and I'll find him," Hatfield said.

Seth regarded the young, determined ranger. If it were him he would feel the same way, but as captain he would have to guide the young man to do the proper thing. "As much as you want to personalize this, and I don't blame you, our job is to apprehend a criminal and bring him before a court of law, if possible."

The gaunt young ranger looked lost in thought.

Captain Gentry knew that Jim Hatfield's perspective was a new one---that of a victim. He knew that the young man wouldn't realize it for a while, but this experience would make him a better ranger.

"Let's go. We have to make the rounds before the funeral," Clements said. "They aren't going to like it, but tell the saloons I want them closed during the services. Seth, take Jim and the west side of the street and we'll meet back here."

"You got it. Come on Jim."

Two lawmen were seldom welcomed with open arms in drinking establishments, so Seth was surprised by the cooperation he received when he said that they must close during the funeral. It seemed everyone had a deep affection for the preacher's daughter. There were sympathetic looks from the patrons at the young ranger and there were strong feelings for Buck Henry to be punished.

Jim Hatfield was quiet. He accepted the sympathetic gestures with a cordial nod and stern look.

As they made their rounds, shops were beginning to close for the funeral. It appeared the whole town was going to turn out. As sad as the event was, funerals were also a social occasion and many of those attending would provide enough food to feed the whole town.

Suddenly, Ranger Hatfield stopped in his tracks and Seth almost bumped into him. "Isn't that Mrs. Brown with that Hayes brother?" Hatfield asked.

Stepping out of the bank, Eli Hayes had a strong grip on Althea Brown's arm; in the other hand he was holding a bank bag. When he spotted the two rangers walking toward him he hesitated a moment, dropped the bag and went for his gun.

The explosion of gunshots echoed through the quiet street, smoke filling the clear morning air. A woman screamed at the abrupt violence, the outcome momentarily in doubt. The governor's wife froze where she stood; ephemeral deafness followed the explosion and she blinked as if to clear the smoke from her eyes. The grip on her arm released and she watched Eli Hayes topple over into the muddy street. Althea began to shake as she peered down the street. Standing there with smoking guns were Rangers Hatfield and Gentry.

The two rangers walked quickly toward the governor's wife. Despite Hatfield's injury, he was as advertised, Seth thought. The boy was fast. Their eyes remained on the gunman in the street and Seth asked, "Are you alright Mrs. Brown?"

Althea Brown nodded, speechless.

Ranger Hatfield took the toe of his boot and turned the Hayes brother over. The outlaw stared vacantly, two gunshot wounds just a couple of inches apart appeared on his small chest. "I never killed anyone before," he said just above a whisper.

Gentry looked at the young ranger. "Might have been mine," he said, "You never know."

Ranger Hatfield picked up the bank bag and handed it to the governor's wife. She took it while staring down at the dead man. "He wasn't a good person," she said quietly.

"No, he wasn't," Seth said.

"Darla's in the hotel room with the other brother," Althea said. "We were supposed to bring the money back to him, but I think this one was going to leave with me and the money."

Marshal Clements scurried toward them. "What happened?"

"Mr. Hayes here forced Mrs. Brown to withdraw her money from the bank. The other brother is holding Darla in the hotel. Take care of Mrs. Brown; Jim and I are going to the hotel."

*****

Ned Hayes heard the gunshots and knew that his brother was up to no good, as usual. "That boy don't know no better, no matter how I tried to learn him," he said to himself.

Darla, still tied up on the bed, stared wide-eyed at Ned, wondering what he would do next and she worried about her mother's safety.

Hayes went to the window and he saw people hurrying toward the bank. He cursed to himself and grabbed his saddle bags and rifle as he left the room. Whatever happened to his brother, he hoped to beat him to the hidden silver, and then all would not be lost.

Halfway down the stairs he saw the two rangers enter the hotel. He dropped the saddle bags and raised his rifle.

Explosive gunshots echoed throughout the hotel. Ned Hayes dropped his rifle without getting a shot off and he tumbled over the stair banister, landing on a Victorian table, crushing it beneath him. Thick gun smoke hung heavily in the air, the acrid redolence singeing the nostrils.

Careful, the two rangers approached the Hayes brother lying comatose on his back. Like his little brother, he stared upward, devoid of life. Ranger Hatfield removed Ned's pistol and shook his head. "Seems like some never learn," he said.

Seth nodded. "I'm always amazed how evil men seem so insignificant when they are taken down. Watch over him; I'm going to see if Darla is alright." Ranger Gentry took the stairs two at a time and entered the half-opened door to the Brown's hotel room. The governor's daughter relaxed with relief when she saw Seth enter the room.

Gentry quickly untied Darla and asked, "Are you okay? You're not hurt are you?"

"I'm not hurt," Darla said in a croaking whisper. "I'm so glad to see you. Is mother alright?"

"She's fine," Seth said, hugging her tightly.

"I was so scared."

Seth held her away and looked into her sparkling, dark brown eyes. “You know it makes my job more difficult if I have to worry about you and your mother getting in trouble all of the time,” he scolded with a smile. He brought her in for another hug. He heard Darla sniff, with her head on his shoulder.

“Mother and I are the least of your worries,” Darla retorted.

“I don’t know about that,” Seth said rubbing her back.

Darla sighed, feeling safe and comfortable.

Ranger Hatfield poked his head in. “Everything alright?”

“She’s fine,” Seth answered.

Darla’s mother rushed into the room. “Are you alright?”

“Yes, mother, I am fine,” Darla said.

“Why is Seth holding you, are you hurt?”

“I’m not hurt, Seth is just comforting me.”

Althea’s eyes narrowed. “It looks like he might hurt you, squeezing so tight.”

The governor’s daughter chuckled. “He’s holding me just right,” she said, looking up and kissing the ranger on the lips.

Darla’s mother, with hands on hips, said, “It’s not proper to show affection in public.”

Her daughter kissed Seth again. “I’m not in public, I’m in a hotel room with this handsome man,” she teased.

The impetuousness of youth, Althea thought. “Let’s get these men out of our room so that we can prepare for the funeral.”

Seth kissed Darla on the forehead. “We’ll finish our business downstairs and get some coffee; meet us there.”

Althea showed the men to the door and said, “We’ll be just a few minutes.”

The rangers descended the stairs and were glad to see Ned Hayes’ body had been removed. “You know it will be longer than a few minutes before they come down, don't you," Hatfield said.

"Yes, I do. Let's get some breakfast. We'll keep an eye out for them; I don't want them out of our sight with Mrs. Brown in possession of her money."

"The marshal said that they found some loot on the two men that came from the Circle J. He's holding it for evidence and will eventually turn it over to the bank," Hatfield added.

Chapter 77

Althea and Darla Brown entered the restaurant as Seth finished his breakfast. Hatfield had wolfed his down and was enjoying a cup of coffee. All eyes turned to watch the lovely women enter the room and a crescendo of whispers greeted them. You would never know that the two had endured a frightful night.

"I told you we wouldn't be long," Althea said as Jim Hatfield pulled a chair out for her.

Seth got up and assisted Darla into the chair next to him. "Uh-huh," he said with diplomacy.

"Darla and I would like a cup of tea," Althea said with a smile.

James Hatfield grinned. He couldn't believe how cool and calm the two women were.

"It's good to see you feeling better," Althea said.

Hatfield nodded.

"I just wish this beautiful day had more happiness," she added.

Darla reached over and squeezed Seth's hand. The impending funeral weighed heavily on everyone.

Althea looked across to Ranger Gentry. "Seth, I just recalled that the two brothers had mentioned hidden silver at the old camp. Do you know where that would be?"

Seth thought for a moment. "Could be one of a couple of places; I heard that the brothers camped just south of the town of Sutter Creek and I know of a campsite up the creek itself."

With excitement in her eyes, Darla said, "We must go looking for it; it would be like a real treasure hunt."

Seth chuckled. "Perhaps we could do that before we head back to Sacramento."

Marshal Clements rushed into the room. "We got things, uh, picked up. The funeral is in about thirty minutes. It looks like the whole county showed up. Me and the boys will be outside while you folks are in the church, on the lookout in case that no-good Buck Henry shows. Reverend Peabody said that he had reserved the front pew for the governor's wife and daughter and young Jim here; he don't have no other family about."

"That was very nice of him," Althea Brown said. She looked across to her daughter. "I so feel for the man losing a daughter like that."

The marshal left as quickly as he had arrived. The funeral of Priscilla Peabody had turned into a bigger event than the annual Fourth of July celebration.

Seth watched the two women finish their cup of tea. "We'd best get over to the church," he said.

"Yes, perhaps the good reverend could use our help," Althea said. "At the very least we can give the poor man some support."

Seth stood and admired the two women. No one would ever know that these beautiful, strong women had been through an ordeal. He pulled out Darla's chair for her and the one-armed young ranger assisted her mother.

The short hike to the church up the undulating streets took a toll on young Hatfield. Seth purposely slowed his walk so that he could catch his breath. The gunshot and loss of blood had weakened the strong young man and only time would bring back his full health.

People were gathered around the picnic area that had been the site of Seth's fight with Buck Henry. Great quantities of food were accumulating on the tables, and though more somber, there was an underlying festive atmosphere that accompanied an unusual social event.

Seth, Jim, and the ladies were greeted by Marshal Mack Wheeler of Amador City. He tipped his hat to the governor's wife and daughter. "Came over to help, and pay my respects."

"Good to see you, Mack," Seth said. "I wish it was under better circumstances."

Wheeler shook his head. "Young Priscilla was like another daughter; they don't come no sweeter." He regarded the young ranger and added, "You all will have to stop by when you come back through Amador City on your way to Sacramento."

"That's very kind of you, marshal," Althea Brown said. "We'll certainly do that."

Endicott Peabody, receiving condolences as he approached, joining them. "I've saved a seat up front for you," he said solemnly. He addressed Jim Hatfield. "I know you cared for my daughter and I appreciate the kindness you showed toward her. We lost her, but God has a new, beautiful angel."

Young Hatfield nodded with glistening eyes. The lump in his throat precluded him from speaking.

The good reverend took the young ranger by his good arm and led him toward the church. The crowd turned silent and the peace was interrupted by the clanging of the church bell announcing the start of the funeral proceedings. The crowd respectfully followed the reverend and his entourage up the hill toward the church.

People already seated in the church watched the reverend and the young ranger walk down the aisle toward the altar. Tears streamed down young Hatfield's face at the sight of the simple flower-covered casket. Light from a stained-glass window shined on the casket as if directed from the heavens. Sorrowful organ music filled the air.

The two rangers stepped back with hats in hand to let the governor's wife and daughter be seated in the front pew. Althea took the young ranger by the hand so that he would follow her and be seated between her and her daughter. Seth sat next to Darla on the end. Darla had a lacy hanky squeezed tightly in her hand, a single tear streaking down her face and she dabbed at it and sniffed.

This is gut wrenching, Seth thought. He bit his lip. It was as if he was soaking up everyone's pain. The organ music stopped and the reverend began to speak. Seth was surprised to hear the preacher's strong voice. Endicott Peabody did not spend a lot of time recalling the virtues of his dearly departed daughter, but did emphasize the importance of leading a virtuous life to enter the kingdom of heaven.

The surprise came at the end of the preacher's sermon.

Chapter 78

On a distant knoll, sitting under a grand oak tree with his back against the trunk, was Buck Henry working on a bottle of whiskey. He watched the throng of people enter the church and observed the lawmen scattered about. He blamed the death of Pricilla Peabody on the arrival of the California Rangers. Things always went his way, eventually, but the arrival of Hatfield had caught the young woman's eye. His woman; her head had been turned and she couldn't see what was best for her. She had the opportunity to be a rich rancher's wife, yet she was blinded by a shiny circled star.

And then there was Ranger Gentry. The guy had been lucky. Buck had never lost a fight before and he blamed it on being hungover. Buck took a drink and pulled his revolver out of its holster. He checked the loads and spun the cylinder. No one had ever beaten him to the draw. In fact, very few had challenged him. If he took care of Gentry and finished off Hatfield things could get back to normal around here, he thought. *Damn those rangers!*

Buck took another pull on the bottle and watched the marshals mill about. A few older women busied themselves setting up for the after-funeral gathering. He took another drink and found the bottle empty. He angrily tossed it aside and staggered to his feet. He knew he couldn't take on all of the lawmen here and decided he'd best go get another drink in town and make a plan. He stumbled to his horse and was about to mount up and head to town when he saw the casket being carried out and put into the mortician's wagon, closely followed by the reverend and the two Brown women, Gentry, and that punk ranger.

Buck couldn't believe who the pall bearers were.

He struggled to get in the saddle and spurred his horse to a gallop down the hill, fighting the urge to turn around and kill him a ranger or two.

Sutter Creek was like a ghost town. Apparently just about everyone had attended Pricilla Peabody's funeral. He tied his horse to the rail and was pleased to find the bartender behind the bar. The feeling was not mutual.

"Whiskey!" Buck demanded.

The bartender poured a shot.

"Leave the bottle."

The bartender left the bottle and walked to the other end of the bar, hoping not to have any trouble and not wanting to associate with a woman-killer. He was also much closer to his sawed-off shotgun under the counter.

Buck poured another shot and swilled it back. Bleary eyed, he looked into the mirror at the empty room behind him. He glared down at the bartender ignoring him. He felt isolated. He might as well have been alone on an island. It was those damn rangers' fault. Everything had been just fine until they showed up. First there was one and then the kid showed with the governor's wife and daughter, turning Pricilla's head. He had been certain that he was making progress in his relationship and then it had stopped. It had not only stopped, but she had rejected him.

He took another drink.

And then there was the captain, taking advantage of his hangover. Until that point everyone in the county respected and feared Buck Henry. That had stopped, too.

Henry picked up the bottle and staggered outside, not bothering to pay for it.

The bartender shook his head. A bottle of whiskey was a small price to pay for being rid of the lady-killer. He made his way over to the window and was disappointed to find Buck sitting on the bench out front. Buck was trying to focus down the empty street.

Chapter 79

At the end of the funeral services Endicott Peabody surprised the contingent by announcing the pall bearers that would attend to Pricilla's casket. He said that Pricilla loved life and all of the people in her life and she would appreciate a depiction of those she cared for so deeply.

The first one the reverend called up was Captain Gentry of the California Rangers. The reverend explained that Pricilla respected law enforcement and had even expressed an interest in being California's first woman ranger; especially after she had met young Hatfield.

A titter arose from the crowded church as they all looked over to the blushing young ranger.

"Pricilla and I would be honored to have Miss and Mrs. Brown and Jim to be honorary pall bearers," the reverend said.

Reverend Peabody then announced the rest of the pall bearers and not all of them were regular church-going members. There was a murmur from the crowd as an old miner was named, a rancher, a store clerk, the town drunk, and old Zeke.

The reverend smiled from his pulpit. "You men, and others of you, treated Pricilla with kindness and she loved you all. I must confess to you that sometimes I found it difficult to share my daughter. She was all I had," the reverend said, choking up. "Pricilla was the sweetest soul I have ever known and it would have been wrong to not let her sow her kind-heartedness amongst you. She had a contagious joy we will all miss."

Sobs and sniffles could be heard as the reverend paused and looked down at his daughter's casket. A loan tear streaked down his face. He took a deep breath. "As we take Pricilla to her final resting place, be cognizant of the fact that she would not want sadness to take over this day. She would want you to celebrate her life and enjoy one another's fellowship. She would want you to be thankful for your blessings and follow the golden rule."

Seth watched as Darla laid her head on her mother's shoulder. Despite the wishes of the reverend and his daughter, a heavy cloud of sadness hung over the church. All stood in respect as the pall bearers carried the casket down the aisle, the reverend in the lead and followed by the governor's wife and daughter and young Ranger Hatfield.

Pricilla's simple wooden casket was placed in the funeral wagon and a procession with heavy hearts followed it up boot hill.

*****

Little Sadie Wilson struggled to keep up with her mother as they hurried toward the church. As they strolled the rolling walks of downtown Sutter Creek, both were short of breath and Sadie's mother would often pick her up until her arms tired. Doris had hoped to make it to the funeral on time but by the time they got there the services would more than likely be concluded. On occasion Pricilla would babysit Sadie and it was important to her to express her heartfelt condolences to Endicott Peabody.

Sadie let go of her mother's hand and stopped. Her mother had continued for a few steps and turned to see what her daughter was doing. Sadie was staring at a man slouched down on a bench, drool running down his chin and snoring loudly. Below the man's hand was an empty bottle of whiskey. Doris hadn't noticed the man as they rushed by. Like other respectful women, she purposely did not notice the presence of drinking establishments and their patrons.

"Mommy, that man is asleep," Sadie said.

"Yes, dear; come on, we have to get to the church."

"He looks scary."

"I know who that man is," her mother said. "He is a bad man."

Buck Henry snorted and Sadie ran to her mother.

Sadie and her mother arrived at the picnic area near the church and helped the other women prepare for the after-funeral social. Doris saw Marshal Clements standing watch and approached him. "I just saw Buck Henry in town," she said.

Clements' eyes widened."Where did you see him Doris?"

"He was passed out outside the saloon; I didn't see anyone else around."

Marshal Clements watched the procession going up the hill. He scanned the area and all was well. As soon as they put Pricilla to rest he would get Ranger Gentry and the two of them would go to town and arrest Henry. He approached Marshal Wheeler. "I just got word that Buck Henry's in town. I'd appreciate you keeping an eye out here and Seth and I will go after him."

"You sure you wouldn't like me to go along?"

Clements shook his head. "With Hatfield being injured and the governor's wife and daughter here I would feel better if you were around."

Wheeler nodded. "I understand. I don't mind hanging around the Browns; Darla so reminds me of my daughter, Beth."

Marshal Clements smiled. "Beth does look like Darla's younger sister. You sure you're the papa?"

Marshal Wheeler grinned. "She took after her mother alright." And then he gazed up the hill with thoughts of his departed wife. "The proceedings are about over."

"I'll go fetch Seth and tell Ranger Hatfield that you and he are to watch everything here," Clements said.

Solemnly, Seth, Althea, Darla, and Jim made their way down the hill toward the church meadow. To Seth's surprise, he saw Marshal Clements marching up the hill with a determined expression. Clements stopped in his tracks and yelled, "Buck Henry's been spotted in town."

Everyone picked up the pace to meet the marshal. "Where was he seen?" Seth asked.

"Passed out in front of one of the saloons; I'm asking Ranger Hatfield and Marshal Wheeler to watch things here while you and I go to town."

Jim Hatfield started to protest and Althea quickly spoke. "Thank you marshal, I'm sure that Ranger Hatfield and Marshal Wheeler will take good care of us all."

Seth smiled at the astuteness of the governor's wife. "I'd appreciate it if you'd save Sam and me some of that good fried chicken."

Wide-eyed and with hands on hips, Darla demanded, "You better come back safe to eat that chicken."

"Yes, ma'am," Seth said with a slight bow.

As Marshal Clements and Ranger Gentry went for their horses, Clements said, "It appears that little lady's got you broke and branded."

Seth chuckled. "And I enjoy every minute of it. I love her spirit."

Chapter 80

Ranger Gentry and Marshal Clements rode into a peaceful Sutter Creek. The stillness was unusual and disconcerting. Seth watched Sam Clements loosen his holstered gun and he followed suit. "You take the right and I'll take the left," Clements said wisely.

With deliberation they slowly rode down the main street paying particular attention to the exteriors of the saloons. Buck Henry was nowhere to be seen. They reached the south end of town and turned around, looked back, and Clements said, "We're going to have to walk the town and check inside the saloons to see if Henry's still in town."

Seth leaned on the pommel of his saddle and studied the street. "We could cover it quicker if we split up."

"Yeah, but we'll have to be extra careful; you take the right and I'll take the left. Remember, Henry is capable of shooting a man in the back," Clements said.

The two lawmen dismounted and slowly began strolling the undulating street, their boots echoing off the rock walks. The jangle of spurs often stopped and the resumption of silence added to the angst as they cautiously climbed steps and peered into the dark crevasses of alleys and empty buildings. Seth was thankful that most of the people were still at the funeral. A crowded street would make their pursuit of Buck Henry more difficult and it would be dangerous for the citizenry.

Marshal Clements approached the first saloon on his side of the street on the tiptoes of his boots. He peered around the doorway and saw an almost empty room. The bartender was wiping glasses and there was a man passed out on a table. He studied the man and realized he was much too small to be Buck Henry. Clements took a quick look over his shoulder. Catching Gentry's eye, he shook his head. They both continued on.

Seth approached his first saloon and saw Clements stop across the street to observe what would happen. With the same caution Clements had used, Seth peered into the saloon. He saw two old-timers playing cards and nothing else. He looked up the street to see some people trickling into town. *I hope we find Buck before more people come back to town, he thought.*

Clements looked into an empty café and continued up four rocky steps. He took a deep breath. He had walked these hilly streets many times and he was beginning to realize it wasn't as easy as it was when he was younger. As much as he loved his community, he was beginning to envy the 'flatlanders'. The marshal's momentary loss of focus was interrupted by excruciating pain and the dark passing of consciousness.

Buck Henry reluctantly holstered the gun that he had used as a club to hit Marshal Clements over the head. He had the urge to shoot the hated marshal, but did not want to get the attention of Ranger Gentry just yet. He dragged the marshal into the alleyway and he stepped behind a rain barrel to watch Gentry work his way down the opposite side of the street. He squinted to focus and cursed the pounding hangover that made him more miserable than usual.

Seth put his hand on his gun. Something was different. The silence was no longer interrupted by the echo of boots on hard walkways. He looked back over his shoulder and saw an empty street. Marshal Clements had disappeared. He scanned the street, pausing at nooks and crannies and dark places to study them. There was no marshal. There was no movement. The silence was deafening. Clements had either gone into a building or had been bushwhacked. He decided not to call out, but to cross the street and backtrack.

Henry watched Seth cross the street and walk toward him. A smile that was more grimace-like appeared on Buck's face. Here was his chance for revenge.

The clatter of a freight wagon arriving behind the ranger caused him to stop and observe its arrival. A few horsemen and a buggy followed, indicating the possibility of the funeral events winding down and people returning.

Buck Henry had considered gunning the ranger down from his hidden location. While it would be satisfying to kill his nemesis in this manner, the only way he would regain his reputation would be to meet the man head on; especially since witnesses had arrived to corroborate his conquest. As he was about to step out into the street he saw the luxurious buggy of the governor's wife and daughter pull into town. The wounded ranger had the reins in his good hand and the governor's wife and daughter were in the backseat. *Even better, he thought, they will witness his victory, adding to his legacy, and he will finish off the young ranger that messed up his life.*

As Ranger Hatfield reined in, he saw Buck Henry step out into the street. He heard Darla gasp behind him and he yelled a warning to Seth. Seth turned to see Buck Henry, legs wide apart, and his hand near his gun.

"You're going to get it now, ranger. You're going to pay for what you done," Henry snarled.

A heavy silence descended on them as Seth slowly moved out into the street, making sure that the governor's buggy was out of the line of fire. "You don't have to die just yet, Buck," Seth said.

"I ain't never been beat to the draw," Buck said. "After I kill you I'm going to kill that woman stealer."

Seth stared at the hulking evil man before him. He didn't get any pleasure out of shooting people but some varmints had to pay for their sins. He knew to watch the gunman's eyes; they always told you when a man was about to draw.

The quiet seconds seemed like minutes. The sudden double whisper of revolvers leaving leather was followed by the singular explosion of both guns firing, followed by a woman screaming. Thick, acrid gun smoke filled the air. The ricochet of a bullet whined into the air harmlessly.

Henry's eyes widened in surprise as he saw the smoking gun of the ranger pointed at him. His gun had gone off prematurely and he tried to lift it in vain. He looked down at the spreading blood on his chest, raised his head, his eyes rolled back and he fell face first into the street.

"Wow, I thought I was fast," Ranger Hatfield said. He watched the grim captain holster his gun and walk toward the buggy. "Think he's dead?"

"There wasn't time not to kill him," Seth said.

Marshal Clements appeared out of the ally holding the back of his head. He spotted the body of Buck Henry. "Good riddance," he mumbled. Clements staggered over to a bench and sat down.

"That was just awful," Darla said to Seth.

"I'll go get the doctor," Ranger Hatfield said after the arrival of Gentry.

Seth nodded. "I'm sorry you all had to see that; there's no pleasure in it."

"You were just doing your job," Althea said with sympathy.

"Yes, but it doesn't make it any easier," Seth added, taking Darla's hand in his.

Marshal Wheeler rode into town and reined in by the buggy. He viewed the body of Buck Henry and contemplated Marshal Clements on the bench holding the back of his head. "You all right, Sam?"

"Got conked on the head," he said.

"Good thing you're so hard headed," Wheeler chuckled.

"Don't mean it don't hurt," Clements groaned.

Wheeler regarded Darla Brown rubbing Seth's shoulders. "He hated having to kill that man," she said.

Marshal Wheeler nodded. “Killin’ is a hard thing to do, but it beats the alternative. This town and everyone in it is better off for it.”

Darla gripped Seth’s hand. “I do hope you never have to do that again, but if it means your life I’ll accept it every time.”

“Thanks,” Seth said gratefully.

Althea Brown breathed deeply. “Well, we can go home now,” she said, considering the young ranger. She knew it would be best to get Jim Hatfield away from here to move on with his life. “You can still drive the buggy with the one arm all of the way to Sacramento?”

“Sure,” Hatfield said succinctly.

“Sam, you’d best have the doctor look at that hard head of yours, and if the governor’s wife and daughter don’t mind, I’ll escort them to Amador City and I’d be right proud to buy them dinner at my daughter’s restaurant,” Wheeler said.

The vision of Beth Wheeler, Darla’s young look alike, brought a smile to Seth’s face. Perhaps she could divert Jim Hatfield’s attention away from the terrible loss of Pricilla Peabody.

“Darla and I will need just a minute to gather our things,” Althea said. “We can stay in Amador City tonight and be off to Sacramento early in the morning.”

Seth took in a deep breath and seemed to relax. “I will miss Sutter Creek.”

“We can return someday soon,” Darla said with a smile. “Maybe we could go looking for hidden treasure.”

Seth’s heart skipped a beat with Darla’s comment. The idea of returning with her was mighty appealing.

“If you ever decide against rangering I heard that there will be a nice ranch available up Volcano way,” Wheeler said. “The word is that John Henry didn’t make it.”

Seth chuckled. “It would take a lot more capital than I make on ranger pay to get that ranch.”

The governor's wife stared at the marshal. "What would it take to get that ranch?"

"I don't rightly know, ma'am. As far as I know there were no other heirs; it might be up to the bank and maybe the judge," Wheeler said. "But I got a hunch it could be picked up for a bargain."

"What happens in the meantime?" Althea asked.

"I guess the judge will have the bank manage it in the meantime. It don't do no good letting it go to pot."

Althea nodded, lost in thought.

"What are you thinking, mother?" Darla asked.

Darla's mother smiled. "Your father can't be governor forever; I think he would like the idea of getting away from politics to own a successful ranch, especially in that beautiful valley near Volcano."

Althea's daughter's eyes sparkled with excitement. "I love that idea!"

"It is a beautiful place," Marshal Wheeler said. "It would be a terrific place for a wedding," he teased.

Seth flushed with embarrassment. "I've been there. There isn't a prettier setting for miles."

"Then it's settled. Before we leave town I'll leave a deposit with Tobias Chandler at the bank and let him know we want first crack at buying that ranch." Althea grinned from ear to ear at the thought of Henry's own money that she had won being used for the deposit.

"Sight unseen mother? What about father?" Darla asked.

"I've grown to love it here," Althea said. "I've heard enough about that valley and ranch. And when has your father ever said no to me?"

Darla smiled and looked over at Marshal Wheeler. "Nice place for a wedding?"

"Yes, ma'am," Wheeler said with a delighted grin as he watched Seth squirm around and tug at his collar.

End